LET'S BE PIRATES

STARSLIDER REJECTS #001

MARK SARNEY

Dedicated to all of the people who got screwed by an impersonal system and couldn't afford to fight back.

ONE

"WE ARE ON THE CUSP," said Captain Barry Spranker of the starslider *Drake*, holding two fingers a centimeter apart, "the very itty bitty *cusp* of fortune and glory of *galactic* proportions."

The comm beeped on the ship's circular command console. It startled Barry because he had routed incoming comms to his bunk. He ignored it, because he was trying to create a moment here.

He shook a finger at Flank, the ship's engineer. "The first ship to chart a circumnavigable route around the galaxy," Barry said. "We'll be the greatest explorers of all time."

Flank scowled, deepening his crow's feet. "So that's why you broke out your best sweatpants?"

Barry grinned. He was indeed wearing his best pair. "Shut up." He said to Tongue, the ship's navigator, "We will easily be the coolest people in the last one hundred thousand years."

Tongue bobbed his head up and down, his long, shaggy hair gently slapping his beard. "The race has been going on for two hundred thousand, but, you know, who's counting?"

The comm beeped again. Tongue reached out to open the message.

Barry slapped his hand away. "Don't you touch it. We're running silent. We are about to slide... into history."

Tongue said, "It's a tight beam transmission to us. Coming through the comm beacon we just dropped. Why wouldn't they use the comm?"

"We can check the messages later," Flank said.

Barry knew what the message said. The first time it came in he decided to ignore it. The crew worked their entire lives to achieve reach Union first. Why would they quit, at the finish line, simply because one of their desperate competitors sent yet another prank message? After the *Drake* became the first ship to reach the Union star system, connecting both sides of the galaxy for the first time, no one would care about who read what message when.

"Can we go already?" Barry asked. He carefully observed his buddies for signs of suspicion. Tongue pushed his shaggy hair out of the way while he checked the navigation math for the final slide to the Union system. Flank glared at the engineering readouts, daring them to reveal a problem, his bare arms crossed.

Barry forwarded all incoming comm messages to his bunk so he could screen them. He had responded to the legitimate ones. He prepped contingency plans for any possible dirty trick the other starsliders might pull to delay, deter, or trick them into losing the biggest race the galaxy had ever seen.

Tongue asked, "What was the comm about?"

Barry huffed. "Nothing. Some loser behind us trying to get us to quit. It would be the third one this month."

This made Flank crack a grin. "Was it Lemonne saying that our drive's about to implode? He's going to suck it when we waltz into Union."

"It couldn't be serious, do you think?" Tongue asked.

Barry waved him off. "Every time I get one of these, I check around. And they don't check out. Relax."

Flank wasn't buying it, so Barry raised an eyebrow to challenge him to say something. He didn't.

The engineering telltales reported in with a beep; they were blue across the board. No ambers, no reds; the *Drake* was ready to slide. She was a long, thin starslider, built and optimized to quickly chart new slide routes in uncharted space. And Flank made it a point of personal pride to make her the top-functioning starslider in the Exchange.

Flank said, "Drive is charged."

Barry asked Tongue, "You got the math?"

Tongue replied, "I do indeed got the math, Captain Sir."

"Wait," Flank said sharply.

The coordinates were locked, the drive was charged, there was nothing else keeping them. Tongue sighed in exasperation.

Flank poked a finger at Barry's chest. "Are you really going to wear this when you record the victory announcement? It looks ridiculous."

Barry inspected his beat-up jacket. Sponsor logos covered nearly the entire surface. Each logo flashed, strobed, glowed, or shifted patterns. "Yes. Our sponsors paid good money for this primo real estate."

"People will be replaying this announcement for the next thousand years, Barry. And they're gonna see these stupid corporate logos for Dinky Donuts, Major Skeeball League, and Spacer Pizza Bros?"

Tongue chuckled. "Flank, the only thing people will remember is his obnoxious gloating."

A smirk danced across Barry's face. "How about we go make some history?"

TWO

"I'M Alan Glown with a very special *Glown Happy Hour* for the entire galaxy today. We were the only Exchange jornos chosen to report the historic events which will happen in just a minute.

"Everybody has been talking for months about the reunion in Union. For centuries our Exchange has worked its way clockwise around the Milky Way from the Ancient Sectors while the GEC, that's Galactic Exploration Corp for you Griddie Kiddies out there who insist on the full name. You know I love you. The GEC has been coming around counter-clockwise. Thousands of years of exploration, tragedies and successes, hopes and dreams, will come together in the next few minutes.

"Let me set the stage. I'm reporting from the Exchange cruise ship *Crystal Temp*, on approach to Union. You won't hear this until this is broadcast, but let me tell you we are totally pumped up hard right now. Everyone's smiling. At the same exact time, the GEC ship *Phisak* will arrive at Union so both sides can win the race together! Isn't that great? "

"For a decade, there's been rumors flying about tensions between the Exchange and the GEC. Can we get along, can we cooperate. It's true: we Exchangers operate differently than you GECers. But it's okay.

There's so much to learn from one another, so many poop jokes to trade. We've discussed this on the *Happy Hour* — remember when we matched up April, the Exchanger chick, with Darien, the GEC gentleman? In the next couple of months we'll see if we can put those together physically, if you know what I mean. Haha. But seriously folks, I'm here to tell you that there's no tension here today. We're in a euphoric mood down here because. This. Is. Connexion Day! Avocado! Avocado!

"We're about to slide into Union and party ourselves silly, but first let's talk to some of the VIPs here. We have an A-list of stars for this historic voyage. There's starlets, retired explorers, and of course, Exchange executives. First up, we're talking with retired Captain Diana Lorne, callname Dinafour, who is the unofficial captain of our expedition. Captain, welcome."

"Great to be here, Alan."

Glown's voice dropped into a serious timbre. "Captain, you've got a glass of stimrose in your hand, tell me how you feel to be here, today."

"Well, Alan, it's a damn honor. Today is the biggest day in human history. After tens of thousands of years of exploration, we are finally linking up on the far side of the galaxy from the Ancient Sectors. Humanity will be able to circumnavigate the galaxy. The galactic frontier will begin to close."

"But there's still a lot left to explore, isn't there?" Glown asked. "For those up and coming explorers in the Exchange."

"It's fantastic out there," Captain Lorne said. "More than half the galaxy is unexplored. Maybe we'll finally discover aliens, with mystical technology and everything."

"Who enjoy deep fried human flesh dipped in hot mustard," Glown interjected.

Captain Lorne laughed. "Yeah, well, the galaxy is big but empty. I think this is the beginning of a golden age for Exchange and GEC explorers."

"Cap, are you ever tempted to return to the life yourself?"

"Every day. Every week you get to be the first humans to ever visit another solar system, a new nebula, discover new constellations."

"Ha! Can you tell us about the GEC ship we'll meet?"

"She's a *Monolith*-class exploration vessel named *Phisak*. She's essentially a mobile refueling station. The GECers take a different approach to spacecraft than we do: metal hulls, inorganic components. She has a longer range than a starslider and supports a crew of several hundred."

"I want to explain to the viewers what it's like to be on board this beautiful vessel, the *Crystal Temp*. I believe the Exchange rented this vessel. She's a big mobile religious retreat, usually, somewhere between a yacht and a cruise ship."

"That's right, Allen."

"To set the scene here, we're on a gorgeous observation deck with a viewscreen tuned to the forward cams. There are big hallways, spacious rooms, and I didn't need to bunk with Farty Arty, our producer and engineer. That's right Art, don't be acting like you don't know what I'm talking about.

"What's that, Art? Cap, Art is asking if life support can evacuate his nocturnal methane. Art, you did too say it! Cap?"

"Uh, it could easily handle the emissions of an entire cattle herd."

"Art's okay. He figured this would be an upscale affair so he put bowties on the mics. Made me not sleep in the nude. He's got class. You're the best, Art!"

"And you two have been perfect gentlemen the entire time you've been on board. I want your viewers to know you are the nicest fellows. You—"

"Cut her mic, cut her mic, Art! We have reputations to protect. Ha ha! She's just being gracious folks, she doesn't know we stole the towels. We're getting pretty close to the big event now, aren't we?"

"We should emerge in the Union system imminently," Captain Lorne said.

"Excellent. I want to thank you for hosting us and for being a good sport on the air with us."

"My pleasure, Alan."

"Next up is Ambassador Stanley Atherton, the Exchange executive. Welcome, Ambassador. I— wait, since when does the Exchange have ambassadors?"

"Alan, someone has to smooth over the wrinkles and waves you make on the air."

"Hoo hoo, very good. Very good. But I'm on my extra good behavior today."

"Originally, the Exchange retained some ambassadors to make first contact with alien races. When we never found any—"

"DinaFour already made the same joke. You're going to bore the audience."

"My apologies. And call me Stan. Seriously, my role is to represent the Exchange. Show how we clean up nice."

"And don't we! Well, Ambassador Stan, give us your take on what today means."

"It's been several millennia since our two peoples began to explore the galaxy in opposite directions. This is a grand family reunion of sorts, a joyous event. While we kept in touch with lightcast communications, this pen pal relationship can become a real friendship. People from the Exchange and the GEC will breathe the same air and be in the same room for the first time.

"In a few minutes, both of our ships will slide into the Union system and drop nav beacons in the names of humanity, not one exploration outfit or another. Together we will complete humanity's quest to reach Union, on the far side of the galaxy from Earth. This day, Connexion Day, will open a new era in human history. We did this peacefully, working together, and when we meet one another in person, I hope we can strengthen the bonds of affection that exist between our two peoples."

"You must be some kind of ladies man. Giving me chills. Art is tearing up over there. Allow me to get crass, Ambassador. The reward for the crew who reaches the Union system first and deploys navigational beacons is unbelievably huge. It's so huge the winner could buy a fully developed planet in the Ancient Sectors. If both the GEC and the Exchange enter the system at the same time, who wins the prize?"

"We'll make an announcement about the prize soon, Alan."

"What? Come on, Stan, make some news here to go along with this historic event."

"I can't say any more at this time. We're working on it, and I think everyone will be pleased with what we've come up with."

Alan sighed. "Okay, I'm afraid we need to leave it there, Ambassador Stan. We'll be emerging from the slide any second. Thanks for being with us. I'll sit in a quiet corner and do a running commentary on this historic event. When we slide out, we'll lightcast live.

"Okay, here we go. There's quite a crowd here on the observation deck. The viewscreen shows what I guess is the inside of the wormhole; smeared starlight, some kind of radiation glow or something. And we're out! Welcome to the Union system."

The crowd cheered.

"The captain has ordered the ship to drop nav beacons. They will make it possible for ships to travel to and through the system. This is the last piece of the galactic puzzle, folks. It's all smiles here as we swing around to head in-system. Union is not really habitable: it's star is too weak and it's planets are either gasballs or rocky cinders—

"Whoa! Something flashed by on the viewscreen! It's another ship! It buzzed us, I think. It is one of ours. Were they here already? People here are shocked, I'm shocked. Ambassador Stan is not happy. There are a few dirty looks coming his way. This is about to get *interesting*."

"Welcome to the Union system," a voice boomed over the comm. "This is Captain Barry Spranker of the Exchange starslider *Drake*, making an exploration claim on this system as of the timestamp of this message. For you runners-up, don't get down on yourselves. You had a good run and you missed by just a day or so." The message began to repeat.

"This is quite a breaking development," Alan whispered, "an Exchange ship beat us and the GEC to Union. The Ambassador literally ran out of here. I'm assuming to figure out what's going on. I guess this qualifies as a situation, huh? Art's feeding me what we know about this other ship. The *Drake* is starslider class, captain is, no surprise, some guy named Barry Spranker. Three-man crew, highly ranked on the Exchange's reputation markets. What's that? They were the odds-on favorite among the Exchange ships to win the race? But the race was called off, right Art? The Exchange and the GEC agreed to enter Union together. We were told the exploration vessels on both sides stopped so we could make this grand entrance together. Whoops, huh?

"The scene here is one of shock. The assembled crowd can't believe the *Drake* has upended this cosmic lovefest. Wow, this is really embarrassing for the Exchange. What? Art says it may be a trick by the Exchange to win. I kind of doubt it, Art, based on these pissed off people I see here. Stay tuned, galaxy, this story is only gonna get more interesting. And we'll stay on top of it and keep lightcasting here at the Alan Glown Show."

THREE

BARRY, Tongue, and Flank huddled by the airlock hatch like they were about to launch an ambush. Barry said, "Let's not get too wasted out there. People will want interviews, anecdotes, maybe even some bumping and grinding, huh? Don't let them down. No pissing in public. Tongue?"

"Never'll happen again."

Flank rolled his eyes.

Barry said, "Right, we're cool, we're professional, and we give as much love as we get." He popped the hatch and stuck his head out. "Hello, hello, *Shogura* Station!"

The screaming, cheering crowd drowned him out with an incoherent cheer. All of *Shogura Station*'s denizens came out to greet them. The crowd spilled from the narrow docking bay into the corridor beyond. The *Shogura* was the mobile operations base for the starsliders and other explorers on the Exchange's frontier. Barry didn't see a single person in the crowd who looked ready to murder him. Which was a pleasant surprise.

"We love you too!" he shouted, waving Flank and Tongue out of the hatch.

The crowd went nuts. "Caught the Grids napping!" someone yelled.

"You're going to be rich!"

"If I could have five minutes of your time for an interview-"

"-Father my children!"

"Be my children!"

The crowd swept them along to a party underway at Grandy's, the swankiest place on *Shogura*. It was two decks above the docking level, spread the width of the station, and it was hopping.

Half a dozen mechanics carried him, Flank, and Tongue, on their shoulders through the casino section of Grandy's. All three of them were deposited on the dance floor, where they obliged to dance for three intense songs. Flank, covered in sweat, was twirling and whirling and having the time of his life. Barry figured he and his crew wouldn't be paying for drinks tonight.

To avoid getting slobbered, seduced, and crushed, Barry kept moving. Jornos kept finding him and asking for interviews. Grubby investors wanted to chat about exciting opportunities. Some pale-faced woman kept appearing, trying to tell him something about the ambassador. Barry high-tailed it to the bar, accepted a free drink from the bartender. People demanded a toast. He stood on a chair and the crowd actually quieted.

"This isn't a victory just for the *Drake* and her crew," he said. "No, it's a victory for every hard working jerk in the entire Provisional Exchange, AKA our beloved Exchange. An Exchange ship reaching Union first vindicates the superiority and preferability, that's a word, I think, of the entire Exchange way of life. Am I right? That's right I'm right. Our loosey goosey band of amateurs and wannabes has triumphed over the GEC's mighty uptighties. I don't see any of my fellow explorers here right now, so I'm going to dedicate this to all you hard working jerks who keep us sliding!"

The crowd whooped and tried to mob him. Someone pulled his hair while another hand pinched his butt. He kept moving, hoping to find refuge outside the bar and casino. He joined a conga line snaking through the restaurant section, out into the station, and through at least a dozen docking bays. The conga line eventually returned to Grandy's which had put out a buffet and offered free drinks.

Every person who slapped his shoulder and congratulated him, he personally thanked them back. Their slack-jawed, confused reaction entertained him. He handed the bewildered well-wisher the drink shoved into his hand by the previous well-wisher and moved on.

He worked his way out of Grandy's and toured around the station. He found himself in quiet corridors collecting congratulations from beaming well-wishers. Exhausted, he returned to Grandy's for a plate from the buffet. Then he pretended to snooze in a booth in the corner, to deter well-wishers. People whispered nearby and took pictures, but no one bothered him. He just wanted to escape the journalists, the moochers, and a pale, unhappy woman who tried to catch his attention several times.

At some point he actually dozed off.

FOUR

SOMEONE SMACKED BARRY'S SHOULDER. He woke up with a snort and looked up at Holly the server. "Ambassador Stan needs to see you," she said. "This woman came by and told me to wake you up."

"Did she look like she had food poisoning?"

"Yeah, miserable."

Barry lifted his head from the table and grunted. Grandy's was nearly empty except for a rowdy table in the corner. Flank was scamming a half dozen drunken fans by betting them they couldn't balance sporks on their noses.

When he saw that Barry was awake, Flank ditched his woozy competitors and beelined to Barry's booth. "You're not picking up our reward dressed like that, are you?" he asked. He could smell money through vacuum.

Other than several small but conspicuous new stains, Barry still wore his usual fashion spread. Sweatpants, t-shirt, a leather jacket covered with the flashing, blinking patches of their sponsors.

"No, no, I'm going to put on a tux."

Flank grunted. "I should come with you."

Barry said, "No, let me handle it. Your fans over there are looking anxious."

Flank scowled but let Barry return to the ship to clean up.

Stan's ambassadorial chambers were just a single cramped office in the bowels of the *Shogura*, past the secondary sewer junction. It was an upgrade for an Exchange official; on other stations they were forced to hold court inside an airlock. Barry knocked and entered.

"What the hell is this?" Stan yelled, pointing at Barry.

"A tux. I have it on good authority that it fits the occasion."

"Just, just sit down, please," Stan said. "You've become quite the media star."

"Yes, such a nuisance. I am currently sorting through the interview requests, the offers for my memoirs—"

"Tell me why the hell you did it."

Barry smiles. "Gonna need to buy the memoir, Stan. I'll try and get you an advance reader copy."

"Do you have any idea how much trouble you've caused? The GEC is livid."

"It was a fair race. Has been for centuries, millennia. And we won."

"I was on that ship you buzzed at Union, that's burned into my memory forever, no thanks to you. This was supposed to be a joint arrival. Both sides win, together. A sign of new cooperation between them and us. Things were already tense between us and the GEC. It's been getting worse for oh, the last three centuries. And then you come in, wave your dick in their face, and pull their pants down!"

Barry scowled. "Wait, how is my dick out when their pants are down?"

"You know what I mean, damn it!"

Barry held up his hands. "Stan, it's over. The only reason the Exchange and the GEC were created millenia ago was to reach Union. It's done, we won, game over. The ancient charters say both organizations must dissolve within two months and let the actual government take jurisdiction. After you all pay us."

"I'm surprised you actually read the charters."

"It's like you don't know me at all. I'm hurt."

"Wait, are you serious about the charters, Barry? Earth is on the opposite side of the galaxy."

Barry read off the section numbers in each charter that specifically addressed the Connexion event. "This is ancient, standing law. The GEC and the Exchange can't pretend it doesn't exist because it makes for awkward diplomacy. In a matter of weeks, there are no more sides. I'm sure you guys and their guys have been preparing for this imminent event."

Stan said, "This isn't public yet, but the GEC is not disbanding. And neither is the Provisional Exchange. We've had two branches of humanity sprinting to explore and settle the galaxy forever. You think they'll stop because of some ancient charter from a hundred thousand years ago? Wrong. We are amending our charter and so is the GEC. With the permission of the 'official government' back on Earth. We'll both keep going, slamming right into one another's territory. We'll compete for settlements and trade routes in the same systems. It could get nasty. My bosses are worried a war could break out between us and the GEC."

Barry straightened his tux jacket. "You're talking out your ass, Stan. You got embarrassed because we spit in your salad bar. Okay? But let's get serious and talk actual business. Let's talk the reward."

Stan said, "You don't get it. People are *freaking out*. The GEC's ships, bases, and settlements are spreading out like a precision military campaign. Guess how long it takes them to build a working city for a million residents on a settlement world? Two weeks. *Two weeks*. It takes us three years."

"Their cities are prison camps, according to the vids."

Stan said, "You weren't supposed to go to Union. You were told to halt."

"Are you saying you tried to call off a hundred thousand year old race for a PR stunt? We were supposed to stop at the finish line so you could have a photo op? Give up on the prize money that has been compounding interest for millennia? And let you breach multiple contracts that are thousands of years old?" Barry asked.

"Yes! That's why we warned everyone off." Stan shook a finger at Barry's gobsmacked expression. "No. Don't play stupid with me. Oh, you're serious, aren't you? You never got the messages, is that your excuse?"

Barry straightened his back and dropped his voice an octave. "Let's talk payment."

Stan held up his hands. "We're not paying you."

A smirk. "That's not funny."

Stan returned the smirk. "I'm not joking. Like I said, the charters are being amended. There is no reward. We're working on how to distribute the money to every explorer equitably."

Barry's body went numb. This foxing bureaucrat was actually serious. The surreality of this weakened his grasp on consciousness. He failed to comprehend the next words Stan's mouth was emitting. No prize money?

For thousands of years, explorers had been scooping up smaller milestone prizes for light years charted, sectors explored. Important stuff, but little stuff. Leading to Union, the biggest prize. And now these jackholes thought they could not pay off? And get away with it? And blame him for honoring the contract?

"The law is really crystal clear on this, Stanley. These are legal contracts backed by the charters. Do you want us to sue both of you for a galactic contract breach?"

Stan sighed. "I'm telling you. The lawyers reviewed this all and approved it. Earth, the GEC, the Exchange: we are the government. We've changed the law, modified the contracts, and added new clauses."

"I never signed these new contract modifications. Never even heard of them."

"Look, you did. There was a clause that allowed for emergency modifications. Bottom line: you are not getting the reward. In fact, since you violated the contracts' rules on following Exchange policy, you won't get anything at all."

So many of Barry's plans revolved around the prize money. He ticked through them one by one and manually cancelled each one. The totality of it amounted to a thorough destruction of his life. And his fiancé Rachel's. And Tongue's. And Flank's. And their investors. And the explorer reputation market.

He didn't lose his cool because what Stan said was absolutely insane. It had to be wrong. The Exchange was built on reputation markets. Barry remembered when he was a kid, a developer named Apsu refused to pay for an office building constructed on his homeworld Shaw. The rep markets crashed Apsu's reputation, siphoned off his capital and destroyed his business. Took out most of the wealth held by Apsu's family, too, with their reputations driven down by investor retribution by association.

Barry stood up. "This is foxing crap. The Exchange government can't renege on a contract, and especially not the most famous contract in history. The Exchange will be finished on the reputation markets. The investors love to punish cheats. The Regulators will probably frog-march you to jail. No one will work for the Exchange ever again."

Stan's tone was resigned. "Yes, they will. The market's not as dynamic as you think. They're not going to blame us, they'll blame you. The media will report that you guys cheated. Or your beacons failed. Or your stunt at Union never happened."

"Never happened? The beacons failed? Are you foxing crazy? No one will believe you."

"The institutional investors already are planning to dump their positions on the *Drake*. Once the news breaks, the rest of the investors will finish you off. You might be forced to sell the *Drake*."

"You've totally murdered us. You're going to scam us by wrecking our reputation to not pay us the reward?"

Stan threw up his hands. "There's nothing I can do."

"Really? We go back a long way, Stan. I've treated you half decently for maybe a quarter of it."

"You don't realize the damage you've done here, Barry. The entire Provisional Exchange is mortified. They're desperate to appease the GEC. They almost cut me loose because of what you pulled."

"Well, how genuinely horrific it would have been for you. I really feel for those children of yours who would be starving." Barry checked around the tiny room for something to smash against the idiot's skull.

Or maybe something to rip apart. But nothing too hard to rip, he didn't want to embarrass himself by failing to pull something out of the wall. But everything was bolted down anyway.

"I never had children," Stan said.

"And to think I doubted evolution once."

Stan said, "The best I can do is call off the investors. And then I'll swing you some lousy exploration contracts. You could drive new slide routes into GEC space. Around Union."

Barry wasn't listening. Stan's sensible offer was a whisper lost in a tornado of anger. Barry roared at the pragmatic squeaky voice in his head that said to listen to Stan. Barry played by the rules his whole life, kind of, just to reach this very point. Only to be screwed over for a diplomacy stunt and told to follow the new, unfair rules designed to screw him.

Barry's mouth curled upward. "I got journos fighting each other for an exclusive with me. If I expose this whole thing, right now, it'll seem like retribution against me. The press will kill you guys."

"Barry." Stan pronounced his name like it was a viral plague. "I'm telling you as a friend — it won't work. No journo will piss on the most glorious day in human history."

Barry spread his arms. "You're murdering me. Murdering us. And you want me to run silent, be a good employee? You can shove this whole thing up your ass."

"I'm giving you the truth here, a full dose. Recognize the gracious favor I'm doing you."

A better favor would be to get lobotomized with rusty crocheting needles.

The Exchange screwing the *Drake* hit Barry like a dizzying slap upside the head. The kind where your scalp tingles before the pain rushes in. There had to be something he could fix, something he could say, something to negotiate.

There wasn't a glimmer of give in Stan's expression though. Stan was informing him of a tragedy, not holding a negotiation.

Barry stormed out of Stan's office. He wasn't usually the storm out type. He always tried to maintain his dignity, unless he could get a laugh. But this was too much.

In the corridor, he slumped against the wall and slid to the filthy deck. His hands and feet tingled because he was taking rapid, shallow breaths. His soul was numb. He loosened his clip-on bowtie and sucked air down into his gut.

The press, the reputation exchange, the investors, they would all ruin the *Drake* in a matter of hours. He couldn't stop any of that from happening.

He scrambled to his feet. He had to do something to cushion the financial blow or to fight back. He didn't know what, but he needed to plot some sweet, remorseless revenge in a hurry. He strode out of the sewer section, his dress shoes snap-clicking on the deck, a sweatpants kind of a guy in a tuxedo with nothing left to lose.

FIVE

BARRY STOMPED up the Drake's corridor to the kick. Tongue said, "Hey Barry, some fuel magnate offered us a free week's stay at his summer place on Krivitsia 179. Flank says he wants to help manage the media exposure in exchange for pitching his product line."

Barry ignored him and looked over the command console's readouts. "Great. Are we charged up?"

"Sure, I guess so," Tongue said tentatively. "What's wrong? How did the meeting with Stan go?"

Barry nonchalantly flipped the comm system off. "Oh, excellent. We'll receive the first installment in a week. The accounting people need to sign off. Is Flank aboard?"

"Yeah, he's still bunked. You know, you don't look so good."

Barry smiled. "What? Me? No. I'm great. But let's go. The vultures are circling, ready to strike. People are eyeing me up like a juicy slab of insect protein. We should have hired a manager to handle the fame."

"Yeah, that's what I'm talking about. This rich guy Jones has offered us the whole package."

"If we're good to launch, let's go. Right now," Barry said.

"Now? We haven't resupplied yet. The only thing in the galley is pepper steak, and I'm not eating that shit again," Tongue said, jerking a thumb towards the galley.

"I'll buy you something nice, later." He watched Tongue back the ship out of the docking bay. The viewscreen showed the *Shogura* falling behind.

"You don't look good at all, man."

Barry blinked a few times. "I haven't slept in a week."

"Yeah, it shows. Where we going?"

"Back to Union."

"Union?" said Flank, charging into the kick. "What the hell is going on?" He put his hands on his hips. "Where the hell's our money?"

Barry stood up and straightened his tux sleeves. "Boys, sit down. There's just a small dollop of bad news." He recounted the meeting with Stan.

The yelling and cursing began, slowly crescendoed, and just shy of breaking into full-on violence, faded. With a roar of frustration, Tongue tried to tear his own seat off the deck, but it was bolted down. He pounded on it with his fists. Flank settled for holding his head in his hands with periodic howls of pure rage.

"What the hell! Why didn't you tell us they called off the race?" Flank yelled. "And rescinded the prize?"

Barry kept his tone neutral. "I ignored the messages. You'd never guess how many cranks, nutjobs, and scammers called us in the last month. I can't be blamed for the GEC and the Exchange secretly cancelling a contest that is literally a hundred thousand years old."

Tongue and Flank exchanged looks and got real quiet. Barry shook his head.

"Why the hell did they call off the race?" Tongue shouted. "They foxing used us. And our ancestors! For centuries!"

Flank stood nose to nose with Barry. "We should have dumped you years ago. I foxing knew you were up to something. But I didn't listen to myself because I wanted the prize. I wanted the fame. You've always been a scheming little shit and it always backfires. Every goddamn time."

Barry shut his eyes and swallowed. He resigned himself to the pummeling Flank was about to deliver.

Flank put a hand on Barry's shoulder. "Barry?"

When Barry didn't answer, Flank slammed him in the diaphragm. Barry dropped to the deck, gasping.

"Knock it off, man!" Tongue pulled Flank away.

"Well, if he can't talk, he can't lie to us, can he?" Flank asked.

"We need to be like, proactive," Tongue remarked. "We should sue their asses for breach of contract."

"We were supposed to be 'the crew who.' We ended up failures," Flank mourned. "Outcasts. Our reps will be lower than dirt."

"Broke outcasts," Tongue added.

Barry crawled to his chair, pulled himself up and rasped, "We return to Union. Stan said the Grids rushed the system already. If they uploaded their charts to the system buoys, it'll give us a complete map of Grid space. We'll keep on going."

"No, I mean, what do we do with our lives now?" Tongue asked. "We were supposed to be rich, famous, you know, free of everything. Instead, it's the three of us, one cramped ship, and no money."

"What do you mean, cramped?" Flank asked.

"That's not entirely true," Barry said. "There's one other payoff coming." He smiled. "I sold my reputation holdings and used the money to short both of your reputations."

"You did not," Tongue said. It was illegal, and career suicide, to bet against your own reputation. The reputation exchanges were fickle creatures already because they were part popularity contest and part honest evaluation of a person's abilities.

"No, this makes sense," Flank said, knitting his brow. "We commit securities fraud on top of being persecuted for doing our jobs. We'll be sure to receive absolutely no leniency. Barry, you foxing asshole."

Barry smirked. "Only if we're caught. Because, guys, our rep stocks are rigged to blow. Stan says the institutional investors will dump us in the morning and our reps will tank when news breaks about us getting screwed out of the prize. The only way we profit off this is for each of you to issue more shares of yourself right now. Then use the proceeds to short the stocks of the other two of us. We'll make serious money off of it. Enough to stay afloat for a long while."

"What about the Regulators?" Flank asked. "If they figure it out before the markets open, they'll freeze trading on the exchange. We'll be criminals, rejects, losers, *and broke.*"

Barry waved him off. "It takes time to trace back these transactions. I have side investment accounts that make these plays. Money moves at the speed of light, but the Regulators have to put their socks on first."

Within a few minutes the other two had shorted each other. Each of their stocks typically hovered around one hundred and fifty. The shorts they purchased would cash in when the price of their own shares dropped below twenty. Career suicide meant their shares would zero out within minutes.

Flank slumped against a bulkhead until his butt hit the deck. "Tongue, slide us the hell out of here," he said.

Tongue sniffled once and engaged the drive.

SIX

JUNIPER M. GRAND relaxed in his office, sipping an early morning brandy. The office was an opulent, wood-paneled gem above Grandy's restaurant on the *Shogura*. Fabric sofas, soft lighting, and choice artwork set the mood for clients and suppliers. His minor ownership stake in the *Shogura*, and management of Grandy's, provided him a home and an office.

He believed he was the vanguard of shady business on the Exchange frontier. For every new route opened, for every planet settled, demand for entertainment and certain comforts increased and he was the first criminal boss to provide it. Very little was illegal in the Exchange, but he still dared to supply what others shied away from: stimulants, escorts, trashy novels, gaming, you name it.

Business was good. He wasn't the only entertainment supplier on *Shogura*. The station's other owners would never permit a monopoly. He owned a majority share of the three legal and the four other than legal entertainment venues.

Yesterday's Connexion Day festivities to celebrate the Exchange's arrival at Union were a gift. He received heavy discounts from whole-salers and suppliers who desperately wanted to attach their brands to the event while he boosted his retail markup. The money was rolling in so fast he could barely keep up with it. The free drinks every hour had paid for itself twenty-fold.

He was perfectly positioned to be the first crimelord to expand into GEC space and to supply their stations and worlds with music, booze, and gambling. Only beginning middle age, he possessed the time, flexibility, experience, and capital to pull it off. But first he needed to learn GEC cultural tastes and mores, a tricky subject when it came to vices. So far they appeared uptight, always wearing drab uniforms and speaking like they were human press releases. He hoped it was a front and the regular GEC folk liked a good time. The Exchangers and Grids would scramble to grab everything around the Union system in Sector 180. The demand for his kind of services would far outstrip supply. He was ready to scale his businesses up and ride the tsunami of opportunity.

An alert flashed on the master screen built into his wooden desk, ruining his pleasant interlude of schemes and dreams. In business, if you took your focus off the details for a split-second the entire galaxy could shift underneath you.

The alert was about his investment portfolio. He rolled his eyes. Turbulence in the reputation exchanges again? And how could there not be? The race to Union was over. The thoughtless herd must be worried about what was next for the Exchange, including the explorers and the frontier businesspeople like him. The herd second-guessed itself with any uncertainty. It never fazed Grand. He was a long-term investor who made informed bets on high quality insider information.

He had parked his expansion bankroll in the exploration-related exchanges. The explorer exchange was one of the least volatile reputation markets given that there was plenty of unexplored galaxy. So long as a starslider didn't explode, it was as close to a sure thing in the frontier sectors. And he had the best insider information that was passed around his restaurants and casinos. His expansion bankroll had been steadily growing for months now.

"Ah, it's only a little market justice," he said. The reputation stocks of the *Drake*'s crew were taking some hits. Their stunt at Union had ruffled feathers and some of the fearful were panic selling. Smarter investors may be profit-taking off the new infamous celebrities who were now heroes on the *Shogura*. And there had to be some contrarians who thought Spranker and company were now overvalued. Share prices oscillated and Grand never let volatility upset him.

But then the explorer exchange collapsed.

The share price on the three explorers fell fifty points in two minutes, trading under eighty. Even fading explorers who turned in a bad quarter never traded below ninety; he invested in these *Drake* guys, years ago at ninety-five. Yesterday they were each at or above one-fifty. His bet to go long on that crew would implode unless their share prices rebounded. But minutes when by and the rebound wasn't happening.

"What the hell," he said, "last night Spranker was prancing around the station in a tuxedo."

His restaurant manager knocked on the door. The large man with blinking lights dangling from his dreadlocks wanted to discuss last night's take.

Grand waved him away. "Come back in an hour."

He couldn't stop reading the exchange's ticker tape. The financial press was chattering nonstop about the death spiral the *Drake* crew stocks were in. The pundits first speculated and then repeated their own unconfirmed rumors about some malfeasance on the crew's part. They began voicing doubts about the *Drake*'s claim of reaching Union first. There had to be some explanation.

"Kroger!" Grand screamed.

Kroger rolled into the office furtively. He was a repurposed health assistant droid. He was better than any human assistant, including the impossibility of betraying Grand by handing over trade secrets to enemies or competitors.

Kroger's soft body was covered with pseudo-skin. It kept Grand's knuckles from getting skinned when he needed to punch the droid in frustration. "What's the matter?" Kroger asked.

Grand pointed at his viewscreen. "These damn star jockey stocks, the *Drake* crew. What the hell is going on here with their share prices?"

Kroger checked the exchange ticker. "There are concerns about the *Drake*'s claims—"

"Damn it, I already know *that*. Who's selling, how much do they hold, how does this match up with the gossip we know? Do I need to do all this research myself?"

Kroger reversed a meter, out of arm's reach. "No, sir. Absolutely not. Institutional investors are liquidating their position on the *Drake* crew. The media reports rumors that the crew may have cheated somehow on their way to Union. Oh my, news just broke that the *Drake* crew short-sold their own shares, and those of the entire exchange the second the market opened. What they have done is highly illegal."

"Shit! They're scamming everyone!" Grand chucked a metal paper-weight at the wood paneled wall, denting it.

Kroger reversed another meter. "The explorer reputation exchange is in free fall. It is down eighty-nine percent. The Regulators have just halted trading."

Grand was titanically screwed. Exchanges were funky things: the herd ran faster when it realized it was moving at all. And now, with the Regulators getting involved, everything on *Shogura* could be scrutinized.

He had missed the insider trading info on this one. Or someone deliberately kept it from him. To ruin him. Yes, someone must have plotted against him.

"Show me my financial position," he said, pointing at the screen. The collapsed explorer reputation exchange wasn't done with him yet. Investors were fleeing anything related to the explorers. The *Shogura*'s share price tanked next. And then the herd dumped Grand's own reputation shares on the hospitality exchange. His own reputation stocks on various unofficial criminal exchanges also collapsed. The 'investors' on those exchanges would blame him for their lost investments and hold him physically accountable.

"What the fox just happened to my balance sheet?" Grand asked.

Kroger's voice quavered. "The margin call on the legitimate exchanges will wipe out your liquid assets. You can't pay your suppliers' bills next quarter. The situation on the other exchanges is worse. You don't have any financing options other than selling assets. Yakov may buy you out. His offer still stands."

"I cufo'ing know about Yakov's offer," Grand spat.

Grand always kept a firm line for acceptable losses and it rapidly approached and then passed by right by. He needed to salvage what he could.

"Kroger," he said in a low, trembling voice. "Sell everything. The casino, Grandy's, the bars, the distribution chains. I'm not shrinking my operation and living with Yakov rubbing his balls in my face. We need to leave the Exchange scene if we want me to live. Where the hell is Spranker?"

"The *Drake* departed the station six hours ago. Rumor has it they slid toward Union."

Grand contemplated this. He had planned to dominate Sector 180 with a head start and a fat bankroll. Now all he had was a head start and a burning need for revenge. "Get me a ship. I don't care how. Make sure it's fast. We'll capture the *Drake's* crew, and I will foxing murder them."

SEVEN

TWELVE HOURS and two slides later, the *Drake* arrived at an unnamed system they'd mapped only weeks ago. A star off the main sequence warming three gas giants and a nasty asteroid belt in the system's habitable ring. The outer system was empty except for a pair of off-ecliptic comets.

Nothing to write home about, or map, or settle, or mine. There were systems like this spread across the Galactic Habitable Ring. The better pickings included habitable planets, easy slide navigation, or an abundance of raw materials. The *Drake* was alone, greeted only by the nav beacons they deployed before.

They were one slide away from Union but Barry wanted to hold here and listen in on the lightcast channels. Interstellar communications traveled via permanent, microscopic zero-mass slides. The messages would broadcast at lightspeed between zero-mass relay slides to provide near real-time communication.

"Check the markets," Barry said, desperate to learn what happened in the last half day.

"We're getting slammed," Tongue observed. "Our share prices are down to the single digits. I wonder what idiots are still hanging on at those prices?"

"Never thought I'd see my share price so low," Flank said quietly.

"Lots of messages," Tongue said. "Most are, uh, wow, incredibly hostile. Remember five years ago when every starslider crew agreed to invest in the other crews so we wouldn't kill each other? We just made all the other explorers lose the money they invested in us and hammered their own share prices."

"Oh, I also shorted their stocks, too," Barry said. "When the exchange shares collapsed, we kind of made a killing. Call it rich-ish."

Flank groaned.

Tongue posted a chart of the explorer exchange's share prices. "The whole exploration exchange tanked before they stopped trading. The media is trashing explorers across the board, not just us. Exchange news says the Exchange deserved it because we played loose and fast with the rules. Man, are they trying to kiss up to the Grids?"

Flank said to Barry, "Congratulations, you've pissed off every one of our friends. Everyone who might help us probably wants to kill us."

"But we're getting *rich. Ish.*"

"Unlikely we're going home, you know," Tongue pointed out.

Barry checked his own messages. One of them made his back stiffen. Rachel. He wouldn't open it in front of the guys.

Barry hurried to his cabin and brought up Rachel's message. Text only. She always got right to the point.

[Barry,

It breaks my heart, but I must end this. End us. It sounds terrible, but I don't have time to rewrite this. It's the only way to avoid being dragged down by you and keep my reputation intact. Oh, and my new album has songs about being dumped. They're not about you, but I might need to say otherwise on tour.

I'm keeping the ring.

-Rachel]

Barry's insides felt like they had been smashed by a spiked mallet. On top of the pain and the rejection, he hated surprises. He told himself that he was the man in touch, with his finger glued to the galaxy's pulse. He positioned himself to benefit from any opportunity on the horizon. Rachel wasn't falling off the entertainment exchange or behind on the fashion exchange. She was smart. She bailed before he could hurt her. Another carefully planned facet of his life dissolved into gooey shit.

What did his eager attention and hard work achieve? The universe shrugged him off like an annoying lounge act. Humanity could barely be bothered to join it for a swift kick to his balls.

Barry sank past apathy straight down to catatonia. He was simply a meat sack, no more special than the plants in the biowall out in the corridor. They mindlessly processed light and water, swished around some chemicals and fluids until they died. Success or failure didn't matter in the end, the striving served as a means to keep his brain cells entertained. But it mattered not one wit to anyone or anything else. Pretending there was a dramatic narrative arc to his life was like imagining a narrative arc for the ship's plants.

He got up stiffly and returned to the kick.

Flank winced. "I'm sorry for you, Barry. The media say Rachel dropped you. But it's better this way. We kind of assumed she cheated on you on the regular."

"No, we did *not*," Tongue retorted. "Why the hell would you say that?"

"Come on," Flank spread his hands. "She's a rock star. She's getting her yo-yo stretched at every tour stop."

Tongue said, "You're not helping here, Flank. She's not the type."

"That's what stars do. That's what I'd do."

Tongue shook his head hard enough to cause his hair to whip around. "She's a woman, not some horny guy. She's not you, Flank."

"Rock stars are rock stars. She cheats, get over it." Flank put his hand on his friend's shoulder. "Barry, you're better off this way. You're free."

"Free?" Barry asked. "Are you two done dissecting my love life? Because I would like to go to Union, if it's not too much to ask."

"We're going," Tongue replied. "What's the plan when we get there?"

Barry said, "We'll think of something once we see the Grid's star-charts." Actually, there was no plan. Maybe cash out his options and hole up somewhere with enough triskey to safely drink himself to death? He tapped some keys randomly at his station.

"Barry," Tongue said, "I'm sorry about this. Everything has changed so fast. I get it: things seem bleak. But it'll, you know, work out. Somehow. Flank thinks so, too. He's too much of an asshole to say it."

Barry Spranker stared off into nothing. For the first time, he began to believe that reaching Union first may have been a mistake. "Thanks."

EIGHT

BARRY DIDN'T SPEAK MORE than five words to anyone for the next several days. He watched the grass grow on his cabin's bulkheads and moaned every once in a while. Guzzling all the triskey onboard diluted his emotional state until nothing was left but existential numbness and a rip-roaring hangover.

The last time they slid this way he and the guys had been practically floating off the deck moss in eager anticipation. On top of the universe. Returning to Union a second time was exciting like, well, like watching deck moss grow.

Tongue stayed in his cabin, too. He needed a calm place where Flank's sourness and Barry's angst couldn't squash his dwindling supply of positive vibes. He didn't avoid them out of spite, but in a kind of emotional quarantine.

Flank lifted weights in the engine room, brooding over his squashed dreams of fame and glory and cleaning and reorganizing his tools and spare parts.

Fame and glory. Barry rubbed the stubble on his chin. It was more like inglorious infamy and aggravated poverty.

"We're at Union," Tongue announced shipwide.

Barry roused himself from his stupor and shuffled to the kick. Getting past Union would require some jawing: it was off limits to Exchange ships, according to a repeating announcement on Exchange comm channels. He didn't expect a warm welcome.

He and Flank arrived at the kick from opposite ends of the ship. Flank motioned at Barry about his rumply appearance. Barry tucked in half of his shirt into his dirty sweatpants.

Tongue ignored them both. "Welcome back." He brought them out of the slide. The *Drake* arrived at a GEC nav beacon at the outer edge of the system, between the orbits of two gas giants. There was nothing out this far. He set the ship to slowly circle the beacon's slide entrance perimeter. They could keep their distance from other ships by staying below the ecliptic.

A ship hailed them. "Unidentified Exchange ship, you are not authorized to be in this system. Travel to this or any other GEC system or territory has not been approved."

Tongue closed the channel. "They took our buoys. They're gone," he noted. The other two took up their stations at the console and studied sensor scans.

"They're beacons, not buoys," Flank grumbled. "Maybe they drifted away."

"Navigators call them buoys," Tongue replied. "And they are locationally-locked."

Barry dug his heels into his eye sockets. "Boys."

Any trace of the *Drake's* initial visit, including the beacons they deployed so triumphantly, were gone. It added another small heartbreak to the growing pile.

"Why aren't there *any* Exchange beacons?" Flank asked. "We're sharing this system with the GEC, aren't we?"

The only nav beacons in the system belonged to the GEC. They floated only in the outer system. Standard practice was to deploy beacons in the inner and outer system, on both sides of the star. The combined telemetry allowed a ship to know exactly where a star system was within the galaxy. The system's beacon network transmitted traffic information for navigational and safety purposes, allowing any ship within slide range of a star system to view the other in-system traffic in real time.

"Maybe the GEC hasn't finished deploying them yet," Tongue said. "They've probably been busy scrapping ours."

"Or this entire foxing system belongs only to them," Flank said.

"I'm not surprised if it does," Barry said. "But who cares? It's not our problem. Let's download the GEC starcharts and get the hell out of here."

Tongue pointed. "Check out the inner system traffic."

Barry sighed but peered at the screen. There were about fifty ships clustered on the far side of the sun. "They must have buoys, uh beacons, in there, how come we can't see them?" Barry asked.

Tongue frowned. "Private buoys not on the network?"

"Beacons. It's not a surprise," Flank said sharply, "They're occupying the system. They're massing dozens of ships here. They're organized and aggressive. There's going to be a war."

"No one's starting a war, Flank," Barry said. "There hasn't been a war in space in, I guess, a million years. Riots over triskey shortages, sure, yeah. But not a war."

"No, they don't need to fight us. They can beat us through logistics." Flank pointed at the count of fifty ships. "Settle more planets, squeeze us out of this sector."

"You mean squeeze out the Exchange," Barry said.

"That's still us," Flank retorted.

"Well, I'm not feeling like the Exchange really wants us any more, you know," Tongue said.

Barry agreed. "Good point. How about we scout the competition a little? Send a probe close to them."

Tongue launched a probe that slid close to the GEC ships in the inner system. It sent back real-time data through a micron-sized slide.

"That is a lot of cargo haulers and Monoliths," Tongue said. "Refuelers and a construction ship, too. That construction ship's arms are deployed, like it's parked here permanently."

Flank wrinkled his bald forehead into a series of ridges. "I'm recording their energy signatures, slide drive design, hull composition, and mass profiles. Huge energy bleeds from those metallic hulls. Their ships are inefficient. Idiotic design."

Other ships began to slide in to the system, around the beacon the *Drake* had slid to. *Starslider*-class, same as the *Drake*. Each starslider's exterior was unique, either because the crew decorated it or because of modifications made to the hull and the bow-mounted slide drive.

"Tongue, right now would be a very good time to get us the hell out of here," Barry said.

The hairy navigator frowned. "These GEC charts, they aren't right."

Flank looked at Tongue's screen. "What the hell?"

Barry ignored them. "Those ships probably spotted us hovering here below the ecliptic," he said, "if we stick around, things could become uh, interesting."

Flank asked, "What does 'interesting' mean? Barry?"

Barry cleared his throat. "I did mention that we shorted these guys' share prices, right? They may be extra unhappy with us."

The comm squawked with an incoming voice. "Barry Spranker, you son of a bitch!"

Tongue asked, "How much did we make?"

Barry sent a financial statement to each of their overhead monitors.

Flank gasped. Tongue said, "You know, you are a son of a bitch."

"Well, in our defense, we're not rich as we should be," Barry said.

"But you cleaned them out!" Flank stomped around the deck. "Did you think, for even a second, about how they might respond?"

"Of course I did. Which is why we need to slide," Barry replied casually. "Why aren't we sliding?"

Tongue stayed focused on his console. "The navigation system has to calculate energy requirements for each slide to judge its feasibility. The GEC doesn't map routes like we do. The *Drake*'s navigation system has to crunch the raw data for our drive's specs. Plus, there's this."

He flipped the GEC starchart to Barry's screen.

"What the hell is this?" Barry asked. "Where's the rest of their routes?"

The only parts of the Milky Way galaxy deemed habitable for human life were inside the goldilocks band called the Galactic Habitable Ring, or GHR. Inside the GHR, radiation from the blackholes at the galactic core wasn't too high and the heavy metal content on planets wasn't too low. The GHR was twenty thousand light years wide and took up over a quarter of the galaxy's volume.

For navigation purposes, the GHR was divided into three hundred and sixty sectors, one for each degree of a circle. The Ancient Sectors occupied thirty sectors at the six o'clock position. Over a couple hundred thousand years, the Exchange and the GEC expanded outward from the Ancient Sectors in opposite directions. Exchange territory spread clockwise up to Sector 179. The Grids explored and occupied counterclockwise, from Sector 345 to 181. Or at least that is what they had claimed.

Union sat near the middle of Sector 180. The GEC starcharts showed only one route hugging the coreward boundary of the GHR through sectors 183, 182, and 181, to Union in 180.

Tongue said, "The good news is we really beat the snot out of them coming to Union. Bad news is, there's totally nowhere for us to go."

The combined galactic map showed that the Exchange had grown organically and haphazardly. Independent explorers grabbed the nearest, choicest planets and laid down the most efficient routes to them. Settled Exchange territory resembled capillaries spreading throughout the GHR. Thoroughly-settled systems resembled the center of a spider's web of slide routes to nearby systems.

The GEC's approach was a carefully orchestrated exploration and settlement program. It constructed long, straight routes, often connected by space stations and supply depots if no habitable planet was nearby. Spur routes reached out to settled systems or just ended in unoccupied space. The organization optimized its resource usage by developing galactic slide 'highways' to minimize the number of slides per thousand light years.

The GEC's galactic footprint resembled straight tree trunks with symmetrical branches growing outward. The two or three main trunk routes curved around the galaxy, slicing each sector into thirds. The 'top' of the tree in the 180s sectors narrowed to a single main route that coiled around the GHR's coreward boundary. It resembled the path of a slow sprinter who took the inside track to make up for lost time in a losing race.

"You know what this tells me?" Flank asked. "It tells me that when the GEC realized how badly they were behind us, they scrapped this branch development altogether. They just mapped a single route across thousands of light years, a couple of sectors. They sprinted for the last century to reach Union. And they still lost to the Exchange. To the *Drake*. To us."

"Guys, can we do the history lesson later?" Barry asked. "Our investors are coming to lodge complaints."

"We settled sixty percent of our territory while the GEC settled only ten percent," Tongue said. "Highly organized, depressingly rigid, and, you know, much less effective. Centuries of lightcast documentaries and vids don't lie."

Flank zoomed the chart in on nearby GEC space. The single route from Union to the GEC's settled sectors consisted of depot stations parked at regular slide intervals. There were no GEC-settled worlds in Sector 180 and in most of 181. "There's nowhere to go," he remarked. "We're not officially authorized to enter their territory. Their slide route is just Monoliths parked at slide points back to their last settled system. What is it? Pergamon? We're fried. You foxing fried us, Barry."

Barry waved his hand. "Okay, okay, can we hurry this up? We slide to the next station, wave hello, and slide again. Not that hard. Better than being destroyed by our old buddies out there coming to kill us."

"At some point, Barry, we're either going to be caught or need resupply or parts. Or we can redline the drive, cause a malfunction, and be stranded to die in the dark interstellar void."

"Guys, I hate to say this, but we need to turn around," Tongue said. "There's a thousand places we could hide in the Exchange. The Regulators and everyone else would never find us."

"But everyone back there hates us," Barry said. Stan tried to offer him a path to redemption, didn't he? Maybe he already knew the GEC would bar Exchangers from its territory. But Barry torched their bridges in the Exchange. Oops.

Flank snarled, "Nowhere to slide to in the GEC, and we're criminals in the Exchange. This is wonderful, Barry, wonderful. You didn't think this through at all, did you?"

Barry rubbed his face and said nothing. He jabbed a finger at the oncoming starsliders who were still sending angry threats.

Tongue shook his head and his hair swung around. "I can't believe the GEC is shutting us out like this. There's got to be another route into their territory." He studied the charts.

Barry closed his eyes as the nearest starslider came within weapons range. A starslider didn't have room for shipboard weapons, but it could wreck another starslider's slide drive, no problem. And a busted slide drive could strand the *Drake* and leave them at the mercy of all the people who were pissed at them.

The comm continued to broadcast their fellow Exchangers' threats, insults, and promises of violent revenge. But despite it, the other starsliders flew past the *Drake*. They each launched a half dozen probes that slid away in every direction.

"What, what are they doing?" Barry asked.

"Looks like searching surrounding space for new slide routes or habitable planets. Maybe the Exchange dangled a new reward for habitable systems in this sector," Flank said.

"They can't afford to take a swipe at us," Tongue added.

Barry exhaled a breath he didn't realize he had been holding.

Tongue shut off the comm and the *Drake*'s transponder. No one else in the system would detect the ship unless they carefully scanned the entire Union system or slid into visual range. "The slide drive is charged, but where to slide next?"

Another Exchange ship slid in at the beacon. It was a small yacht typically used as an interstellar shuttle or personal transport. It identified itself as the *Sluicifer*.

"Who's this guy?" Flank asked Tongue. Tongue looked at Barry.

"Beats me," Barry said. "Probably not an explorer. What? I don't memorize the ownership records of every little dinky shuttle in the

Exchange. I'm turning the comm back on." He sent a canned greeting hail.

The comm crackled with a live reply. "Spranker, you owe me a hell ton of money."

The *Drake*'s navigation alarms chirped. The yacht was on an intercept course.

NINE

"WHO IS HE?" Tongue asked.

Flank threw up his hands.

The voice was familiar, but Barry couldn't place it. He recognized the anger though. Their luck at Union was not improving.

He keyed the comm, saying, "Stand by, uh, *Sluicifer*." He said to Tongue, "Start her up."

"So this is what it's going to be like, outrunning investors?" Flank asked. "And where are we sliding, exactly?"

Barry was perplexed. "We don't *owe* money to anyone."

"We ought to introduce this guy to the people who stiffed us," Tongue suggested bitterly. "Let them work it out."

Barry activated the comm. "We're kind of in the hole with everyone, *Sluicifer*. Mind introducing yourself?"

"Juniper Grand," was the reply.

Tongue pushed Barry's hand away from the comm. "You pissed off Grand? He's—"

"I didn't—"

"—the head of *Shogura's*-"

"—don't even owe him a bar tab."

Flank sighed. He hated organized crime because he considered them cheaters unable to compete within the rules.

The drive status board showed blue: they could slide right now. Tongue asked, "Where we going, guys?"

Flank replied, "We need to stay and we need to settle this. I don't want gangsters chasing us across the galaxy."

Barry considered letting Grand board the ship. Nah, Barry had never seen Grand on the *Shogura*, just the brutes he employed. Better to keep some cold vacuum between them. "Let's get out of here. What's he gonna do if we slide into the GEC? He'd be in the same trouble if he follows us, but less able to get away."

"We can't piss this guy off," Flank warned.

"We already did that," Tongue said.

"Really, what's one more gangster in addition to the entire Exchange?" Barry asked.

Tongue laughed at Flank's discomfort. "We do need to disappear. Like immediately. Do we slide toward Pergamon?"

Barry scrunched up his nose like the idea smelled like wet compost. "Grand would assume that's where we went. So, let's not go there. We need to lose him."

"Back to the *Shogura*?" Flank asked with resignation.

Barry switched the main overhead display to the live feed from the beacon stationed in the inner system. "You wanted a closer peek at their ships, Flank. If Tongue can slide us 'in on the probe' without hitting anything."

Tongue grinned. Sliding 'in on a probe' was a lot riskier than emerging at an actual nav beacon. The nav beacon continually broadcast exact parameters for constructing a safe slide in the nearby area. It continually updated the safe areas for sliding into in a particular volume of space.

A probe was a tiny slide drive with sensors. It was designed only to see around the local area. It estimated the necessary structural integrity and energy investment needed to create a ship-sized wormhole, in addition to locating obstacles or other navigational dangers at the exit.

Probes sent real-time feeds through a zero-mass slide back to the ship. To slide in on the probe, a navigator needed to shut down this zero-mass slide and hope the area around the probe was still safe to slide into.

Once you lost contact with a probe, you couldn't be sure the slide's exit point was still clear. If the exit point was blocked after the slide was begun, the supraspace wormhole would collapse and crush the ship. Or strand it in the nether space that wormholes existed in. Either way, it was unpleasant.

But sliding down a probe was what exploration vessels did several times a day. For an experienced navigator like Tongue it was like running across a busy street. But those slides back in their Exchanger days were into uninhabited space, not smack in the center of a cluster of large ships arriving, departing, and in flight.

The challenge made Tongue grin. "Just a sec," he said as he concentrated on his screen.

The *Sluicifer* rapidly closed the gap between herself and the *Drake*.

Barry said, "About the other ship…"

Tongue waved him away. "Shhh. What'll they do if they reach us? Ram us?"

Flank growled. He and Tongue stabbed at their respective consoles.

"*Drake*, you better let us dock," Grand said over the comm.

Tongue muted the comm. "How's this?" he asked, and the overhead display showed a projected slide path to the inner system probe. The locations of GEC ships in the system were listed. The probe itself was a hundred thousand kilometers out from the ships and still on the ecliptic.

The slide path arced below the Union ecliptic, staying well clear of the Union star, and rose sharply to end about a million kilometers below the probe, but directly under the GEC ships.

Barry nodded like his neck was a loose spring. The *Sluicifer* was almost on top of them.

"First we gotta get clear of Grand's yacht so we don't, you know, take them with us," Tongue mumbled.

The *Drake* surged forward as its bow-mounted slide drive created a gravimetric trough in the fabric of space, causing it to fall forward. The yacht fell behind them another thousand klicks in a few seconds.

Tongue activated the slide drive and a high-pitched whine came from the bow. The *Drake* slid.

TEN

THE *DRAKE'S* drive deactivated in less than a minute. The ship exited into normal space, and its forward scopes displayed a star-studded sky again. The dorsal scope showed the probe above them and a cluster of GEC transports, shuttles, tenders, and Monoliths.

Flank posted the recharge countdown: twenty-five minutes, less than half the normal recharge time. Intra-system slides didn't need as much juice.

Tongue made the ship rise to retrieve their probe. The comm blinked with an incoming message. He unmuted it.

"*Drake*, this is the Galactic Exploration Corporation ship *Beatrix*. We regret to inform you that you are not authorized to enter this area. Leave immediately or we will detain you and impound your ship. *Beatrix* out."

"Well well, it's great to finally meet you too, Beattie," Barry said with a smirk. "How are things going over there?"

Beatrix replied, "You are not authorized to be in this system, *Drake*. Please return to Exchange space."

"Oh, is this GEC territory?" Barry replied. "I seem to remember the millenia-old treaty says otherwise."

"This is heavily trafficked space and your presence contravenes our safety margins," *Beatrix* replied.

"Well, we're sure very sorry about being contraveniers," Barry said, "but there are no nav beacons here to mark this as a slide destination. Show us the beacon and we'll be on our merry way."

Tongue gave Barry a thumbs up when the *Beatrix* didn't respond immediately. Barry bopped his head to a jazzy tune in his head while he waited.

"Ah, *Drake*, this is your last warning to vacate the area. Please return to an outer system location marked by one of our beacons."

"I told you they're taking over," Flank said.

Tongue agreed. "Yeah, we didn't do anything here. Well, at least not on this trip. They can't, like, restrict our freedom of movement."

Grand would assume they slid deeper into GEC territory. Hopefully the GEC would bust the angry crime boss at wherever GEC he slid into. In the mean time, the *Drake* needed to run out this recharge time regardless of what they did.

The proximity alarm sounded. A Monolith slid in above them. A mammoth blue metal floating city dropping on them. But all their scope showed was the Monolith's hemisphere-shaped slide drive on the Monolith's bottom. To Barry it resembled a massive blue butt cheek coming down to smother them.

The comm chirped. "This is the *Beatrix*. Stand by for boarding."

Tongue asked, "Uh, Bare, what's our play here?"

Fear won out over apathy in Barry's head and kicked his selfishness into gear. Toying with corrupt restauranteurs from *Shogura* was one thing, rotting away in the hold of one of these GEC ships was another. He wrinkled his nose. "Are they packing weaponry?"

The navigator squinted at his screen. "That's a huge freaking heap of metal, puking out EM in every wavelength. I can't tell yet what's an antenna or a cannon, an airlock or a missile tube. I need a few minutes."

Flank threw his hands in the air. "We don't have a few minutes. This is stupid; it won't work. The *Drake*'s not built for tactical maneuvers or combat. She's built for exploration and stellar cartography."

Barry ignored him. "Open up the throttle. Let's zip right by them, fly right into the thick of their ships there. With the mass that blue tin can is hauling, by the time they delta their v, we'll be far past them. They won't tractor us with the other ships nearby. And we can sneak a real close peek at their ships."

Tongue maxed thruster speed and the *Beatrix* rushed closer. Its circular slide drive filled the view from the *Drake*'s forward scopes. Barry braced himself against a bulkhead.

Flank tapped at his terminal. "Twenty percent chance of Tongue screwing this up and ramming them. Sixty percent chance they catch us."

Tongue scowled. "But how will they catch us? Throw a net around the ship?"

Flank replied, "Meh, energy weapons, missiles, tractor beam, rail gun, any law enforcement tech."

Tongue angled the *Drake* to sideslip the Monolith. It took forever, but they flew past the *Beatrix*'s keel. Tongue was skimming the Monolith's blue metallic hull so close they could see the seams between hull plates.

"We're recording this, right?" Flank asked. The ship's sensor suite could produce a detailed schematic of the ship from such close range.

"Yeah, whatever," Tongue said, wrestling with the controls to avoid the pointy superstructure on the *Beatrix*'s dorsal side. "What do we do when we're clear?"

"Run like hell," Barry replied.

Flank's voice dripped with disgust. "Run?"

"Like hell. Beats staying."

"And if we do escape, then what?"

Barry slapped his shoulder. "I don't *know*, Flank. They didn't cover this situation in school."

The bald engineer grumped but said nothing else.

The *Drake*'s drive needed another twenty minutes to recharge. But the *Beatrix* banked around and would reach them in less than ten minutes. Barry needed to kill time.

"Let's buzz the other ships," he said. "Scan them and jink around so

Beatrix doesn't corner us. Then we slide to the next GEC depot. Check out Pergamon."

Amazingly, no one argued with him.

The *Drake* flew toward an automated cargo hauler pulling a train of modular, linked compartments. The compartments were connected to the spine of the long, narrow cargo hauler, with a small snub-nosed control module on the bow.

Tongue banked the *Drake* over it, putting it between them and the *Beatrix*. Their pursuer continued to send threats over the comm, but he muted it. "Check out the sensor readings," he said, "These automated containers are individually pressurized. A huge waste of energy and air, because there's no life signs aboard. If we weren't being chased, we could clean it out. None of these patrol craft could stop us."

Barry and Flank gave him incredulous looks. But Tongue's eyes gleamed with mischief.

"That's nonsense," Flank said cautiously. "What would we do with it? Ransom it back to the Grids?"

Tongue shrugged. The *Beatrix* continued to close the distance. He slewed the ship around in a diving corkscrew at right angles to the *Beatrix*'s course toward a boxy construction platform repairing a Monolith.

"Careful," Barry said, magnifying the view from the forward scope, "I see individual workers out there."

Tongue nodded. He swung them wide around the platform and the Monolith under repair. The *Beatrix*'s momentum made it harder for her to change course in response.

"Check out this stupidity," Flank said. "They really do use thin metal plating on a polymer skeleton. Highly conductive, easier to pierce. Costs them a ton of energy to keep heated and shield it from radiation and micrometeors."

"Maybe they just have a soft spot for the ancient ways," Barry surmised.

Tongue swung them hard around the docked Monolith. "Sorry," he said, when everyone had to lurch to stay upright. The *Beatrix* was forced to jog around around her sister ship to pursue the *Drake*.

Flank said, "Well, I got an early read on *Monolith*-class armaments. The closest thing to powered weapons I see are the tractor ability of that big ass slide drive. They could overload an active sensor array to create a beamed weapon, but it would be pretty weak. They may have projectile launchers or other physical weaponry, but they would produce an energy signature."

"*Drake*, this is GEC Security Cutter Fifteen. Stand down for boarding and inspection. Or we will damage your vessel. It'll serve you right for acting like you won the race."

"Security cutter?" Barry asked.

Flank, the self-appointed tactics expert, highlighted the approaching cutter on their screens. It was about the size of a starslider, but seemed to be mostly thrusters. No slide drive signature. Two life signs aboard. A small, winged shuttle followed it, waiting to ship them to a GEC prison. Both ships were the same gunmetal blue as the Monoliths.

The *Drake*'s recharge countdown was still above ten minutes.

"Lose this ass," Barry ordered.

Tongue nodded. When the *Drake* came around the docked Monolith, he set her on an intercept course with Cutter Fifteen.

Beatrix vectored to box them in the against the cutter.

"You chasers don't quit, do you?" Cutter Fifteen taunted.

"Chasers? Is that some kind of insult?" Flank asked.

Barry replied, "You'll get angry if I tell you. Tongue, toss this turkey aside when we pass."

Tension tightened in the kick as the cutter and the *Drake* rushed towards each other.

"Tell me what 'chaser' means, Captain Spranker," Flank said impatiently.

"It means they don't like Exchangers," Tongue said through gritted teeth.

The *Drake* cruised at its maximum sublight velocity. Hundreds of kilometers between the two ships plummeted to dozens.

Tongue partially juiced the slide drive's output. A little squirt of power slammed the underside of the cutter with a massive gravitational pulse. The pulse tossed it off-course, away from the *Drake*.

Three enormous clangs echoed through the *Drake*'s hull. Barry checked the dorsal scope. Three cabled clamps had bounced off the hull and fell behind them. The cutter spun from the gravimetric disturbance the *Drake* threw at her, and she fired her oversized engines to regain control.

"Bastards hit us with clamps. Magnetic clamps," Flank said.

"Magnetic clamps?" Tongue laughed hoarsely. Against a metallic hull, those clamps would latch on and the cutter could reel in its prey. But these guys were apparently unaware of the nonmagnetic ceramic hulls on Exchange ships.

The shuttle following behind the cutter peeled away, clear of the *Drake*'s gravity cone. With its pursuers safely astern, the *Drake* passed the stationary Monolith that had launched the cutter and the shuttle. Barry wanted to moon them, but the *Drake* had no windows or viewports on its hull.

Tongue's analysis program highlighted the GEC starship's bays, sensors, and energy signatures. "No one in the Exchange has this kind of detailed data on a Monolith. Maybe we can sell it?"

The *Beatrix* birthed three more cutters from a hangar bay on the far side. They came streaking in at maximum throttle.

"Tongue."

"Yeah, I see them."

The countdown clock slipped under four minutes. Barry knew Flank shaved every millisecond he could off the *Drake*'s recharge time as a matter of course. He bit down on the urge to ask him if he could shave off any more.

Tongue flew the *Drake* towards a pair of the GEC passenger liners. An Exchange *Chandelier-class* passenger liner glittered like a crystal shard in space. The GEC reused the *Chandelier* blueprints but stripped off any elegance or beauty. Their passenger liners resembled a Monolith stretched into an ugly grey oval, but with more viewports.

"We'll slide when we're between these passenger liners," Tongue said. The *Drake* flew along the starboard side of the nearest one. The GEC loved windows on the hull; there were hundreds on this passenger liner, all bleeding light and heat. The port scope showed people at the windows, staring at the *Drake* whizzing by. It felt like flying past an ugly GEC office building.

"Gods these are ugly ships," Tongue said.

The nav board showed that the math was ready for the next slide. The next GEC waypoint was a depot of some kind in deep space. There were no other destinations this far out.

The cutters were nearly within Flank's rough estimate of their magnetic harpoon range. Tongue rolled the ship upwards, using thrusters to kill their momentum and sipping energy from the slide drive to change direction. The *Drake* crested the liner and flew over its immense dorsal side.

The cutters were thrown off. They lost ground when they banked to a new intercept course. Barry monitored the port and starboard scopes while they flew between the liners.

"I think we're crashing formal night," he said.

The nav board showed they were perfectly lined up for the slide, but they were half a minute shy of being recharged. The Beatrix, the cutters, and the passenger liners left them no room to maneuver. Barry asked, "This countdown clock is killing me. Flank, can you do something?"

Flank shut down lighting, sensors, ventilation, thrusters, everything except the recharge clock. Its red numerals were the only dim light in the kick. It dropped to to five, four, three…

In the dark, Tongue activated the slide drive.

ELEVEN

PERGAMON.

"This is the first settled GEC system we've ever visited." Grand indicated the large beige planet on the monitor. "And would you look at this shitshow."

Kroger, in *Sluicifer's* pilot seat, displayed a worried emoji on his faceplate. "The planet has one small city of about a hundred thousand residents. There are approximately eleven thousand vessels in orbit. Most are cargo transports. Two thousand shuttlecraft are in flight."

"Is the *Drake* out here?"

"No sir, no Exchange vessel signatures in orbit other than ours. Maybe they landed. Or slid further into the GEC."

The comm chirped. "Unidentified Exchange ship. You do not have permission to be in this system," squawked a nasal-sounding female dispatcher whose ID said System Control.

"Ask them if another Exchange ship came through," Grand said.

Kroger engaged in a spirited debate with System Control for half an hour. He requested an orbital slot and news about other Exchange ships. System Control denied both requests, citing the *Sluicifer's* lack of flight plans, GEC permission to be in the system, orbital slot permits.

There was so much bureaucratic jargon Grand believed she made up half of it on the spot.

Kroger took them over the planet's north pole, avoiding the crowded orbital paths. At a distance, those orbital paths resembled metallic planetary rings.

Grand took a closer look at the city on the surface. Beyond a small urban core, most of the city consisted of prefab trailers on dirty streets. He grinned. Vids of the GEC's gleaming cities never featured backward dumps like this one. This looked chaotic and disorganized. A perfect place for Spranker to lay low.

Usually Grand ignored this flight control mumbo jumbo. But he stayed in the kick and smacked his droid on the shoulder. "Tell them we're landing."

"What? Why?" Kroger asked. "There's nothing down there."

"Just tell them."

Kroger keyed the comm. "Permission requested to land on the surface. At your very small city?"

"Fine. Do so at your own risk," System Control said. "You can be the city's problem." She went on to list a number of potential dangers and problems for an Exchange ship expecting any kind of refueling or repair. She passed them off to Orbital Control for landing instructions.

Kroger set course. He said, "The *Drake* is not down there."

"Maybe not on the official records. The thing is, the GEC has lied about everything," Grand explained. "They lied about how close they came to Union. They lied about this situation in orbit here. I mean, see those decaying personal transports?" He pointed at a line of transports floating by in the nearest orbital path. Their metallic hulls were patched with scrap plating and dark orange foam used in emergencies to plug leaks. "It means there may be another way to find Spranker. There must be an underground who can help us."

"So, you're not angry?"

"Angry? No, you idiot. This gives me *hope*. I can work with this environment. I can make money in it. I can leverage it for revenge."

Kroger requested a landing slot from the city's orbital dispatcher. The dispatcher refused and suggested they leave the system. Kroger politely insisted that they could travel freely in GEC space, and cited the exact centuries old regulations.

Grand leaned over. "Ask them where the *Drake* went."

For the past several days the *Sluicifer* slid through one empty GEC star system after another. The only sign that these were GEC territory was a lone nav beacon. Once every few slides they found a Monolith serving as a navigation beacon and resupply station. The Monolith would tell Grand and Kroger to get lost. No settled worlds, no residential space stations. Just a single, long, straight slide route through nothing.

Ergo, the *Drake* had nowhere else to go but Pergamon. Kroger pitched the question. The dispatcher insisted there had never been an Exchange ship in this system until now.

"She may be lying," Kroger said. He cringed, waiting for Grand's reaction.

"Huh," was all Grand said. *Spranker wouldn't return to Exchange space*, he thought. The slimy bastard would get pounced on by the millions of other cheated investors. The explorer exchange was the highest profile reputation market in the Exchange. Betting on the starslider jockeys mapping the galaxy was nearly an obsession for Exchangers. "If he didn't slide here, he's waiting out in the void for things to cool down. Or he slipped past Pergamon and he's deeper into GEC turf."

"Any Exchange ship can only slide in to a GEC beacon," Kroger pointed out. "System Control tracks every ship coming in. For example, three transports left the system since we arrived, bound for Union. But seven more arrived during the same time period. As an aside, the GEC is starting to unclog this backlog."

The *Sluicifer* left Pergamon's orbital mess of habitats, cargo containers, and Monoliths to land on the surface. System Control managed a titanic traffic jam in a space ballet. *It may not notice a small Exchange starslider*, Grand thought.

Kroger argued with Launch Control in Perga City during the entire descent. The planetside GECers unleashed multiple layers of bureaucracy on the *Sluicifer*. Customs, health inspections, landing orientation, flight plans, credentials verification.

Grand let Kroger handle this minutiae. He studied Perga City on the ship's cams. The city core consisted of prefabricated government buildings and two office towers. The other buildings were repurposed transports, trailers, and shipping containers. The farther out from the gated city center, the cruder the real estate.

A nervous eagerness leapt into Grand's throat. Fear melted to anxiety which crystallized into a nervous energy. *Learn the rules around here. Adapt. And discover where the easy profits are hiding.* His old instincts gave him a focus and an overwhelming desire to get the hell off his ship and get started. If the *Drake* had skipped out to another system, Grand would need funds to continue chasing it.

The assigned landing pad was a sun-baked slab of uneven concrete. It was walled off from the rest of the spaceport by two-story lime green dumpsters. He and Kroger exited the ship. There was no welcoming committee to greet them.

The air was pleasantly warm but the dumpsters emitted a sickly-sweet stench of rotting fruit baked at high heat.

Grand chucked Kroger on the shoulder and said, "Fox me, this is a vaunted GEC world? Let's have a look around."

Grand's first impression of Pergamon's surface was a mix of obnoxious smells. Beyond the stank dumpsters, the spaceport proper reeked of chemicals: engine exhaust, burnt plastic, and solvents. Grand gagged when his lungs tried to close up shop. No Exchange world or space station smelled this bad. The Grid way of life was built upon harsh, acrid chemicals and metallic polymers.

And pipes. Everywhere there were different colored pipes for ventilation, waste, and water labelled in ugly, block white lettering.

He and Kroger emerged on a street behind the spaceport, lined with loading docks and dumpsters in both directions. They waited twenty minutes for an automated tram to arrive.

When they boarded, the other passengers went slack-jawed. The GEC didn't use droids. Kroger's torso and arms resembled a humanoid. But his treads and his cartoonishly robotic head, made it clear he was a droid. The Grids couldn't stop gawking at him.

The Grids appeared exactly like the vids had portrayed them. Physically, Grids and Exchangers were the same. The differences were in the clothes, hairstyles, speech, and bearing. The Grids dressed in either utility coveralls or business suits. Some were impeccable and some were threadbare at the cuffs and knees. The hues in their clothing ranged the spectrum from dark grey to grey with a beige tint. To a person their hair was short and neatly trimmed. Exchangers called GEC citizens 'Grids' because they lived in such a boxed-in, rigid society and resembled droids with broken emotion algorithyms.

Grand usual business suit cost as much attention as Kroger: dark purple slacks with light-emitting threads shimmering in ever-changing colors. Jacket of the same light-threaded purple fabric with gold bands shot through. Glowing fire-red marble lace at the cuffs. Underneath the jacket he rocked an aqua undershirt so bright it had once ruined an evening outing to stargaze.

"Hi. We're from the Exchange. So happy to reach the GEC," Grand said to a man in the tram's next row.

"Um, are you joking?" The man asked, gaping at Grand's outfit. He gave Kroger a once over. "Welcome to Perga City, I guess."

The rest of the passengers pretended to ignore them.

Perga City's urban core consisted of a marble and steel compound filled with landscaped gardens and well-dressed people. It was separated by a three meter-high fence and a security guard who wouldn't let them enter.

"If you don't have an appointment, it doesn't matter what planet you're from," said the guard. "Leave, or we take you in for trespassing. I'm surprised the spaceport allowed you to land."

Grand bowed with a pleasant smile and led Kroger away. "Let's get a drink."

"You're in a good mood," Kroger remarked cautiously.

Grand saw another tram coming up the street. "Yes. Not sure why. Don't you go and ruin it."

Kroger stayed quiet.

The city center made up only a third of the city. The rest consisted of worn plastic slums and fenced-in settler camps. Their existence made a joke of the word 'temporary' with their crude brick additions and cemeteries. The tram was free, so Grand played tourist.

The tram line ended at a slum on the city's north side. Grand and Kroger exited, the only passengers left, and the tram went out of service.

The air was filled with dust and different stenches. Something was frying that should never be fried. The sewer technology left a lot to be desired, beginning with burying the pipes underground. Red and yellow sewer pipes sat alongside the dirt streets, under the sun, baking and reeking.

The streets were filled with residents who were poor, idle, and anxious. Their coveralls were drab and threadbare. Everyone in the GEC supposedly was fully employed, but Grand doubted it. Too many people were milling around aimlessly in the middle of the day. Maybe they had jobs taking olfactory air samples.

Grand and Kroger stuck out in this crowd like apricots in a box of nails. The locals gathered around them in a thick crowd of the curious.

The GEC didn't have anything like Kroger, apparently. Full employment meant no need for droids. The neighborhood's kids emerged and crowded around him.

"Can I touch your skin?" one kid asked.

"Certainly!" Kroger replied. He opened his arms and the kids squeezed, groped, pinched, and touched them. "I am not ticklish," he said to a girl who tried to scratch at his armpit.

"Take us for a ride," yelled a boy.

Kroger let the kids climb on him. "Hang on," he warned. He rolled around randomly and the kids squealed and tightened their grips.

The adults ignored Kroger and focused on Grand. Some asked if he was a failed lounge singer or a clown. Others pointed to his fashion choices and straight-up asked about his mental health.

Others, filled with panicked desperation, pushed the snarky onlookers aside. "Can I get offworld passage," one woman asked. She waved GEC currency cards at him. "You must own a ship if you came here. Please."

Others joined in. They begged, they offered currency, they cried. Another woman kept calling him captain. A man began to yell when Grand didn't respond to him immediately.

Grand was amused at first, followed by a brief sympathetic pang. But the first whiff of other people's desperation made him greedy. He couldn't help it. He began scheming how to leverage this desperation to separate them from their money.

"Wait, wait a second. Aren't you about to be shipped out to settle new worlds?" Grand asked the crowd.

Some began swearing or muttering under their breath. "If we won the race to Union, how come you showed up here already?" bellowed the angry man. A woman next to him rapped him on the shoulder.

"It's hard believing the company line when none of us are going anywhere," the angry man added.

Kroger was ferrying kids around the perimeter of the crowd. He chimed in and said, "We noticed transports going to Union when we arrived."

"That's foxing great. How long until they clear them out of orbit and get to us?" angry man asked. "Years?"

Kroger swiveled his torso and the children giggled, hanging on to keep from being flung off of him. "My estimate is twelve to fifteen years."

There were serious business opportunities here. These hopeless people were loaded with GEC currency but couldn't spend it. The only thing they valued was getting the hell off Pergamon.

Grand could quickly recapitalize here and then mount a serious search for Spranker and his idiot crew. People were shoving money at him. He should grab it and make some sweet promises, then skip town. Oldest scam in the books. Except there was nowhere for him to go either.

These people believed if the Exchanger in a flamboyant purple suit owned a ship, what other choice did they have but to trust him?

He could cart these people anywhere outside this GEC hellhole and charge them a ton per trip. Locating the ships to carry them would be tough, but the *Sluicifer* would do for the early going. He could dump these poor losers at *Shogura* or at the embryonic Exchange settlements back in Sector 179. There could be an arbitrage opportunity here: vacuum up GEC currency while it was worthless and convert it to Exchange credits when the two sides figured out a conversion rate.

If only he could get his hands on larger ships and some place to dump these Grids. Maybe he could work with the smugglers and cargo transport crews he knew from the *Shogura*. There must be dozens of Exchanger ships at loose ends with the big race finished.

But, but, but. The GEC probably wouldn't approve of Exchange ships stealing away their colonists. The crazy backlog up in orbit meant fighting a losing battle with the GEC to secure scarce and valuable orbital slots. Once they figured out what was happening, the GEC would do more than sternly deny them landing clearance. They could try to prevent their own people from escaping. And Grand didn't know anything about how to work over the GEC bureaucracy.

No, he would stick to what he understood. New business lines were always fraught with surprises and hidden learning curves. He wasn't operating with enough capital to afford those lessons. He didn't need distractions and side ventures to finance chasing down the *Drake*. He liked customers who got well pickled and then became spendy on more entertainment.

But he needed this crowd to leave him be. He spread his arms. "I'm sorry I can't help you. Our ship was damaged and we're stranded here like you. I actually came out here to ask *you* for *your* help."

The crowd shut up. Half of the people instantly pocketed their currency cards and walked away. Others tried bartering help for him in exchange for transport offworld.

Finally, he said, "I can't help you. They won't let me in the city center to talk to someone. Where can I go to make the high and mighty listen to me?"

"Go to the entertainment complex," the angry man said. "Third floor clubs. For all the good it will do you."

TWELVE

THE REMAINING CROWD MELTED AWAY. Grand lifted a kid off Kroger's body. "We need to go."

"Bye children!" Kroger called. Grand ushered him down the street in the direction of the city's core. The city's entertainment complex occupied an entire city block just shy of where the paved street ended.

The GEC owned everything, including all the legit entertainment venues. Perga City's night life was officially housed in this cavernous prefabricated building, three stories high with nondescript double doors. Its lobby had a line of kiosks where house tokens for gaming, food, and drink could be purchased.

"Tokens are a great way to make customers overspend," Grand noted. "Kroger, get us enough for a meal and some games."

Kroger rolled up to the nearest kiosk. "There is no gambling here. And these machines only accept GEC currency cards."

"But no cover charge. Let's walk around."

The ground floor included six individually-themed watering holes or bars. The themes were all childish: jungle, desert oasis, nautical, cartoonish aliens, a pub with swanky brass and wood decor, and a gleaming minimalist wine bar. They had zero ambiance.

The second and third floors housed the upscale clubs. They were dark; they only opened at night. The clubs' exterior walls were opaque to signal their privacy and exclusivity.

Grand settled for perusing the clubs' glossy promotion sites online. The dance club had a sturdy steel industrial design, glammed up with lights. The cocktail club had a live music stage, plush beige seats, and faux wood paneling. The walls were printed separately and joined together; the place was built of separate modules.

He rejoined Kroger on the ground floor. The droid handed him entertainment tokens he bought with currency some kid had given him for the rides he gave.

They entered a pub with a 'corner bar' theme. Grand was surprised to find people inside. They wore business attire and most were eating rather than drinking. The ones who had drinks chatted over untouched wineglasses.

The chewing and chatting ceased when he and Kroger entered. The raised eyebrows suggested none of the patrons had ever encountered a droid or an Exchanger.

Grand ignored them and ordered an ale from the bar's order kiosk. It cost five entertainment tokens, which was vastly overpriced. Someone came up behind him and when he looked, he was nose to nose with an unhappy GEC gentleman.

"Can I ask you how you got here?" the man asked, with his hands clasped behind him.

Grand smiled. "Landed today. Came from Union." The bartender handed him a pint of clear ale with a greenish tinge.

"Exchange personnel aren't permitted here in Perga City. Right, Brewster?" The GEC official asked an older woman behind him.

The woman named Brewster scowled. "There's no security bulletin allowing it," she said. "I would know, since I'm the one who writes them."

Grand ignored her and sniffed the ale. It smelled of grilled fishplant harvested downstream of a chemical factory.

"I'm afraid you're not authorized to be here," the man finished.

Grand sipped the ale — it tasted thin and watery, which in this case was a plus. The initial taste mixed tomato with something he struggled to remember. Maybe rotting asparagus? His tongue detected no alcohol, only preservatives and artificial flavorings. He swallowed it, to better capture the bitter taste on the back of his tongue. It wasn't alcoholic. More like a soggy vegetable. Kale. It was kale ale.

"According to the really old agreements between the Exchange and the GEC," Kroger said, "there is free movement for both peoples."

"Maybe in the Ancient Sectors. But there are no enabling regulations implemented in this sector. What are you supposed to be, exactly?" Brewster asked Kroger.

Kroger stood up taller on his tread feet. "I am Mr. Grand's major domo, named Kroger. Pleased to meet you, Brewster."

"There are regulations about bringing foreign computing hardware into GEC territory without a computing hygiene inspection certificate." Brewster said. "You may need to come with us to get this sorted out."

"Orbital Control informed us of no such requirement," Kroger said. "If you could send me the requirements, I'll make sure we comply."

Brewster shook her head. "No, we should do this in person. I'm afraid I'll have to call this in. We will have to head down to the office to sort this all out."

"What kind of hospitality are you extending to the first Exchangers you've ever met?"

The man snapped, "Why should we? You look like a homeless fortune teller with a broken mannequin. When did you last shave your face?"

Grand rubbed his neatly trimmed beard. No male Grids had facial hair. "I trim it regularly."

Grand set his glass down but clenched his fist around it. He never wanted to taste kale ale again. He really wanted to smash it against this asshole's skull.

Kroger said, "I think we should leave."

"Your robotic lackey isn't stupid," Brewster said.

Kroger physically tugged Grand out to the street. "If this is the only entertainment in town, it's only a matter of time for you to outcompete it," Kroger said.

"That place was awful," Grand remarked out the side of his mouth.

"But it was filled with bureaucrats. They would never let us serve them. We need people less interested in spouting GEC regulations in their off hours."

"We should go to the outskirts. Officially, there are no bars but they must have something." Kroger displayed a map on his faceplate. "The poor service back there is an opportunity," he said. "You could run circles around them."

Grand said, "One of my cardinal rules is never compete with city hall. Government monopolies are unbeatable."

"The GEC is not a government. It literally has a corporate monopoly on everything," Kroger pointed out.

Grand clenched his fist. He hated when the robot tried to one up him. Kroger shrank away from him and Grand unclenched his fist. "It's damn foolish to expect the Corporation's right hand will help us put its left hand out of business, Kroger."

Kroger studied his own right hand, followed by his left. Was he screwing with Grand? Kroger understood figures of speech. The day's frustration with the Grids disrespecting him, still no sign of Spranker, and now this upstart circuit breaker foxing with him was simply too much.

Grand punched Kroger in the gut. Kroger's faux-human torso folded in half from the blow and he emitted a grunting gasp.

"Knock it off before I knock you off," Grand growled through gritted teeth.

"Sorry," Kroger said and straightened up. Everyone on the street was rubbernecking at them.

They left the city's paved streets for the outskirts, where the buildings were made of old trailers and ramshackle one-story structures made of old hull plating. Thousands of Grids lived out here. In the blazing mid afternoon, everyone outside but them stuck to the shade.

"Come on," Grand said, striding off toward what must be a bar. A dim red beer mug glowed in a darkened window.

The door was locked and a voice yelled, "This is a private club and you can fox right off."

It was a shame: the voice sounded like his kind of people. He found he was actually thirsty, too. The sun was making him sweat.

He and Kroger made a circuit around the slums. Grand saw landing craft, old furniture, and shipping containers recycled into homes and shops. And most importantly, there were makeshift bars. He and Kroger entered the largest one, called Blast's, housed inside an old shipping container. The patrons cleared space at the makeshift bar for him and Kroger.

"Never seen an Exchanger. What the hell brings you to Perga City?" asked the bartender.

"A chaser owes me a lot of money," Grand replied. "You heard of any other Exchangers around here?"

The bartender served him a half pint of a ginger-colored ale with a head of foam. It smelled like deep-fried popcorn. "Not a single one. I guess more of your people are coming here. And your droids?"

Grand sipped the ale. It was blood warm with a sweet caramel taste. It went down like a lager should. The aftertaste was earthy and blossomed across the roof of his mouth. "Kroger is my droid assistant. Does all the dreck I don't want to."

"What did you do in the Exchange?" the bartender asked.

"Casino owner and entertainment provider. This is the first half-decent drink I've had here," he said. "A little fruity. Much better than what you can buy with these tokens." He dumped out two tokens from the entertainment complex.

The woman on the next stool chuckled. "No one goes there to drink. It's business meetings and being seen. Gods, the food is even worse."

"How come the good booze is in the worst part of town?" Grand asked. "I expected cat piss to be served out here. The good stuff costs too much."

The bartender replied, "it's simple. Alternative distribution channels. And no regulation by the fun stoppers."

"An unofficial exchange?" Kroger asked. "We are very familiar with the concept. Do you brew this locally?"

The bartender replied, "Yes, out back. The shed is labeled sewer waste. Keeps people away."

"I could help you sell this in the Exchange," Grand said. "It's a mid-range ale, but you'd be the first GEC drink to hit the Exchange." He took another gulp. "I know wholesale distributors. What do you call this?"

The bartender smiled. "Carruthers 5. Named it after myself. I wasn't planning on distributing it."

"And those must be skeeball machines," Grand pointed to the far end of the shipping container. The bar took up half the length of the narrow container and the other half was filled with skeeball machines ablaze with flashing high scores and blinking lights.

"Oh, have you played?" the woman asked. "I'm Margaret. Resident skeeball champion."

Grand smiled at her. "Do you ever play for money?"

She smiled and said, "Only when there are people stupid enough to challenge me."

Grand hopped off the barstool. "Free round on me!"

The GECers cheered.

Grand leaned closer to Margaret. "A free round or two and you'll get some takers." She smiled and said she was in.

Grand organized an impromptu skeeball tournament and clued the bartender in on what he was doing. From Carruthers' dazed expression, it never occurred to him to vacuum up more money from his customers. But he nodded eagerly when Grand cut him in on the proceeds.

The sun was setting and the crowd grew. He and Margaret hustled petty cash from easy marks. Sometimes he acted like an old man with trembling hands. Other times, he won a stack of GEC currency from Margaret and then she beat a string of guys who assumed she was easy pickings.

Word spread around the neighborhood and the bar filled with people wanting to see what the commotion was about. Kroger managed the side bets on who would win. Carruthers was serving up drinks as fast as he could pour them. The tournament ended before one in the morning. Margaret won the top prize, a stack of Grand's Exchange currency.

Carruthers closed the bar with Kroger's help. The droid wiped the bar and cleaned the glasses while Grand counted up the night's earnings.

Grand handed over Carruther's share of the profits. The GEC man gestured to the stack of currency cards. "That's more than I made last year."

Grand smiled broadly. "Eh, I was trying to have some fun. Doesn't every bar run games and challenges?"

Carruthers shook his head. "Usually a good night here is when a fight doesn't break out." He said to Kroger, "You two really can distribute booze through, uh, non-official channels?"

Kroger nodded in an exaggerated up and down motion. "We regularly used covert shipments to stock our restaurants, bars, and casino. I've used twenty-three different methods for hiding alcoholic beverage containers on a cargo transport."

Carruthers smiled slyly. "There's someone who may have a business proposition for you. If you're interested, of course."

Grand interlaced his fingers on the sticky, plexiwood bar. "I am."

Carruthers tapped the stack of currency cards against the table. "Give me a day or two to send word. In the meantime, what other tricks do you know to keep people coming in like they did tonight?"

"Another skeeball tournament. But this time, there's an entry fee and a minimum bet on the players. If it works, we do a cover charge the next night."

They ran the skeeball tournament for two more nights. Grand and Kroger stayed in a boarding house three blocks away. The other bartenders in the slums wanted Grand to show them how to do the same thing in their establishments. He declined, but told them how to run some small games of chance where the house would usually win. Gambling was illegal in the GEC, of course, but in the slums security only responded to spilled blood.

The fourth day they were in Perga City, Grand ran an all-day skeeball tournament. The next day he made the tournament bigger, more complicated, and more dramatic. Two more days later the tournaments featured multiple brackets and a qualifying round where the average of a contender's three best games needed to beat the bar average.

Blast's stayed crowded the whole day, with patrons coming and going between their work shifts. People would roll their three games in a given round, check out the competition, chug a Carruthers 5, and leave.

In early afternoon, during the last qualifying round, Carruthers waved Grand to the bar. Grand was inspecting a custom-painted ball while a small crowd waited for his judgement.

Grand handed the ball to a big guy next to him. "Sorry, Bill. Tell those guys they must play with the house balls or they're out. God knows how they modified these. I can see the drill holes where they added weight."

Carruthers led Grand and Kroger out the back door. The smell of something boiling made Grand realize he was hungry. Four green kettles simmered with food in a makeshift kitchen. Slum cuisine apparently heavily favored soups and stews, which Grand disliked, but Carruther's yellow bread was like cake. He sent Kroger inside for another decent-sized chunk. There was something about chewing food that boosted Grand's thought process. Kroger returned with a hand-sized hunk.

Carruthers kept his voice low. "There's a criminal organization looking for a savvy operator to manage some of its businesses. I told them about you and they'd like to talk. They were really interested in the idea of Exchange distribution of my brew."

"Criminal organization?" Grand chewed and thought. In Exchange space, he would worry about a scam or a sting operation. He assumed criminal activity simply didn't happen among these uptight Grids. "Do you know these guys?"

"Yes, they're the ones who supply the ingredients for my brew. And the bread. The yeast is pretty special."

"How long have you known them?"

Carruthers said, "Seven years. They've treated me well. I pay them cash on delivery. No debts, no strings attached."

"I probably *am* the first Exchange criminal to reach GEC territory,"

Grand mused. He asked Kroger, "What's happened on the criminal rep exchange?"

Kroger adopted a blank facial emoji, which meant he was tapping the Exchange networks for a market update. "You fell off the exchange entirely. Lymanther, Porthole, and Cross Boss are the top three. The scuttlebutt is the three are playing things conservatively, and aren't expanding to Sector 180."

"The Exchange has a reputation market for criminal bosses?" Carruthers asked. "Why doesn't the government arrest everyone who is on it?"

Grand laughed but the bartender was serious. Grand asked, "We wouldn't deserve to be at the top if they could, now would we?"

Carruthers opened his mouth to respond but then nodded.

Grand asked Kroger, "Any change in my Exchange financials?"

Kroger's faceplate displayed a negative symbol.

Grand chewed over his options. He expected to work his way up from skeeball tournaments to running half the bars in town in short order. Worming his way into the GEC criminal element would probably build the capital and the connections to track down Spranker. And reestablish him financially, too.

But this offer could shortcut all that work. It could also be a trap, meant to wipe out any Exchanger competition poking around in GEC space. But it was too interesting to pass up entirely.

"Did this contact give you any bona fides? I may be desperate, but I'm not jumping into an trap."

Carruthers handed over hardcopy of a prospectus of sorts of an interstellar criminal organization. Kroger held it up for Grand to skim and handed him a bowl of stew. The prospectus listed booze, entertainment, illicit cargo, and other businesses spread across dozens of GEC systems beyond Pergamon.

"Okay, I'm willing to at least meet with them. I want you to do the introduction."

Carruthers blanched. "Me? I can't go with you. The meeting isn't in this star system. It's on Royada."

"Royada. Never heard of it. Kroger?"

The robot said, "It is not on any of the GEC starcharts."

Carruthers smiled. "I hope not. It's not an officially charted system. There's a lot not in the official GEC records."

"Like the yeast for this bread?" Grand swirled his bread in the stew. "I'm glad to hear it.

Carruthers rattled off a galactic coordinate. "Don't file a flight plan to it."

"And who are we meeting there?" Grand asked.

Carruthers shrugged. "My contact wasn't sure."

Grand handed the bartender his bowl. "Your stew tastes like shit, but this bread is heaven."

"Hehe, screw you, Grand. It's in the yeast. Where's my tournament money?"

Grand handed over a pile of GEC currency cards. "There's more where that came from if you run things smart. Thanks for the hospitality."

"Thanks for making me a casino operator. How am I supposed to keep this going without you?"

Grand touched him on the arm. "You size up each patron and how you can make them *excited* to spend every last credit. If you need inspiration, study how we do entertainment in the Exchange. You'll be way ahead of your competition."

The barkeep smiled sheepishly. "I don't want to be a casino owner. I want to be a master brewer. I want the major business suits at the Complex downtown to be ordering cases of my brew."

"I suggest you offer them a free bottle," Kroger said. "Maybe they'll let you ship it offworld."

"Better yet, give them a case." Grand said. "When they come sniffing around about this skeeball scheme, and they will, welcome them in. Give them a free taste. If they cut you slack, send them another free case. They'll become regular customers."

"Good idea," Carruthers said. "Do you really need to leave? You could be running these slums in another week."

"Thanks, but I came here on a mission," Grand said. Without the orbital jam above, Perga City would eventually shrink into a sleepy backwater. No point being the local gangster of a ghost town. He handed another currency card to Carruthers. "Give me a case of Carruthers 5. I'll do some hand-selling for you on this planet Royada."

Carruthers hefted a case into Kroger's arms.

"All right, you go run your tourney," Grand said with a grin.

Grand and Kroger took the tram to the city's spaceport. They waltzed into the spaceport's front entrance this time. The currency cards and a couple bottles of beer bought them prompt maintenance. Grand felt it was a good omen. When he and Kroger strapped in to the *Sluicifer* to launch, he felt they were back on track to find the *Drake*.

THIRTEEN

"HOW LONG UNTIL we reach whatever the hell the next settled system is?" Barry stood at the entrance to the kick with only a bath towel wrapped around his waist.

Tongue pointed at the overhead display. "Soon. Hey, don't use up the hot water again. Kill time some other way."

"Screw you." Barry stomped off to the bathroom. So what if his last shower was two hours long? There was nothing to do. It was either booze or hot showers to keep him from going nuts.

Barry and the guys were used to months-long jaunts with only each other's company. They were long-time friends so things went smoothly. Usually.

Not this time. Since they left the *Shogura* weeks ago they were sniping at each other. Everyone was miserable and sulking. Every GEC system they entered required them to dodge Monoliths and cutters. There was no place to refuel, retool, or get off the damn ship for a quick break. The GEC depots were stuck in interstellar voids with very little scenery. It was like a recurring nightmare of sensory deprivation mixed with existential terror.

Rather than run a gauntlet of GEC stops straight to Pergamon, they built their own parallel route. They would slide near the GEC beacons but out of range of any nearby GEC ships. Or launch a probe and stop a few light hours or two away from the GEC ships. They were tired of being hassled by a Monolith every time they slid to a GEC beacon.

The ship couldn't keep this up much longer either, Flank reminded them. He monitored every system, waiting to pounce on the first malfunction, aberration, or odd growth on the hull fungi. When he climbed around the hull to fix things, Barry suspected it was mostly to get away from him and Tongue for a while.

"Why don't you check out what's happening back home?" Tongue asked. "That always keeps you occupied."

"Too depressing. The GEC reports that Exchange ships keep intruding in systems they've claimed. The Exchange reports that its planting flags and footsteps everywhere in Sector 180. The diplomats are yelling at each other."

"Flank says a war is going to happen," Tongue replied. "I don't believe it. All these competing routes and settlements around Union, it will quiet down. There's so much empty space out here. I mean, the sectors on either side of Union are barely touched."

"We probably could have grabbed five systems on this trip," Barry said sourly. "If anyone valued our claims."

"You'll perk up. This next stop is the last one before we reach a settled system."

"We just keep on sliding, numbed and irritated. My only joy is relishing the chaos in the GEC. Things are so foxed here, it's really amazing. A good thing they have all of these traffic jams at the nav beacons. Gives us a place to hide."

"Nav buoys."

"Tongue, don't make me drop this towel."

"Go take your shower. We'll be there soon."

The *Drake* slid in at the outer range of an outer system beacon to avoid being chased away. It usually took hours for anyone to bother with them if they slid in so far away.

This depot consisted of four Monoliths parked at an inner system beacon. The last stop had only two of the hulking GEC ships.

"You ask me, they got these ships here to hunt for habitable systems nearby," Tongue said. "They don't need this many Monoliths sitting there, you know, pretending to be stations."

Flank emerged into the kick from engineering, swinging a tool and whistling a little ditty, satisfied with himself.

"What?" Barry asked, if only to interrupt the whistling.

"I was right," Flank said. "I replaced the sensor band on the third inducer array. It returned some strange diagnostic values and I knew it was the sensor, not the array. Lucky, too, because the array is a Drepper and they're damned expensive. But at least they print them right. Remember how you tried to talk me into getting that Bistyll crap instead?"

Barry shrugged. If it were up to Flank, they'd spend every point of their market capitalization on expensive parts. The Bistyll model was two classes above what most of their competition used.

"Yeah, uh huh. Still," Flank waved the tool at him, "it's another sign the drive needs maintenance. Performance is already off thirteen percent. Our recharge time is up twenty-two percent."

Barry said, "One more slide should do it."

"You're doing an amazing job keeping her together," Tongue said. Flank grinned at him and went aft to the galley.

Barry said, "Laying it on so thick means it slides off that much faster."

Tongue threw his hands in the air and returned to his station.

The comm chirped.

"*Drake*, this is the Monolith *Ponzington*. You are not in compliance with flight control directions. You do not have permission to enter this system."

Tongue pointed at Barry to speak. Barry said, "I talked last time."

"Um, *Ponzington*, we need to make some minor repairs, recharge, and then we'll leave," Tongue commed.

"Negative, negative. You are instructed to leave the system when you can slide, which we estimate to be twenty minutes. You will slide out beyond the heliopause and make repairs there. Please proceed toward the heliopause on thrusters while you recharge. *Ponzington* out."

"Hey," Tongue said into the comm, "don't be such an ass about this. We haven't slept in a while and we need to make repairs."

"Who do you think you're talking to? I don't know what kind of anarchy you are used to in the Exchange, you chaser, but we don't put up with it here. I'll bring you up on charges."

"Just, like, can your static for a minute. It's not helping." Tongue shut off the comm.

Barry smiled. "Nice going, T. Very diplomatic."

"What do you want? I hate it when people get like this."

"You're overdue for a break. You get cranky when you're tired. Go punch a bunk."

Tongue waved him off and got up. "I just need a snack to perk me up." He lumbered aft to the galley.

Two automated cargo ships slid in at their beacon. The *Drake* was parked twice the minimum safety distance away, because the local area was packed. There were half a dozen of these cargo ships at the same beacon. The depot's navigation net showed almost thirty ships within a light minute from the Monoliths. *The GEC had some aggressive expansion plans*, Barry thought.

Tongue returned to the kick, gnawing on a cranberry bar. He unmuted the comm. The *Ponzington* was no longer bothering them. His expression brightened substantially. He hated being yelled at.

"So what are we doing once we reach Pergamon? Get jobs?" he asked Barry.

Barry shrugged. "Doubt it. The news says they dismissed about two million employees because the race to Union is over. The last people the Grids would ever hire are Exchangers, especially tainted ones."

"Okay then. We could circumnavigate the galaxy. No one's ever been able to do that until now. Might take the rest of our lives to do," Tongue replied. "Of course, it would cost a lot of money."

Thing was, Barry didn't really care any more. He was tired of caring intensely about his career, his status, the Exchange's prospects, and his personal relationships. What good came of any of this effort, worry, and responsibility? Staying on the run was bound to take up loads more of his energy and attention. He wanted out of this game but he couldn't afford it. And he was at a loss on how they could make any money in the GEC.

"These Grids will keep kicking us until the ship falls apart and we're starving," Tongue said. "Don't sugar coat this, Captain."

Barry grinned. "Yeah. I wouldn't be surprised if they handed us over to the Exchange once the two of them are on better terms."

"God, I hate the stress," Tongue lamented.

"Prison food probably isn't *that* bad."

Tongue pointed at the scope showing the nearby ships. "I mean, are you seeing this? Automated ships, filled with valuable products. We're like rats who wandered into an abandoned warehouse. We could take anything we wanted and no one would notice."

"We're not thieving rats," Barry said.

Flank came back into the kick. "We shorted our own stocks," he said bitterly. "We are rats. Or did you forget what you did, Barry?"

Barry rolled his eyes. "We stiffed them for a little because they stiffed us for a lot."

"And we get to starve to death because of it," Tongue said. "Let's do something fun and let the universe worry about us for a change."

Flank was nonplussed. "What are you on about?"

"These cargo containers. They're unguarded. Their supply line is highly constricted and easy to target. They're going to hunt us down anyway. What's there to lose?"

Barry could only guess how competent GEC law enforcement was or how they would react to space lane robbery. But here were these shipping containers, unprotected, unsecured. There was really nothing to lose. They might be sacrificing long lives of drudgery and disgrace. It was completely irresponsible. Luckily, he was completely sick of being responsible.

He smiled. "Let's be pirates."

FOURTEEN

BARRY SAID, "Here's the rules. We don't get involved with the Exchangers and we don't get involved with the Grids. No quests, no passengers, no smuggling, no getting ambushed, and no falling in love. That's pop entertainment shit. It's about the money. Avocado?"

Tongue slapped his hands excitedly. "Avocado!"

Flank said, "Avocado. But it's also about the fame. We need to stay infamous. The best pirates ever. And I lead the boarding parties."

Tongue swung the ship around and eased alongside one of the cargo ships. Barry hoped the *Ponzington* and the other Monoliths weren't powering up their drives yet.

"*Drake*, this is *Ponzington*. You are not cleared to approach those ships. You are ordered to leave the system."

Tongue's hand hovered over the button to transmit.

"Don't answer it," Barry warned.

Tongue pulled his hand away. The starboard airlock's telltale switched from red to blue. With a smirk, Flank left the kick. He signaled for Barry to come over to the cargo ship a minute later.

Barry passed through the mated airlocks and into zero gravity, pushing off the floor into a cavernous hold filled with crates. There was a passage between the stacks of crates too narrow to carry anything through. The gravity meant that Flank could slide crates over the rows and aisles.

Flank shoved crates at Barry, who hovered near the airlock and redirected them into the *Drake*, where each crate dropped with a thump on the starslider's gravity-encumbered deck moss. The crates were labelled only with cryptic inventory labels and the contents were a mystery.

"Hurry guys," Tongue said over the comm. "The Grids are incredibly pissed off."

The *Drake* didn't have a cargo hold and the airlock quickly filled up. Barry climbed over the pile and began dragging crates all over the ship: engine room, galley, the bunks, the kick, everywhere. They might need to steal entire ships if they wanted to make off with any serious freight. Or they needed to rethink the piracy business.

At least the crates weren't too heavy.

"What is this stuff?" Barry asked when Flank reappeared in the *Drake's* airlock.

Flank grinned. "Space pizza."

"Come again?" Barry asked.

"Space. Pizza. Dehydrated, vacuum-sealed space pizza."

Barry said, "The old ship rations. Space pizza! Yeah. Okay. Great. Why are we stealing ship rations?"

Flank scowled at Barry's lack of enthusiasm. "What did you expect? Gold, ice, dancing girls? This is brilliant. It's condensed food. You just need water and heat. It may be cheap to us, but the Grids need to ship this stuff from five sectors away. It will get top price. You should think these things through, Barry."

"Maybe you ought to be captain," Barry replied in earnest as they closed the airlock.

"Maybe I ought to be."

They returned to the kick. The drive was almost charged and the *Ponzington* was not screaming at them anymore. *This piracy thing isn't too hard*, Barry thought.

"Tell me we struck gold." Tongue said, his feet resting on a stack of crates labelled 'GEC property.'

Flank scowled. "You think the Grids are stupid enough to ship currency in unsecured containers, out to a frontier where they can't spend it? Are you really that stupid?"

Barry stated flatly, "We got pizza."

Tongue furrowed his brow. "Uh, what?"

Barry smiled the fakest smile he could fake. "Don't you worry your shaggy little head. Flank says we'll be richer than we can imagine. Who knew piracy would be so simple? How are we doing on getting out of here?"

His normally upbeat navigator was uncharacteristically melancholy. He thought he could cheer up poor Tongue when a giant blue ship filled all of their scopes. Bow, stern, dorsal, ventral, starboard, port.

"Thrusters!" Barry cried dropping into his seat and strapping in. Flank stumbled out of the kick toward the engine room. The *Ponzington* either violated safety protocols to slide in so close or was uncharacteristically bad at navigation.

Something thumped off the outer hull. The starslider wobbled but stayed on course, pulling away slowly from the Monolith.

Tongue worked the controls. "Are they firing at us?"

"Magnetic harpoons," Flank replied on the intercom. "Bounced right off. Morons. They never talked to the *Beatrix*."

Tongue threw the ship into a tight bank to the left, putting the container ship between them and the *Ponzington*. The *Drake* built a lead but its drive needed two more minutes to charge.

Tongue wrenched the ship around to keep out of range of magnetic harpoons or whatever else the GEC might fire at them. "We can't slide unless I fly straight. These guys will catch us if I fly straight. And we're low on thruster fuel."

Barry sighed. "So get us away from them and then fly straight."

"We're not gonna escape," Tongue muttered.

So they kept charging ahead. The *Ponzington* needed to climb over the cargo transport, which stretched the *Drake*'s lead to over a dozen kilometers.

The recharge clock dropped under a minute. Barry's hopes rose. The recharge clock reversed and then flashed and reset to all nines.

Flank roared with anger from engineering. "The foxing drive is offline," he yelled.

Tongue gasped. "Shit."

Barry keyed the ship intercom. "Flank, can you tell us, in a calm voice, what's wrong with the ship?"

"Yeah," the engineer yelled, "the fail safe tripped on the beam collimater. We can't fire the beam that creates the wormhole we slide into. I'm working on it. Don't ask me when it will be fixed."

"So what can we do in the meantime?" Barry asked Tongue.

"We're foxed," Tongue said. "The *Drake* isn't built for, like, high speed maneuvers. Or combat. She's a delicate lady."

"Go faster."

Tongue said, "We're already at max velocity. See this?" He pointed at the tac display. The *Ponzington* was closing. And with the *Drake* in open space, there was nowhere to slide to. Nowhere to hide.

Barry heaved himself out of his seat and took too long for his feet to touch the deck. Arty grav wasn't working right either? This was doubly serious. He bounced awkwardly to engineering.

Flank's entire upper torso was jammed inside the drive. Parts were spread out on a towel. Barry sort of recognized the pieces. Creating a beam to rip space open and form a micro-wormhole required really complicated machinery.

He sleptwalked through the classes on slide technology. He always told himself he could probably get by with the manuals. He kept meaning to ask Flank a couple of questions, to study up.

"What can I do to help?" he asked.

Flank grimaced. He considered himself the best engineer in the Exchange and the best member of the crew. So for his area of responsibility to be letting down his crew grated on him. Worse was Barry offering to help and being nice about it. "Stay out of my way or I'll kill you."

"There's no time for bruised egos. I'll tighten a nut, grease a ball bearing, whatever you need."

Flank growled at him. "Okay. Check the other collimator assemblies. The failsafes went off on them. Follow the damn checklist and pay close attention this time. I don't want to repeat what happened on Krivitsia Prime."

Barry picked up a scanner. "Are you ever going to let it go? I'm not drunk and delirious from venereal humidity plague."

The failsafe checklist was open on a nearby display. Poking holes in the fabric of space was dangerous work. Without a highly controlled procedure, a malfunctioning drive could easily rip a ship in half. The failsafes tripped if the beam collimators were unaligned and wouldn't direct the gravimetric pulses in the correct direction.

Barry was vaguely aware that the slide drive allowed for sublight flight as well as sliding. Bank the ship left by creating a gravimetric source off the port bow and the ship would slide, or fall, towards it. The slide drive could be used in combination with the thruster system to increase maneuverability and to make sublight propulsion more reliable and safer. You wouldn't use the slide drive for exact tactical maneuvers, that's what thrusters were for.

But for the drive to provide any directional control, the beam it produced had to be targeted precisely. The *Drake*'s drive consisted of two dozen vertical beam projectors that worked together. Each one had triple-redundant failsafes. If those failsafes tripped, the ship wouldn't tear itself apart, but it would fail to slide. Which, in this case, would fail to keep them safe from the Grids.

Barry opened the access panel for collimator assemblies twelve and thirteen. He wrinkled his nose at the burnt toast smell of fried organic wiring. Rather than use the checklist he chased the stink instead. He scrambled around the compartment, tracking the smell to the junction of the collimator assembly and a specific vertical emitter plate. The junction allowed the plate to swivel without compromising the flow of gravimetric energy from the collimator assembly.

But his nose couldn't find the source of the stink. He started working through the checklist. He made it halfway through the checklist before it was clear the junction was fried on both the twelve and thirteen assemblies.

"Multiple junction failures," Barry said.

"What? How? Hang on," Flank replied. He rummaged around in

the machinery and his bald head popped into view a couple of assemblies down. "Son of a bitch," he said. "I got three more down here. No wonder it tripped the failsafes — the computer believes the main trunk is misaligned. We were supposed to refit two months ago — I told you we were nearly redlined when we reached Union the first time."

They last discussed ship performance issues on the final sprint to Union. This wasn't Flank being his usual extra nutty about his efficiency stats. "Can you replace them?"

Flank was busy disconnecting and winching up the main trunk to access the broken block. "Yeah, I can fix it. But we need to get this whole thing overhauled really soon. I need to shut down four emitters."

"Guys!" Tongue barked from the kick. "Another Monolith slid in. No pressure though."

Barry sighed and stomped into the kick. Maybe kicking off their pirating career with a banged up ship was something he should have considered. He glanced at the overhead board. The new Monolith was the *Poplar Revue* and she was cutting them off so the *Ponzington* could catch up. "Flank needs a few minutes."

Tongue was busy plotting a course away from both GEC ships. His tongue was hanging out. "Great, but if we're caught in one of their grav cones, we can't slide. Too much gravimetric disturbance."

Barry didn't know what to say. His usual smart-assisms seemed inadequate to the task. He studied the tac board. The situation was hopeless. Where was a pretty crystalline passenger liner to run interference when you needed one? "Do whatever you can to stay clear of their drives," he said.

"Trying to. Watch."

They buzzed the *Revue*, circling its super structure, sensor pods, and hangar bays. The *Ponzington* couldn't bring its drive to tractor them without damaging her sister ship.

They were so close to the *Revue*, and flying so fast, the *Ponzingtons'* magpoons couldn't reach them either. The *Drake* reached the *Revue's* pinnacle, a thin mast blistered with multiple heat vents. Tongue reversed course. They circled downward around the *Revue*, toward its wide-bottomed slide drive.

"Aren't you flying too predictably?" Barry asked.

Tongue grinned.

The *Revue* launched nasty-looking tugboats to chase them down. The tugs had strong enough slide drives to grab the *Drake* and hold it, if they could isolate it from the Monolith it was hugging. Tongue did another orbital pass around the Monolith and put the *Drake* into a steep dive for the Monolith's equator.

Barry saw the plot Tongue was executing and grinned. "Flank," he said into the intercom, "we ready to slide?"

"Almost. Last replacement junction… okay, it checked out."

Tongue pulled away from the ship to swing wide underneath it. The *Revue* was already powering up its slide drive to snag them. A magpoon thudded against their stern. The tugboats were now in range to add their slide drives' gravity as well.

The *Drake* flew straight into the Monolith's gravity cone. With enough velocity and a parabolic course it could use the Monolith's gravity to sling shot around its keel. It placed the *Revue* between them and the *Ponzington*.

The slide drive telltales flipped from red to blue. They were good to slide if they could get clear of all the gravimetric disturbance.

Flank ran into the kick and fell up to the ceiling. The internal gravity was losing a fight with the *Revue*'s slide drive. The gravity snapped back on and he somersaulted to the deck.

Inertia took hold when the *Drake* swung through the slingshot maneuver. Barry's insides tried to push out of his right side. Tongue was smiling confidently though.

Suddenly, the *Drake* zipped away from the *Revue*. Tongue's nav board went from bright red to bright blue.

"Hit it," Flank said.

Tongue activated the slide drive.

The bow scope showed space constricting in front of the ship as the drive formed the wormhole. The wormhole pulled the ship in and the image dissolved into rainbow static and snow when the ship slid inside.

Flank stood and puffed out a breath of relief. "That was too tight."

Barry tapped a finger against his cheek. This piracy business needed more thought and planning. He needed to get on top of the situation, which was rapidly evolving. They couldn't blunder around like this again. It was dumb luck they didn't end up adrift or captured. Even worse, if they didn't step up they could fail to achieve revenge on the foxing foxholes who screwed them.

FIFTEEN

PERGAMON.

The *Drake* had no choice but to stop at this settled and busy GEC system. Flank announced that any additional sliding would likely cause the drive to implode or strand them permanently in the deep black. The next GEC world, Andiron, was several slides away. They needed to stop here even if it meant they were arrested for pizza larceny.

It fell to Barry to talk their way past Pergamon's authorities and to some repair facility. So on the way to Pergamon, while Tongue tried to eat the incriminating evidence of larceny, he consumed vids of real-life GEC citizens, their mannerisms, dialects, and how they lived. They didn't act stiff like Exchanger entertainment portrayed them, but there was some truth to the stereotypes. He practiced talking like a weaselly-mouthed PR hack for a morally-bankrupt corporation.

The rest he would improvise, because he rarely failed when he ad-libbed. Or at least he rarely failed ad-libbing without also entertaining himself.

Tongue dropped them into Pergamon right at the nav beacon. Unlike the previous stops along the GEC main line, this nav beacon was in geosynchronous orbit around a habitable brown planet.

The *Drake*'s nav screen filled with intrasystem traffic. Over eight thousand distinct craft were in-system. It reminded Barry of Rachel's homeworld: an urban multiplanet system which was such a crowded sector transit hub that it needed flight control stationed on every major celestial body to handle the flow. The difference here was Pergamon was a chaotic mess.

Tongue zoomed out the view to take in the totality of ships at Pergamon. "Well, isn't this place hopping?"

System Control messaged a request for identification. Barry affected a nasal accent and said, "Yes, we're the *Grimy Spikes*, and this old tub is carrying our comedy troupe."

Grimy Spikes Happy Kid Hour was a children's show broadcast in certain Exchange sectors over twenty years ago. These Grids would never get the reference.

System Control responded, "We're assigning you to an orbital path. Please proceed to these coordinates and wait for further instructions."

Tongue grunted. "It's a weird elliptical orbit, far from the planet. There's no other ships in that orbit."

"Should we worry?" Barry asked.

Tongue threw his hands in the air. "Beats the hell out of me."

With each passing hour they stayed in their assigned orbital segment, Flank made happier-sounding grunts from engineering and Barry watched as other ships were cleared to land on the surface or park at one of the orbital stations.

No one on the *Drake* wanted to state the obvious: the GEC was holding them there until they figured out what to do with them. The GEC must be hunting for pepperoni pirates flying a starslider. *Coming here was really, really stupid*, Barry suspected. But what other choice did they have? Flank needed time to replace parts on the drive until they could reach a legit repair facility. And who knew if the Grids knew how to fix Exchanger tech?

Finally, the comm beeped, startling Tongue from a nap. It was a text message containing coordinates followed by a short message: *Pergamon unsafe. Slide to these coordinates to avoid GEC. Meet your fan club.*

Tongue entered the coordinates. "This goes nowhere. Maybe an uncharted system or just deep space? You know, at least unexplored on the Grid charts. I'd need to send a probe to make sure nothing dangerous is waiting for us on the other side."

"We can't. The damn ship is broke," Flank said. "I'm patching her up here as best I can but I can only print so many parts. Don't give me that look. Yes, she probably can slide one more time. But every slide brings us closer to a total fry job."

"You're so sour," Tongue said, exasperated. "Do you ever stop worrying about how things can go wrong?"

"No. I foxing don't," Flank said. "We were supposed to get a reward once..."

Tongue shook his head violently.

Barry shrugged. "Maybe this other system has free printers. And ship repair facilities. Maybe it has an entire exhibition of the latest ship tech happening."

"Are you kidding me?" Flank yelled. "Aren't you slightly concerned about who the hell is asking us to leap into the deep black? Huh?"

"Tongue, is their a habitable system or any sign of technology in this system our strange rescuers want us to slide to?"

Tongue scrolled around his navigation screen. "I don't see anything."

"Why should we trust them?" Flank asked.

Barry said to Tongue, "Ask them who they are and what they want with us."

Tongue tapped away and a response came back less than a minute later. He posted it on the main screen.

We're friends. Not GEC. We need to buy your cargo, Drake. *Here are probe feeds proving the Batik coords are legit.*

Tongue posted the live feed from this secret Batik probe to the main board. The Batik system consisted of one habitable planet with at least two ships in orbit. The beacon would bring them near an orbital path.

"It's the right coordinates," Tongue said. "No surprise, no ambush."

Barry texted a reply: *We need repairs. Drive refit. Can you accommo-*

date? Accommodated was one of those GEC words Barry picked up on to blend in.

Yes, was the reply.

Flank shook his head. "I'm surrounded by idiotic bastards."

Barry smiled broadly. "We could sit here and wait for the GEC to figure out who we are. I nearly crap my sweatpants every time they call us."

Flank pounded the bulkhead and returned to engineering.

"Are you getting scans of these ships around us?" Barry asked Tongue quietly. There were unfamiliar ship classes in orbits above and below them. They resembled boxy cargo container ships. Juicy, undefended cargo container ships.

"Oh yeah. We're developing quite the unusual database. Could be worth a lot back home. Hey, you want to grab anything while we're here?"

Barry said, "No. But look at this." He pointed to the ship identifications on all the ships on the most crowded orbital path. Half were automated cargo haulers. Another third were piloted, but by a small crew.

"Easy pickings, man," Tongue agreed.

Barry asked, "But can any of these outrun us or fight back?"

Tongue queried their intel on GEC ships. "Only the Monoliths and their security cutters."

"We need to refit quickly," Barry said.

"Okay, we're good to slide," Flank reported from the bow.

Tongue carefully followed Pergamon System Control's procedures for leaving their weird elliptical orbit.

Barry's eyes flitted from one patrol ship on the navigation board to the next. He gripped the side of the console with both hands.

Tongue's hand hovered over his console.

"What's wrong?" Barry asked. "Is the math okay?"

"Yeah, it's totally solid. Drive is ready. Coordinates are good. I'm just, you know, not used to sliding blind like this."

Barry said, "Every second you delay, my heart's ready to explode." He came around to Tongue's side of the circular console. "Is this the button here?"

"Yeah."

Barry slapped it. The *Drake* slid out of Pergamon.

SIXTEEN

THE *DRAKE* SLID into the Batik system and, for a change, no damn offi-
cious Monoliths were there to boot them out. There were only five
other ships in system, two small GEC freighters and a trio of shuttles
huddled around a small space station. A single beacon broadcast the
system ID on a non-GEC frequency.

Batik's only habitable planet was a cloud-covered snowball at the
outer edge of the solar habitable zone. Its distance from the sun
resulted in a relatively small temperate zone around the equator and no
tropics. The *Drake*'s long-range scopes showed it was barely habitable,
but not desirable, other than being a short slide from Pergamon.

The only sign of humanity in the system was the ancient orbital
station. It was patched together into a letter 'H' from repurposed shipping containers, old ship sections and a motley arrangement of docking
slips, extendable repair arms and one functioning shipyard dock.

The sun rose over the Batik's horizon and bathed the station in light.
The hulls of the containers reflected bright white and gray, free of
scoring and pitting. They looked new.

"Maybe it's a repair depot, not a habitat," Flank noted.

"Come on, I'm sure it's fine, better than Yagotell," Tongue observed.

"Yagotell had its charms," Barry said. "The food was exquisite."

"Religious cult, not so much," Flank retorted. "But tough fighters."

"These people did say 'friends' in their message, so maybe we shouldn't worry so much," Tongue said. "After all, we're the pirates."

The flight controller welcomed them to Billy's Station and directed the *Drake* to an extended docking slip on the station's port side. Tongue slipped the ship between a battered orbital shuttle and a triangular yacht and connected to the station's airlock.

A crowd waited for them on the other side of the airlock. On first glance, this motley welcoming committee was no different than Exchangers physically; a multitude of skin shades, facial structures, and ages. They all were a slice too thin though. Their clothes consisted of coveralls and jumpsuits that looked like they came from a rag bin. They had the wide-eyed, curious look that signaled mental disturbance or excessive boredom. They resembled starving patients from a fifth-rate mental institution.

"What's wrong with these people?" Flank asked.

Barry winked at Flank. "Look zonkers. Maybe they're going to kill us and eat our fresh corpses."

Flank gave him a look. It was an old ooga-booga story: the derelict habitat full of zonkered stir-crazy denizens that dine on unsuspecting visitors. The thing was, these people and their station fit the description perfectly.

Barry popped the hatch and winced when the acrid bite of solvents and toxic cleaners filled his nostrils. No one in either group said a word.

A short man with bristly graying hair slipped through the station's awkward gawkers. "I'm Sean Clasker. I sent you the message," he said. His mouth was set like an iron trap but a lopsided smile escaped. He was wearing a business suit.

Barry made introductions. A skeletal woman came up behind Clasker and he introduced her as the station owner, Billy. She had long black hair and a permanent grimace.

Clasker turned to the gawkers. "Can everyone give us some space?"

The gawkers blinked and dispersed down the corridor.

Clasker asked Barry, "Only you three?"

"We're pretty versatile," Barry said confidently.

"Right. Welcome to the Underseed."

"I thought this was the Batik system?" Tongue asked.

Clasker nodded. "It is, it's one system in the Underseed, which, let's just say, *complements* GEC territory. But we're separate."

"Never heard of it," Flank said suspiciously. "Does the GEC know about you?"

"Yes. But it's complicated."

"How come the Underseed isn't on any of their charts?" Tongue asked.

"Officially, we don't exist," Clasker said. "Pretend we are off-Grid." A tight little smile. "We attract people who dropped out of the GEC. Or are forced out. People ready to embrace living with less structure, bureaucracy, and restrictions. We actually emulate the Exchange way of life to some degree."

"Grids sick of the Grid. Who'da thunk it?" Barry joked.

Clasker said, "We brought you here because otherwise the GEC would have confiscated your cargo. You'd be rotting in an interrogation cell. Exchangers willing to raid GEC shipping could be a great help to us."

"Oh, really? Do we agree, guys?" Barry said. Tongue gave a thumbs up. Flank was bored with the small talk and motioned to get on with it.

Clasker shrugged. "If you want to sell any of the cargo you lifted, you do. I represent an import/export business here. Barry, shall we repair to the local drinking house? We have business to discuss. Flank and Tongue could show Billy and her gang around the ship, get started on repairs."

"Uh," Flank said, "actually we'll come along with you and our dear captain. Make sure he doesn't treat you too roughly."

Clasker led them deeper into the station, through several cramped shipping containers packed to the support struts with equipment and supply cabinets. These outer containers provided rough shielding for the living spaces on the center level, he explained.

They walked through a poorly lit housing unit of sorts, each cabin not much more than an enclosed cubicle. Next to it was the segment housing the station's retail and administrative space.

'The Bar,' said a battered cardboard sign tacked above the door. Inside was a hodgepodge of mismatched furniture and a bar made of faded plastic crates. A very thin man working a still behind the bar nodded when Clasker held up four fingers. Apparently there was only one drink available at this establishment.

Clasker showed them to a back corner walled off with strips of sound proofing. When they pushed through the sound proofing, white noise crackled from each strip. Inside was a makeshift desk with garish fluorescent lighting.

"My temporary office," Clasker explained, taking a seat on a three-legged stool. The bartender delivered the drinks: a small juice glass filled with a foamy, sparkling purple liquid.

Tongue took a sip and nearly gagged.

"Pretty strong, huh?" Barry asked.

"Tastes like liquid plaster and sour greens," Tongue said, wincing. "No offense."

Clasker laughed and held up his glass. "Cheers. We're short on food here. This is what we have to eat. It has protein, calcium, and uh, other nutrients." He sipped it and needed a minute to compose himself. "So, argh, sorry, what did you steal?"

"Space pizza," Barry whispered like it was a state secret.

"Really?"

Tongue held up his glass. "Tasty, unlike this shit."

"How much space pizza?"

Barry said casually, "Oh, only one hundred flats, fifty packets each."

"Wow. You hit the cargo convoy at D-NH4, I hear. I'll pay ten per packet. GEC script, I'm afraid. It's the only currency in the Underseed."

"God, only fifty thousand?" Barry said. "It would barely cover our fuel costs, wear and tear on the ship, docking fees, not to mention the risk premium for bringing the Grids down on us. Thirty per packet."

Clasker drained the rest of his cup in one swig and winced. "They go for about two per packet in the GEC economy. But things are different here. You're new here, so I'll be gracious and say twelve."

"We'll keep that in mind for the next convoy," Barry said. "We're happy to help, assuming we can make a decent profit. Twenty-five."

"Fifteen apiece and I throw in our starcharts," Clasker replied.

Tongue laughed. "We already got GEC starcharts. And a lot of good they are: there's only routes for half a dozen settled systems in this sector."

Clasker grinned. "Charts of the Underseed, not GEC. There's dozens of Underseed systems in this sector. They may be the only safe places left for you to go now. No GEC law enforcement, no trouble. This is a good deal, because food is scarce out here, and you can't slide into any GEC systems for supplies." He pulled out a personal screen displaying a Grid starchart.

The starchart showed the single, straight GEC main route from Union to Pergamon in yellow. It hugged the inner coreward boundary of the GHR. Clasker tapped the screen and a web of green lines appeared alongside the yellow line. The web connected to Pergamon and Andiron and extended to the Way Back sectors, all rimward of the GEC route.

Clasker was handing them the key fob to the Underseed. These green lines on the starchart went where the Grids couldn't find them.

Flank asked, "How does the GEC not know about this?"

"They know it exists, but they don't have the slide coordinates. They've been in such a rush to reach Union, they have not explored most of the volume in the last two sectors. The Underseed actually stretches all the way back to the Ancient Sectors."

Barry grinned. "Have people been unhappy with the GEC for that long?"

Clasker returned his grin. "Smugglers, cranks, small traders, misfits, entrepreneurs, thrill seekers, everyone who doesn't fit in. They headed out to make a life for themselves outside the Corporation. None of our systems in sectors 180 through 182 are well developed. But they're home to us. And you can hide here. Fifteen a packet and these starcharts."

Barry leaned forward. "We could take the time to have Tongue verify that these starcharts aren't fake charts. Or you can take twenty plus the charts."

Flank looked ready to bite off Barry's arm and shove it up his ass. Tongue still played the cool cat.

Clasker said, "Deal. And to show my gratitude, I'll introduce you to my boss. If you guys start hauling in a lot of freight, my boss will buy it from you."

"A fence pays wholesale and sells retail and keeps the difference," Barry said in an accusatory tone.

"It's not a charitable service. If you're going to be pirates, you'll need someone to sell the goods for you," Clasker pointed out.

"We're not interested," Barry replied.

"The hell we aren't," Flank said. "Did you figure out how we convert stolen goods into cash, Barry? We can't waste our time searching for buyers."

Barry said, "We're not going to be indentured to any organization, Flank. The *Drake* is an independent operator."

Clasker said, "Oh, we're not hiring you."

Flank chugged his drink. "Ah. The taste grows on you. Contractors. Better yet. What percentage do we get?"

"Depends on the product and its market value. Like you said, she buys wholesale and sells retail. You can go elsewhere if you don't like what she offers. Try and sell it yourselves if you want. This is a strictly mutually beneficial, transactional relationship. So when you're caught, we aren't implicated." Big smile.

"Out of curiosity," Flank said, "how many other pirates are out there raiding the GEC?"

Clasker took Barry's untouched drink and downed it in one gulp. "You're the first. The only pirates I've heard of are centuries-old legends from the Ancient Sectors. Self-loathing hedonists or idiotic adventurers, right?"

"Hey, we're not self-loathing," Tongue said hotly.

Clasker said, "We're fine with you being pirates, but we would like... an accommodation."

"An accommodation," Barry repeated warily. Here came the strings that would ensnare them.

Clasker held up his hands. "It's simple. Don't attack Underseed ships. In return, you'll be allowed to stop at any Underseed world or facility."

Barry smiled. "We got this hang-up about rules, okay? If Underseed ships are off limits, we're limited to these GEC crates. Kind of makes us Underseed privateers, not pirates. We aren't choosing sides, or becoming anyone's foot soldiers, or joining political crusades."

Clasker barely smiled. "Pirates with principles, how nice. And if you rob everyone, where will you sell your winnings and repair your ship? You might not want to make enemies everywhere you go."

Tongue kicked Barry's shin.

Barry nearly took the bait, especially with Flank boiling at the word *repair*, but he refrained. Clasker seemed savvy so he would play things straight. "We hit who we want, when we want. On the other hand, I can't see why we'd *want* to raid poor starving Grids in the Underseed. Unless there's a seller's market for very used coveralls."

"Call it what you want," Clasker said. "Just don't attack Underseed ships. Choose your targets deliberately so we don't starve more."

"What is there to eat around here?" Tongue asked.

Clasker hoisted his glass. Tongue sighed. Clasker said, "We have some other concerns about your new business venture, if you don't mind."

"Sounds a little bit nosy," Barry said.

"Not at all. If we're buying your stolen goods and giving you aid and comfort, we should know what kind of risks that entail. For instance, what is your strategy for raiding GEC shipping?"

"Whooping a lot, maybe some flourishes," Tongue said.

"Everything we do, it's with class and style," Barry added.

Clasker said, "No, no. How will you slip in and out of GEC systems without any trouble? How will you avoid capture? You'll need several sets of transponder codes, fake ID to get by customs and the traffic control guys. And weapons."

Barry clucked his tongue. "And how much will that junk cost us?" he asked.

"Don't pepper us with a list of additional expenses," Flank sneered.

"Flank, will you shut up," Tongue said. "They could have fed us to the Pergamon cops. Man! Show some damn gratitude here."

Flank retorted, "I didn't say it was a threat, moron, I don't want us totally foxed on the price. It's a negotiating tactic, get it?"

"Maybe for someone who's hit their head on the emitter arrays too many times," Tongue muttered.

Barry slapped them both on the backs of their heads. "Boys, must we do this in front of Mr. Clasker?"

The man across from them raised his hand and grinned. "It'll cost ten thousand for ID for each of you, plus another ten for the transponder codes."

Barry said. "We'll take the transponder codes, but not the IDs. We're not sneaking into the GEC." Flank raised an eyebrow at him, but he ignored it. He figured they could steal IDs. Transponder codes were harder to fake.

Clasker said, "Another thing. We survive off of harassing the GEC. You can't let them chase you back to Underseed worlds. Understand? They'll kill us." There was an earnest fear in his eyes.

Barry replied, "We won't bring them to your doorstep. You're afraid that there's a fight brewing."

Clasker said in a low tone, "There are rumors of a conflict looming on the horizon, yes. Question is: what kind of conflict?"

"The Exchange is totally not our people," Tongue said.

Flank raised an eyebrow at that.

Clasker said, "Quite right, I guess. Exchange ships are already showing up at Pergamon. Won't be long before they reach Andiron and stumble into one of our systems. The GEC is pushing hard into Sector 180. We'll need to monitor developments on a going forward basis."

Tongue scowled. "On a what?"

"On the basis of going forward. As time progresses."

Tongue rolled his eyes. "If you mean the future, why not be clear about it?"

Clasker laughed. "Welcome to the GEC side of the galaxy. It's great working with you Exchangers. You're probably itching to fix your ship."

Flank nodded. "We are. There's a lot of work to do."

The guys declined to toast their deal with another round of drinks. Instead, they returned to the *Drake* and brushed their teeth several times.

Billy's office was just a walled off corner in the station's oldest shipping container. Barry and Tongue had to sit in chairs in the narrow aisle outside and lean around a stack of boxes to hear Flank and Billy talk shop.

Flank said, "I need to do a ton of work on the ship and I need parts and a hand. No offense to the two clowns sitting out there in the hallway."

"We're not offended," Tongue replied.

Billy said, "This isn't an Exchanger repair depot. We don't know much about your ship or your tech."

"It's a standard starslider, only very well maintained. Wait, what's it typically cost to refit and refuel here?" Flank asked suspiciously.

Billy replied, "Look, I'm not winding you up to fleece you. Couple of thousand, mostly for labor. Batik is a mining settlement, so thruster fuel is cheap. This station doesn't have the equipment to be a repair depot. And not for what you need. You'll have to bring your ship down to the surface to repair it. You can deliver the food to the settlement at the same time."

"We need to bring her down anyway," Flank said, starting to stand. "We need a lot of organic matter to print replacement parts. The sooner we get started, the faster we can get out of here."

Billy motioned him back to his seat. "Yes, about that. We should discuss the bigger picture. You see, your ship isn't fixable."

SEVENTEEN

"THE FOX ARE YOU ON ABOUT?" Flank asked Billy.

She said, "It's a form-factor problem. A starslider is a racer, built for sliding long distances and exploring new systems quickly. Not carrying cargo. Astrometric sensors and probe storage are useless for pirates."

"I was afraid of this," Barry said with a groan. The logic clicked into place for him. "She's right."

Flank leaned back out of the cubicle. "Shut. Up."

"Show me your drive's performance profile," she said.

Flank sent her the *Drake*'s numbers. "These our top numbers for slide time per light year, minimum recharge time, and maximum slide range."

Billy's eyes widened. "Damn, there isn't a single GEC craft that could approach these stats. Congratulations. But they're irrelevant now. Your ship needs to be optimized for fast in-system flight, hauling big cargo containers, and combat. Every one of the ships in the Underseed is better configured to flee GEC security than you."

"It *is* a totally different scene out there," Tongue agreed, leaning into the cubicle.

Without looking, Flank shoved his face out. "So what do you have in mind?" he asked.

Billy said, "We've retrofitted every GEC boat to flee the security cutters and Monoliths. And you can't retrofit a starslider. It doesn't have the cargo capacity. You need a different ship."

Barry shook his head.

Flank said, "Let me guess: you just happen to have the perfect ship."

"I'm not a ship dealer," Billy said. "You need to steal a cargo hauler."

"No. We're using the *Drake*."

Billy paused. "How serious are you three about succeeding as pirates? Is this a lark? Are you just fooling around?"

"We're serious," Barry said. "We may not have figured out how to do it, uh, competently. What are we missing?"

Billy said, "Okay, okay. You need to slide into a point where there's cargo you want to steal. You need to reach the ship, disable it, board it with enough people that the crew won't fight back, take the cargo or the entire ship, then get the hell out of there before you're caught."

Flank said, "You sound like you have a lot of experience outfitting pirate vessels. How many have you actually done?"

"Zero. I'm explaining how GEC cutters operate on contraband stops. It's a close analog to piracy."

Barry stared at the wall, his eyes twitching back and forth in thought. Billy was making a lot of sense to him, which made Flank grind his molars.

Tongue waved his hand in front of Barry's eyes, in case he was having a seizure. Barry grabbed his hand and held his finger to his lips.

Billy continued, "To do all that, you need an overhauled slide drive, more capacitors, more cargo capacity, weaponry. For starters. All that won't fit on a tiny starslider frame."

The *Drake* was optimized to be a slick racer and Flank optimized himself to keep it optimized. Reconfiguring the ship to be something else meant meant reconfigure his own way of working. Starting over. Learning a whole new set of mission parameters and how to make the *Drake* exceed them. It made him itchy. Made him want to walk away.

But he saw that Barry looked receptive to Billy's sales palaver. Flank needed to do something. He said, "I think it could. We optimize the drive for fast, responsive maneuvering. Recalibrate its emitter configuration for a wider wormhole, so we can tow a cargo container. Swap storage space for probes for more capacitors. And replace the astrometric sensors with weapons."

"Even if all that is feasible, and you can pay for it, that doesn't fix the problem where you need a dozen or more crew to take control of the other vessel and move the cargo," Billy said. "Or do you think the GEC will let you steal automated cargo ships forever?"

Flank grunted in agreement. Billy knew her stuff. She realized Flank was attached to the *Drake* and would drain their accounts for a gold-plated refit. Flank had been played by drydock salespeople before. Barry was always on his ass about not needing the latest model hardware when the previous model was good enough.

Tongue said, "She makes a good point. If we're serious about ripping off GEC ships, I think we need to make truly profound changes. Our approach. Our hardware. All of it."

"I don't want to keep leaning on luck," Barry added. "We're lucky we made it this far. Don't tell Clasker, but he probably saved our asses by pulling us out of Pergamon."

"Don't worry about it," Billy said. "You're not the first ones he's saved."

Flank waved his hands. "This won't work. We're not bankrupting ourselves."

"I'm not trying to pick your pockets," Billy said, reading his face. She shook the flappy coverall that she was lost in. "This thing used to fit me. That's why I recommend you go steal a bigger ship that needs fewer upgrades."

"You'll have to excuse bald and cranky here," Barry said. "We're new to piracy. We were hoping to keep doing the same thing until our luck runs out. Then we'd just, I don't know, improvise. But that sounds like an incredibly bad strategy."

"Yeah. And honestly, we need you out there stealing food for us. We need you to succeed."

"To be financially viable," Barry said, "we may need to expand what we steal and how we steal it."

"What do you have in mind?" Tongue asked.

"Not sure yet. But I think we need the *Drake* to be, uh, *versatile*."

"That's not going to be cheap, *Barry*," Flank said.

Billy held up her hands. "Touchy about cost, are we? I can't give you an estimate until I see what I'm working with, inside and out. Maybe a tech swap can lower the cost, too. We'll have to do this planetside. That's where the food is going and we can't do spacewalks up here."

"Why not?" Tongue asked.

"We're short on spacesuit valves. That's life in the Underseed."

Flank transferred a quarter of the space pizza crates to the station, and then the *Drake,* and a shuttle carrying Clasker and Billy's people, landed at the planet's lone mining settlement.

Barry was unusually quiet during reentry. He got that way when he was thinking big thoughts.

Flank let him be: Barry got them into this spot, he could figure out how to get them out. Flank feverishly worked on the puzzle of how to refit the ship for an optimal pirate performance. As Tongue lined up for the final approach, Flank began smiling.

Batik's sole settlement was tucked into a temperate rain forest at the base of a mountain. It was the staging area for a mining operation in the mountain it was snuggled against. The landing area was a dirt clearing carved out of thick, dark green pine trees covered in lacy yellow hanging moss.

Barry and Tongue unloaded the cargo by hand, setting the crates on the dead pine needles.

Clasker, wrapped in a thick cloak, came over and watched them struggle down the ramp with the unwieldy crates. "If you had an actual cargo hauler instead of that tiny scout ship, there'd be loading equipment to do that."

Barry grunted. "No, this is, uh, great exercise. You going to stand there and watch or help us?"

"I already worked out today, thank you. Billy couldn't talk you out of getting a more appropriate vessel, I see." He nodded to Billy and her crew, who were walking around the *Drake*, taking pictures, measurements, and running their hands over the hull.

"We're sticking with the *Drake*. Flank insisted," Tongue said, stretching his back muscles.

"Then you'll be here a while," Clasker remarked and walked away.

Billy ran her hand over the *Drake*'s hull. "Is this rock behind the ceramic plating? It's not metal."

Flank shook his head. "Coral. The hull is a coral reef ecosystem that thrives on deep space vacuum and radiation. It includes several species of space marine invertebrates, coral, lichen, barnacles, all living off each other. It provides structural integrity and shields the living quarters."

"It's alive?"

"Sure is. The ceramic plating isn't bolted on. It's secreted by the outer layer of barnacles. They smear it uniformly across the surface, except where we have sensors, the drive arrays, or an airlock hatch like this one."

One of Billy's techs said, "This is insane."

"You should watch some documentary about Exchange shipbuilding before you touch my ship," Flank said.

"We're not the documentary-watching types," Billy said. "I suppose we can't remove parts of the hull to swap out ship compartments." She exchanged looks with her crew. "How do we add weapon bays and new sensors?

Flank handed her a handheld screen with a rotating schematic on it. "We can remove *some* of the hull. The little buggers will grow back. I've worked it all out." He walked to the stern of the ship and pointed to a spot on the tapered stern. "See where a magnetic harpoon scraped the hull? The coral, the lichen, and the barnacles are already growing back. They self-repair. Only downside is the time it takes to grow back. When it's done, we'll patch up the ceramic skin around our sensors there."

Billy said, "Our hull plating is only a couple centimeters thick. You're hauling a lot of mass to get that same protection."

"GEC ships need their hulls replaced or their radiation shielding burns out, right?"

Billy said, "Every ten years, on average."

Flank patted the hull. "The *Drake* is over eighty years old. Its coral replaces itself. A starslider can last up to two centuries, with proper maintenance. And the coral and fungus are light. You can keep any bits we remove, cultivate your own starship hull garden."

Billy nodded. "How long does it take you Exchangers to 'grow' a ship?"

"Depends," Flank said. "Five to ten years, depending on the builder and what mix of organisms they use."

"A Monolith takes three months," Billy said. "I worked on the assembly line. A security cutter, which is about the size of your ship, takes around thirty days."

Flank crossed his arms. "That's final assembly. How long if you include building the custom printers, mining the minerals, printing all the parts, and pre-assembly?"

Billy shook her head. "Don't know. But I do know that my crew can overhaul a GEC wreck in a week. You probably don't want to wait a decade for your living hull to grow out to three times the volume of this thin pencil."

"We can make do with the existing dimensions," Flank said. "I've worked it out. Step into the central corridor here and you can see most of the interior."

Billy and her engineers oohed and aahed. "There isn't a straight line in here," Billy noted. She ran her hand along the smooth but irregular bulkheads and the curved ceramic structural beams.

One of the crew pointed at the garden wall next to the galley. "You really use plants and bugs for life support." She scrunched up her nose at the humidity and the peaty smell.

Flank raised a brow. "Those aren't typical houseplants. This ecosystem is symbiotic: it supports us and we support it. Everyone eats and breathes everyone else's waste products and eggs, anyway."

Billy batted away a lumbering insect. "I can't imagine depending on a flimsy greenhouse biome to survive."

Flank chuckled. "Seems crazy to me to survive in a thin metal box with canisters of compressed oxygen and processed food."

Billy's scrunch-nosed engineer smiled. "We don't have to breathe in spores, mold, or insect feces."

"Where does your water come from? Huh? Let's go to the kick. Kick stands for center of integrated command. It's not big enough to be a 'bridge'."

Billy and her team crowded into the kick. Barry was standing there waiting for Clasker to transfer the money to their account. "Welcome," he said.

"How do you see outside?" someone asked, looking around at the solid walls.

Flank replied, "Scopes, scanners, and cams." He clicked through the various feeds on the screens around the kick.

"What if that equipment malfunctions?"

"We have redundant backups. If they all failed at once, we'd be dead anyway." Flank said. "The drive is this way. Do you really think your drive tech will work with ours?"

Smiles spread across Billy and her techs. "We use the same blueprints. We bought the licenses to print the new 5800 series emitter arrays and the R2300 capacitors."

"R2300?" Flank gasped. "That's the first major advance in capacitors since I was a kid."

"My question is how much will all this fancy R2300s cost us?" Barry asked, noticing Flank's eagerness. "We still need to eat, like, occasionally."

"Don't you eat bug poop and leaves?" one of the techs asked.

Barry pointed. "Flank does. My point is, we don't need the fanciest parts."

Flank retorted, "Being versatile doesn't come cheap. We're factoring the value of Exchange tech for them."

Billy said, "Being the first to have Exchange tech is worth a lot to us, I'll be honest with you. We're not part of the GEC supply chain. Whoever leans on self-sufficient Exchanger tech first will have an advantage."

"So maybe you'll pay us for the work," Barry said.

"I don't play psych tricks on customers and I don't negotiate,

Spranker," Billy said. "I give honest estimates when I know what work I have to do. And I don't know enough yet."

Flank gestured for Barry to back off.

Barry rolled his eyes. "Fine. Go show them the drive. Our guests are drooling on the deck moss in anticipation."

Flank rubbed his hands together. He led Billy's crew into the engine room and popped off access panels to expose the hardware. He placed each panel in a particular spot on the deck. "We may be plant-loving bug chewers, but the components are the same. It's just that they're printed from different materials."

Billy and her techs stuck their noses in the hardware. Billy said, "The parts look the same to me. What are these arrays and junctures made from?"

"Synthesized cellulose polymers. When you're out mapping new routes in the deep black, you don't wait to for new parts to arrive. We can print everything ourselves from organic feedstocks."

Billy raised an eyebrow. "I don't know how the hell ground-up twigs and seeds can be made to poke holes in space."

She pulled a diagnostic tool from her thigh pocket and plugged it into a data port. "It can get a reading. But this port isn't metal or plastic. Feels like my grandmother's old wicker-caned chair. But it transfers power and data just like our equipment."

"So our tech is interoperable," one of Billy's techs said.

"Maybe. One data port hook-up may not be a true test," Flank said. "We need to test more. I'm not keen on hooking your chemical and metal inorganics into my drive."

"Is that a printer?" Billy pointed at Flank's small workbench in the corner. The bench actually sat on top of the printer unit, which was two meters long and a meter tall.

"It is. Prints almost anything out of almost anything. But only organic parts. Bamboo board, cellulose conductors, superconductors, and so on."

Billy and her crew stared at the machine. Flank smiled. "You could use one. This settlement is literally surrounded by feedstocks."

"Can it print edible materials?"

Flank chuckled. "Sure. But nothing you'd *want* to eat. Bug protein is preferable, trust me."

The techs exchanged hopeful looks with one another.

"How long would it take to ship one of those from the Exchange?" Billy asked.

Flank snapped the access panels back in place. He scowled. "Are you foxing with me? The Exchange doesn't deliver out here. We'll just print you one from this one. You can take the price off of our bill. Open up a printer business line on the side."

"Impressive. Our printers are prohibited from producing more printers. They have to be shipped from a manufacturer. GEC regs."

Flank snorted. He showed them the rest of the ship, using his refit schematics to point out where sensor assemblies and probe storage would have to be replaced by additional capacitors, weapons, and storage room. Billy and her techs took extensive notes and commented on possible engineering issues.

They ended the tour in the galley, the only place on the *Drake* with enough seating for Billy's crew.

"Can we do this?" Billy asked her techs.

One tech shook his head no. "I don't think the tech will work together. Safest bet is to use their printer and do this with all Exchanger versions of parts."

Another said, "It seems feasible. But we'll run into a lot more unexpected problems. Flank, how much of your drive hardware is original?"

Flank rubbed his jaw. "I've rebuilt it twice. My father rebuilt it maybe five times, I think."

Barry and Tongue came back to the galley. "Clasker paid us, but it's not like we're rich," Barry said.

Tongue asked, "How's the refit going?"

"Spranker, you didn't tell us about your pot of gold in engineering. A printer that can print more printers. Maybe we'll owe you money after all," Billy said.

Barry smiled. "Is that a promise?"

Flank scowled at him. "I think we can work something out. The tech heads here have to figure out if we can do this refit, first. My biggest concern is printing weapons."

Billy said, "Ship-mounted weapons are, of course, illegal in the GEC. We don't have any plans for them to print. In the Underseed, we've re-engineered active sensors and boost the power throughput enough to knock out the target's electronics. We're not trying to disabled ships, just defend ourselves long enough to escape."

"But those weaponized sensors only work on targets with a conductive hull," Tongue pointed out. "Not so good against Exchange ships unless you hit an exposed sensor or scope."

Billy asked, "Are you planning on attacking Exchange ships?"

Tongue looked at Barry, who shrugged, before he replied, "No, I mean, I guess not?"

"Definitely not." Flank said. "What is a typical GEC weapons load out?"

"They don't need them, honestly. They can disable a ship through a software backdoor by taking control of it. So if you're stealing an entire ship, you need to be careful that they don't make it your prison cell. The newer Monoliths are armed with disabler cannons that overload the electrical systems. Plus, we've seen them use their drives to trap ships by preventing them from sliding."

Tongue nodded. "Yeah, we saw that. Can you print what Flank asked for? Dorsal and ventral disabler cannons, recessed in the hull?"

"The cannons, yes."

"What kind of personal firepower do the Grids carry?" Barry asked.

"Monolith crew carry stun guns or zappers," Billy said. "We never carried weapons on any civilian GEC ship I served on. Did any of you?"

The techs shook their heads.

"Zappers are just small underpowered capacitors with a beam projector on the end. We can print you a crude versions." Billy tapped on her pad and stared at the result for a moment.

"So what's the damages?" Barry asked.

She held the pad close to her chest. "Let's just say this should be really affordable. We'll do the refit and throw in a case of zappers. Lifetime warranty on the work. If you build us a copy of your printer, we'll call it even."

Barry nodded in surprise. "No charge, huh? We can do that."

Billy said. "That printer will make us more money than this refit job. Don't misunderstand me, it's still a bad idea for you. She's the wrong form factor. You'll be back to pay us to refit a proper GEC ship."

Barry smiled wryly. "No we won't. We're not playing by the old piracy rules."

Flank had no idea what the hell he meant by that, but he didn't care. He just wanted to get to work. "Barry, sign off on this and I'll spin up the printer."

EIGHTEEN

JILL STAMP, Investigator Second Rank, noted that the Andiron system's orbital traffic had grown substantially in last three weeks. Her transport joined a lengthy queue leading from the nav beacon to the only inhabitable world in the system. Two orbital stations and a shipyard were under construction, despite the recent mass dismissals of personnel in the space divisions. Streams of tender ships, construction craft, freighters, personnel transports, and logistics ships crowded six separate orbital paths. The logjam at Pergamon had outgrown that system and now reached all the way back to Andiron.

The GEC was in transition: for the first time in centuries it could do things other than obsess about reaching Union. The new mission, announced in corporation-wide broadcasts and departmental all-hands meetings, was to claim every habitable planetary system in the sectors around Union. Otherwise, the GEC would be surrounded and over-whelmed by the Exchange.

The transport touched down at a brand-new makeshift launch field outside Andiron City. Unlike the other passengers returning home, she didn't natter on about the shock of seeing so many changes. Growing up, her family never stayed put in a frontier system more than two years. She was inoculated against rapid change and new circumstances.

She could absorb the customs, practices, idioms and manners of a new world like other people changed outfits.

Andiron City was fifty percent bigger. People fresh off the transport milled around, lost, trying to orient themselves to an unfamiliar city. The quiet outpost Jill first saw five years ago was now a small city. It smelled like spilled engine lubricant and the body odor of people working double shifts.

She led a dozen lost lawyers to the correct tram bound for the city's administration complex. Chatting on the way over, one of the lawyers explained they were newly-assigned prosecutors. The GEC recently upgraded Andiron's administrative level in the sector government and that meant expanding the judicial infrastructure.

She noted his name for future reference. Good working relationships with the court monkeys was key to closing cases quickly.

The utilitarian glass administration building at the city's center was eight stories high, the tallest in the city. The lawyers wandered in a pack toward the Justice wing while she went up to the fifth floor to Investigations.

The Investigations office hadn't changed at all. A dozen colleagues were engrossed at terminals, sitting in the same chairs. They reviewed video footage, shipping manifests, and accounting spreadsheets, and called it police work.

"Look who came back," said Leonard Bozell, Investigator First Rank, from his desk in the center of the open office. He'd hit on her when she first arrived as a new Fourth Rank. She reported his harassment, he was reprimanded, and things between them went downhill from there. "Cleaning up the Corporation one crooked cafeteria worker at a time."

He was trying to goad her into spilling something about her case. His version of work was talking shop with everyone else, to appear knowledgeable about every investigation in the unit.

"You're still here, Leonard?" Jill asked, feigning surprise. She couldn't stop herself from skewering the jerk. "You always say you're going to retire and make a fortune in real estate." She waved at the construction cranes dotting the city skyline. "There's a huge land rush out there. You didn't screw up something so easy, did you?"

He grimaced. "Yes, well, I don't see First Rank insignia on your chest. You got a huge expense account and nothing to show for it. Unlike everyone else here." He indicated the investigators tapping away at their terminals.

Jill conducted investigations differently than her colleagues. They relied on the GEC's data warehouses and heuristic models to flag possible criminal activity and then digitally chase suspects. This was mainly because they were introverts who preferred statistics to interacting with people.

She liked building relationships and talking to her network of confidential informants. She enjoyed undercover work and was comfortable anywhere in the Underseed or on the GEC frontier. Yes, her expenses were quadruple theirs, but her case closure rate was double. Her cases also recovered about ten times more money on average.

Jill bee-lined it to her boss' office. She was in too good a mood to let Leonard's stupidity aggravate her. She'd progressed from resolving purchase card abuses to ending the black market trade in medical equipment in Sector 182, while he played the office jester. Someday soon she would be wearing First Rank jewelry over those breasts Leonard could only dream of catching a glimpse of.

Lieutenant Sandra Wheeler was the reason Jill came out to this outpost on the edge of nowhere. The middle-aged woman was tough but kind, methodical, and results-oriented. She fought for the resources and cooperation Jill needed for an investigation. More than once, it was Jill's fear she would let Sandra down which kept her plugging away when a case verged on falling apart.

"Leonard is an ass," Sandra grumped apologetically when Jill closed the door. The two women didn't discuss certain cases through electronic communication. "He's only good for citizen complaints anymore. I'm glad to see you. What was in those warehouses?"

"I was the first person to put my hands on the actual inventory in years; the managers rely on automated inventory management systems rather than personal inspections. But their portfolios are ten times the recommended tonnage for them to supervise."

Sandra shook her head. For over a decade, tons of food rations disappeared from the dusty confines of GEC warehouses. The food was tagged spoiled or damaged in the accounting systems shortly before it vanished. With only a few ships needed to stretch a navigable course out to Union, food was a low priority for shipping, despite the hungry refugee camps on Pergamon. As a result, warehouses in the Way Back sectors were crammed with rations, seedstock, and agricultural equipment. A higher than average loss ratio could be expected, considering the conditions. The thieves exploited those expectations.

"You identified the suspects?" Sandra asked.

"Yes. Consumption pattern analysis didn't ID them; they were within a standard deviation of the mean consumption levels for their pay grade. But they worked in Logistics and their coworkers noticed." If you stole from the GEC, spending the profits in the GEC economy was not the sharpest play. Automated consumption analysis would pick it up. But there weren't a lot of other places to spend money; the Underseed's black markets were off-limits. And people around you noticed when you were living too large for your pay grade.

"Someone built loopholes right into the inventory systems to hide the theft," Jill said. "It was compartmentalized; the perps weren't aware of each other or who was running things."

"You're implying a *criminal network* was behind it," Sandra said. The GEC bureaucracy was impenetrable when people refused to be helpful. And Sandra and Jill suspected Sector would block them from exposing a particular organized crime ring.

Jill smiled. "The suspects talked and implicated the FGM's subordinates."

FGM was their codename for Fairy Godmother, AKA Ms. Eden Overhead. Overhead ran the Underseed and the most wanted criminal boss in the GEC. The only person more notorious was the mysterious crime lord called 'The Name'.

"Is there enough evidence to prosecute?" Sandra asked. She saw Jill's expression. "I assumed not. Keep digging. There's pressure coming down to cripple the Underseed, since we're now racing to settle systems in Sector 180."

Jill said, "The Underseed is about to collapse. Its short on food, fuel, and medicine. If we shut down a little more of the stolen resources flowing through Overhead's organization, the entire Underseed should collapse and return to the GEC."

Corruption in the GEC was not an epidemic. Every young adult was tested with ability targeting exams and carefully slotted into employment matrices to determine optimal career possibilities for them and the Corporation. It maximized productivity and employee happiness and minimized the number who were unhappy in their work. Few people felt the need to cheat the benevolent GEC.

But trouble could be found in the GEC's conformity distribution curve, specifically in the tails of that distribution. The stupid ones managed their unhappiness with larceny, bribery, and other minor crimes. The relatively smarter criminals decamped for the grimy Underseed. This kept corruption and inefficiency at a minimum, or so the theory said.

Sandra said, "You've been going at Overhead for two years. You haven't cracked the mid-level people in her organization yet."

"I expected the food thefts would bring them around," Jill said. "The Underseed desperately needs the food, which means it's a critical resource for Overhead."

"The data jockeys out there are predicting you'll get convictions but not confessions. None of Overhead's people are willing to implicate anyone else."

Jill replied, "Forget court, squeezing her organization and the Underseed will pay dividends. People will talk."

"On another topic, have you heard anything more about Endor?" Sandra asked.

"Not since my informant reported it over a month ago. He was speculating, connecting rumors from Pergamon. What do you know?"

Sandra showed her a chart of mentions on the GEC's comm networks. "The term 'Endor' has begun appearing on the frontier. The predictive guys," she pointed to the keyboard tappers outside the office, "say it's because of tough times. When things get tough, there's an uptick of chatter about religious and mythical paradises."

"The Lucasians are not the type to have visions or spread rumors about discovering paradise," Jill said. "Are they claiming they found Endor?" The hairs on the back of her neck stood up.

Sandra nodded. "The Endor system does not actually exist. Not in the GEC and not in the Underseed. But if someone named some station out in the deep black, we need to figure out where it is."

"In my more cynical moments, I say it's wishful thinking by half-starved Underseeders. Or a deliberate misdirection for smuggling. But I'll run it down."

"Thank you. The bosses at Sector HQ want an update on mentions of Endor. They didn't say why. You ask me, they're afraid of a mass psychosis event like twenty years ago." Sandra shuffled things on her desk. "Anything else?"

The way Sandra said it meant she needed to tell Jill something unpleasant.

Jill said, "The Name came up again."

Sandra leaned in conspiratorially.

"Nothing solid, unfortunately. Another claim that he's very high up in the GEC but no one can say *who* he is. I chased down three leads." Jill spread her hands. "They evaporated. I couldn't do any more without blowing my cover."

Eden Overhead was atop the GEC's most wanted list. If Sandra and Jill dared add 'The Name' to the list, he would go ahead of Overhead. But they didn't dare. His corruption network was entrenched throughout the GEC.

"Speaking of The Name..." Sandra began with a pained expression.

Well, Jill thought, *here it comes, bad news.*

NINETEEN

SANDRA SIGHED IN PURE FRUSTRATION. "Sector has ordered me, yes, *ordered me*, to switch you to a new assignment. The corruption case has grown big enough, according to Sector, that they should take it over. It's bigger than our operation can handle, they say, and requires more resources. They want you to work the Exchange problem."

Jill furrowed her brow. "Do they think Overhead's corruption is connected to The Name?"

Sandra promised she wouldn't tell Sector about Jill poking around The Name. Even mentioning The Name tended to cause Sector to shut down any related inquiry. He seemed to have substantial influence over the GEC's most powerful. "No, I promised you I wouldn't tell them."

This made the Exchange assignment change worse, actually. It meant Sector 181 executives didn't believe corruption was a priority any more. Sector HQ was not as near the frontier as Andiron. Jill had never worked there and was ignorant of its office politics.

"Your sole assignment now is collecting intel on Exchangers in our space," Sandra said, announcing it like a death sentence.

Jill's stomach seized. Her career centered on corruption-busting.

Contract-fixing, theft, bribery, falsified reports, black market shenanigans; she was an expert in nearly every way to rip off the GEC. "Six months ago, Sector asked me to delay taking my First Rank exam because corruption was such a priority."

Sandra held up her hands helplessly.

"Who am I handing over the case to?" Taking her off the corruption investigation was bad, but at least it would continue. Overhead and the Underseed would have a free hand if the investigation ended. Her mission here was to protect the GEC, even if the GEC bureaucracy seemed to temporarily lose interest in that goal.

Sandra said, "They didn't say. The grapevine is aflutter with rumors. Shake-ups at Sector, across the board mobilizations, new rules, crackdowns. The investigation might be overtaken by other events."

"Other events? If I could have a little more time, we can take down Overhead. We're really close. A month away. If I'm pulled off it, we'll lose the whole thread here."

"Jill, there's no choice. No options, no wiggle room. I begged for it. I burned some capital asking for it. And I was turned down."

"My informants won't talk to anyone else," Jill noted. Most of her informants were reluctant to deal even with her. It took time and effort to earn their trust. "They trust me, they believed me when I offered them deals for leniency or immunity in exchange for their help."

Sandra came around her desk and sat in the other visitor chair, close to Jill. "Keep the informants, keep everything. The brass are damn near panicked about these Exchangers. Our sociologists are saying this whole quadrant could go Exchanger. We could be pushed back to the Way Back sectors.

"They gave me more resources for the Exchanger work. Sector hinted this could be a career-maker: next stop is First Rank for you and a promotion to Sector HQ for me."

Which would be something. Corruption investigators were not well liked and didn't advance quickly. Jill said, "A mentor once warned me the way brass quietly ends a corruption investigation is to promote the investigator or make it career suicide. He called it carrot and stick bribery."

Sandra shook her head. "The brass right now, they are focused entirely on the Exchangers. The less generous explanation is they are shortsighted or ignorant. Or are covering for The Name."

Corruption, fear, or ignorance. Jill hated it all; she joined the Investigations unit to protect the efficient, smart, overachieving GEC. It felt like a long time since the GEC had acted that way.

Sandra smiled. "Chin up. There are multiple ways to peel a banana."

A dark part of Jill's mind cackled evilly. But she didn't know why. "Meaning?"

"We want to take down Overhead, but the theme of the month is stopping the Exchangers. So instead of graft and corruption, we take her down for harboring Exchangers. Keep using your informants, but change their focus. The Exchanger angle may be easier to prove anyway."

The dark part of Jill's mind chuckled with satisfaction. "The Exchangers' only place to go is the Underseed," she said. The GEC was blocking them from its own systems. And the Underseed was lousy with Overhead's people and operations. She would need to deal with the criminal organization there to reach the Exchangers.

Sandra smiled. "Yes, Investigator Stamp, the Exchangers will likely hide in the Underseed. But don't forget Sector would love to exile troublemakers to a Monolith at Union, eating canned stew and hand-checking sensor logs. They shipped Duanski out to Pergamon that way. Stay away from The Name for both of our sakes."

Jill tilted her head skeptically. "And what am I supposed to do with the Exchangers I round up? And what do I charge them with doing in the Underseed? Trespassing?"

Sandra waved off her sarcasm. "Legal is working on it. This is a scouting mission only. Determine if the rumors of Exchanger infiltration are true. More instructions will follow."

Fine, Jill thought as she left Sandra's office, I'll *take the assignment at face value and poke around for Exchangers*. If they wanted to throw First Rank at her for doing it, great. But wouldn't it be nice if Overhead's fraternization with Exchangers *forced* GEC Investigators to pursue her?

The idea prompted a smile when she passed Leonard's desk. He bolted to Sandra's door to find out what Jill was up to. Maybe the dark part of Jill mind wasn't ready to return to the shadows yet.

TWENTY

GRAND AND KROGER'S coordinates led them out of the thin stretch of GEC-occupied space in Sector 181. They slid to a series of unofficial beacons that led to the Royada system. Royada had one habitable planet that had near perfect attributes: temperate climate, big oceans, and plentiful vegetation.

Their contact would meet them at Royada City, a coastal city at a prime location in the planet's tropical belt. Beach-front estates lined the shore and sported different interpretations of the GEC's boxy, straight-lined architecture.

A thunderstorm was soaking the spaceport when the *Sluicifer* landed. These blows, the local weather forecast called them, could last hours or days when weather systems were trapped against the mountains to the north. A covered exitway extended to the ship's airlock and they stepped into humid air that smelled of ozone from nearby lightning strikes.

Grand didn't give a crap about the weather; he smelled something else: money.

Their contact sent a small, bright orange ground vehicle for them. Their escort was a big guy named Bixby who reminded Grand of his bouncers from *Shogura*. Bixby took them on a long slog into the city.

Rain assaulted the car's windows in angry sheets, obscuring the few office buildings and one-story shops along the street. Boats bucked and bobbed on the ominous gray waves. The city was built like a resort and the storm whipped the beautiful landscaping unmercifully.

Since the scenery was lacking, Grand chatted up Bixby, alternatively telling tales about Exchanger life and pumping him for information.

"What's your pleasure, Bixby? What do you enjoy?"

Bixby was nonplussed. "In my off hours, you mean?"

"Yes. Girls, booze, boys, gaming, sports? I ask everyone when I'm on a new world, to gauge the entertainment demand."

Bixby said over his shoulder, "I collect video clips of circuses."

Grand was dumbstruck. Collecting himself, he scoffed, "What the hell is that? A fetish? I can't make money on it. Haha, get yourself a new hobby, Bix."

The big man laughed.

Once outside of the city, they spent half an hour chugging around the base of a lush green mountain. The storm clouds broke up and sunlight made the ground steam. They picked up speed despite the road surface going from smooth pavement to crushed stone. They arrived at a low-lying compound between the base of the next mountain and the sea. Several low, maroon brick buildings were surrounded by a natural fence of bamboo trees concealing a stouter, two meter fence of polymer posts.

They were buzzed through the front gate and parked in the circular flagstone drive. Bixby ushered them into the house through giant white double doors. The windows consisted of flimsy wooden blinds and the house was cooled by ceiling fans and the breeze that had blown the storm over the mountain. Grand didn't see any noticeable security measures and assumed it was there, but tucked out of sight.

Bixby handed them off to a pleasant, neat little man named Clasker, who Bixby claimed was the boss' right hand man. Clasker had the observant eyes of a schemer and the cool demeanor of a skeptic.

Grand stowed his usual bluster when he was around others like himself. In the old Exchange days, he tussled with Cross Boss and Lymanther, who were also fellow schemers. These untrustworthy types needed to be watched closely. It was clear Clasker was the loyal lackey, the major domo, the Kroger. But unlike his own droid, Clasker had bigger ambitions. Grand distrusted him completely.

Clasker took them through winding corridors to a stately library with a bar in the corner. It opened to a veranda with a splendid view of the sea. Tropical plants waved in the breeze and the room smelled like citrus.

Clasker took a seat and motioned for Grand to do the same. "Welcome to Royada, Mr. Grand. Royada is part of the Underseed, which winds through the entire GEC, but it's separate from it. It's been built by dissidents who left the GEC for one reason or another. We have a kind of side civilization. Sleazier, poorer, but a much freer life than in the GEC. Like your Exchange."

Grand snorted. "A pale imitation, at most."

Clasker smiled but continued. "One of the entrepreneurs in the early days of these sectors was Eden Overhead. She blazed trails and launched businesses in the burgeoning Underseed. Kept parts of it going almost singlehandedly."

He expected Grand to be impressed, but Grand simply looked at him.

Clasker continued, "When the GEC decided something needed to be done about it and instituted a blockade, she lobbied her government contacts and the GEC laid off. Food prices spiked anyway and she retailed it at wholesale prices to keep people fed."

Grand fought the urge to sigh. Charity was a poor business practice.

"She runs a several-pronged enterprise," Clasker said. "Most of the legal and illegal activities in the Underseed are run, protected, and encouraged by her organization. Being invited to work for her is a rare honor."

Grand said, "Well, it sounds more promising than hustling skeeball in the Pergamon slums."

"What are your plans for this side of Union?" Clasker asked.

"I want to establish my own enterprises here ahead of my Exchanger competitors. Corner the market on the Exchange way of running certain businesses, you see. In the short term, I'm interested in keeping tabs on fellow Exchangers in the area while learning about the GEC business environment. Or this Underseed business environment, I guess. Market research."

Clasker smiled. "You realize the GEC is a monopoly? They don't tolerate competition."

Grand said, "I bet. I usually fill niches where there's no competition. On the shady side of the Exchange, you don't squat over someone else's turf."

"Excellent. I'll go get the boss," Clasker said and left him and Kroger to admire the view.

"Was that some kind of stupid test?" Clasker asked.

Kroger raised all of his arms in a shrug.

TWENTY-ONE

CLASKER RETURNED WITH EDEN OVERHEAD. She was older than Grand but walked at the faster clip of a much younger person. She had thick iridescent white hair and friendly gray eyes. She reminded him of the crime boss Lymanther, who strangers recognized was boss when he entered a room.

"Mr. Grand, Eden Overhead," Clasker announced.

"Juniper Grand, welcome," she said. Her voice was sweet, and he liked her immediately.

"Thank you for inviting us," Grand said smoothly.

"Please sit down, everyone. Drinks will be by in a minute."

Overhead sat in an ornately upholstered chair, her back straight and head held high. Clasker stood off to the side, ready to take notes or run errands if needed, a pleasant facsimile of a human being. Grand still distrusted him.

"Mr. Grand, your reputation precedes you. Your recent misfortunes could prove fortuitous for both of us. I must attend to new opportunities in other sectors, what we call the Way Back sectors. They'd distract me from my ongoing concerns. I need an experienced hand to manage my businesses in the surrounding sectors while I'm away. Not a caretaker. I expect that you'll streamline and modernize according to your Exchanger experiences."

Grand nodded appreciatively.

She continued, "In return, you get a crash course in GEC culture and Underseed economics. Plus you'll make more contacts than you'll be able to handle. When I return, you would be free to pursue other opportunities, no feelings hurt, or perhaps take on a permanent position in the organization."

Clasker handed Kroger a data card that was compatible with the droid's data interfaces. Clasker had scoped him out, done his due diligence.

Overhead said, "We're giving Kroger a summary of the financials. Most of our businesses operate in the grayer areas of legality since we operate in the GEC and Underseed. Shipping, retail, entertainment, plus consulting and financial services."

She continued, "The organization could use a dose of someone with more logistical… ruthlessness. We're operating at a steady profit, but there's plenty of room to tighten things up. Ah, here are our drinks. I've talked myself dry."

They sipped berry-flavored spiced coffee and she rattled off numbers. Kroger sent them to Grand's wrist display a split second later. Her organization was profiting on everything except food, which she lost money on.

Grand asked, "Why are you losing money on food?" Food was a profit center in the Exchange's restaurant industry. People overpaid for it, especially if it was prepared by someone else.

"I sold it at a loss to keep several Underseed settlements afloat. I consider it a long-term investment."

Long-term players in the Exchange would accept losses just to drive out competitors and gobble up market share. In the Exchange, if you were legit you couldn't grab too much market share without the Regulators coming down on you. Outlaw entrepreneurs could drive out competitors with cheaper, heavy-handed tactics that didn't require a negative cashflow.

It was odd the financials didn't include any organizational efficiency metrics. GEC culture was supposed to be obsessed with both efficiency and effectiveness. Everyone worried about making their performance numbers. But this quasi-criminal outfit apparently tossed away the metrics of the efficiency pinchers.

It was a mistake, in Grand's opinion. Her organization had middlemen for middlemen. He could be a goddamn hero to the bottom line by making some common sense changes.

"An intriguing offer," Grand said. She was hiding something. He wasn't surprised. He expected she would hold a lot close. "How much control would I have over personnel, logistics, practices?"

"You'll have complete control over the entire organization. I won't interfere and my people will be loyal to you, not me."

Clasker nodded. Grand didn't buy it.

They waltzed through the usual subjects like compensation, security procedures, the competition, market analyses, and the like. He needed to be certain she wasn't handing him a failing business and setting him up to blame. He paged through the historical data. She was the queen of a small, interstellar criminal empire. And she wanted him to play CEO for a while.

"So what's the catch? Is the GEC about to take you down, and I get hit instead?" Grand asked and sipped his coffee. Kroger twitched nervously at his boldness. "Or are the businesses about to crater? Because, Eden, I'm struggling to believe you would pluck the first shady Exchanger who crossed the border and hand over everything. Why me? Why now?"

She appeared relieved he asked. "Only the propaganda mouthpieces say the Underseed will 'disappear' once the GEC settles planets again. Carruthers said you got a taste of Pergamon: it's an overcrowded refugee camp. Immigration to the Underseed has tripled in the last five months. We're predicting exponential growth for the next ten years.

"My allies inside the GEC are deflecting investigations into my organization, but it's becoming harder to do. The GEC is gunning for this organization only because they are after me." She smiled eagerly. She enjoyed flexing her insider connections, Grand noted. They meant a lot to her.

"Like I said, there are matters, unique opportunities, that I need to deal with in the Way Back sectors. Me leaving will take the heat off the organization. If you manage things here, prepare for the expected growth, and handle competition from other Exchangers, we'll both benefit."

Her smile was feral. "But remember, our operation irritates the GEC because it smuggles supplies and people to the Underseed. Law enforcement might come for you anyway. The Investigators are very good. But you can deal with them, and I'll be helping out behind the scenes."

Despite those potential pitfalls, this job would provide an excellent start for his new life outside of the Exchange. Streamlining Overhead's operations would make them more profitable and easier to assimilate if he decided to make this a permanent arrangement.

A lesser man might be tempted to abandon his pursuit of Barry Spranker and the *Drake*. With an opportunity like this, why bother holding onto an old grudge? Ah, but he wouldn't let his reputation be shredded like that and walk away. Crushing them would tell everyone that Juniper Grand would cross the entire galaxy to wring your neck if you screwed him.

And this position would make tracking the *Drake* a whole lot easier. It gave him more eyes and ears than he could ever have otherwise, plus the resources to pursue Spranker in every sector, every star system.

"I'm in," he said.

———

BY THE TIME the sun set, Grand was in charge of Eden's organization. She had told her lieutenants that Grand was the new boss and that she would be unreachable, effective immediately.

Eden, Clasker, and Grand enjoyed a quiet farewell dinner while staff ferried her luggage out the front door.

Both she and Grand received agitated messages from underlings. "Some of them need a lot of hand holding," Overhead admitted. Grand remembered their names. They would be the first ones to go.

After dinner, Grand and Kroger escorted Overhead and Clasker to the circular driveway, where bug zappers were getting a workout from the local insects.

"I'll touch base from time to time," Eden said. "Contact Clasker if you need anything. Thank you for doing this."

Grand put both hands over his heart. "I'll take good care of your baby."

Clasker and Overhead both left, leaving Grand an interstellar criminal empire that he could use to crush Barry Spranker into paste.

TWENTY-TWO

THE NEXT AFTERNOON Grand met his new underlings. There were over two dozen of them spread across several Underseed systems, as well as embedded on the GEC worlds of Pergamon and Andiron.

He memorized their personnel files in the morning. Eden assigned her minions to jobs the same way Grids did everywhere: based on psych profiles, personality tests, and ability measurement tools.

Exchange criminal organizations operated on loyalty, family ties, or good old greed. The available labor supply might not fit the available jobs, which made things bumpy. But if you were yelling at family and friends it made up for it. In some of the Exchanger outfits, this led to the stereotypical idea of a bunch of buddies hanging around with nothing to do. In Eden's case, her minions performed adequately in jobs they didn't want when they could excel elsewhere. But a smart crime boss, and Grand considered himself such, matched her people to the right work. There was a lot of low-hanging fruit to be plucked from the profit tree by giving these people room to excel.

He met with them as a group on the back lawn, snacking on veggies with a fiery dip. He wore his flamboyant purple business suit to play up every Exchange stereotype used in GEC entertainment.

"I operate on one simple rule: cut costs," he said to them. "We use the savings to open new markets, to build up a big cash reserve to hedge against uncertainties.

"I delegate authority and responsibility. I do not tolerate fools. I want all of you to excel." He made a mental note of each person's reaction. Some didn't buy it; others merely pretended to. Some acted like he was a breath of fresh air. Others looked confused. He called for questions and a few feckless ones made 'mother may I' queries which only identified them as the most useless.

Next, he met with Bixby, his new security chief, and the team Bixby just hired. The team included a new security consultant who changed the locks and advised on how to beef up the defenses.

With Kroger in tow, Grand, Bixby and the security consultant toured the palace defenses inside and outside.

The consultant pointed out the diamond shard fence — a deadly, almost invisible fence that resembled an ice sculpture. It ran around the perimeter of the grounds. There was a closet-sized armory in the house that contained stun guns and projectile weapons. The consultant pointed out several other hidden features and suggested half a dozen upgrades. If the GEC wanted to storm the compound, they would need much more than a single tactical assault squad.

Dinner was roasted local fruit and a factory-made nut steak. He, Bixby, and Kroger retired to the living room to work on his primary goal, capturing the *Drake*.

"The bounty hunters are waiting outside," Bixby said.

Grand preferred to hire ex-Exchange Regulators, but no Regulators had ventured into the GEC yet. He was willing to settle for savvy Underseed pros who knew Sectors 180 through 185. However, Bixby hired two bounty hunters who were available, experienced, and cheap. Their names were Risko Walter and Mercedes Potts.

When the bounty hunters came into the living room, Grand scowled. "I need you two," he spoke slowly, because Risko appeared lost already, "to locate an Exchange spaceship named the *Drake*. Don't blow it up. Don't kill the crew. Don't tell them who sent you. Just catch them and bring them here."

Risko asked, "Here?"

"Yes, here. How can I make it any clearer?" Grand's patience was waning.

"We'll do it," Mercedes said. "What kind of ship is it?"

"*Starslider* class."

"Starslider," Mercedes repeated.

"You get half the bounty up front: fifty thousand. But this is an incentive payment plan. For every month you don't bring them in, you lose ten percent of the remaining fifty thousand. For each additional month beyond the first ten months *you owe me* ten percent of the advance. With interest. If you can't locate them, in twenty months, you'll owe me fifty thousand. Plus interest. Understood?"

Risko played it cool, nonchalant. He asked, "What about the *Drake* itself, do you want the ship, too?"

Grand waved his hand. "Keep it. There's a rumor they call themselves pirates, so you can take whatever property they have, too."

Risko and Mercedes negotiated with each other through nods, chin jerks, and eyebrow wriggles. Mercedes appeared to be a little intelligent while Risko was greedy and stupid. Grand wished Risko was a mark and not a contract employee.

Risko asked Mercedes, "How much loot can they bag with us after them?"

"They could be dangerous, Risko," she warned.

Grand chuckled. "Kroger, they're afraid of Spranker and his boys. Isn't this rich?" He said to Mercedes, "They're star mappers, sweetheart, not pirates. A couple of half-decent bounty hunters can scoop them right up." To prevent another round of silent bickering, he said, "If you don't want the job, I'll go to the next on my list."

The bounty hunters agreed and left in an excited rush. Grand went on the veranda and watched the ocean lapping against the beach. Not a bad first day on the job.

Kroger rolled up the sand with two dozen new problems for him to solve. The hapless lieutenants with the half-assed questions wanted to check with him on everything. He smiled sadistically. He could straighten out some of them with a gentle rebuke. Others would need a swift kick in the ass, or would need to be sacked. It was like when he first bought the restaurant on the *Shogura*.

"Kroger, where did Bixby find those bounty hunters?"

"His security consultant recommended them. There are no bounty hunter exchanges yet in this sector or the 179."

"A shame. I'm not confident in those two foxwits. We need a way to bring the *Drake* to us."

"Very good, sir. I'll make a note."

TWENTY-THREE

THE PIRATE SHIP *Heckler* slid into the PineStar system. The ship was a converted GEC *Chandelier*-class short haul freighter, boxy and tall. With the race to Union over, the GEC's space divisions decided to surplus freighters and dismiss their crews from corporate employment. Naturally, both the crews and the ships gravitated to the Underseed.

The *Heckler*'s metallic hull sported menacing skulls and stripes and three cartoonishly large, fake blaster cannons. The pirates also installed a wet bar in the galley because legend had it that pirates drank a lot of triskey.

PineStar was an Underseed system with one point of interest: the fantastic atmospheric storms on the gas giant PineStar III. The other two planets were tiny burnt rocks orbiting close to the star.

The *Heckler*'s target was the *Aksamma*, an old WalshX 90 yacht, built for intrasystem pleasure cruises and short distance slides. It was designed to provide good viewing angles for sightseeing passengers. Many were still in service because the GEC stopped shipping newer yachts to the frontier when it needed to catch up to the Exchange. The WalshX 90s moved nicely through spacecraft dealerships and eventually some of them found their way to the Underseed where any craft that could slide went for a premium.

The *Aksamma's* passengers noticed the arrival of the *Heckler* right away since they were packed into the yacht's dorsal observation bubble. The passengers were from Andiron and consisted of ladies who lunch and young couples who wanted a romantic cruise. One second they were gazing at the visually stunning storms and the next they faced the business end of *Heckler*'s blaster cannons. Getting boarded and robbed wasn't on the itinerary. Such was life in the sparsely-populated GEC frontier these days.

The *Aksamma's* captain, an elderly man named Stivex, frantically tried to call for help. The *Aksamma's* comm system was out or the *Heckler* was jamming it, he couldn't tell. So, he decided the *Aksamma* would make a run for it.

On paper, a WalshX 90 was rated faster than a freighter, but it became clear to all taht the *Heckler* had upgraded engines. The *Aksamma* tried to use its extra maneuverability to compensate for its lack of speed, but the gas giant was like a wall in space, boxing it in. And the gas giant's radiation belts and its rings of micrometeors gave the thinly-shielded *Aksamma* nowhere to run.

Captain Stivex cut the drive and surrendered. Was there any other choice? The *Heckler* could disable the yacht and let it get fried by the storms or the radiation belts. Rather than announce this unpleasant news, he let the passengers watch the *Heckler* approach.

Three pirates swaggered aboard, each rocking long hair and shirts open to the navel. They brandished stunswords, dull metallic blades that could deliver a knock out charge. No projectile launchers: even first-time pirates understood firing explosive projectiles inside spaceships was a bad idea.

Two of the younger passengers squealed in terror when these rough characters came through the airlock. The older ladies were split between those who grimaced and those who welcomed some drama.

Captain Stivex instructed the passengers to stay in the main cabin and to comply with any of the raiders' demands. He tripped over the word 'raider' and it sounded more like 'rattler.'

"All the belongings, in the bags, make it quick!" yelled Dean, the handsomest pirate of the trio. Dean had long golden locks and a lightly stubbled jaw. He put a lot of work into the muscly, hairy drama happening on his chest. He was pleased when several of the ladies took notice.

Another pirate named Brash stuck his heavily-pierced visage into the face of each passenger. When Stivex regarded him with obvious contempt, Brash proceeded to beat the old man mercilessly until Stivex managed to crawl away and lock himself on the bridge.

"If a single maneuvering rocket farts, old man, your passengers will regret it," Brash growled at the locked door.

Over in a corner, the third pirate, a raised middle finger of a man named Billy Tusk, brandished his stunsword at the passenger holding the loot bag. "Hurry up, hurry up. You don't want Mr. Brash to get pissy."

Billy hurried the bag down the line of passengers collecting personal electronics, jewelry, and currency.

When he reached the final passenger, a nervously grinning young woman, a young man leapt out of a galley closet near Brash. The young man swung a stunstick at Brash.

The youthful, misguided attacker was Georgey Stivex, the copilot and son of Captain Stivex. His stunstick was half the length of the stunsword Brash swiped at him. But Georgey was determined.

Dean failed to hide a smirk while Billy Tusk shoved the bag under the nervous woman's nose, ignoring Brash and Georgey exchanging blows.

Georgey retreated from Brash's longer reach and took up a fighting stance. With all the loot collected, everyone turned to watch.

Brash tried to circle and crowd Georgey into the ship's center where the other pirates could help. Georgey feinted towards the center. He pivoted to jab at Brash, forcing him to retreat.

A blow, a parry, stun devices reverberating against one another, like two tuning forks arguing over which played the same note better.

Georgey took a swipe at the nearby Dean, who chuckled and scrambled out of range. Brash took advantage of the opening and charged. He swung his sword up and it glanced off George's shoulder. With an electrical snap the copilot collapsed to the deck.

"Got any others in there, miss?" Billy Tusk demanded of the last victim. She was still smiling nervously at him.

"F-fresh out of copilots," she said and giggled despite herself.

Dean slapped her loudly. The other passengers gasped in horror and became deathly quiet. The woman slid to the deck and cried quietly. The mood became serious.

Dean asked them, "Anyone else?"

The terrified passengers shook their heads no.

"Time to leave," Billy said. He made the passengers lay face down and gave a few butts a weak zap or two to make sure they listened. He also tossed more insults at the Captain through the locked door on the bridge before exiting through the airlock.

TWENTY-FOUR

THE PIRATES DISENGAGED the *Heckler*'s airlock and prepared to leave the *Aksamma*. Billy frowned at Dean.

"Did you need to hit Lisa?"

"It was her idea, to make it more realistic," Dean said. "At least I didn't knock anyone out cold."

Brash snorted. "Barely tickled his funny bone. The sword was on its lowest setting. He's a good actor."

"So is Lisa," Dean said. "Because I didn't actually hit her."

Captain Stivex steered the *Aksamma* away at max velocity. Within a minute, it slid for home, leaving the *Heckler* alone to recharge by the gas giant. The two ships would reunite later to return the loot to the passengers. Another easy day of playing pirate to bored tourists who got more than they expected on this sightseeing trip.

An alarm buzzed on the console. It was an unfamiliar sound: a navigational proximity warning. Despite ten years in the GEC space division, Dean had never heard it go off.

Billy said, "Ship slid in, right the hell on top of us. Some kind I've never seen. She's armed, too."

Dean and Brash exchanged looks. It was insane to slide in this close to another ship. Safety rules mandated a hundred thousand kilometer minimum separation. Five hundred thousand was recommended.

"Maybe they need help," Dean said. "Call over to them."

"No response. Trying secondary communication methods. Still nothing. And she's coming towards us," Billy said, his voice tight.

Dean asked, "Well, what kind of ship is it?"

Brash was tapping like a madman on his terminal. "An Exchange ship. Not sure what class though. It's small."

Brash's hand shook when he paged through information on his terminal, like a big kid who faced a bigger kid for the first time.

Dean said, "Let's work through our procedures for a situation like this."

"There are no GEC procedures for this," Billy said. "The closest is a procedure for close approaches during rescue and salvage operations."

"Where are we on the communications protocols?" Dean asked.

"Hailed, not answered, and no response to light beam communications," Billy said. "And they're coming around to dock. We could run."

"Run?" Dean tapped his thumb on the armrest. "There's no procedure for running."

The docking alarm sounded, followed by the familiar thud and hiss of a clamp sealing against their airlock. Too late to run.

Brash grabbed his stunsword, ready to run for the airlock door.

Dean waved him off. "Let's not scare anyone. Billy, you're with me. Button your shirt. Brash, stay here on the bridge."

Dean and Billy hurried to the airlock. They found two men strolling onboard, in the middle of an animated discussion about space pizza.

"Can you believe they're pretending that *this* is a pirate vessel?" said the shorter one, who was wearing a beat-up leather jacket and sweatpants. "I'm embarrassed that we invested in something sight unseen."

The other man stroked his shaggy beard. "It's not that bad. Its decrepit condition allows it to sneak up on other ships without drawing attention. Course, then there are these guys dressed, you know, like that violently bad lounge act from Grandy's on the *Shogura*."

"Ah, the good old days on *Shogura*," the leather jacket man said.

Dean asked, "Excuse me. Who are you and what are you doing on our ship?"

The bearded one said, "I'm sorry, he's Captain Spranker of the *Drake*. I'm Tongue. Oh, you've heard of us. Good." To Barry he said, "I get it now. They're, like, our tribute band."

"We're not real pirates," Dean said. "We're entertainers. This is a set piece, to give the customers a good scare. We don't really steal from them."

Tongue pointed at Billy's loot bag still slung over his shoulder. "What do you got in the bag?" He pawed through the contents and held up several items. "What are these, trinkets? You didn't steal any food packets? Anything actually valuable?"

Brash, who didn't stay on the bridge, thumbed his stunsword on and charged.

"Take it easy, twinkle cheeks," Barry Spranker said. He was holding a stun pistol and waved its targeting laser over Brash's chest.

Dean said, "We return their belongings after we dock. It's a show. We're insured against losing it."

Barry laughed. "Normally we wouldn't care, but it's a pretty poor pirate who steals phony diamond bracelets. We're not here to steal anything. We're your new business partners."

Dean, Brash and Billy Tusk exchanged bewildered looks. Dean said, "Keith Dalston already owns this business."

Captain Spranker said, "Used to. We saw Keith a few days ago. Persuaded him to sell to us for a super reasonable price."

"You pirated a whole company?" Brash asked.

"Bought it. From the proceeds of pirating," Tongue said. "It's totally different."

"Don't get us wrong, we're not investing a lot of money," Barry said. "Maybe a new paint job and some more realistic cannon props on the hull—"

"And the yacht looks like hell," Tongue added.

"—the yacht looks like hell. But we will be drawing dividends from this cute operation of yours." Barry ticked items off his fingers. "First, there's a small monthly protection payment, so we can keep the other pirates from bothering you. And there will be a lot more pirates."

"Always a lot more pirates," Tongue agreed.

Barry shrugged. "It's a nominal fee. Second, we take fifteen percent of the gross. Third, we oversee the business."

"So real pirates want to own a tourist pirate adventure company," Brash said.

"Own? Did we say own?" Barry asked.

"We didn't say 'own', I'm sure," Tongue said.

Barry said, "You own the business. Keith sold the business to us. We'll sell it to you if you agree to those three easy conditions. Here is the contract." He held out a handheld with a blinking signature field.

Dean asked, "You're giving us the business?"

"Well," Barry said, "we certainly don't want to work for this tourist trap."

"We should have a lawyer read the agreement before we sign," Dean said.

"Man, you don't need a lawyer," Tongue said. "This is in the Exchange's Legal Simple language. No contract longer than a page, simple terms. In the Exchange, we only need lawyers for lawsuits."

Dean took the handheld and read the contract. "Us and Lisa, and the Stivexes will all be part owners?"

"You're the ones who work for the business," Tongue said.

Billy Tusk asked, "Why would Keith sell to you? Did you force him?"

"No," Barry yelped incredulously. "He contacted us, said he was tired of starving in the Underseed. He's heading for Exchange territory. He had to sell his investments to pay for the trip."

The three pirate entertainers each read the sale contract with a skeptical frown. But they signed.

Barry handed over the records, including a plan to expand the business. "We included the account numbers in there to pay us. So *happy* to do business with you guys."

Barry and Tongue bowed with a flourish and returned to their ship. The *Drake* undocked and slid away.

Dean looked around the corridor. "We really should clean up this ship some."

Billy Tusk stood there, dumbfounded, holding the bag of the customers' personal property. "What just happened?"

TWENTY-FIVE

JILL STAMP FELT a frisson of thrill when she boarded the Underseed space station named the *Leggett Rose*. The *Leggett* was a giant passenger liner long past the end of its service life. Underseeders had converted, retrofitted, and towed it out to empty interstellar space between Andiron and a nearby Underseed system. It was the closest Underseed transit hub to Union and the nexus of several Underseed and GEC slide routes.

She had boarded the transport under the name Jess Forrester. Jess was a glum, unlucky GEC divorcee hoping to start over in the Underseed. By the time Jill buckled into the transport, she'd become Jess. She was comfortable in the Underseed's drab clothing, idioms, and customs. She grew up with engineer parents who moved constantly to inspect space stations close to the frontier. Blending in with the locals was a muscle she enjoyed flexing.

She shed her GEC mannerisms, slumped her shoulders, and barely contained her wiry hair in a rough pony-tail. She consciously set aside her hard-boiled corruption investigator persona like she hung up a cocktail dress. This included unclenching the cop muscles which made her do-gooder colleagues terrible at undercover work.

Overhead's organization ran a gambling operation out of a

converted ballroom on the *Leggett*'s top decks named The Chateau. Jill expected Exchangers to show up on the *Leggett* and eventually join Overhead's operations. So Jess Forrester would settle down on the station and keep her eyes and ears open.

The *Leggett*'s owners retrofitted hangar bays and gangly docking arms to handle the ship traffic. Jill dropped her meager belongings in a low-rent apartment no bigger than a bedroom which was simply a poorly-partitioned passenger cabins. She toured the ship and found that everything she may need to live onboard could be found at a chaotic bazaar on the lowest deck.

Jill wandered the corridors from the classier upper decks down to the busy but freezing bazaar. She gravitated to the areas with constant bustling crowds where she could hide among the crowds and observe the people, the culture, and the economy. That led her to the bazaar on the lowest deck.

It was icy cold because the hull insulation was old or non-existent down here. The lights flickered frequently. Jill noticed everyone stepped around numerous rainbow-sheened puddles on the uneven metal decks. It was clear that the lower the deck on the *Leggett*, the worse shape it was in.

No one paid her any attention in the bazaar: she was just another new arrival. Until a scrawny, frowning woman waved her over to her flimsy table of used clothing for sale.

"Name is Murray. You pretend like you're invisible, but I can see you're spying on everyone," the old woman said. "You're new here and you're afraid. Skulking around like a wet dog who lost his owner."

"Uh yes, I just arrived today. Jess Forrester. I guess you got me figured out, huh?"

Murray shrugged. "It's not hard. There's some dark corners of this place you want to stay clear of." She listed a number of locations. "Plenty of people ready to victimize a vulnerable, stupid girl like you. You don't want nothing to do with any of those assholes, trust me."

Murray liked to blab, probably because she was lonely, or trying to talk her into buying something. And her caustic mouth probably kept people away.

Jill said, "What do you suggest?"

"There's a diner by hangar three. Someone curious like you can sit there and people watch for hours. Meet people. Figure out your next steps. Or you could talk to me, but no one listens to old Murray. I know everything and everyone on the station. But bullshit doesn't buy food." Murray gestured at the clothes for sale on her plastic table.

Jill picked up a thick shawl with cold fingers. "What about working in the Chateau?"

"Run by organized crime. Glitzy for the customers, but you don't want any part of it."

Jill did, but Jess was not supposed to be interested in the criminal underworld. She bought the shawl and thanked Murray profusely. When Murray pressed her for Jess' life story, she innocently divulged. Murray would probably tell everyone who would listen.

Jess became a regular at the diner outside hangar bay three. Murray was right; it was at the crossroads of the station's heaviest foot traffic. It was the perfect vantage point to observe comings and goings on the *Leggett*. People and cargo came in from the hangar bays, locals passed by all day, and it was close to the stairs leading up to the Chateau above. The diner was run by Tammy, a woman who never stood still. With food in short supply, people gravitated there because Tammy's prices were barely above wholesale.

It also meant Tammy was overwhelmed by hungry patrons. When Jess Forrester offered to bus tables, Tammy almost cried.

"Thank you, Jess. I can't keep up," she said. Her graying hair was in a more ragged ponytail than Jess' and dark circles lurked under her eyes.

No one was cleaning the dishes either, so Jess just started to do that, too. When Tammy buzzed by for more omelet mix, Jess said, "Do you mind if I clean these?"

"Mind? Hell no. Fernando was supposed to be my dish cleaner, but he has better things to do, apparently."

"He your brother?"

"Paramour," Tammy said. "We came here by way of Andiron.

Fernando had to go and punch the captain of our transport. I thought we'd be stuck on Andiron permanently. So I arranged passage here."

"For me it was a bad divorce," Jess replied.

Tammy said, "There's a lot of divorces happening these days. With the dismissals and so many refugees. Do you want a job here?"

"Yes! I really need it. Is it only you or does your boyfriend work here, too?"

"Fernando is off running 'errands' for the Chateau," Tammy said. "I told him to stay away from those people, but he chose them over me. If I'm honest about it, he and I are over."

Tammy needed the help: business was booming. New arrivals carrying a bag and total confusion wandered out of the hangars hungry. Tammy scrounged up more tables and put them out in the corridor to handle the overflow.

Jess became a full-time server within a week. It was the perfect cover to observe this Underseed community. She made a point to learn a few basic things about each customer, where they were from, where they were going. The interest and attention boosted the tips and she recorded the info in Tammy's beat-up order-taking tablet. She became an apron-wearing data collection bot feeding a database on the diner's customers.

The database was a snapshot of the *Leggett*'s visitors and residents. Tammy was so impressed, she talked about opening another location off Bay Six, which had been closed until recently because a bulk freighter hit it.

Jill also learned a lot about the residents who ended up here. Tammy's story was fairly common. Many of the diner's regulars had left settled worlds in the GEC's Way Back sectors. Overpopulated systems were a nasty side effect of sacrificing settlement to keep up with the Exchange. With the galactic frontier wide open, the GEC's overpopulated worlds were geysering people in every possible direction, including into teh Underseed.

Most of her customers were just passing through, only here for fuel, food, and a hot shower. The *Leggett*'s permanent residents were an odd collection; the deviants, non-conformists, paranoids, loners, and hedonists. It was like someone put a filter on a pot of GEC coffee and they were the grounds left behind; hard to tolerate but the source of actual flavor.

The days were long, and Jill's feet protested mightily. But she heard about everything: family squabbles, current events, GEC raids, trade deals, Exchanger pirates, rumors, commodity prices, gambling woes, gossip, advice, and tall tales.

She used it all to map the political and economic power structures on board. Overhead's organization ran the Chateau and handled a large share of Underseed commerce. The *Leggett* was run by a grungy station manager who answered to a loose council of business owners, but the real power was Overhead's Chateau operation. The customer database told her which ships carried more Exchangers than GECs. She identified the major shippers and sussed out most of their shipping schedules and manifests.

She categorized the criminal gangs by number of illicit activities, threat level, and connection to the Overhead organization. She even had a list of the most crooked gaming tables based on which ones the bellyaching gamblers complained about the most. She shared this information with Tammy, for Fernando's sake.

Despite GEC policy prohibiting Exchanger ships past Union, more Exchangers at the *Leggett Rose* arrived every day. They took bypass slide routes around Union leading directly to the Underseed. She reported to Sandra about their growing numbers and the new bypass routes. She also reported an Exchanger rumored that one of their own had joined Overhead's organization.

Exchangers differed from GEC folks in their accent, more relaxed attitudes, and flamboyant fashions. They liked to bargain, desired fresh rather processed food, and tipped generously. Jill found if she matched their energy and body language, it boosted tips from Exchangers. The Exchangers also laughed at themselves more easily than GEC citizens.

Sandra didn't care about the cultural differences or how Exchangers interacted — or not — with Overhead's organization. Division's new concern was Exchanger *pirates*. She told Jill to confirm reports of Exchanger ships pirating GEC supply ships. The GEC media channels were mum about pirate activity. Since they never reported on corruption, Jill wasn't surprised. GEC Legal was still unsure what to do about Exchangers, pirate or not, roaming GEC territory.

Exchanger pirates were just one of many groups practicing what Jill knew was the Underseed's favorite pastime: stealing from the GEC. Tammy's plastic lunch counter made its way from a GEC restaurant supply depot, Tammy admitted once in a nonchalant, offhand manner. Where would everything in the Underseed come from other than GEC inventory?

Nonetheless, Jill dutifully reported Exchanger pirate raids. She chased any leads hinting at a connection between Exchanger pirates and Overhead's operations. She befriended Exchangers who passed through Tammy's, especially the regulars. They all told a similar story: they were figuring out new lives here like everyone else, living hand to mouth. Most came to the Underseed because they had no other decent options. Some were fleeing a particular person; others hoped to turn-around bad luck that landed them at the bottom of a reputation exchange back home.

No one called themselves a pirate, a thief, or a raider. It was an odd thing to ask when you were taking their breakfast order. She didn't get much out of any of them, until she met a goofy Exchanger named Jon.

TWENTY-SIX

JON WAS an Exchanger who delivered food and supplies to Tammy's diner every couple of weeks. For a slice of fruit pie, he would stock the deliveries on the correct shelves in the store-room. His laugh was raucous, he was relaxed and pleasant, and he always asked Tammy if he could do more to help.

When Tammy asked Jill to bring him a slice of pie, Jill found him wedged in their tiny pantry, shoving crates of mangapples onto the top shelf. He wore a GEC mechanic's coverall but any resemblance to a GEC resident stopped there. His hair was long and unkempt, he had a beard, and his posture was terrible.

"Why don't you have a seat at the counter," she said.

He smiled at her and followed her out front.

"Food is pretty expensive," she said as she put the pie in front him. "Shouldn't you be armed or escorted when you make these deliveries?" There were sections of the *Leggett* where you could be assaulted for a protein bar. Tammy actually kept an array of weapons under the counter and closed the place with roll-down metal bars each night.

"I doubt anyone *here* wants to kill me," he said, with a half smile.

He dug into the pie. It was sherryberry and apricot, a local favorite. He closed his eyes as he chewed.

"I'll buy you a cup of spiced coffee in exchange for your life story," she said.

"Spiced coffee? Yeah, sure. But my life is too boring to be worth a whole cup."

"Exchangers are interesting to me," she said. "You grow your hair out without fear of being locked up. You must have run the Union blockade to get out here. The GEC is kind of boring, if you haven't noticed. It feels like we all grew up on the same planet."

He flashed a guarded smile but offered her a seat next to his. It was the lull between the lunch and dinner rushes. The only other people in the place were three old men playing cards on the far side of the diner's counter.

Jon shrugged and took a sip, burning his tongue and cursing. "I signed up for this milk run on a short-range hauler which supplies the *Leggett*," he said. "You know, until I get my act together. I make these deliveries to keep busy while we're docked here."

"Not into gaming or gambling?" she asked. The *Leggett* didn't lack for entertainment.

"Nah. Anyone who can do math knows better, right?" He gave her his undivided attention, leaving his fork hanging in mid-air. "What about you?"

"My parents are station engineers," Jill said. "They were always following the exploration push." Sticking as close to the truth as possible was always easiest. "Had a couple of bad experiences with the GEC. My ex, for one. And GEC employment requires being pushed around a lot. So, I came here to wait tables until I figure out my next step. What brought you to this side of the galaxy?"

He was focused on the pie. Finally the fact that she had asked a question registered. "Oh, it's not that interesting."

She smiled. She wasn't sure if she was working an informant or flirting for real. She could play the flirt just like she could play the hard-core cop. But to play any role you had to believe in it a little. "It has to be interesting. Come on. The Exchanger side of the galaxy is full of bandits, plagues, risky reputation markets, daring rescues... orgies."

Jon grinned sheepishly. "If it was really that fun, why would I be out here? Ha. No. I was crewing an oxy resupply freighter. We came long after all the hotshot explorers mapped the routes for us. We helped build the infrastructure. Never wanted to be a captain or anything, I go with the flow. But my buddy got into gambling trouble betting on a 'sure' thing. I told him, you know, the house always wins, the math never lies, but he was hooked. He lost everything to this total ass of a criminal bookie. Creep wouldn't let it go either. So, we bailed. We signed on as contract janitors on a diplomatic vessel headed to Pergamon. Then we quit when we heard about this Underseed scene."

"You did that for your friend?"

Jon was surprised. "I mean, yeah. It's what friends do, right? Until one night when the friend takes all your money and disappears. Can you believe that crap?"

"It depends. Do you get swindled often?"

"What's 'swindled'?"

Jill waved her hand. "Conned, ripped off, tricked..."

Jon said with a grin, "Sorry, those must be some kind of uptight GEC terms."

She punched him on the arm. "You're conning me." There was more to this man than get-along, go-along.

He shrugged. "I guess I have been tricked a few times. I trust people too much."

"Are you here to find him? Your con artist ex-friend?"

His brows knitted together. "No, not with the dogs he's got chasing him now. Thank you no."

"Oooow," Jill said, resting her chin on her fist. "Shadowy Exchangers. Bounty hunters? Criminals? Tell me more. I'm into bad guys."

"Sounds like you're ingesting too much fiction, Jess."

Her eyes widened. "You heard anything about these pirates?"

Jon said, "Come on, don't tell me you believe these stories about pirates."

"What? Are you serious? You haven't heard about this?" Jill pulled up an audio clip on her handheld.

"And we're back on the Alan Glown Show. We have a weird story for you. Remember the little starslider that nearly upended Connexion Day? The crew

has returned, but not in the way you'd expect. When we last heard about them, they tried to snatch the mythical Provisional prize for reaching Union first. What? Oh, after that scam failed, they apparently bet against their own reputation stocks and skipped town.

"But we haven't heard the end of them. So these so-called explorers, these con men, have become — can you believe it — pirates. That's right, they knocked over two ships in two weeks, and they're the terror of the GEC shipping lanes.

"The first attack was on an automated convoy and there's been no report of what was stolen. The second attack was on a charter tour yacht showing off the Purple Turtle Nebula. What the hell is a Purple Turtle Nebula? Arty says its a GEC tourist fad these days. Okay. We should poke around the GEC some more, we really should. Pergamon is such a class act, really, very classy. Purple Turtle. Back home, they'd probably call this the Twinkling Clit Nebula. We're so crass in the Exchange. What? what's the problem? You can't say 'twinkling' on the air? Ha!"

"So, the Drake's captain is a guy named Barry Spranker, they board this charter yacht and what do they do? They didn't want the yacht, or the passengers' trinkets. They forced the passengers to transfer money to a dummy account. All they wanted was currency. So the passengers do it because I guess these guys threatened them.

"The ancient tales about pirates, stuff we heard as kids, remember the old stories about pirates stealing proprietary software? And luxury items, like spiced coffee? Did they take hostages then? Yeah, okay, then these guys are a little different. We have one of their victims on the line with us, a Betsy Yuffaren. Betsy, welcome to the Alan Glown Show."

"Hi, Alan."

"So, you were on a tour of celestial sights and got attacked by pirates. Were you scared?"

"Oh yes," Betsy replies. "They were polite, but they were slobs."

"Ha, Betsy, you haven't met enough Exchangers yet. Did they take any hostages or hurt anyone?

"No. The captain said we were being boarded and for safety reasons we should comply with their demands. They carried stunguns, but they weren't threatening, really."

"What did they take? I heard this wasn't a simple robbery."

"No. They wanted us to deposit money in their account in exchange for not harming us or blowing up our engines. And they gave us presents."

"Gave you presents?"

"Yes. Little cards saying we'd been robbed by the Drake. *It was a funny thing to do."*

"Rumor says they're pissed over not getting paid for reaching Union first. Did they say why they chose to be pirates?"

"No, Mr. Glown. They acted pretty nonchalant about the whole thing."

"Thank you, Betsy. This isn't the only incident. Shipping captains are nervous because the Drake *has been popping up from Union to Andiron, picking off unguarded shipping.*

Jill turned it off.

Jon held up his hands. "I hope I never run into them. Had enough of Exchange criminals: Lymanther, Squish, Porthole, and Cross Boss. I just want to make some deliveries, eat pie, live my life."

She knew Exchangers with high profiles chose names for easier branding and marketing. Division's briefing on Exchanger society made the point that investing money in LeMarcus Frank the accountant didn't instill the same confidence as the name DecimalPlace.

"Oo, tell me about them."

Jon said, "Squish is supposedly a sadistic provider of adult entertainment. Lymanther throws the best parties. Grand is an ambitious restauranteur. Porthole is a loan shark and speculates in waterfront real estate. Cross Boss runs some criminal enterprise and has, like, severe anger issues."

"Any of them coming to the Underseed? Spice this place up some?"

"Rumors say some of them are sliding toward GEC territory," Jon said. "Lymanther was supposedly spotted on Andiron. Squish's advance people were scouting the Underseed. Grand was rumored to be on Pergamon. Cross Boss may have disguised himself as a cook on a ship. You realize most of these people spread stories about themselves just to pump their share price?"

Jill filed away these names and details. Her memory was photographic, a talent which helped her to skip quickly to Rank Three. These

Exchanger crime bosses might be her way to pursue Overhead. If they set up shop, they would most likely clash with GEC law enforcement. If Overhead co-opted them or even contacted them, Jill would have probable cause.

Jon was studying her, puzzled at her delay in processing this. Too much introspection for a server? She felt a brief guilt pang for pretending in front of this guy. The way he tried to figure her out, like she was an interesting science experiment, made her want to toss aside her masks. This had never happened before when she worked undercover.

"Yes, yes, self-promotion," she said belatedly. "Still, it's fascinating. Exciting."

"Hey, Miss, are you still working?" yelled a grumpy old guy across the diner. "I could use a bowl of chocks." His pals elbowed him, embarrassed, and he fell to arguing with them. "She can date on her own time," he said.

"I better get back to work." She got up and smiled at him. "Why don't you stop by again, and tell me more stories? Coffee will be on me."

He gave her a toothy grin and hoisted his mug. "You can count on it."

TWENTY-SEVEN

"JEBUS LUCAS ON A STICK, will you dock already?" Flank said. His feet were propped up on a pallet wedged between his station and Barry's. He had been awake thirty-six hours straight, nursing the *Drake*'s systems to keep them from breaking under the strain of dragging so much extra mass. She was towing two freighters and her interior was jammed full of stolen cargo.

Tongue replied, "Don't interrupt me. This is delicate." The *Drake* was on approach to *Leggett Rose*'s largest docking arm.

The mass of the *Drake* and two freighters made the maneuver clumsy and too unpredictable for Tongue to leave it completely up to the ship. The delicate metal docking arm would crumple like cloth if he hit it.

Tongue learned this the hard way from jacking a ship in the Foster system. Luckily no one was killed when he hit their airlock. The *Drake* had no equipment for cutting through a hull or repairing these rigid metal airlocks the GEC used.

"Don't mind cranky, he needs his nap," Barry said. "And don't wreck the take."

"Utter... calm..." Tongue muttered, deep in concentration. He was choreographing a difficult ballet here. It was exhausting to figure out how the *Drake* could slide with two freighters which were wider and longer than it. Mass, momentum, orientation, speed, and torque on the tow cables didn't leave mental space for chatter. When this was over he needed to lubricate his neurons with sleep.

The board of docking indicators flashed blue. Clanks, thumps and hisses reverberated through the ship's ceramic hull. They were docked. The freighters drifted a few meters and came to a stop relative to the *Drake*. Tongue slumped in his chair.

"Our biggest haul yet," Flank said proudly.

"Let's go sell the take," Barry said cheerfully. "Drinks are on me."

Tongue held up his hands. "I'm out. I'm going to bed. No good getting drunk when I'm this tired."

"Me too," Flank said. "The drive is redlined because of dragging those freighters. I need to sleep before I try to see how bad it is."

Barry didn't like negotiating solo. Without Tongue's soothing presence and Flank's spastic bouts of outrage and implied violence, it wasn't fun. They acted cool as hell when they strutted around the *Leggett Rose*: Tongue's Zen attitude and Flank's shiny angry dome. Without them he was a scam artist on a corner trying to fence hot goods.

Barry said, "Come on, guys, this is the best part of the trip. We've been stuck on this ship for three weeks now. It's no fun to do it by myself."

"You slept the whole way here," Flank said incredulously. "We're tired as fox. Biz off."

"Let's wait till tomorrow," Tongue said. "Maybe the demand will go up if we let everyone wonder what we got here."

"If we do that," Flank snapped, "it will sit there for a couple of days. Don't forget the fifth rule of pirating: sell the loot fast."

"Sorry, man, I can't keep these rules straight," Tongue said. "What was rule two? Only steal what you can eat?"

"Screw you. Rule two was no drunken pirating without pants," Barry said when they left the kick.

"You nearly got caught on the passenger liner because of that,"

Flank pointed out, "and it's rule twenty-two not two. You foxing losers would be lost without me."

Barry said, "He's talking about when you messed up his tools, Tongue."

Tongue shuffled down the corridor towards his bunk. "You know the space between your ass and your shoulder blades? Yeah, well it was itchy and I needed something to reach that spot. So what, I didn't memorize where everything was."

Flank punched him in the thigh when he passed by, causing Tongue to howl and curse him energetically. Barry left them to it and crossed over to the station.

The *Drake*'s docking arm connected to the Leggett's lower decks. *Leggett*'s day cycle was midday but down here the few working lights meant it was no brighter at noon than the rest of the ship at midnight.

Barry zipped his jacket for the first time since Batik. He headed for the station's darkest bowels. The lowest decks were never a place to conduct legitimate business. The engines, ship's stores and other utilities made it the perfect place for shady business deals.

He learned the hard way to check in here first before approaching Clasker or the other buyers. Market conditions were evolving fast in Sector 180. He needed to gauge the market before trying to sell anything. And this time, with freighters full of product, investment in gossip would net a payoff higher by an order of magnitude, he figured.

Mixed in with the shady types on the lower decks was the station's riffraff. Some panhandled in the misguided hope of using a tiny stake to rebuild their fortunes up in the casino. Barry fully expected to end up like them someday, except he might get lucky and end up in prison instead. Some, like his contact, belonged down here, and seemed to enjoy the ambiance of desperation.

His contact was a thin woman with short dark hair and a bright pink jacket. She leaned against the wall like she owned it and the real riffraff kept clear of her.

"Jasmine, milady, how's the rumor mill?" Barry asked.

She smiled at him from under a set of heavy dark bangs. "Ah, the pizza raider returns."

"I prefer 'pirate.'"

"I've never heard that word. Where's your better halves?"

"Sleeping off some extra shifts." His pocket was full of loaded currency chips to keep *Leggett* denizens talking. He tossed a chip to her. She deftly slid it into her own comlink, transferred the sum, and tossed it back to him.

He put his hand against the wall next to her head, leaning in like he was about to kiss her. "What's the word?" he whispered.

"The media is now calling Sector 180 'The Mix'. Because the Exchange and the GEC are tripping over themselves and the Underseed, grabbing territory. It's a mixed up mess."

"Cute. How are things on the *Leggett*?"

"Lots of new people. Most are hungry and wearing all that they own. Two transports of GEC refugees docked yesterday and everyone stayed here. Said they saw their GEC settlement world and took a pass. They might stay; there's plenty of room. Exchangers are showing up more and more, too. A pawn shop opened on four, an electronics kiosk in the Chateau. A new fence named Beater is working out of the Chateau: a high roller, he's connected to Overhead somehow."

More customers was good, and a new fence might drive down fencing fees. He could demand higher prices from the usual suspects. "He any good?" Barry asked.

"No one's really sure yet."

"Clasker around?" Clasker was minimally trustable but maximally reliable. So long as none of Clasker's schemes included him, Barry didn't care. Clasker usually took whatever they were selling, minus a twenty percent handling fee. But with new competition around, maybe he would be willing to lower his fee.

"I saw him a few days ago. Probably still onboard." She indicated the corridor he came down. "You scored quite the load, I hear."

Barry smiled. "Only for you, J."

"Seriously, I can help you unload this stuff. The whole station notices when you guys come in now. You need someone to manage the station side of the business for you. Do you want to spend the time looking for the best deal, vetting all the fences passing by? You haul two full freighters in, I can send the buyers to you."

Flank would probably agree, because it would shorten their turn-around time, and snatch more ships in the same amount of time. Barry smirked. "I don't think we can afford to support the lifestyle to which you are accustomed."

She cocked her head to the side. "You're rolling in money, I hear."

Barry shrugged sheepishly. "Our profits are tied up in investments, like vital organ sales, robbery futures, that kind of thing. I'm not doing this the rest of my life. I have plans. Any mention of us in the GEC news?"

"Their sites only said there was an accident with a convoy. But no details."

Barry snorted. "They can't admit we exist yet, huh?"

"It's better for you this way," Jasmine said. "Once they admit it, they'll come for you. And when they do that, what happens to this place? It'll become a derelict if Investigators start crawling all over it. I hope you are retired before that happens."

The GEC dropouts throughout the Underseed sweated Investigators like a crooked Exchange stock broker feared the Regulators. Barry ought to fear the Regulators, too, considering the crimes he committed against the explorer exchange. "Don't worry," he said. "I don't only stop here. There's a dozen other ports like this one with two women in each."

"My sources tell me that you only jack ships and jerk off." She smiled. "You don't have anyone in any port."

"How do you know *that*?"

"Time's up. Got to leave you wanting something more. Unless you want to shoot another chip my way."

Barry grimaced. Jasmine always had the upper hand when they talked. She might be one hell of a distributor for them. Or a possible replacement for him, when the time came. Like he said, he had plans, or at least plans to make plans.

"You're too pricey for me. You take care of yourself, J."

"Stop by Tammy's. She may know where Clasker is."

Barry raised an eyebrow. "Free information? Is Tammy paying you to send customers her way?"

Jasmine smiled and nodded.

Barry took the stairs up to the main deck. The *Leggett*'s elevators were iffy at best and he needed the exercise. The crowds on the main deck were full of dazed GEC refugees wandering around. A sprinkling of equally dazed Exchangers stood out like sparklers in a morgue.

Tammy's was full-tilt busy. The diner was so close to one of the main hangars that its aromas lured the disembarking crowds who needed get their bearings and fill their bellies.

He dodged past the full tables and a young server trying to keep up with the rush. He leaned against the counter where Tammy was slinging java like a pro while tending to a sizzling grill. She would stir the hash, crack an egg, flip over some pink meatish substance and make three coffees and a juice from the beverage machinery. Pour, flip, dice with the side of the spatula. She ladled dripping pasta into two bowls with one hand while the other worked her spatula on the grill.

"Tammy, is Clasker aboard?"

A smile curled her lips but she concentrated on splitting a roll with two fingers and flipped the meatish stuff on top. She handed him three plates. "Table four."

He saw a family of two dirty kids and a scrawny woman who needed a stiff drink and a babysitter. They were expecting him to acknowledge them, and maybe help them.

He trudged toward them, speeding up when the plates began burning his hands. He dropped the plates on the table, jostling the food but not spilling it. The mom warned the kids to wait for the food to cool while the kids burned their mouths on the pasta and cried.

"Is there anything else I can do for you, milady?" Barry asked.

The woman replied in a weary tone, "I'll wait for the server."

"Good call," Barry said and walked away.

Someone at the next table flagged him down. "Excuse me, could we get another round here?"

The table held an empty glass, a drained coffee mug, a full glass of something red, a shot glass, and a half-empty coffee mug. Tammy offered about a hundred different drink options, but ninety of them tasted the same.

Barry asked, "What can I get you?"

"Oh, uh, I was drinking a double spiced coffee, no sugar, two-thirds of a packet of creamer, she was drinking sweet milk no ice—"

"—And a cherry," said the woman next to him.

"Sweet iced tea, with a cherry—" the man repeated.

"Wait, you said sweet milk, whatever the hell that is," Barry said.

"Yeah, no. Why can't you put order tablets right here on the tables?" the man asked.

"We are very deeply committed to personal service here," Barry said. "We wouldn't want to deny you this personal interaction with our friendly staff."

"It makes it very inefficient to get our orders in," the man explained pedantically. His thinning blond hair was in a pathetic combover. "Okay, the double spiced for me, the sweet milk for her, with a cherry, and Bob?"

The other man at the table said, "Oh, right, what do I want? Uh, a caramel coffee, pepper spiced, the guava juicer with extra ice, and a triskey."

"Coming right up," Barry said. He made it only two meters when a woman tugged at his sleeve wanting red pepper for her oatmeal. He made it half a meter when another customer asked for a menu.

Tammy grinned at him when he returned to the counter. "Was it a good cruise, Captain?"

He shrugged. "I have a full hold and an empty credit balance. Are you going to tell me if Clasker's around or should I go scare off more of your customers?"

"He left for Royada three days ago," Tammy said. "Not sure when he'll be back. But he bought a bag of his special coffee blend, so probably not soon."

Barry thumped the counter in frustration.

"Oh, he's been sending everyone wanting to talk to him up to some new guy in the Chateau named Beater. I hope the name is a sick joke."

Barry's hopes for increased competition among the local fences dropped. "Thanks Tam, you're a peach."

"Hey, what about those drink orders?" she asked.

"Just give them water," he said while he walked away.

The customers waiting for their drinks looked expectantly at him as he left the diner. Barry faked a loud fit of hacking coughs on his way out. No one bothered him.

TWENTY-EIGHT

THE *LEGGETT'S* owners designed the Chateau to resemble an open air Earth courtyard with false doorways, real plants, chandeliers, and wall murals to create the appearance of more buildings and shops. Birds chirped over the hubbub of people, games, and dealers.

Overlaid on this scenery was the latest in GEC gambling technology. Role-playing quest contests, fantasy sports, competitive tabletop gaming, and betting pools on anything where the house liked the odds.

The Chateau's entrances were clogged with freelancing con artists and grifters promising better odds than the house. The Chateau's proprietors tried to keep this low rent competition away but it was like fighting weeds growing in rich soil. The best they could do was to keep them just outside the Chateau's multiple entrances.

The weeds in this case were the very young and old con artists who loitered at the entrances, with dirty dice in hand, soliciting the gamblers or demonstrating impossible card tricks to draw in suckers. Barry couldn't blame them: the sweet smell of easy marks and quick money was pungent within a hundred meters of the Chateau.

The grifters no longer bothered with any of the *Drake* crew. All it took was Flank loudly explaining to the crowd how a twitchy young dice shark was scamming them.

Barry never met Clasker in the Chateau. The fence preferred quite, business-like settings. But Barry liked the Chateau's atmosphere. It put some zip in his step being amongst all the action and money changing hands.

He stopped at the sword and sorcerers quest game. Along with Jasmine and Tammy, the players at the fantasy-fantasy RPG were the most knowledgeable on the station. Something about the multi-layered strategies in the competitive fantasy RPG drew the deep geeks who knew everything about everything.

The game was a fantasy-fantasy RPG: the bettors chose fantasy teams of the players at the table who were playing in a competitive fantasy RPG. Sometimes the bettors teamed up with specific players and sometimes they backed an entire team of adventurers. The winning RPG player and anyone who picked her for their fantasy team split the winnings.

He asked the least freakish player there if they had heard about a guy named Beater. The player wore a leather cap, chainmail bikini, and a purple cloak. "Ask the DM," she said, pointing at the busy man behind the long u-shaped table with a rainbow ponytail trailing down his back. "My code-slicer thief is getting slaughtered in the open while my asshat boyfriend here lets his Dwarf Jedi cleric get stunned every damn round."

Her boyfriend frowned at her.

"Next round," said the DM, juggling two ten-sided dice. The screen overhead showed a battle against a giant yellow lizard in progress. The bettors prowled around the table, assessing their fantasy teams of twenty-odd player characters who were bent over small screens.

The DM rolled the dice, presumably for the lizard, and the number was high. Onscreen, the lizard whipped its tail and swept the remaining adventurers over the side of a cliff. Total party kill. Game over.

The DM triggered payoffs to bettors who took the long odds on a total party kill. The rest of the bettors were swearing under their breath at the DM's dice-rolling skills.

Barry caught the DM's attention. "Here to see Beater."

The DM relayed the request through his comlink. The answer squawked into his ear prompted him to motion to the turret. Beater seemed to be part of the operation.

The corner of the Chateau consisted of a stone castle turret. Chip exchange windows occupied the narrow slits on the ground floor. Security officers escorted carts of chips in and out of a side door. The turret's portcullis raised to admit high rollers and other VIPs. The turret led to the specialty games and back offices where the big time action happened.

Barry hung around the castle for five minutes until a well-dressed tough guy emerged from the turret. He was a pillar of calm muscle a foot taller than Barry. He was a backdrop, elbow steak for some Underseed goon. From the neck up, Elbow Steak appeared completely uninterested in talking to Barry. "What's your business?"

"Captain Barry Spranker, great to meet you. I specialize in salvage and recovery, wholesale distribution and redistribution. I usually deal with Mr. Clasker, but I'm looking for a, uh, Mister or Miss Beater."

Elbow Steak simply replied, "Follow me."

Rather than go through the portcullis, they exited the Chateau and took a private elevator in the corridor. Unlike the public elevators, the doors closed cleanly and began to rise without any jerky stops and starts. It was because this elevator went to the upper decks.

Passenger liners and cruise ships inherited a vertical hierarchy from their days afloat Earth's oceans. Height equaled higher status and better amenities. The elevator rose for fifteen seconds and Barry was sure he had never been this high up in the *Leggett*.

Beater might be a bigger big shot than Clasker. Maybe he was about to meet Eden Overhead? Her assistant Clasker usually handled their business arrangements. Barry and the guys hadn't rated direct access to the lady herself yet.

Perhaps the *Drake* pulling in two entire freighters merited a personal audience. Maybe she was unhappy with the *Drake* stealing so much and selling it here. Maybe Barry's remains would end up in the recycler by day's end.

Elbow Steak preceded him into an empty waiting room and

scanned him for weapons. Had something happened to spook Over-head? He racked his brain for the recent news and nonsense and came up empty-handed.

Elbow Steak gave the all clear and led him to an apartment next door, guarded by someone Barry tagged as Elbow Steak 2. Eden Over-head was not among the occupants inside.

"Barry Foxing Spranker," said an angry man on a couch, "Finally."

Something about this angry man was familiar. He was medium height, pushing into middle age, silvery gray hair and big murderous eyes that drooped to his jowls. His tailor-made purple business suit practically shouted: flamboyant Exchanger who thought highly of himself. Or wanted to pretend to be an Exchanger but was overdoing it.

Barry said, "Great to meet you. I specialize in salvage and recovery, wholesale—"

"Sit down and shut the fox up," the man demanded.

Barry acted hurt. "Usually I get a warmer reception from Clasker or Eden herself."

"Momma Overhead is currently indisposed. So is Clasker. They put me in charge to take advantage of my unique skills. Don't expect them to save you," the man said. He signaled to Elbow Steak 2, who shoved Barry down onto the couch.

"Hey, don't scuff the jacket," Barry admonished. "It's made of fabric that actually rubbed against real leather once."

"Pay attention, ass clown," Grand said. "This is wildly important to you. You owe me a metric shit ton of money and I've been waiting to kill you for a long time."

Barry squinted at him. "Are we skipping the introductions then? That's a shame. Because now I just gotta ask: who the hell are you?"

TWENTY-NINE

ELBOW STEAK 2 pinned Barry in place on the couch. The pissed-off man in the ridiculous purple suit came over and loomed over him.

"I am your nightmare come to life, Spranker. I was one of your investors on the reputation exchange. Oh, yeah, I'm one of the people you totally foxed. I bet five to one on you reaching Union first. And I bet that you'd finish in the top three at two to one.

"Then you went and foxed it up. Insider trading on your own shares to tank them! I lost everything. *Everything*. What I didn't lose on the exchange I lost when my credit dried up, my contacts didn't return calls, and my business evaporated like piss on a plasma fire. Nobody wants to deal with a crook who gets conned!"

Today was not Barry's day for getting easy answers. He said, "Back up there, friend, and start by telling me who the hell you are."

The man brought his nose within millimeters of Barry's. "Are you jerking me? Are you? What kind of a stupid question is that?"

"The kind," Barry said calmly, "where I'm asking a stranger for an introduction. Politely, which, to be honest, is taking a lot of effort on my part."

The man leaned in so close Barry could smell his breath. "My name is Juniper Grand, you foxing ass clown."

Grand? The crime boss? From the *Shogura*? Barry never met him, much less stole from him. Well, stole directly from him. The blood drained out of Barry's face.

"Thank you. It's just wonderful to meet another Exchanger out here at the end of the galaxy. How are you boys doing?"

"I came all this way out here to kill you, that's 'how us boys are doing.' I hired people to search for you, the fox good it's done me. And here you walk right in. I've wanted to kill you ever since you left the *Shogura*. It had consumed my every foxing thought."

Barry feigned sympathy. "I understand. You were boned like the rest of us. We made Union first and the Exchange refused to pay. Can you believe that? They were going to destroy us: our reputation share prices, the value of our bonds, everything." He shrugged, "Yeah, I shorted our stocks before the news broke. They were about to crater in a few hours anyway. Your investment was gone either way. We ran for our lives, with nothing to show for years of work. Just ruined reputations, disgrace, our ship and yeah, some pocket cash. But we're still hustling out here."

"Pipe down. I was speaking in the past tense, Spranker. Pay attention. Kroger!" He yelled to the next room. He waved at the elbow steaks and Barry regained ownership of his shoulders and arms again.

A worn-out droid rolled into the room, casting nervous glances at Grand and the elbow steaks. It was one of those care-giving models that shoddy nursing homes chained to an old person's ankles and called the arrangement 'assisted living.' This one's pseudo torso was scuffed and it wobbled uncertainly on its treads.

"Like I said, you're lucky, Spranker. My assistant Kroger here tells me you produce a dependable stream of income to the Overhead organization. Nothing which could repay what you owe me, but still, respectable. The thing of it is, your take has been climbing since you started this pirating thing. You dolts really muddled through learning how to steal from these helpless Grids. Something that any five-year-old could master, by the way. Kroger, tell him about the trends."

The droid handed Barry an e-page with the *Drake*'s pirating history summarized in money terms. The *Drake*'s week-over-week take grew about fifteen percent at first. But lately the take drifted down to six percent. It matched Barry's own numbers, more or less, which he would never admit that he kept careful track of. Flank wasn't the only one keeping score.

Grand tilted his head. "I'm working for Overhead, so I must act responsibly. Focus on the bottom line. Here's the deal. You keep your ship. I'll take thirty percent for Overhead's organization, but it's thirty percent of a baseline growth rate of your loot of four percent per week. Anything above the four percent growth rate, I take only ten percent. Give you a proper incentive to be a better pirate."

Barry asked, "What's the catch?"

"The catch is these Grids don't understand incentives. The faster your take grows, the more you keep."

Barry scoffed, "But we need to keep increasing the take. Which increases the chances we get caught. Your baseline will compound at four percent a week. We can't keep up with that. Our growth rate will plateau soon." Barry was lowering expectations. How much longer could the *Drake* increase its take? The Grids were unexpectedly inept at stopping them. But if they kept raising their profile, the GEC would eventually crush them, or their luck would simply run out.

"Barry, Barry, Barry. If I were a vindictive shit, you'd be right and I wouldn't care about driving you into prison. But I would be throwing away money. I won't do it, because I am an ambitious and greedy bastard."

"What a relief," Barry said.

"The baseline will be set at the average for all pirates. The *Drake* won't be the only pirate ship out there. There's competition emerging already, but they're mostly buffoons. It's easy pickings for any half-competent pirate right now. Every GEC ship has no choice but to slide down the main GEC route. But as more routes develop, and more pirates pile on, you'll lose your advantage. Classic pirate bubble. You need to read up on your ancient history.

"Bottom line, your loot growth will eventually drop to zero. It's simple economics. Just stay above the dropping baseline and we both make extra money."

It was refreshing to compete with another Exchanger who could think strategically. It had been a while. The Grids were entirely incapable of it. Flank was focused on the short-term and just wanted to be the best at whatever. Tongue existed entirely in the present.

Grand was right; the pirate market would not remain a bonanza forever. But Barry didn't care to plan out how to benefit from those changes. If the pirate business turned into another hyper-competitive exchange or ended altogether, it didn't matter to him. He didn't expect to be a pirate forever. Grand may assumed that he, Tongue, and Flank were in it for the long term though. Barry may have an advantage over him because of it.

"Overhead will figure out that you're lining your pockets," Barry pointed out. "You do *not* want to get on her bad side." It was misdirection to pull focus away from long term concerns, but they were legitimate concerns: he didn't want to be caught in the middle if Grand was scamming Overhead.

Grand grinned. "Don't you worry your tiny brain. You'd be amazed how inefficient these GEC criminal organizations are. I started so many new revenue streams and have so many cost-cutting changes in play that she won't mind. I'm keeping fencing fees low while this Mix gets settled. Won't last forever, so the key for you is to maximize income in the short run. Which is one of the reasons I'm developing a new revenue stream based on betting on pirates. The *Drake* will be the blue-chip asset of the new pirating reputation exchange."

Barry blinked a few times. Another speculative market that paid him based on his reputation in the business was the last thing he wanted. The whole point of pirating was escaping others' expectations and the responsibility to meet those expectations. It didn't matter if he was a dog turd in the public's opinion, he was sick of strategizing about his public appearance to maximize his net worth.

Having to work at keeping investors happy turned Barry's stomach. Pirates needed friendly ports to hide from the GEC. They needed to depend on the public's generosity. What would angry pirate shareholders do? Dump their shares and call in the Grids if they didn't think the *Drake* brought in enough pizza?

Grand smiled. "I'm the bookie, so win or lose, I make money. And since you'll be working for me, I'll cash in on side bets on the *Drake* and on the fencing fees for everything you steal."

Barry said, "You can't be a pirate when you're worried about your own share price. What if we jack one of our shareholders? What if we blow a run and you lose one of your guaranteed side bets?"

"Oh, I'm not letting you put any money in this exchange," Grand replied. "And no one can short anything. I'm keeping it simple. If I lose a bet here or there, that's fine. Good even. It'll appear like it's an honest exchange."

"Meanwhile, we still need to worry about keeping our bettor/investor happy," Barry noted sourly. "Are there reputation dividends?"

"Unlikely. If you stay on the exchange for a whole year, we'll see."

"Pirates have no skin in the game then. Not a smart move."

"Here's what you do," Grand said, "gather your fellow degenerates and you hit the heavens. Be outlandish, be bold. Attract copycats and competition so my piratical reputation exchange gets up and running."

Barry chewed his lip. He desperately wanted to tell Grand to cram this deal into a tight, hairy hole. But his inner voice of reason said there was no choice. Grand was grasping them by the scrota. He sighed.

"Good," Grand said, clasping his hands together, "let's talk about this loot you brought me. Two freighters. I'll get someone down there to appraise it, cut you a chip for your seventy percent."

"Whoa, whoa, whoa. It's worth a lot more than our four percent growth rate. You don't get thirty percent," Barry said.

Grand scrunched up his nose, irritated. "Fine, the more you keep, the more it jacks up your growth curve. Which means I take more from you in the future, smart guy," Grand replied. He motioned to the elbow steak twins.

Barry's beefy escorts ushered him out of the office and back to the Chateau. They left him in the sea of desperate gamblers sweating their fortunes at the gaming tables.

The familiar icy bite of responsibility clamped down on his shoulder blades. He was an owned man once again. Unlike the fools gambling at the tables in front of him, he harbored no ridiculous hope of working his way out of this jam by playing by the house rules. Those rules were as stacked against him as the gaming rules were stacked against the bettors in here. Barry put his hands in his pockets and began a slow walk of despair back to the *Drake*, trying to delay the moment he had to deliver this shit nugget of news to Tongue and Flank.

THIRTY

THE RECENT RUMOR of a space shark attacking ships in the Farris was not what brought the *Drake* to the system's outer reaches. It was a report that the *Drake* itself was making big bank by pirating grain and vegetable shipping there.

Barry found the report odd, because the *Drake* had never been to Farris before. It was one of the few settled GEC systems a little ways off of the GEC's main route between Andiron and Union. The GEC settled Farris' lone habitable planet three years ago to extract heavy metal deposits from the planet's crust and that brought a lot of transport convoys to it

"The convoy should be here in five minutes," Tongue said. "We're outside the range of Farris' nav buoys, so we should be virtually undetectable by the Grids."

Barry grunted his acknowledgement.

"What, this is going to work."

"So what?" Barry asked. "Grand thinks we're shorting him on what he thinks we already stole from this system. Whatever we get here today won't help us pay him back."

"Digs the hole deeper," Tongue said, "I get it. But this is where we turn it around. I can feel it."

"I told Grand that this system has had a problem losing supply convoys long before we even reached Union," Barry said. "Jasmine said insider theft here is a poorly-kept secret."

"Of course he know's that," Tongue retorted. "The GEC's bean counters publish how much tonnage is lost in each system. It's disappearing here for, you know, *a reason*."

"If it isn't us, then who's doing it? Another pirate would want the credit on Grand's new exchange."

"From rumors I heard on the *Leggett*," Tongue said, "the crews run off to some uncharted paradise planet and are living out of cargo containers. Or this system has navigation hazards and those crews were crushed into, you know, photons."

"You heard all that puttering around on the *Leggett*?"

Tongue smiled. "People like talking to me. I don't insult them. You should try it."

"How boring. The old lady who sells clothes on the bottom deck, Murray? She told me there was a space shark attacking ships," Barry said.

"Come on."

"Honest. She said a space shark bites through the hull, digests the entire ship, doesn't leave any debris. A friend of a friend of hers saw it happen."

Tongue shook his head. "You don't believe that grown adults in the GEC buy that. Back home, we stopped believing in those tales at what, seven years old?"

"For me it was when I learned no one had ever found anything bigger than a groundhog on any habitable world. And the biggest things in space that eat ship hulls are microscopic pain in the ass bacteria. I don't think she likes me."

Tongue snapped his fingers. "Just like I said."

Time to change the subject. "Our loot growth rate is only three percent. You think Grand will buy the space shark excuse?"

"Who cares? We still have the biggest market capitalization on the pirate exchange. We're fine."

Barry groused, "If we get the credit for jacking a ship, we should get the cash, too. The rest of that exchange is a bunch of wannabes and posers. I think Grand is setting us up to get caught. Or owe him money forever."

Tongue held up his hands. "Bare, it's not that bad. Grand has thrown us a lead here and there, right? He doesn't want us caught - it would wreck his pirate exchange if the top guys get caught."

Barry sucked in his lower lip and let flub out of his mouth with a wet pop. "I'll bet my balls that Grand has a way to win if we lose."

"We'll catch up on the loot growth, you'll see. Flank wants to daisy-chain raids to optimize our loot per day average. Our contacts are giving us new leads every day. My super-precise navigation has already cut our raid time by, like, a lot. I don't know, Flank told me it was some high percentage."

Barry nodded along but bit down a response. Tongue was their optimist, their cheerleader. Barry didn't tell him that he had amped up the theatrics so media coverage would boost their share price a little higher than it should be. He hadn't told him how he sold off captured ships piece by piece to maximize their haul. They were focusing on more lucrative targets now, realizing that five freighters of toilet paper wasn't worth a single freighter of frozen dinners.

"You're sure Flank is onboard the *Baddings*?" Barry asked.

"Relax," Tongue said. "What's with you? Worst case, Jasmine is wrong and the *Baddings* slides somewhere else. But there's really nowhere else around here to go. It's the GEC main line or nothing. Their schedule said they're coming here."

Barry nodded and went to the galley. He drank three fingers of orange juice. He knew Tongue was right but it didn't stop the anxious bees buzzing in his chest. Planting Flank on the targeted ship was the best way to track the ship through a slide. Each slide was a highly variable affair that unfolded outside of the space-time curve and was un. Without a stowaway, you had to attach a tracker to the ship, wait for the ship to exit the slide, and then slide to the tracker's updated position. Flank could relay the slide coordinates right before the ship slid so the *Drake* could be waiting when the Baddings exited. If it was the faster ship.

The *Drake* was plenty faster. In theory, it should be able to catch the *Baddings* while the latter was heading for the planet's surface. Even without Flank to nurse every ounce of speed he could from the *Drake*.

"Nothing better break in here," Barry muttered.

The intercom in the galley chirped. "Flank's signaled," Tongue said. "He sent coordinates. They're on the far side of the system."

Barry grinned. "Good good good."

The *Drake*'s slide drive was already charged. Tongue activated the drive before Barry hurried into the kick. The *Drake* slid.

THIRTY-ONE

THE SLIDE across the Farris system was so short that it ended right after it started. They exited a hundred K-klicks from Flank's coordinates.

"Can Flank keep quiet?" Barry asked. They were so close to cracking this mystery.

Tongue shrugged unconvincingly. "Eh, I'm sure."

The *Baddings* was a segmented blue column, barely visible in the dark. Most of the ship was cargo containers with a small pilot ship on the bottom.

it. Tongue throttled up the *Drake* to full and the distance shrank. Slower GEC ships like these cargo vessels required a seventy to ninety-minute recharge time. If they tried to flee, the *Drake* would grab them in five minutes.

"Stand down, *Baddings*," Barry radioed, and began his piratical spiel. No one would get hurt, please don't resist, don't call for help, because it won't arrive quickly enough. Ya ya ya. His mouth was on automatic pilot, sounding like a personal service announcement.

The reply from the *Baddings* was a burst of shouted argument, cursing, and a crash. The crash sounded like something breaking through a equipment on the bridge.

Barry scowled. "Did you hear Flank's voice?"

"I'm going to say no," Tongue said.

Flank was supposed to hide until they boarded. They both stressed to him how important it was to let the Baddings be stolen as planned so they could discover who was copying them. Flank revealing himself could spook them into acting stupid.

The *Drake* was in weapons range, and Tongue did the pro forma shots across the bow. The *Drake*'s homemade beam weapons were too weak to puncture bulkheads, but they could overwhelm a ship's power system and fry the fuel cells. A powerless, cold ship was easier to sell than an exploded one.

"*Baddings*, your last transmission sounded, uh, weird," Barry said. "We are coming aboard."

No response.

"We may need to cut through the airlock," Barry said to Tongue.

"We?" his navigator said in mock surprise, "I have to guard the ship here." He got very busy with something at his console.

"Great." Barry needed Flank's cutting torch and a sidearm. Flank's engine room was always disgustingly neat. Angry, Barry spread tools over the engineering console and sprinkled very tiny spare parts liberally over the deck. Finally, he found the torch from a clearly marked cabinet.

Standard procedure was to secure a surrender before boarding, to avoid any in-person resistance. Barry would explain to the victims how things would work, including that they would get a small prize at the end of they complied, so everyone could experience the most comfortable pirating possible. It reduced the victims' will to resist and it made the interaction more orderly.

Tongue flagged him down when he returned to the kick. "Bare, something strange here. This ship is missing several cargo containers. Standard number for a freighter is ten. It has eight."

"So maybe a couple were damaged and left behind?" Barry offered.

Tongue squinted at the manifest. "The manifest says ten. Ten modules of spork-knives? Spork-knives. Hahaha, hoo boy, maybe Flank found that out?"

"Hey, they *are* the ultimate utensil," Barry chided. He tapped his finger on his chin. Something was very off about this, but he didn't know what. The *Baddings'* airlock was closed. He banged on it — a final warning if they didn't want him mutilating their airlock with his rusty torch skills.

No answer. Barry lit the torch, it's white flame whooshing to life. He took a breath and guessed the right spot to cut through. But before he could scorch it, the airlock cycled.

Flank was on the other side, breathing hard and with a cut bleeding down the side of his head. "Bout time," he snarked.

"I couldn't find the torch," Barry held it up.

Flank grunted. He retreated into the *Baddings'* cramped corridor and stepped over what Barry hoped was an unconscious man.

"Don't start with me," Flank said, "I've been knee-deep in scumbags for the last fifteen minutes."

"You agreed to behave yourself until Tongue and I showed up," Barry said. "What's this?"

"There's a situation," Flank said. "It's not really clear what's going on here." He led Barry past several more inert bodies and a few others who began to stir.

When they were three meters shy of the bridge, someone shrieked and grabbed at Flank's head.

Flank pivoted to his right. He swung around behind the attacker's momentum and drove him headfirst into a metal bulkhead.

The nineteen year old attacker slid to the ground whimpering.

"And stay down, you spunky little asshole," Flank crowed. "I knew there was one missing."

"You're getting old, Flank," Barry said sardonically, "you used to beat up an entire ship's crew in under three minutes."

"Drunken console jockeys, maybe."

"I'm remembering the *Belladonna*," Barry said. "But you weren't much good against their five wrestlers."

"They ganged up on me. And they were passengers, not part of the crew."

Barry grinned. "So what's the story here?"

Flank frowned and showed him to the bridge. "Maybe you can figure it out."

Barry's mouth hung open. "What the hell?"

THIRTY-TWO

THE BRIDGE of the *Baddings* was trashed. Chairs tossed and displays cracked. The bridge crew sat on the floor, bound up and bloodied. The captain was a man in his twenties with bright fluorescent orange hair.

"You from the *Drake*?" the captain lisped through a split lip. "So *you* must be Willard Bailey."

"Yes and no," Barry said.

Flank sighed. "I've already played this game with him."

"Captain Barry Spranker, at my service," Barry said. He strolled around the bridge. "I'm here to inspect your work environment, make sure it meets GEC standard. And frankly, we have a lot of violations going on here."

"Listen Orangey," Flank said, leaning down. "Barry and I are who's jacking your ship."

"But—you can't," Orangey said and swallowed noisily. "You, you're not the right pirates."

Barry scowled at Flank. Flank misinterpreted this and grabbed Orangey's collar and wound up to hit him. Barry waved him off.

Flank yanked the man close. "What are you talking about? My patience has worn very thin."

Orangey said, "We're supposed to be attacked by the *Drake*, which will steal our cargo and sell it to Underseed gangsters."

"Which Underseed gangster?" Barry asked.

Orangey shook his head. "They didn't say. We used to report a couple of lost shipping modules. Damaged during the slide or while docking. The money we received for selling them to the Underseed plugged holes in our budget. But the GEC has made us purchase pirate insurance, and getting raided pays off better for us. Especially since the Space Division cut its budget again. This has been the only way to maintain our ship."

Barry loomed over Orangey. "You've added an insurance scam on top of double embezzlement? Yes, double. We noticed that you're missing some modules."

Orangey looked sheepish.

Barry crossed his arms. It was odd for one part of the GEC to fake pirate attacks to score reimbursements from a different part. What was odd and incomprehensible was Underseed pirates paying for the privilege to pretend to be him and his crew. And wrong. Barry smelled franchise fees he was getting screwed out of. He asked, "Okay, so you're skimming some on the side. What I don't get is why pretend it was the *Drake*?"

Orangey said, "We get a fee for claiming the *Drake* did it."

"Someone is setting us up," Flank said.

Barry wasn't sure, at least not yet. Too many angles to sort out. Someone could be trying to throw off investigators tracking them across the Mix. He said, "So we can't take the insurance payoff. If we take the cargo we rip off the fake pirates, who will arrive momentarily. How do we make money on this trip?"

Orangey shrugged. "We didn't expect the actual *Drake* to show up."

"Who pays you the fee?" Barry asked.

"An Underseed outfit. Maybe organized crime," Orangey said. "Hurting them is probably a bad idea."

"You could be right," Barry replied. "Unless they are doing this to set us up. Pretend that we're taking more than we claim."

Flank asked, "Can we take hostages? We should take hostages.

We're taking hostages. Instead of selling whatever trinkets they're hauling for next to nothing." He grabbed Orangey's collar. "You better hope that whoever pays your ransom is smarter than you are."

"Ransom?" Barry snorted. "We could turn them in to the Grids and collect the reward. The GEC *hates* embezzlers and con artists." He squatted on his haunches and regarded Orangey. "You're already in enough trouble. Consorting with pirates, property theft, falsifying insurance claims, dying your hair that color."

"I, I dyed it to fit in better with Exchangers in the Underseed," Orangey said. "Maybe you could split the reward for the cargo with the other *Drake*."

"Screw this," growled Flank, "I want hostages."

Barry acted like he was seriously considering Flank's suggestion. And he really did take it seriously. Taking hostages would not be only good for laughs, it would ensure the fake pirates cut in the real pirates on the action. And no one wanted that many spork-knives.

He said to Orangey, "Fifteen thousand per head."

Orangey flinched. "Ten."

Barry said, "Twenty-five."

"What?!?"

Barry leaned against a smashed console. "This is not a negotiation. This is you purchasing your freedom. If you waste my time haggling, the price goes up. Plus, you acted relieved at fifteen, so you can pay more."

"Okay."

Barry made him thumbprint the payment. GEC money flooded into a holding account Barry had created for these transactions. He ran a program that shuffled the money out of the Grid banking system in very small amounts via person to person transactions.

Flank scowled. "We're letting them go?"

"For three hundred and fifty thousand. Yeah." Barry turned to Orangey and gestured at the bridge. "I'm giving you a pass on these health and safety violations, just this once. Don't look so dour, you've got to set an example for your crew."

Orangey took a step towards Barry and Flank clamped an arm on his shoulder.

"Look, I'm sorry about the digs about your hair color," Barry said. "If you want to dye it the color of a safety vest, we support and affirm your fashion choice. Here's a little thank you gift." Barry handed him a small gift bag with chocolates. "Flank, let's top off our cells before we leave."

Flank drained the *Baddings'* fuel cells through a power cable running through the airlock. The *Baddings* wouldn't be able to slide, but had enough juice to limp into Farris orbit. It would require a humiliating rescue by the Grids there.

When Flank and Barry returned to the *Drake*, Flank immediately went to the engine room to return his torch to the proper location. Barry gleefully anticipated his reaction when he saw the mess.

"We going?" Tongue asked.

Flank came thundering towards the kick. He appeared to be in a full rage but then smiled evilly at Barry and sat at his station.

Barry was fully prepared to flee, but did a double take. He said to Tongue, "Yeah. Right now."

"We're really not taking the cargo?" Tongue asked.

Barry held up a currency chip. "Looted bank accounts today."

"You don't want to meet the other pirates?" Tongue asked. "See who they work for?"

Flank and Barry exchanged glances. "They probably work for Overhead, which means they're Grand's people," Flank stated, adding, "They're setting us up to take a bigger fall. Knock down our looting growth curve."

"Son of a bitch," Tongue said, "Grand's grabbing loot directly and pinning us for the piracy? He'll probably pay us less for our own loot."

"And running an insurance scam against the GEC," Barry said with a smile. "Plus Grand's bidding up our share price on his reputation exchange." Barry admired the entrepreneurial genius in building multiple profit streams from a single screw job.

The GEC's pirate insurance presented a new opportunity for the pirates, too. The GEC was encouraging its crews to avoid piracy on their own by dinging their pay for insurance premiums. But if some of the crews were already 'losing' cargo to the Underseed, the insurance provided a separate scam to run against their employer. Until the premiums increased to cover the payoffs. Or the GEC started going after their people for insurance fraud.

Profit-maximizing pirates should grab a piece of the insurance fraud payoffs these GEC crews were pulling down. Stealing cargo was nice, but Grand's exchange was really about the money. In fact, money was preferable, because Grand didn't get a percentage of funds secretly transferred, only physical cargo he could sell at retail. Like the pirate tourist business, it would be yet another revenue stream Grand didn't have his claws in.

Barry figured the GEC would eventually deploy claims adjusters to investigate the mounting piracy-related insurance losses. The scammers would need evidence of a pirate attack. And the *Drake* could do these scammers a favor by producing realistic evidence of a pirate attack. For a hefty slice of the insurance payoff, of course.

The *Drake* left the *Baddings* behind at maximum velocity. When they were clear and charged, they slid out at the same moment the fake *Drake* slid in. It was some boxy GEC tugboat. Barry smiled at their imitator's amateur look.

"Guys, this could be a better business model for us."

THIRTY-THREE

"KROGER, sometimes you know what you're talking about," Grand said. Their shuttle banked over the green mountains of Royada's coastline. A small storm was showering the mountains to the north on its way out to the ocean. Everywhere else the sunlight transformed the deep greens of the tropical forests into a dazzling vibrant emerald.

"Sir, one of my more basic services is monitoring health levels. Your sleep was inadequate and your heart rate was elevated."

"How many days were we on the Leggett this time? I get so wrapped up in things I lose track. Hard to tell day from night in the Chateau."

"Three. A month ago it took two weeks for your system to recover."

"A month ago I didn't have a pirate reputation exchange with that foxwit Spranker giving me lip." The *Leggett* used to remind him of home on the *Shogura*. But he had been an established institution on *Shogura*, he had a nice routine there, and the stakes had been lower.

"The gaming operations on the *Leggett* are operating at twice the volume they did before you took over," Kroger said. "The new manager seems to be performing well. The pirate exchange is established now and the casino's financial people have it well in hand."

The shuttle touched down on the mountainside landing pad.

Grand slipped off his seat restraints. "If you're just saying all of this to make me feel better, and it's not true, I'll just get that much angrier. At you."

"Well aware of that, sir. But I think you understand the organization is in a good position."

Grand couldn't argue that. He watched the outboard camera feed as the shuttle circled to land.

Within an hour, Grand was relaxing on the tropical print couch in his living room, sipping his pineapple rum and enjoying the mid-day sun glinting off the waves. A breeze from the ocean tickled the hairs on his legs. The late afternoon was hot and sunny and he was tempted to take a dip in the rolling waves. A quick swim always cooled him off and cleared his head.

But he never swam for long. There was always work to do. Even on vacation.

Kroger was in the other room dispensing with low-level administrative issues. As Grand's major-domo and chief of staff, the droid handled the crap that would waste Grand's time.

It was the kind of relationship Grand couldn't build with the carry-overs from Overhead's crew. The cultural divides were too great. The denizens of the Underseed and GEC citizens were driven by rank and proper procedure. Grand quickly tired of their questions about how he wanted them to do something or worries about the proper chain of command. He sent more and more of these nervous rule followers to Kroger.

Overhead's bottom line was in great shape. Grand fixed the easy problems and impressed the hell out of Overhead's lieutenants in doing it. He needed these quick, easy victories to bank loyalty for when he made the bigger, harder changes.

"Kroger, send my screen the latest Underseed population estimates."

Kroger obeyed and Grand's small handheld populated with the most recent trends. The Underseed population across the three closest sectors was exploding in size. It was both wonderful and terrible news. Thousands more fled the stumbling GEC every day. But it was up to

Grand's organization to keep dozens of Underseed stations and settlements supplied with food, water, and other necessities.

When he took over, Overhead's organization was only two weeks away from putting the Underseed in Sectors 180 through 182 on rations. Kroger found and attacked the logistics bottlenecks while Grand used his entrepreneurial skills to separate refugees from their money and use the money to feed them. Hungry refugees with wads of GEC currency were an unexploited opportunity.

The new pirate exchange helped, too. The pirates were increasing the amount of stolen GEC supplies funneled to the Underseed. And their notoriety distracted GEC enforcement's attention away from Overhead's network of embezzlers and smugglers.

"Sir? You're making that face you make when you're upset," Kroger said.

"Yeah. When were you going to tell me the Underseed is about to foxing starve again?"

"I wasn't projecting that it will. My projections show the refugee numbers dropping soon and our food uh, 'imports' increasing in a linear fashion."

"But if one of those things doesn't happen, we're foxed, aren't we? Yes, that's what I figured. If we continue on our current trend, without your rosy assumptions, the Underseed starves. Or food prices skyrocket. Can we buy more food from the Exchange? No? Call our contacts over there again to make sure. It's a damn odd problem to have too much money and an empty belly. Did either of these damn fool organizations plan to feed the people coming into this sector?"

"Bixby told me that the GEC assumed that settlements in Sectors 181 through 184 would supplement food shipments to 180," Kroger said. "But when the GEC stopped settling worlds in those sectors to rush to Union, food production didn't increase as they expected."

"Ah, those total idiots. Food prices are going up from Sector 179 to 184. The GEC and Exchange are struggling to get the food to follow the people."

Food prices in the new Exchange settlements in the Mix had started high and only climbed. The Exchange's shippers and food reputation markets were swiftly adjusting but no amount of incentives could magically haul food through multiple sectors faster. They couldn't feed everyone flooding into the Mix, either.

"What about the currency conversion rate?" Kroger asked. They had built an income stream by converting GEC 'utilitons' into Exchange 'dividends.' The lower deck dwellers did conversions at outrageous exchange rates. Kroger had set up kiosks all over the Underseed to offer slightly less ridiculous rates. Given the desperation of food-poor, cash-rich GEC exiles, it was a seller's market for Exchange dividends. "We could manipulate the currency supply to make Exchange imports cheaper, including their food."

Grand grumbled.

"Or, we could ramp up Exchanger food development practices," Kroger said. "They can produce food three times faster than the GEC. An Exchange settlement becomes food independent very quickly."

"How do they do that?"

"They rely on insects for food and recycling in phase one and two settlements."

Grand sighed. Even his own droid was grasping at straws. "That's not gonna fly in the Underseed. Pun intended."

"They would rather starve?" Kroger asked. "Using insects to consume human byproducts and become a food source themselves is a cheap and sustainable food source."

Grand shook his head. "Tell that to the rioters we had on *New Prince Station* when we tried substituting bugs for plant protein. The Grids only will eat food processed from slow-growing crops."

"I suggest running a public service announcement campaign to change the culture," Kroger said. "Offer the 'bug food' for free or at a reduced price. You could reduce portions of processed GEC food at the same time. Hungry humans become less finicky."

"Another lesson from working in the old folks' home?"

"We always maintained the highest standards of service and care at our facility," Kroger replied.

"That's what it said on that place's brochure, smart ass," Grand said. "We can't *push* people to eat mashed bugs. We have to *pull* them to it." He snapped his fingers. "Let's spread a rumor about food poisoning in the GEC. Scare people a little. Make them want good old Exchange bugs, beans, and greens. We did this once when I was young and wanted to undercut a certain brand of triskey. A couple scary rumors, some fake episodes of people being hospitalized, and we snatched their market share."

Bixby came into the room, but rather than interrupt, he waited. Such a good guy. Grand fed him a steady stream of circus video clips from the Exchange's most exotic circuses. Three rings of fornication, stripper clowns, bestiality with robots. Got a laugh out of the big guy every time, and no complaints. Grand almost regretted making Bixby wait on him.

"You'll have to walk me through how we create a fake scandal about food poisoning in processed food," Kroger said. "And when we depend on that food for eighty-seven percent of the Underseed's diet."

Was that disapproval in his voice? "I'm open to other options, if you have them, Kroger."

"We could increase the premium we pay for food."

Grand shook his head. Paying extra for foodstuffs, water, and medicine hadn't increased supply enough. Overhead had relied on disgruntled and dismissed Grids to bring along a cargo hold of food with them. But it wasn't working any more.

"Put the word out to our GEC contacts. We need them to grab as much food as possible."

"The GEC may stop tolerating the Underseed's presence, especially if it causes them shortages," Kroger warned. "It is a topic of much discussion on every station we visit."

Grand waved his hand, "We don't have any other options. Between the Exchange, the pirates, and their own logistical problems, the GEC may not notice an increase in spoiled or lost cargo. Let's risk it." He motioned for Bixby to speak.

Bixby said, "One of the sensor rings in the back lawn went out."

Grand peered into the back lawn of soft, spongy short grass which ran down to the beach. "There's nothing out there."

"Right. We're looking for a malfunction. But I wanted you to be aware."

One of his constant irritants with GEC tech was the inferior quality. The GEC sloppily manufactured components with inorganic metal wiring, highly processed plastics, and metal alloys. The equipment failure rate was double the Exchange's bio-mechanical versions. He missed his old life at times like this.

"Are you increasing security?" Grand asked. He employed four times more security personnel on the estate than Overhead, and spared no expense for additional sensors, gates, and other security measures.

Bixby said, "Already done. Doubled the patrols, deployed snipers, and we're running an unscheduled drill in two minutes." A surprise drill was a way to throw off surveillance or impending raids. To someone on the outside, the whole household suddenly scrambled in unpredictable ways. A caravan of vehicles would leave carrying unknown passengers. Guards switched to new positions. Security went on alert and changed their entire force posture.

It was partly to spook any nearby surveillance and partly to inject enough randomness to make hostiles think twice about storming the place. It also kept their own guards on their toes.

"Mike and Susie were pulling up when I came in here," Bixby added.

Ugh. These moronic bounty hunters had begun to perform almost adequately after Grand lowered the bar for them. They didn't need to pin down the *Drake*'s location anymore. They only needed to learn where it had been already and what it had stolen. He didn't trust Spranker in the least and feared he wasn't getting his fair share of the *Drake*'s haul.

Susie sent regular reports on the *Drake*'s whereabouts, but not specifics about how many raids the pirates conducted, tonnage stolen, and estimates of the haul's worth.

Grand motioned for Bixby to send them in. Mike and Susie were dressed in GEC business wear and trying to play it professional. Grand listened to their report calmly. They really were trying to claw their way to competence.

"We've been a little confused about the media reports about the *Drake*," Susie said. "A couple of times we've tracked them to a certain system at a certain time, but the media reported they were raiding ships somewhere else at the same time."

"Uh, don't worry about it. Those are copycats," Grand replied. "I'm boosting the *Drake*'s reputation on the exchange with a couple of well-placed stories."

Mike was relieved, but Susie grew more concerned. "Then we can't be sure we're following the real ship. It would help if we knew which reports were the fake ones."

Grand bit his tongue instead of barking about how stupid those words sounded coming out of Susie's mouth. They wanted *him* to tell *them* which reports about the *Drake* were fake? Who was working for who here?

Susie caught her mistake and quickly added, "If we hear the *Drake* is docking at the *Leggett Rose* but was also in the Pergamon system at the same time, what are we supposed to do?"

Grand frowned. If these two morons could puzzle out the presence of his copycats, then anyone paying attention could. The impersonators could undermine his pumping of the *Drake*'s share price, not to mention the entire pirate reputation exchange. He said, "Kroger, send our intel on where the real *Drake* plans to go to our copycats so they won't be spotted somewhere else at the same time."

"Yes, sir."

"Why don't you tell us, too? We can't get near these guys," Mike said.

"It's called doing your own detective work," Grand sneered. "What am I paying you for? Make some contacts, talk to people, learn what information Spranker is getting to decide which ships to raid. Think like him."

He leveled a finger at them. "They can't know you're working for me, or that I'm behind these copycat raids. The pirate exchange needs double the crews it has now. I would be very disappointed if it collapses. Got it?"

They both nodded, but neither one emanated confidence. Grand supposed that he could simply require Spranker to report his plans ahead of time, but he didn't want to push the sleazeball pirate too far.

A commotion started outside. Guards ran across the lawn, drawing their weapons. Grand motioned for Mike, half out of his seat, to sit back down. "It's a training exercise."

"Honestly, we can't follow the ship," Susie said. "They know we're tracking them. They have friends on every Underseed world, warning them, or misdirecting us."

Grand smelled the pungent bitterness of burning plastic. The odor disappeared but returned stronger a second later. While he debated figuring out what it was, Kroger shot into the room like he was rolling downhill.

"Flush," the robot said and took off down the hallway. Grand's hands turned cold. 'Flush' was their emergency word. It meant trouble. It meant run.

An explosive thump came from the front of the house. A rattle of gunfire followed.

Grand jumped out of his seat. He hurried after Kroger to a safe room behind Overhead's study. It was in the rear of the sprawling house.

Gunfire came from every side of the house now. Windows shattered.

Mike and Susie whipped out their stunguns and crouched behind the sofa. Grand was relieved they weren't following him; hopefully they would buy him time, slowing down whoever was gunning for him.

He passed a room where armored troopers were climbing through busted windows and trampling the cream-colored drapes. One of the troopers fired his weapon and something hissed by behind Grand. Too close. He ran faster.

Kroger opened the massive stone-polymer door when he reached the study. Thank hell no one was coming through these windows; they opened on an enclosed courtyard.

There was yelling in the hallway. Something about the GEC. Followed by more gunfire.

He punched a button and the massive door slammed shut. The power cut out and a brownish emergency lamp turned on. This used to be Overhead's vault, but without the shelves and crap she cluttered everything up with. It could comfortably hold an angry man and his terrified robot while the battle raged outside.

Grand didn't know what was happening out there. Bixby said the mansion's security provided a better than fifty percent chance of repelling most assaults, including not losing power. This was apparently foxing unusual. There were GEC goons in the next room, for one. Maybe Bixby didn't know security after all.

He and Kroger waited. Twenty solid minutes ticked by with occasional muffled noises coming from nearby. Finally, there was silence that stretched for a minute and then two. Grand expected Kroger to do something, but the robot remained still.

Without power, Grand couldn't see the feed from the camera outside the door. He and Kroger received nothing in here; no signal, no comlink, nothing.

"I need to speak with Bixby first thing when we get out of here," he snarled at Kroger.

Kroger backed up. "Perhaps you should talk less. To conserve oxygen."

Grand shoved a finger into Kroger's faceplate. "Screw you, you bucket of fake flesh. I should have sold you off for parts years ago."

The power turned on. The monitor inside showed Bixby and his security team waiting outside the safe room. "Flushed," Bixby said. The safe code.

Grand hit the release switch and the stone door retracted. Bixby and half a dozen guards stood there with their weapons drawn, aimed down the hallway. Grand remembered having a lot more than half a dozen guards.

THIRTY-FOUR

"WHAT THE FOX HAPPENED?" Grand asked, hands on hips.

Bixby said, "Yeah, uh, it was a GEC raid. They waited for our drill to strike. But they withdrew after the motorcade rolled up their rear."

"How did they get in here? With the security upgrades, this is what I get?!" Grand indicated the trashed furniture, the bullet-pocked walls and floor. His voice shook with anger, adrenaline, and fear. He wasn't entirely faking it, because damn it, these guys needed to understand this was completely unacceptable.

"Was anyone injured or captured?" Kroger asked.

"Um, I got two guys wounded, one was arrested. Which is not bad," Bixby said. "This was a crack GEC team. Investigator Jill Stamp led the raid."

The name sounded familiar. Stamp was a GEC cop who hassled Overhead and many limbs of her organization the last couple of years.

"Are they gone?"

Bixby said, "Yes. I—"

"—I want to talk to our guys," Grand said curtly, and left the room. Kroger and the security team rushed to follow him.

Every square meter of the house was stained, chipped, shot,

fragged, or torn. Most of the shots, Bixby said, were stun rounds which scorched the stucco walls.

The injured guards were about to be whisked to the hospital in town. One broke his leg and the other was hit in the back with grenade shrapnel. Grand told them some dirty jokes and tried to put them at ease. They chuckled weakly for his benefit, acting tough. He went around and personally thanked the remaining guards.

Meeting the men and women who had just risked death on his behalf twisted something deep in his gut. White-hot indignant rage welled up in his stomach. Not at the GEC cops conducting a legal raid. He was pissed at whoever ratted him out to the GEC. Somebody would pay dearly for this, he began muttering.

"Where's Mike and Susie?" he asked Bixby.

"They left at the first chance they could. Sir, the tactical situation here is pretty bad. You're not safe," Bixby said.

"No. Someone set us up, Bix. I need to figure out who." Grand wagged a finger at his security chief. "Don't you tell me this was a coincidence." Especially because of the situation here on Royada. Royada was Underseed but high rollers in the GEC owned places here too. They had a gentlemen's agreement: none of them would bring the GEC law to Royada, the age-old maxim about not defecating where one dines. Perhaps the changing times, such as his arrival from the Exchange, made someone believe this maxim was now null and void.

"We need to get you out of here first," Bixby said.

Kroger added, "We should listen to him."

Bixby had planned several emergency departures routes. Cars, vans and floaters would stream out of the compound, drive to different destinations and return by other routes to confuse any GEC surveillance. Bixby ordered security to execute RapDep 6. Within two minutes, Kroger, Bixby and Grand were in a utility van climbing into the mountains to the east.

"How did they break in so fast?" Grand asked Bixby.

The big man shrugged. "They disabled each of our alarm systems. This is the first time anyone has attacked the place."

"An inside job, then?"

Bixby was taken aback. "Uh, no, I mean, I doubt it. But I'll double check on that. The GEC was surprised by our firepower. They would have brought more force if they knew. If someone informed them. But they came with only enough force to take the place with the prior defenses. Those upgrades saved us."

Grand began exploring other possibilities. Maybe one of his GEC neighbors ratted him out. The Grids on Royada were not the most upstanding members of the GEC. They wanted to avoid attention and keep a low profile. They wouldn't bring the GEC here if it could be helped.

Eden was connected high up in the GEC ranks — which might protect her but not him. Or maybe, maybe she set him up. Handed over her organization to him right when the GEC was about to take it down. Invited him into the GEC's crosshairs. The speed and the ease with which she handed over the reins continued to needle him. There was an angle he wasn't privy to. Maybe this raid was the angle.

The higher up the mountain they drove, the more convinced Grand became that Overhead had betrayed him. How many others knew about the compound? Who had the most to gain by focusing Investigator Stamp on him and away from her? Stamp underestimated the force needed because Overhead wasn't aware of his latest security upgrades. Who put him in the position to be targeted? Who had conveniently disappeared? Who failed to warn him the raid was coming, despite her powerful connections in the GEC's upper echelons?

He held his tongue until they reached his ship. He didn't want their driver to overhear anything in case his loyalties were still to Overhead. The *Sluicifer* was parked under camouflage netting in a clearing.

Plan Six was to get offworld fast. Grand would miss the compound on the beach, but he couldn't wait around for the next wave of GEC commandos to attack. He would sell the repaired compound to a subsidiary in the organization and make it sell the place back to him. It was likely Investigator Stamp would search elsewhere for him, if she was actually interested in him, not Overhead.

Bixby stayed outside to pull off the netting while Grand and Kroger went aboard to prep for launch. It was such a relief to be on an

Exchange ship again. More comfortable, less sterile, more reliable. It was like going home.

Bixby boarded, eyes boggling at the interior, and belted himself into a seat. It dawned on Grand that his stalwart chief of security was leaving behind his home and family for who knew how long. "You okay, Bix? With leaving?"

Bixby gulped. "I don't like spaceflight, but yeah, my family understands. This is the job."

"Good man, I can use you. Because we have an Eden Overhead problem," he stated.

Kroger exchanged glances with Bixby. Bixby said, "Ms. Overhead?"

Grand explained his reasoning. Bixby wasn't the kind of guy to argue. These kind of chess strategies were something he didn't care about. They reminded Bixby of the complicated friendship dramas his young daughters enjoyed watching and he wanted nothing to do with them.

Grand engaged the launch sequence and the ship rose through the twilight. "We need to be ready for her. She's wants her old job back. I should hit her first. Any problem with that, Bix?"

The other man said, "I work for you, Mr. Grand, not her."

"Is it, is this a wise thing to do?" Kroger asked, piloting the ship higher.

A fireball of liquid anger exploded in Grand's gut. He didn't like being shot at, or being set up, or being questioned by a piece of shit droid. He punched Kroger in the torso. Hard. The rubbery fake flesh gave way under his hand, like it would with a human. Kroger grunted in surprise.

"You're damn right it is," Grand retorted. "Someone tried to kill me today. If you had any sense of mortality, you might understand!"

Grand rose out of his seat and pummeled the droid.

"But… what… if… you… are… wrong?" Kroger asked between blows.

Bixby half rose out of his seat to intervene.

Grand grunted and punched Kroger right out of his seat. The droid toppled, appendages flailing, and landed on the decking with a soft thud.

Grand kicked him in the rear. "Ouch," Kroger said in a flat voice.

Kroger was mocking his kick's effectiveness? Grand kicked harder. This foxboxing tin shitbox didn't care if Grand was gunned down in a hail of bullets. Some hospice droid he must have been.

Grand continued kicking furiously, and soon sweat trickled down his temple. Kroger played a metronome, in time with the blows. This only drove Grand madder.

"Enough," Bixby said quietly, putting his hand on Grand's shoulder. Grand let out a long, tortured sigh. The liquid anger inside his chest was burned off. He stalked off to his cabin while Bixby helped Kroger stand back up.

THIRTY-FIVE

JILL WASN'T surprised when Sandra ordered her to return to Andiron for a debrief on the failed Royada raid. There was a price to pay beyond having the failure noted on her performance record. What Jill feared was that Sector HQ politics would determine her next steps. She, and the investigation itself, could be sacrificial pawns.

She didn't leave Tammy wondering where her best server went. 'Jess' told Tammy she needed to leave to take care of her mom in the Way Back. Mom was hurt in a big fall and needed help recuperating. Jill made a point of proving she would return by paying the rent early on Jess' tiny sleep compartment. She had made the compartment, which was little more than a bunk with storage, cozy and homey.

Andiron had changed again since she had last been there. In orbit, security cutters escorted cargo haulers. At the spaceport, there was a new credentials check to verify her GEC citizenship. Guards were doubled at the administration building and they did a second credentials check.

She reached her apartment early in the afternoon. The bare white walls and untouched kitchen were more like a hotel room than a home. She never settled in because she was never there long enough. She opened the window to let daylight and sound from the congested streets fill the dead quiet inside.

To stay awake, she ran a refresher over anything with fabric, cleaned her dress uniform, and studied her briefing. But her mind was tired and kept wandering back to the *Leggett Rose*. Her tiny, inadequate bunk there felt more familiar, more like home. And she missed Tammy, Jon, and even Murray. It happened on every undercover assignment. She collapsed into bed at an appropriate time and woke fearing an inquisition.

Despite the additional security in the lobby, Jill found the Investigator office unchanged. Except Leonard was nowhere to be seen. The Sector VIPs must be here already, she assumed, and he was probably shining their shoes.

Sandra was in the conference room and cracked a smile at her, her version of a warm hug. Her boss' subtle emotional display put Jill on edge; when Sandra wasn't gruff, it meant something was wrong.

The something wrong was the two Sector VIPs. They came into the conference room carrying hot coffee with Leonard close behind. Leonard smirked knowingly at her until the men closed the door on him.

The two men wore GEC formal dress uniforms, something that people on Andiron only did if they were getting married or buried. Maybe they were here to bury her career.

The younger one, name tag read Thomas Hewell, wore the insignia of a marshal, second class. He stood with his chest puffed out and his knees bent slightly, ready to rocket into action.

Nigel Rutland was a senior official with a practiced smile, wavy hair turning sliver, and an immaculate uniform. He looked like the typical Sector special assistant without portfolio who lived to have his fingers in everything.

"Call me Thomas," Marshal Hewell said. "Pleased to meet you."

"I prefer Mr. Rutland," Rutland said.

Jill briefed them on the Royada raid. She explained how much time Grand spent aboard the *Leggett* and that it was not a secret when he traveled to Royada. She listed all of the intel Sector provided on the

Royada complex. Floor plans, guard patrols, wiring diagrams, and threat assessments.

She showed them a side-by-side comparison of what security the intel said the compound had versus what the raid encountered.

Jill finished by saying, "The strike team was assessing the tactical situation when the compound went on alert. The team accidentally tripped a sensor outside the compound's property line. Lieutenant Fancher decided to launch the raid. He estimated that Grand's people were off-balance and we could use surprise to counter Grand's superior numbers. I didn't object."

"So why did the raid fail?" asked Thomas.

Jill put up a schematic of the Royada compound on the wall screen. "The overhauled security systems were deployed to avoid surveillance. It was unlike anything the strike team encountered before," she said. "The passive sensor posts were on the neighbors' property, which the strike team hadn't anticipated and so accidentally tripped them. Grand doubled the guards. Half were barricaded inside the house. The other half were in blinds and bunkers tucked into the foliage and partially underground."

"Instead of two perimeter defensive systems, there were eight, including automatic turrets hidden in these shrubs here. The strike team was caught in multiple fields of fire. There was no way they could all reach the house. We did breach the house here and here, where a firefight began. We did not catch Juniper Grand. The team withdrew with five killed in action and ten wounded. The primary lesson learned is that the Exchangers are qualitatively different than us. Different perspective, different tactics, a lot more military-grade firepower."

Thomas said, "To take the house in that situation would require a siege, or a full-on military strike, backed by more extensive intel gathering. This could have been a trap for a strike force your size."

Jill was glad this Sector guy concluded this on his own so she didn't have to sell him on it. "If we extrapolate Grand's effect on the compound's security to the criminal underworld in the Underseed, we'll need substantially more resources to counter Exchangers throughout the sector. The raid was a good example of how thin our resources are in the Mix, as they're calling it."

Rutland's smile faltered. "There were concerns raised that you actually targeted Eden Overhead, not Juniper Grand." He spread his hands apologetically to imply such a suggestion was not his, necessarily. "I would like to take something to headquarters to reassure them that this is a *mistaken impression*."

"Certainly," Jill replied. "I was targeting Juniper Grand because he's a high-profile Exchanger with a history of criminal activity. My sources say he runs the largest criminal enterprise in the Mix. He may have taken over Overhead's operation, which means his reach could extend across several sectors. Or he may simply have pushed her organization aside. No one has heard from her in a long while."

Sandra cleared her throat. "I approved this raid because of the threat Grand presents. It's highly probable he's facilitating the immigration of Exchangers into the Underseed. Taking him out of play would have a positive multiplier effect across the Mix."

Rutland said to Jill, "Investigator, you and Lieutenant Fancher performed well under those circumstances. There will be repercussions for the loss of life, of course. Both of your records will include your role in this incident."

Jill nodded. It would matter more to Fancher's career than hers because strike teams were his business. But both would have blemishes on their performance records.

"It may be serendipitous that this raid failed. Sector HQ has changed its posture on stopping criminal activity against us. Going forward, with a forward-looking lens, we will no longer pursue Juniper Grand and his organization. We need to stop alienating the Underseed, given our issues with the Exchange."

Anger and relief ripped through Jill in opposing waves, nearly causing her to shiver. Relief at avoiding blame for the raid failing. Anger at dismissing Grand's threat to the GEC. She willed her body to remain very still.

"Our top priority is stopping Exchanger piracy. These attacks impact our ability to transport people and materiel. They forced us to slow shipments, assign protection along slide routes, and add layers of security at all entry points. Our settlement progress has stalled. Existing settlements are facing food and medicine shortages. Pergamon's backlog has worsened. We're losing strategic advantage in the sector."

Jill had heard about the pirates, of course. The tourist industry on *New Price Station* was cashing in on the fad. It was the ironic novelty of the Underseed. She knew that pirates brought in stolen GEC food shipments which had helped alleviate the shortages. It didn't occur to her that they were making the shortages *worse*.

She'd probably waited on pirates at Tammy's. Or passed them in the *Leggett's* crowded corridors. They probably looked more or less typical, both Exchangers and Underseeders alike. No different than Murray, Jon, Tammy, or any of thousands passing through the *Leggett*. Hunger, dislocation, and a breakdown of social order could push the marginally compliant to become criminals.

"The Underseed is swamped with GEC refugees," Jill said. "Food is in short supply and every station and world is stretched even thinner as more people come in."

If the pirates were part of an Exchange campaign to undermine the GEC, then they were exceedingly dangerous. Suddenly, she wanted to crush the pirates. Murray's paranoid fears about someone deliberately starving the Underseed didn't seem so paranoid. Crooks like Grand were a lower priority, so long as they were helping to feed the Underseed rather than starve it.

Rutland nodded. "We believe the Exchange is using piracy to undermine us. The pirates are only targeting GEC shipping. Headquarters has officially deemed these Exchanger pirates a *fundamental security threat* to the GEC."

Jill straightened her back.

"The fundamental security threat tag means that it supersedes all other priorities," Rutland said. "Protecting the GEC is why we're here. Investigator Stamp, you'll take charge of our forward anti-piracy operations. Marshal Hewell will assist you. He's a fast-rising star at Sector and has experience with search and rescue."

"I'm happy to have your help," Jill said to Thomas. "We really need an entire task force to counter a fundamental threat. Tactics, intel, logistics, training, recruitment, analysis, command. Pool resources from multiple departments, and from neighboring sectors."

Rutland replied, "Sector is working on that. But for the near term, you and Mr. Hewell are our feet in the door."

Sandra asked, "Have you considered that Juniper Grand could be behind this, too? If someone is orchestrating piracy against the GEC, it could very well be the man running the Underseed's pirate exchange."

Rutland's ever-present smile faltered again. "Moving forward, with a lens to the near term, we want you to target only the pirates. Ignore the rest, including Underseeders and those profiting from them, like Grand."

"What about Underseed criminals who have raided our warehouses from the inside?" Jill asked. She meant the ones that survived off of GEC corruption and embezzlement. The original pirates the GEC faced, in a sense.

"No, I'm afraid not."

Sandra gave Jill an apologetic wince. Jill had been only a few walls and a couple dozen meters shy of capturing Grand. His trail was cold by now and would grow colder still. She could only hope the campaign against the pirates would turn back to him.

Rutland said, "Your first task, Investigator Stamp, is to infiltrate the pirates. Determine if the Exchange is behind them. We need to recruit Exchanger vessels and crews from the Underseed. To incentivize recruitment, we can offer GEC citizenship and financial bonuses."

"GEC citizenship?" Jill asked.

"Yes," Rutland said. "We need to co-opt disgruntled Exchangers who have left the Exchange. We won't be allowing free access to our worlds and Monoliths any longer. Citizens will need to use their IDs to enter security or land on one of our planets."

Jill absently felt for the ID badge hanging from her neck. She rarely thought of it unless she was coming into the administration compound. She needed to remind herself of its new importance. "They will all need the card rather than just biometrics?"

Rutland said, "Everyone needs the card. Your face and the ID will be the new security requirements."

Thomas said, "I'll assess their tactical capabilities and assemble ships for the squadron. I've studied the entire history of this type of cargo piracy. Once we apprehend the most successful ones, they will be more reluctant. And once economic conditions stabilize on both sides, the appeal of piracy should disappear."

"Should disappear? What's your thought about this plan, Investigator?" Sandra asked. She only addressed Jill by her title when she wanted the unvarnished truth.

"This is the second major change in strategy since we reached Union," Jill said. "We already threw away years of work to focus on Grand's organization. The fundamental threat status commits us to fighting pirates. Nothing else. Is Sector HQ going to stand by that?"

Nigel Rutland kept smiling but the warmth was gone. "Marshal Hewell expressed similar reservations. Believe me, Investigator, I understand. The circumstances in this sector are changing rapidly, though. We all need to become more nimble."

Which meant they could rescind the fundamental threat designation next week. Or name more of them. She and Hewell shouldn't hold their breath on a task force forming.

"Jill, what do we know about the pirates from your perspective in the Underseed?" Sandra asked.

"They're popular," Jill said. "They're bringing in desperately needed food. Grand has created an exchange betting on which ones will be the most successful."

"Food stolen from the GEC, you mean," Thomas said.

Jill nodded. "Yes. People in the Underseed believe the GEC has abandoned them and maybe even wants them to starve. Food shortages happened long before the Exchangers showed up, but they're growing worse."

Rutland said, "My logistics people estimate that one ton of food stolen from the GEC delays another twelve tons from reaching this sector due to the extra security precautions we have to take. The pirates and the embezzlers are starving us and the Underseed."

"I haven't heard that this is deliberate. People assume the pirates are working for anyone other than the Exchange," Jill said. "Including Underseed crime syndicates. They may not understand the effect their thefts are having on overall food supplies."

Thomas said, "I've analyzed the pirate attacks. The *Starslider*-class ships easily evaded our Monoliths and security cutters. The only ships we have that can keep up with a starslider is our fast-attack patrol craft. We have requested that three for the squadron. Sector is considering our request."

"Just considering it?" Sandra asked.

Rutland waved his hand. "Once they saw the ship performance analysis, Sector became concerned about giving up these craft. The squadron will need to add starsliders and their crews. And you will have to recruit them, Investigator."

"There's a lot of Exchangers showing up in the Underseed," Jill said. "The exploration and cargo crews are at loose ends. Exploration work is down because the Underseed already settled several choice systems."

"Like Royada," Rutland said.

Sandra changed the subject. "Luckily, the Exchange publishes its exchange data in real-time. They think we may want to throw money at their reputation casino. But that means we know which explorers are hard up for work." She sent Jill two dozen dossiers of Exchange explorers who could be potential recruits. None of the names were familiar.

"Can you recruit them while maintaining your cover?" Rutland asked.

"I've done this to a couple of crime rings that were more careful than this lot," Jill said. "When I infiltrate them, I earn their trust with some good leads. And then we can trap when the squadron is ready."

"Explain how that works, please," Rutland said. "I'm intrigued."

"We'd have to give them actionable leads and let them steal some cargo. When they're trusting the leads I feed them, we set a trap. They slide in for a raid and the squadron is waiting for them."

Rutland said, "Brilliant. I'm confident you both have this well in hand. I'll be in touch about better resourcing this operation. In the mean time, do your best, Investigator Stamp, Marshal Hewell." He stood and bowed to them.

They both returned the bow and Sandra saw Rutland out of the office.

Jill knew only three things for certain. Sector was lurching back and forth at threats, but they may have finally figured out the foremost *external* security threat. Second, it occurred to her that Overhead and The Name benefited from this new assignment, and that may not be a coincidence. And third, somehow, she was indispensable enough to be given a chance to prove herself after Royada.

THIRTY-SIX

MARSHAL HEWELL DEPARTED for Union on a Monolith passing through Andiron. He had a contact who could help secure three patrol craft for the squadron.

Jill checked in with her Underseed contacts, informants, and confidants on a winding route back to the *Leggett Rose*. She made stops on *New Prince* Station, Woodshed, and Batik.

As Jess Forrester, she returned to work at Tammy's with a tale about her mother having improved but might require follow-up care visits from her.

Tammy had added two shifts to serve the growing throngs of hungry refugees packing the *Leggett*'s corridors. She gave her pal Jess regular hours on the dinner shift. Jill's mornings and afternoons were spent around the hangar bays and the Chateau, surfing the waves of conversation, rumor, and reports of Exchangers arriving in their own ships.

She didn't have to worry about seeming out of place by expressing interest in the pirates: the Underseed had become obsessed with them. Murray told everyone who would listen that pirates made passes at her every time they bought one of her flashier and pricier scarves. The pirate mania was fueled in part by the *Alan Glown Show*, now the top talk show in the Mix. Alan covered each new pirate raid and exploit, and his light-hearted interviews with victims became the highest rated entertainment in the Mix.

Speculating on Grand's pirate exchange was all the rage in the Chateau. The exchange's pirate crews were ranked by the monetary value of goods they had stolen, but investors also rewarded the pirates for style and outlandishness. The *Drake* crew continued to lead the exchange. Their latest stunt was to humiliate a GEC gossip columnist who questioned their manhood by shipping a transparent box of sex toys to his work cubicle.

Every day, Jill slipped past the con artists at the Chateau's door to join the crowd watching the pirate exchange board on a giant overhead screen. She could have looked at it on her personal screen, but the scrum of bettors, spectators, brokers, and on-lookers were a juicy source of piracy gossip and rumor. The loot statistics removed any remaining doubts she had about the pirates posing a fundamental security threat. The pirates were cleaning up, and the highest priced item they were stealing was food rations.

"Every half-assed thief with a shuttle is trying to outdo these Exchangers," said one bettor talking to a couple. "The number of pirate crews on the exchange quadrupled in the last month, Mike and Susie. Every Exchanger with a slide drive thinks they can make a fortune."

It was true. Two more of Jill's potential recruits had joined the pirate exchange since she returned to the *Rose*, taking their starsliders with them.

"Let me see if I understand this," Mike said. "We buy shares in a pirate crew. They don't get the money, the person who sells us the shares does. How do they get paid?"

The broker said, "They get a dividend each month that equals a small percent of the total value of all of their shares. Paid by the exchange itself. The more their shares go up, the more they get paid. When the share price goes up, you and Susie here can sell your shares to someone else and the profit is the difference between your sell and buy prices."

The woman, Susie, asked, "What if they get caught?"

"Their share price drops to zero and they are de-listed from the exchange. And the investors lose their investment. You need steady nerves and lots of smarts to make money here. You two are a lot smarter than people I've helped make a killing here. You've been out there unlike these fools. You have experience to gauge the risks."

"I don't know if we should bet on any Exchangers, honey," Susie said to Mike. "They're reckless."

Mike, watched the share prices fluctuate, itching to jump into the action. "Is there a way to buy into all of them for a little bit? Hedge our bets?"

"Smart man, Mike. I'm working on just such an index. Give me a little more time and I'll set you up."

Jill's comlink buzzed with a new message in her hip pocket.

"If there was some way to know where the pirates would strike next, I would feel a lot more comfortable," Mike said. "These fluctuating prices, it's hard to tell whether any of them are a good buy or not. Is there some way to know where the pirates generally operate? Do they have their preferred areas of the sector?"

The broker shook his head. "There's lots of rumors around here, but nothing about this ship will strike in this place at that time. Only the pirates know that. And Grand won't let invest in the exchange."

"I don't know, honey, we should just keep an eye on things," Susie said. "Think about it more." She put her arm through Mike's and tugged him away.

"You heard the boss. I'll be in touch," Mike said over his shoulder.

"Excuse me," Jill said to the broker. "Do you think the shares will drop because the GEC is only letting citizens into GEC facilities?"

The broker turned and looked at her. "Could be. It's not like pirates try to slip past a badge check. Are you looking to invest, miss? My name is Barnsy."

Jill laughed. "I'm a broke server, Barnsy. I'm worried that these guys who won't keep us fed if they find something to steal that pays better. Rumor is that these guys are desperate for bigger payoffs and they'll jump on the next big commodity."

"Kilo for kilo, food is the highest priced item in this whole sector right now," the broker said, pointing at the loot statistics on the board.

She started to leave. "I hope so. Because we can't eat precious metals and gems. They only thing worth more than that out here are GEC ID badges." Only gems and precious metals were listed on the exchange's loot statistics. She kept walking away and was satisfied to see the broker squint at the board, his lips mouthing 'ID badges.'

She checked the message on her comlink. Her confidential informant in the Pinestar system wrote that she had a potential recruit dock his starslider at the *Leggett Rose* to meet her. Jill stopped by her hovel, swapped her Jess Forrester disguise for a close enough facsimile of Murray.

This potential recruit was the highest-rated one she and Hewell had on their list. An Exchanger named Charles Lemonne who had a starslider and an interest in the GEC. Thomas Hewell compiled a dossier on Lemonne that found the Exchange explorer was driven, competent, and highly compliant with authority. On the other hand, he was difficult, touchy, and gruff, an acerbic complainer who didn't tolerate other people. But, he was vocal in his dislike of the Exchange, the Underseed, and Barry Spranker.

Jill contacted Lemonne through a burner account and arranged a meeting aboard his starslider that night. At night, the crowds in the corridors dropped considerably and her version of Murray could slip aboard his ship while the real Murray was asleep.

She had seen pictures and vids of starsliders, but never one up close. The *Charles* was fifty meters long and twenty meters wide. The hull's polished white porcelain was covered in elaborate black vines that stretched and curled over the entire ship.

Lemonne was a thin, slouchy man, with black curly hair framing a long, pinched face. He dressed in the Exchanger version of formal wear, a tailor's fever dream of combining a jumpsuit with a tuxedo with tails.

"Captain Lemonne?" Jill was careful to pronounce it 'lay-moan' rather than 'lemon.' Her Pinestar informant had learned the hard way that mispronouncing his name was a sore point with him.

He gave a stiff nod of greeting, which she returned. "Ma'am. My pleasure. Please, come aboard."

"You fly this thing all by yourself?" she asked, walking aboard. GEC regulations required a certain crew complement based on the ship type plus redundancies. A one-man ship was unheard of.

Lemonne followed her up the boarding ramp and closed it. "I own a quartet of droids I custom-programmed to streamline operations. I bought out my partners years ago because of, to put it politely, managerial differences. Please take off your er, muddy boots, when you get inside."

Growing up on a series of GEC stations meant Jill had seen the interior of every GEC spacecraft. Every interior was metal and metallic polymer bulkheads, painted in neutral colors, with bright overhead lighting, sparse furnishings, and the ever-present hum of the ventilation.

The *Charles'* interior was something out of a cozy fairy tale. It was lit with soft, indirect light. Plants, shrubs, and lichen covered every bulkhead. Creeper vines sparkling with dull orange fireflies wrapped around coral support beams. The sound of water gurgling came from multiple directions but she couldn't any water. Her bare feet sank into spongy moss carpeting the slightly uneven decking. The air was hot, moist, and rich with the pungent scents of a greenhouse.

The warm air prickled her nose. "Nice ship," she said. Her sinuses were filling up; she was allergic to something onboard.

A droid swung towards them on the curving overhead coral beams. Twelve bamboo tentacles radiated from a small spherical body made of dark wood. At the center of the body a large eyeball fixed on Jill without blinking.

"This is my first officer and engineer, Jenkins."

Jenkins said in a humanlike voice, "Welcome aboard." It resumed swinging aft, its long arms holding on to the support beams.

"Did you grow it?" Jill whispered when it was out of earshot. "Is that thing alive?"

"Oh no no. Droiding is a whole profession unto itself in the

Exchange. It's a cybernetic being constructed from biological materials."

The tour began in the bow, in a small engine room where Jenkins worked on the slide drive. Lemonne called the bridge 'the kick'. The closest thing to a seat in the kick was Jacob, a navigation droid that rolled along on treads and resembled a high-backed captain's chair.

The crew quarters each contained private bunks, a common bathroom, and a tiny galley with seating for four. One of the bunks was a med bay run by Genny, the medical droid. Genny had powerful hydraulic lifts for limbs and a human-shaped head. Her white tile chest cavity bristled with an array of health sensors and medical equipment.

She studied Jill for a moment. The medical droid could probably see right through the added padding, the wig, and the facial prosthetics. It probably noticed Jill's heart starting to hammer in her chest. Genny reached in a side compartment and offered her a pill. "This antihistamine will help. Your immune system is not used to the ship's pollen."

Jill took the pill.

"Aren't you warm?" Genny asked Jill.

"I'm used to much colder than this. I'll be fine," Jill said.

"Please, let me make you a drink," Lemonne said from the galley. He went to work with a pitcher and several pieces of fruit. "How do you like the ship?"

She gawked at the strange Exchanger technology. Where the GEC used metal and plastics for bulkheads and console interfaces, the Exchange used living biofiber, wood, and stone-like coral. The electronics looked the same to her, but it was odd to see viewscreens encased in pink and yellow coral. "Never been inside an Exchanger ship," Jill rasped.

Lemonne offered her a cup of fresh-squeezed fruit juice. It was warmer than room temperature, yellow, with a thick, pulpy texture. She sipped it and discovered a sweet taste with a tart bite on the end. "Delicious. You could sell this. Make yourself some extra cash."

Lemonne smiled proudly. "The starslider's superiority stems from more advanced design than your GEC engineers can achieve. It's biological interior creates a symbiotic, mutually-life-supporting relationship with the crew." He gestured at the bulkhead. "The ceramic exterior provides comprehensive cosmic shielding. And my own conscientious attention to detail results in top-level performance."

"You weren't rated at the top of the exploration exchange though, were ya?" she said in the old woman's scratchy voice.

"Your reputation precedes you, Ms. Murray. I am a cutting-edge explorer in the Exchange," he said with a flourish. "My specialty is optimizing routes my sloppier, attention-stealing competitors cobbled together in haste." He snorted. "Exchanges are popularity contests and not based on merit. They are whipsawed by impatient investors and sleazy marketing. Route optimization pays better, but it's not as glamorous."

"Pretty honest of ya there." Jill said. "The GEC only approves of properly-mapped routes or the cartographers get downgraded. I grew up on frontier stations. Saw several cartogs wash out."

She said, "I'm reaching out to you, Mr. Lemonne, because the GEC is recruiting fast Exchanger ships to catch pirates. They're especially interested in starslider crews who wouldn't hesitate to apprehend fellow Exchangers."

He said with disgust, "These 'pirates' are the same idiots who ignored the rules, for years, in the Exchange. They don't respect authority, other people, or themselves."

Jill said, "We'd probably classify them as narcissists with sociopathic tendencies and opposition defiance disorder. I'd love to hear, how exactly the *Drake* wronged ya?"

He shook his fist. "They stomped on decency and dignity like they hated the very concept! The rest of us were supposed to laugh off a 'prank' that stranded our ships in deep space. They were dreadful gloaters when they won a milestone reward. Humiliating treatment, just foxing humiliating. Whenever I complained, the authorities accused me of being jealous!"

The fastest way to a griper's heart was through commiseration. Jill said, "Captain, I'd like to offer you a chance for some payback. Old fashioned revenge. These pirates are treating the entire GEC like they treated you."

"And in return?"

"You'll be rewarded, beyond just financial compensation. GEC will upgrade your ship, pay you for your service, and give something even more valuable: GEC citizenship." She flashed a temporary ID badge. "The GEC has closed its borders in the Mix to non-citizens. The Way Back sectors are where the true GEC is: orderly, civilized societies stretching all the way back to Earth. Not like this chaotic mess."

He rubbed his chin. "Why me? Why my ship, in particular?"

Jill indicated the ship around her. "We need your ship, its speed, and your experience. That is, if you don't mind chasing down Exchangers."

He waved away her concern. "I would relish it."

She produced a contract for Lemonne and his ship. Citizenship was conferred by dint of signing the contract, because GEC procurement had no mechanism in place to contract with non-citizens.

Jill said, "You'll be joining a GEC anti-piracy task force. Bound by operational secrets, you understand. You'll be part of an organization and be expected to follow orders. Violation of those rules will not only forfeit your citizenship but land you in permanent detention."

He said, "Yes, yes, absolutely." He signed and said, "The *Charles* needs more than passports and promises. What upgrades did they have in mind?"

"Light weaponry and military-grade sensors," Jill replied, "Our shipboard weapon systems are limited. Mostly converted mining beams that overload a ship's electronics and disable it. Magnapoons were originally meant for search and rescue but can grab a metallic hull at close range. We're working on a harpoon that can embed itself in nonmetallic Exchanger hulls."

Lemonne snarled. "I can't wait to haul in that rat bastard Spranker. Is the *Drake* going to be our first target?"

Jill replied, "Possibly. Can this ship overtake the *Drake* in open space?"

Lemonne sneered. "This ship is ten years newer and better maintained. It's sublight speed is rated twenty percent faster."

"How did they beat you then?"

"We never raced in sublight. Mapping new routes is a scattershot exercise. Send probes in a dozen directions and maybe one is a safe route segment. If not, you try another dozen. It's luck."

"Got it. This GEC squadron will remove the *Drake*'s luck from the equation." Jill pocketed the signed screen. "Welcome to the GEC, Mr. Lemonne. Wrap up any business you have in the Underseed. Marshal Hewell will be in touch with further instructions. Here's the temporary GEC ID. You can get a permanent one from the Marshal. It is probably worth as much as your ship. Guard it carefully." She stood up with a grunt. "I should be getting back. Gotta grab my spot in the bazaar early in the morning."

"Thank you," he said. He walked her to the ship's hatch and extended the boarding ramp.

"Your first operational secret to keep is that I work for the GEC. Now that we're on the same team and all."

He shook his head. "I doubt anyone would believe me if I told them. Your reputation for sharing all your secrets must be excellent cover."

Jill smiled. "Trick of the trade. There are eyes and ears everywhere, down at the stalls and up here in the hangars."

"I see. You don't want word to spread that you have been visiting Exchanger ships."

"You got it. My business depends on gossip flying faster than light. But not gossip *about* me. People don't really want my shitty second-hand clothes. They want to hear what I've heard, with some extra embellishment. Now, if you visit my stall, I'll act like we never met. So don't expect a discount on account of this meeting. Understand? I knew you would. Good night then."

She limped out of the hangar.

THIRTY-SEVEN

BARRY AWOKE in his bunk from a recurring dream about yelling at Stan and fruitlessly searching the *Shogura* for the hidden Union reward. The dream left a bitter taste of disappointment in his mouth. Or maybe it was the triskey from last night, when he drank himself blotto.

The hangover settled into his bones like an old friend dropping by. The type who borrows money and never pays it back. He and the guys had a hell of a good time on the *New Prince*. The second they arrived the Underseed crowd treated the *Drake* crew like touring rock stars. Things got too raucous even for Barry, which was saying something.

New Prince's locals were thrilled to buy up a portion of *Drake*'s ID card loot. Jasmine had sold him a hot tip that GEC IDs would be selling for more than food now that the GEC had barred outsiders. The New Princers heard the *Drake* knocked over the courier and were bringing legit GEC IDs to the masses. With the stolen IDs, Underseed denizens could go home again. Everyone wanted to buy a round of triskey for the *Drake* crew. With the *Drake*'s share price climbing on the pirate exchange, some of their well-wishers were also investors or bettors on their investors.

Some foxhole jacked up the gravity, Barry thought. *If Flank wants a better workout, he should buy heavier weights.* He tried to sit up. *Fox me.*

He was surprised to find himself on the booth seat in the *Drake's* galley. He remembered stumbling home from the party last night; he must have passed out here, evidently. He needed something to flush his gums of triskey aftertaste.

Someone was rummaging in the galley across from the booth. Barry caught a glimpse of an attractive ass. The only other asses on this crate belonged to his two ugly male friends. Was he still drunk? Did someone spike the triskey? The booze came off a GEC supply convoy bound for Andiron. He didn't remember ever being so sloshed that Flank or Tongue became physically attractive.

But this ass was indeed a woman's. He briefly wondered if his hangover had erased memories of taking someone home. Or hiring a female crewer who wasn't modest. Uh, no.

"Can I help you?" he mumbled.

The woman whipped around, trying to pull her shirt down over her thighs. It only made her nipples protrude from the fabric. If Barry's mind wasn't a dyslexic Greek chorus slurring its way through a Gregorian chant, he might appreciate it.

"It's okay," Barry said. "I'm relieved a rear end so nice doesn't belong to one of my best friends."

She was on the tall side, dark haired everywhere and growing very, very angry.

Maybe she'd stayed with him last night? No, no, he'd remember it. How long had it been since someone slept with him? Ugh.

"Jess Forrester," she said defensively.

"Hi. I'm Barry Spranker, supposed to be captain of the *Drake*." The galley spun around him, so he plopped down. "Argh. But if I were captain, my crew would tell me about visitors boarding the ship. Sorry, I'm usually ruder than this. Let me get you a robe so you can get comfortable while I go on a rant."

"Jorge Lucas on a stick, Bare, you're too fried to rant," Flank said, walking in. He tossed a towel at the girl. "Morning, Jess."

"Thank you, Flank."

Barry was totally lost. Was she with Flank? Something about how they acted suggested no. "Was everyone but me aware she was aboard?"

"I'm sure Tongue would have said something," Jess ventured.

Tongue.

"I'd remember if he did," he squinted at Flank. "Wouldn't I?"

Flank shrugged.

"Are you a paying passenger, by chance?" Barry asked.

"She helped us on the ID run," Flank said, reaching in the fridge for the juice. He emptied the carton. "She's Tongue's contact. She got the courier's delivery schedule. I guess Tongue, ah, returned the favor."

She scowled at him.

Fox it, Barry was still thirsty, but the fridge was about a light klick away. He slumped against the booth. "So why are you aboard our ship?"

"My ship," Flank said with a growl.

"I've been on the run, kind of," Jess said guardedly.

Barry winced. "You're about to tell me a whole story now, aren't you?" He wasn't ready for story time. If he managed to stumble to his bunk last night, he could've avoided all of this.

"You know a Grid cop named Stamp?" Jess asked.

"Investigator out of Andiron. Ballbreaker, yeah," Barry replied.

Jess smiled. "She took down Eden Overhead, Murray said. She's hunting pirates. Did you know about this?"

Flank and Barry exchanged clueless glances.

"Rumor was, she wanted Eden to expose every Exchanger operating in the Underseed. Jasmine said that Stamp's about to tear up the Underseed for pirates. Probably only a matter of time before she shows up on the *Leggett Rose*. Jasmine suggested that anyone who hangs out at the pirate bars should get scarce. And if everyone on the *Leggett* has seen me with Jon, I mean Tongue—"

"—You're a pirate groupie, be proud—" Flank interjected.

Jess smiled sheepishly but continued anyway, "I had to leave. Not going to rot in some penitentiary after what I've been through. I hope you guys don't plan to either."

"How long have you and Tongue been together?" Barry asked. It seemed like Tongue should have mentioned this news in conversation. Normally there weren't any secrets among three men living hip to hip in a narrow ceramic terrarium.

"A while," Jess replied with a shy smile. It reminded him that she was wearing nothing but a short t-shirt. "Tongue told me to grab the next shuttle to *New Prince.*"

Barry blinked. He believed he could smell a con across vacuum, and she didn't worry him. She really did like Tongue. The Underseed was full of Way Backers like her who the GEC shoved around until they developed a weary, fatalistic worldview. They were like Exchangers, minus the ambitious optimism and self-confidence.

Her story checked out, too. There had been furtive raids on stations by armed bands purporting to act under Stamp's authority. GEC fast attack craft had begun boarding Underseed transports, searching for contraband. There was talk of a GEC squadron searching for pirates. Another wrinkle in paying off Grand made Barry's head throb.

He had been on such a high when they docked at *New Prince.* The locals assumed the *Drake* crew were as thrilled as they were to have access to legitimate GEC IDs. But none of the three of them cared about visiting a GEC world. That's not why the guys were jazzed.

Flank sold out of the portion of ID cards they reserved for *New Prince.* He handsold the cards, right at the bottom of the boarding ramp. Such a historic haul of high-priced ID cards boosted them on the exchange. Put a nice dent in what they owed Grand. That dent was why Barry let himself get truly, celebratorily drunk for the first time since Union.

Barry squinted at Jess. "How did you get the courier routes? They're secret. The corporation randomizes the schedule." He didn't mention that he could have bought the info from Jasmine, but she wanted too much.

"I work at a diner on *Leggett.* People tell me everything, especially if I slip them an extra slice of instapizza. There are plenty of mechanics and parts suppliers stuck in the GEC who looking to sell info to escape to the Underseed. You think Pergamon is bad? You should see the Way Back; it's a lot worse."

Barry said, "I'm not fond of having company aboard."

"Uh, morning," Tongue said, walking into the galley. He was wearing sagging underwear, exposing his paunch. "What's going on?" He slipped an arm around Jess' waist.

"Your captain wants to toss me out the airlock," Jess said.

"Flank drank the rest of the juice," Barry said miserably.

Tongue's shoulders sagged in disappointment. "Damn it man, you know we want juice in the morning."

"Quicker ship grabs the system," Flank retorted.

Tongue asked Barry, "What's your problem with her?"

"She's pretty, but she's a security risk," Barry said.

"You know, Bare? Don't be an asshole. She's a Grid, sure, but she's been in the Underseed like, a long time. She's clean. I've known her for months. So lay off, she's really freaked out."

"I came to warn you guys," Jess said. "I've told Tongue you guys need to lay low for a while. I'm worried."

"Aw, isn't love sweet?" Flank cracked.

Tongue ignored him. "Baby, let's not get into this. We're fine. We're professionals. We have financial obligations."

Jess looked distraught. "But things are getting worse out there. You'll have a harder and harder time. Your luck won't continue forever."

"She's right," Barry said. "There are more checkpoints, security procedures, and the pirate exchange keeps pushing us to be more bold. We need to pay Grand off and retire."

"More hauls like those ID cards and we could do that," Tongue said.

"And do what?" Flank asked. "We're infamous criminals in the GEC and in the Exchange. Hide in the Underseed? Hide in the Mix? For the rest of our lives?"

"What will any of us do?" Jess asked. "So much is changing, so fast. But it's still worth it to stay out of prison, and to not get killed." Her eyes misted. Tongue pulled her close but she hurried out of the galley.

They let her go — three pirates, no snappy comebacks.

"You really serious about her?" Flank asked Tongue.

"I mean, yeah. But I'm not bailing on you guys."

"New ship policy: no more surprise guests," Barry stated. "It's probably not safe for her to be on board. She needs to go somewhere safe, if you're that into her."

The *Drake* was enroute to the Hydrangea system, their last stop on the ID card sales tour. There was a small Underseed mining base on an airless moon who had cash-flush miners desperate for a visit home.

Tongue said, "She wants to talk to me about, you know, our future. What should I tell her?"

"If we're going out of this business, we're going out on top," Flank said sharply. "We need to go big. Pay off Grand, become legends, then disappear."

"I kind of figured we'd be cornered and rot in prison," Barry said. He filled a glass of water and shuffled towards the kick. The tacky moss massaged his bare feet. "Flank, figure out how to escape Stamp's squadron. Tongue, deal with Jess and for fox sake don't let her disinfect the ship's flora. She's a Grid, she probably doesn't understand that these smells are a good thing. I'll be in the kick, trying to remember how to produce saliva."

THIRTY-EIGHT

"WHY ISN'T THE COMLINK WORKING?" Grand asked. He was at the dining room table, overlooking Royada's ocean. "I can't a get a damn call out. Kroger? Hey! Kroger!" The droid was on its way out of the dining room.

"Yes, sir," said the droid.

"Did you hear me? I can't call out. Can you?"

"There is no net access," Kroger replied. The droid waited for his reply. When there wasn't any, he rolled away.

Damn construction work. Ever since the raid, there'd been construction crews in every corner of the compound. These crews replaced the safe room, upgraded the perimeter sensors, and patched the bullet holes in the walls.

He considered abandoning the compound and building his own compound somewhere Eden and the GEC didn't know about. But he was attached to this place. And already invested a lot in it. He strolled the beach every night, and sometimes during the day, too, when the clattering and banging of the construction workers irritated him. He was friendly with the neighbors: he was settled. And he could do business from anywhere, provided he could get a damn signal.

He could *feel* business getting screwed up because no one could message him. The witless bounty hunters tracking the *Drake* didn't make their required check in yesterday. Revenue reports from the Andiron operations were due today. His old Exchange associates needed his help slipping past Union. And his GEC underlings were digging into business opportunities in the Way Back sectors.

Bixby sat next to him, eating a mango. A family guy, low-key, dependable, unassuming, no drama. Grand liked him. He was the obvious choice for a right hand.

"Bix, can you run next door and ask if the Hudsons lost their signal, too? And pay attention while you're out there."

Bixby wiped his hands and stood. "What should I bring them?"

Grand smiled. If he had Bixby's calm, he'd nap all day. He needed low-level anxiety to keep him wired, keep him at the top of his game. "Nothing. Invite them over for dinner, once the construction is done."

In his spare moments, Grand schemed. He couldn't help himself. It usually paid off because he could act quickly when things were cruising again. His spare moments equaled the number of competent underlings answering to him. More of his underlings now resembled Bixby. He had weeded out the incompetent, the obstinate, and the unwilling from his predecessor's regime. Most of Eden's nervous twits may make their quarterly numbers, but they could never figure out how to double them.

The GEC's situation in tha three sectors that made up the Mix was foxed. It had barely reached Union and was woefully unprepared to settle the sector. It would be months before the it could match the Exchange's frenetic pace of exploration and settlement, if it ever could. That created an opening for the Underseed, and Grand's people, to move in.

Kroger had suggested the idea of returning to the Exchange. The notion held little interest for him. For one, there was plenty of criminal competition back there. And he had left behind plenty of enemies.

The Mix was fertile ground to operate in only in the short term. How the GEC and Exchange may co-exist in the Mix made made his organization's revenue projections look all screwy with uncertainty. There was talk of these two galaxy-spanning juggernauts coming to blows, but he couldn't bet on war, peace, or something in between. If the Mix did erupt into war, his organization could profit immensely in the confusion and chaos. But a muddled peace that allowed the Underseed to fill the gap between the two was even better..

Either way, the under-developed sectors between the Mix and the GEC's Way Back, roughly sectors 183 through 186, was riper territory for expansion. The GEC presence was minimal since the corporation dropped everything to scurry past them sector 180 and Union. It was now rushing people and equipment into the Mix sectors from the Way Back.

The situation offered innumerable opportunities for an Exchange criminal bastard like him. He would have a competitive advantage. Eden Overhead was the Underseed's de facto leader until he showed up. Sure, maybe she tried using him as bait for the Grid cops, but it backfired.

He had doubled the size of her enterprise by expanding to the Exchanger settlements popping up in the Mix. He jacked up profit margins on the non-food businesses. He was bringing reputation exchanges to an Underseed population desperate for entertainment and social advancement.

Maybe he could shovel some exploratory work to Spranker and other itinerant Exchanger crews. Make them scout out his business opportunities beyond the Mix. The most important thing in the settlement game was to be first. Those who were first could control the illicit markets and be a folk hero by feeding the hungry. He needed his organization to become the dominating criminal institution from the Mix to the Way Back, to scare off the Exchange crime bosses who would take him down otherwise.

Hell, with her resources, maybe Overhead bankrolled the Underseed herself. Maybe he should found his own settlements between the Mix and the Way Back, an Under-Underseed. If he played his cards right, with a fleet of former Exchange starsliders, he could scout the best planets, the best slide routes, and essentially control his own section of the galaxy.

But first, he needed to accrue capital fast. Every starslider he sent out of the Mix was one less that would be ripping off GEC shipping and feeding him a piece of the proceeds. He needed to get this pirate reputation exchange firmly established. Then let the betting on professional role-playing games, skee-ball and other little ventures shower him with capital.

Kroger rolled into the dining room, his treads slapping the floor. The spare moment was over and Grand resigned himself to dealing with whatever nonsense the droid was unable to handle.

"You have a visitor," Kroger said. "Eden Overhead."

THIRTY-NINE

WHEN GRAND WAS COMFORTABLY ENSCONCED in his office chair he told Kroger to bring in Overhead. He tried to forget his anger at her for setting him up. This office was one of the few rooms in the Royada estate not pock-marked with bullet holes. It effused a quiet serenity he hoped to tap into.

"Ms. Overhead," Grand said. "Please excuse the construction. We were raided by the GEC. Or maybe you already knew that."

"I learned of it afterwards. And I'm sorry it happened." She took a seat. "You can't believe I'd set you up. My god, I don't have any reason to, for one thing. Plus, I don't control Jill Stamp or Sector HQ." She picked up a skee ball from his desk. "You changed the décor." The skee ball was a memento from Carruthers back on Pergamon. She didn't seem displeased.

Grand had auctioned off her personal items a week after moving in. Kroger said the collection fetched a good price, considering it was mass-produced GEC trinkets.

"Never spend money on decorations: you accept gifts from those you've helped out," Grand said. "It keeps costs down."

"Is this an Exchange business practice?" She asked, amused.

"Gangster 101. A guy named Pinhole showed me how much you can amass without stealing or buying, just by cashing in on goodwill."

"Will Pinhole be a competitor at some point?"

"Naw, he died in a freak deli sandwich incident twenty years ago," Grand replied.

"Oh." She changed the subject. "Juniper, I am not here to take back the organization. I have too many other things to attend to. You're better at running it than I ever was, anyway. You can walk away, too. It's your choice."

Bixby appeared in the doorway, zapper at the ready. Grand signaled him to wait. "You understand my suspicion, right Eden? You installed me, a total stranger from a strange society, to run your baby. That made me a prime target for law enforcement. And the GEC comes down on me. Now that the dust settles, you reappear. Excellent timing to take it back."

She didn't lose a shred of poise. "I had other business that required a low profile. I suspected there might be a plot against me. But the raid ended up hurting the Investigators, not you. Stamp failed miserably and her superiors have now 'refocused' her and the other Investigators away from this organization and both of us."

She may be right. Stamp's interference in his businesses had disappeared. Even if she arranged for Stamp to get her wrist slapped, he wasn't going to dredge up a thank you.

Eden raised a finger. "But you'll still get wiped out by the GEC because you're an outsider," she said. "Anti-Exchanger feelings are growing in GEC exec circles. That's why they closed their borders to non-citizens. The piracy you're sponsoring helped push them to it. I was never so overt in taking on the GEC."

"The organization's balance sheet is healthier now," Grand retorted.

"Yes, but your piracy exchange has raised your threat profile. I can offer some help there, by the way."

"Oh really? I'm so intrigued to hear this."

She greeted his sarcasm with a thin smile. "I have a business proposition for you. The GEC is greatly concerned about Exchanger expansion in the Mix. The Exchange is expanding faster than the GEC. The more tensions rise between the GEC and the Exchange, the bigger the target on you. The GEC believes you're working for the Exchange."

Grand chuckled at the idea he would kowtow to the Exchange's pathetic bureaucrats. "The Exchange government, to the extent there is one, thinks I am a criminal and a thief," he retorted.

"Appearances, Juniper, are hard to deny, especially when people are scared, suspicious and prone to miscommunicate. And the top people in the GEC are very scared by what's happening in the Mix. Especially with these pirates. They see Exchanger plots everywhere."

Grand chuckled.

"But I have something which can clear your name, Juniper, end the piracy threat, and help maintain the peace between the GEC and the Exchange. You can probably profit off it quite well, too."

She produced a chip and connected it to his office monitor. It was a map of Sectors 180 to 183. The GEC systems leading up to the Mix were bright yellow lights snaking along the coreward boundary of the Galactic Habitable Ring. The Underseed systems were green dots peppering the center of the Ring.

There was a solitary blinking yellow system on the outer edge of the Ring. It was thousands of light years from anything else. She pointed to it. "That is the Endor system."

"Bullshit." He shook his head. When she didn't respond, he crossed his arms. "Do you take me for a gullible religious twit?"

"It's not the name that matters, it's what's there. These coordinates are a closely-held GEC secret. I've talked to high-level GEC officials who've seen what's there."

She zoomed in on the Endor system and pointed out a thin line of beacons dotting a zig zag path from the GEC main line route. "There's only one slide route in. You send the *Drake* there and they'll be captured."

"Captured? They're at the top of the pirate exchange. I'm making a foxton off of them in a lot of different ways. Why the hell would I want them captured?"

Eden raised an eyebrow. Ah, she knew his history with them. "I'm sure you can find a way to profit from their capture. You have bigger plans than just ripping off pirates forever, don't you?"

He definitely did. And he had zero concerns about betting against the *Drake*'s share price, if he knew he was sending them into a trap. "What's out there? Why would these guys drop everything else and go there?"

"The system has several GEC shipyards. Dozens of ships are finished with upgraded slide drives to better compete with Exchange vessels. They are ripe for the harvesting."

Grand motioned for Kroger to vet the video she was showing, to look for signs of editing or tampering. Kroger nodded at him. The video appeared legit.

"Your pirates need bigger, more outlandish prizes to keep their investors happy, right? They'll be crawling over each other to raid Endor."

Rumors swirled about the top pirates planning heists so extreme and lucrative that their share prices bubbled upward in anticipation. Eden understood the pirate exchange pretty well for a Grid.

Grand regarded her coolly. "Who are you, exactly?"

She smiled. "A faithful GEC employee employing unofficial means to advance the good of the Corporation."

"Are you foxing with me? I can't trust you. Can you guarantee that the GEC will leave me be if I hand it the *Drake*?"

She shook her head. "No. Occasionally the more repressive faction in the GEC get their way. They don't like me at all and I have no influence over them. A guarantee from me would be worthless."

He had hit a sore subject. Those repressive elements must be the ones who botched the raid on his home. He rubbed his chin. He didn't want to check over his shoulder every minute. Eden was too much of a player, a double agent, to trust. But she was also a player without the juice, or interest, to protect him. And no doubt she had loyalists lurking in the organization, wanting to help her. Her reappearance would only strain their loyalty to him.

He motioned to Bixby. The big guy strode into the office and zapped

Overhead. He caught her before her head hit the desk. He lowered her gently to the thick rug.

"Put her on a refugee transport sliding toward Pergamon. No ID, no money, nothing." Pergamon was a prison in every aspect but name. Escape was slim to impossible thanks to the GEC's decades of practice keeping people trapped on the surface and in orbit.

Bixby asked, "You sure you want to leave her alive?"

Grand said, "Effective gangsters never kill. It's counterproductive. Bad for business. Better to shunt threats to less damaging walks of life." He said to Kroger, "Inject her with GBS though. Feels worse than Malaria Twelve. It'll Keep her down and out for a while."

FORTY

"WHAT'S YOUR BIGGEST HAUL BEEN?"

Barry splashed in the clear aqua surf, pointedly ignoring the question of the scantily-clad woman. Her name was Sharon. He figured she and the other woman swimming nearby were testing him. They wanted details about the *Drake*'s travels and adventures. He didn't trust either of them.

Barry flipped onto his back and let the waves of Margarita's largest ocean toss him around. He pondered how far these women may be willing to go to wring secrets out of him. Would it be worth it? Nah, he decided, gazing up at the brighter bits of the Waterfall Nebula, visible through the blue sky. He had to stay focused on the gig.

"Barry Spranker, are you trying to ignore me?" Sharon asked, snuggling up to him and pushing him underwater.

Her hand brushed against his crotch. "Hey now, *hey*," Barry said.

"Is this bothering you?"

He chuckled. "No. Yes. I mean, why can't you dial it down a smidge, like Peggy over there?"

Peggy was nude, lazily paddling backwards in a backstroke.

"It's not every day a living legend visits us," Sharon said with false meekness.

"Okay ladies, time to take a break," he announced, wading toward shore. Peggy pivoted and swam his way.

Further up the beach, Flank jogged alone, his biceps pumping away with weights in both hands. He'd driven off the pirate groupies, or whoever they were, hours ago. An example Barry should follow — he really should. Flank nodded at him and continued down the beach.

Barry didn't know where Tongue was. Probably meditating in the verdant rainforest encroaching on the beach. If anyone would spill secrets, it was Tongue. Both guys had told the locals to come bother him rather than them. Barry relished the attention.

The planet's ruling committee, which consisted of a dozen suntanned seniors who lived in grass huts at the end of the beach, told Barry to hang loose while they debated his request. They were taking their time and Barry sensed he wouldn't hear from them until tomorrow.

Was the council actually deliberating or were they waiting for Peggy or Sharon to pry secrets out of him? The residents prized secrecy, since even in the Underseed almost no one knew about their barely settled planet. He couldn't blame them: the planet was an unknown gem. It was in a system close to nebula and its solar system was hard to see from a distance. Within a couple of slides of here were the few GEC systems in Sector 181. It was not listed on Underseed slide route maps.

Tongue had only found it because they searched for a habitable planet to hide on if things went bad. He poked around the edges of the nebula hoping for a planetoid or asteroid the ship could hide on for a few days of laying low. Even Flank admitted that there would be times they needed to stay off the slide routes.

In the past month, the *Drake* had turned its first ID shipment theft into a booming business. A shipment of blank GEC IDs was currently the hottest item in the Mix because of the GEC's entry restrictions. And an entire shipment fit easily inside the *Drake*. No need to tow a freighter.

The ID cards were shipped from the Way Back sectors, to Andiron and on to Pergamon. But which ships had them and when they were sliding into and out of each stop along the way were the huge unknowns. A pirate ship had to be there when the ID hauler slid in, grab the cards, and leave before the law arrived. Naturally, the ID shipping schedules themselves had become treasure of their own. The scammers outside the Chateau were selling schedules to the clueless new pirates flooding onto the exchange. Jasmine was charging Barry four times her usual rate for this intel.

Jess' intel had held up though, and the *Drake* had racked up a nice series of raids. The GEC was adapting quickly. After their next raid made them metric fox-tons of money, they would need to hide.

Barry plopped down on the blanket under the beach umbrella. The women laid down on either side of him. One laid a hand on his shoulder, the other traced lazy circles on his bare gut with one finger.

Barry noticed the beach umbrella's shadow now stretched towards the water. The afternoon was almost over. "I'm not having any fun with either of you until you tell your committee I can keep a secret."

Not a word was uttered. Both women rolled away, gathered up their beach bags, and left. He listened to the surf rolling in and the screeching of tropical birds. He opened one eye and swiveled it around. Nope, he still couldn't name a single thing that would make him want to leave. Damn. He dozed off.

Flank roused him with a kick to the shin.

"Yowww!" Barry sat up, holding his leg.

Flank grinned at him in the golden light of the setting sun. Tongue stood next to him, dressed in palm fronds. "Committee is ready to talk."

The trio trooped down the beach and into the jungle where a makeshift pavilion was made amongst a cluster of giant palm trees. Four women and two men dressed in the natives' standard sun-blocking mesh robes waited for them.

"We need to make sure that you won't divulge the route here, or this system's coordinates, to anyone," one of the women said. "Discretion and confidentiality keep this settlement alive. Is that understood?"

"You know, totally completely understood," Tongue said.

"We only will come back here if we need to disappear for a while," Barry added.

"We're giving you the coordinates to other routes we use to come here." She handed a chip to Flank. "You can't sense the beacons unless your sensors are pointing at just the right coordinates," the woman said. "That route can take you to the GEC main route much quicker than the way you took to reach here."

"Thank you," Barry said.

"But that route also has a number of dead-end slides for those who aren't careful. A slide beacon maze of sorts."

"That sounds like a nightmare," Tongue said.

"I like the idea," Flank replied.

The bushy-bearded man said, "We are concerned, what with your reputation, that you'll bring trouble here."

"And by trouble," another woman said, "we mean more than the GEC. Exchanger scouts and Underseed settlers are just as much trouble. We don't want people coming here and paving the place."

Barry cleared his throat. "Honestly, most places I wouldn't care if the GEC flattened it two seconds after we left. But this, this is a special place. I get why you wouldn't want anyone else to know it exists. We'll keep it a secret. Maybe we'll join you some day. Turn our ship into a beach house."

"My ship," Flank said.

The committee chair said, "You must not come here directly. There is only one viable slide route direct from the direction of Union. We only use it for emergencies."

She posted a slide route map to a small screen hanging from the pavilion's roof. The map showed several alterate routes to Margarita from the Underseed and the GEC. But all of them detoured to tricky, hard-to-reach spots in the middle of the Waterfall Nebula first. The maze seemed to go inside and outside of the nebula.

Tongue wrinkled his nose. "It means crossing or stopping on the GEC main route, what two, three times? It goes practically over to the next sector. The other path, let's see what you have here: it stops at Andiron? That's uh, a lot more cop-heavy than I think we want."

The committee stared at Tongue for several long seconds, and then looked at Barry for a reaction.

Barry blurted, "We accept your terms. Thanks." He pulled Tongue out of the pavilion.

"We could map a better route ourselves," Tongue said.

Flank marched him down the path to the beach.

"Barry. I'm not kidding. We should talk about this," Tongue said over his shoulder.

"We have a shipment to catch," Flank said.

FORTY-ONE

AS NIGHT FELL on the tiki huts the *Drake* launched from the Margarita villa. On on the external scopes the villa slipped away and the sounds of chittering animals and the soft whoosh of the tide rolling out was replaced with the wind.

"Very nice vacation," Flank remarked.

Barry added, "Back to work."

The rendezvous with the ID shipment required several slides. Tongue used the down time to avoid the other two and study the new plant specimens from Margarita. He was the caretaker of the ship's biome and hoped he could transplant these new plants to the *Drake*.

The *Drake* exited into empty interstellar space near a low-powered nav beacon. Flank called to the rear of the ship to tell Tongue to do his job.

"We didn't reach Union first because our chakras were aligned," Flank cracked when Tongue entered the kick.

"We won Union because of our botany, not because you knocked the recharge time down by a fraction of a minute," Tongue sniped.

"By two minutes, dirtbag."

Barry sighed. These two had been arguing about this since they were all teens. They were tense about this job. How come he understood that but they didn't?

"Give me an asteroid, or one of those Grid metal boxes," Flank replied. "I'll outfly anything with just a box of nutrient bars. I don't need to waste time on a stupid garden."

"Only an ignorant turd discounts synergistic symbiosis theory while living in a successful example of it," Tongue muttered.

"Eh, maybe there's fungus growing in your skull again," Flank said.

"That organic comlink would have worked if you didn't rip it out."

"How about let's not do this now," Barry said.

Tongue ignored him. "Kiss my ass, man. You know how many tries it took to perfect bamboo steel? A quarter of a million."

Flank shrugged. "They teach you at the orientation for the Lucasian brotherhood?"

Tongue opened his arms. "Oh, you want to go there? Ha. Really? Some humans are more sentient than others chose to be. Certainly more self-aware. But it doesn't mean we can dismiss them."

Flank scowled. "Just like a Lucasian. Talk about enlightenment and higher forms of living, but still condescending to everyone else."

"You're one to talk, you know," Tongue shook his head. "At least the Lucasians have a reason to condescend to others."

Barry said, "How much longer are you two arguing about this? Enough. Hit the slide so everyone can return to ignoring the others."

Tongue verified that his triple check of the next slide parameters matched the ship's calculations. He posted the countdown on the main board.

Flank scowled at Barry. "Oh, where would we be without your wise counsel, Captain? We need to rethink this whole power structure someday."

Barry smirked. "You're just tense. Both of you."

Flank replied, "You piss off everyone you meet, just for laughs. It's a big foxing joke for you isn't it? When you screwed the pooch on Union, it was a big laugh."

"Hey, we did this together," Tongue said, tapping his forehead. "Lucasian memory retention technique."

"He shorted our shares without asking us, idiot," Flank retorted. "Don't try to spread the blame around for the sake of peace."

"Don't drag me into this, Flank. I'm just saying. You're too toxic to be captain. You're not likable sometimes either. Barry's a jerk, but at least he's good with people. You treat everyone like they're beneath you, without giving them a chance to prove otherwise."

"They *are* beneath me. Sometimes they're too stupid to realize it. They need my help coming to grips with reality."

Tongue snapped his fingers. "Exactly what I'm talking about. And you say the Lucasians are stuck up. Man."

"Hey, you're welcome to the job when I'm out," Barry said.

No one said anything.

Barry said, "Hey, I'm only in this to make up what we lost. Then I'm gone like I always planned to be when we won the race."

Tongue squinted in confusion. "You been planning to bail on us?"

"Barry," Flank said, "back then you had a life to return to."

"And I lost it, thanks for reminding me of that painful fact. I want to live in a nice quiet place where no one expects me to do anything."

Flank frowned. "Sounds like you got too much sun and fun on Margarita."

"Good for you Bare, I guess, having a plan," Tongue said.

They slid in to where the GEC courier carrying the ID cards would arrive, a single beacon floating deep in interstellar space. No other spaceship, station, or star system. Just another stop needed to let ships recharge on the long slog from the Way Back sectors to Andiron.

"And now we wait," Tongue proclaimed.

They waited overnight and into the next morning. They drifted away from the kick. Tongue lost a Margarita flower but kept the other specimens alive and learned more about their chemical interactions with the environment. Flank ran tactical drills and lifted weights. Barry lay in his bunk, bored, plotting shortcuts to pay off their debts to Grand.

An alarm trilled before lunch: a ship slid in. The courier. The courier ship resembled a comet that had been dipped in molten metal and stood on its round head, the hemispherical slide drive.

Scans of the courier's scrolled across the overhead monitors in the kick when the guys rushed back in. One monitor showed an estimated recharge countdown for the courier, which was their window to grab the ship.

Barry activated a broadcast to the courier. "This is Captain Barry Spranker. Stand down or we will fire on you. You are outgunned and I hope you see how foolish it would be to resist."

The courier banked away from the *Drake* and accelerated. Tongue gave chase.

The courier continued to pull away. Tongue accelerated and the distance between them edged downward. Before the refit on Batik, the *Drake* would have been slower than a GEC courier in sublight space. It was rated twenty percent faster now.

"I should mention here," Barry said to Tongue and Flank, "that we shorted the stock of the courier subsidiary and its insurance company. If this job gets the publicity Grand says it will, we should profit from this a couple different ways."

Tongue grinned manically.

Flank hunched over his board, intense as usual. "Nice. Weapons and defense systems are hot, damage board is cool," he announced with some hand-twisting flair. He posted the sensor feeds from the courier ship on the main display.

When they pulled within weapons range, Flank fired a warning shot near the courier's port heat baffle. The courier returned fire, hitting the *Drake*'s drive grill. The grill drank up the extra power and shaved almost a minute off their own recharge time. Which was helpful. This far out from Union, the Grids hadn't yet heard that Exchange ships hit with energy fire routed the power surge to the drive's capacitors.

Barry again demanded the courier to surrender. Again, he received no response. Instead, the courier pilot engaged the slide drive at a low level to add speed at the expense of recharging faster.

"Their weapons went cold. They're shunting power from the drive capacitors into propulsion," Flank said. "With their drive engaged they can't recharge enough to slide."

Tongue asked. "I guess they're happy to just stay out of arms reach for now."

"Can we catch up?" Barry asked. "Close enough to disable them?"

Tongue added the slide drive's power to their local thrust. The *Drake*'s recharge clock slowed its descent, paused, and began to climb.

Flank sent a barrage into the courier's rear. A baffle melted on the ster and the starboard running lights flared and winked out. But the courier didn't slow.

"Don't disable them completely," Barry warned. "We don't want to tow them."

"Maybe we don't tow them," Flank muttered. "Just leave them out here."

Tongue shook his head. "Don't say that. They aren't calling for help. They must realize no one will come in time."

Another volley overloaded the courier's weapons capacitors. The small ship cut acceleration and signaled its surrender.

As the *Drake* pulled alongside to dock, Flank said, "There's a dozen additional people on board, waiting by the airlock. They're armed with zappers. Should've guessed this wouldn't be easy."

"We can win a fight from outside the ship, but not from the inside," Tongue said.

Barry looked from Flank to Tongue. "So, what's our play here? We need to get those cards and the clock is running."

Flank said, "Force them to lock themselves in their bunk room and stay there while we board, do our thing, and leave."

Barry nodded quickly. "I like it." He relayed the order to the courier ship.

When there was no response, he said, "Flank, fire a little warning shot, high and off their bow. To show them we're serious."

The *Drake*'s cannons fired a blast in front of the courier ship. Flank said, "The crew left the weapons in the airlock and are inside the bunk room. The captain, too."

Barry said, "Flank, guard the bunk room door. Barricade it, use their own weapons, whatever you need to keep them in there. Time's a wasting."

The three of them boarded the courier ship. Tongue searched for the cargo and began shifting the cases of ID cards to the *Drake*.

Flank stood across from the bunk room door, holding two weapons on it.

"They staying quiet?" Barry asked.

"Not a peep," Flank replied. "Nobody wants to eat vacuum."

"Huh," was all Barry could say. He wanted to argue but couldn't pin down why.

Without anyone to mug for, Barry stomped around the courier's tiny bridge. He was at loose ends and full of adrenaline. He paced the small room in jerky steps. He wasn't this nervous when they reached Union. It was an unfamiliar feeling.

Tongue flashed a message to Barry. Thirty cases of ten thousand ID cards on board. They were three minutes into the boarding. Flank budgeted five minutes to steal the cargo, but they were late catching the ship.

"Are we set?" Barry yelled up the corridor.

"One more thing," Tongue replied, coming into the bridge. He slapped a chip into a reader and copied the ship's logs, schematics, performance data, and transponder codes. He installed back doors to allow the *Drake* to track the ship and tossed in a couple of decoy viruses for grins.

As it uploaded the contents to the courier ship computer Tongue whistled tunelessly and browsed through the ship's comm logs.

He stopped whistling.

"The last entry," he said, "a message tightbeamed to the nav beacon. They called for help."

Alerts on the scopes distracted him and Barry. A motley collection of Exchanger and GEC ships slid in to the nav beacon. Three GEC patrol craft, an assortment of other GEC craft, and a starslider.

The ships commed to the courier ship and the *Drake*. "We're the GEC's new anti-pirate squadron." Charles Lemonne said. His voice was more condescending and irritating than Barry remembered. "Surrender, Barry, and make this easy on everyone."

FORTY-TWO

FLANK WAS the last one to sprint through the *Drake*'s airlock. He slapped the manual release and the airlock banged shut. He raced to the kick.

"I knew something was rotten about this job," Tongue muttered. "Didn't like the slide routes."

Flank shoved Barry away from his tactical station. "The courier ship tried to slow us down every way they could, until help arrived. Someone set us up." According to the recharge countdown, the *Drake* was twenty minutes shy of sliding.

"No shit," Tongue rasped. He had the Drake moving at full speed away from the squadron. The faster ships in the squadron came barreling after them. The slower ones throttled up and spread out.

"Come on you guys. We can beat them!" Barry exclaimed. "It's a bunch of tin GEC boxes with power supplies built by the lowest bidder!"

"Um, that's the *Charles* out there," Tongue said, pointing at the white starslider with black stenciling. Her transponder was broadcasting a GEC signal though. "Not all of these are GEC tin boxes."

"Fox," Flank muttered, studying the tactical screen. "Those fast attack craft are moving too fast for their rated speed."

Lemonne was still spouting orders over the comm, "Pirate ship *Drake*, this is the GEC ship *Charles*. This squadron has been commissioned by the GEC to apprehend you. Surrender your ship and prepare to be boarded."

Barry muted the comm. "We can't get caught by Lemonne, guys," he said. "I mean, I'll surrender to anyone but that stiff."

"They're trying to box us in. This won't be like running from a Monolith," Flank warned. "Those GEC clunkers are modified, too. They all have weapons, based on their power signature readings."

The *Drake* rocked violently, like a log kicked by a kid, hard, but not enough to roll over. Tongue and Barry fell over.

Flank stayed upright. "The *Charles* shot some kind of grappling hooks into our hull. I can see the monofilament lines on the dorsal scope. They're dragging us to a stop."

"Oh boy," Tongue replied, his voice pitching unexpectedly higher.

On the main display, thin objects shot out from a crab-like GEC rescue ship. The crab ship had fallen far behind the fast attack craft. Missiles. They streaked past the fast attack craft and curled in toward the *Drake*'s port side.

"Grab hold of something," Flank warned.

They missiles were solid objects that plowed into the hull and knocked the ship off course with a thundering boom. The *Drake* almost rolled over from the impact, shedding hull fragments.

Even Flank was thrown to the deck. He popped up first though and checked the damage report. "The hull has been blown clean off in three spots. Fungi scraped down to the ceramic skeleton in at least one place. No ruptures or leaks."

"Get us the hell out of here," Barry ordered angrily, rubbing a banged knee.

Tongue nudged the drive right up to the edge of draining power from the recharge. The *Charles* pulled the other way, killing their momentum. They weren't going anywhere with cables embedded in their hull.

"We need to lose those cables, like, right now," Tongue said.

He swung the ship around to be parallel with the *Charles* and engaged the drive to pull them towards it. The monofilament lines between them slackened, glinting in the running lights of both ships. Flank's cannon fire found the lines and sliced them to ribbons. The *Drake* was loose.

Tongue banked away, presenting a minimal profile for the *Charles* to fire more grapplers. He kept the fragile, disabled courier shuttle between the *Drake* and the crab-like missile platform. He opened up the throttle all the way, using the drive to build a lead.

The recharge clock began climbing as he drained the capacitors. "Um," Barry said, pointing at it.

"Worry about it later," Flank said. He began a steady rain of fire on the *Charles* and the three fast attack craft, which were now well within range.

The squadron's slower ships were almost in range, too. Tongue swore under his breath. "I can't get a slide solution." He sounded desperate.

"Did they disable our navigation system?" Barry asked.

"No. All of their ships are engaging their drives, creating local gravimetric disturbances. It prevents any of us from forming a slide."

Tongue posted a graphic of slide potential around them. The last isolated pockets they could escape through dwindled and disappeared.

"We need to fight our way out," Flank said.

Barry bit down a sarcastic retort. "Good idea."

Tongue was surprised at his response. Barry shrugged helplessly. What other choice was there?

Flank fired every weapon at the nearest GEC ship, an oblong passenger shuttle packed with human heat signatures. The shuttle was angling in towards the *Drake*'s starboard airlock. The energy cannons swamped the shuttle's hull with excess energy. The shuttle's lights went out as its electrical systems overloaded. With its propulsion knocked offline, the shuttle fell behind them.

Their pursuers were now aware of how much firepower the *Drake* was packing. The gravimetric net they wanted to tighten would force them to close within the *Drake*'s weapons range. They needed to choose whether preventing the *Drake* from escaping was worth a life-threatening pounding?

Flank's threat analysis program highlighted the crab-like missile ship as the next target to hit. The crab was trying to get a clear shot at the *Drake*. Flank was about to target it with their disabler and main cannons when it fired a volley of thirty missiles.

Flank was ready this time though. He let the *Drake* target the inbound projectiles. They were small ballistic missiles, not much more than thrown rocks, and Flank vaporized one after another like it was a game. But there were too many coming in too fast.

Tongue rolled the ship to expose the undamaged ventral hull. Three missiles made it through Flank's barrage. There was an ear-splitting crash from the collision that shoved the ship upward.

Tongue kept rolling the ship so Flank could return fire at the crab. He checked the roll when the dorsal weapons were lined up. Flank aimed for the crab's underbelly, its rounded slide drive. His threat assessment software discounted the *Drake*'s ability to damage what the crab's armored missile tubes. Flank hit the crab's slide drive, slagging a third of its emitter plates.

Tongue rolled the ship again. The *Charles* surged towards the *Drake*. Lemonne closed while firing his overcharger cannon at the *Drake*'s fragile stern sensors. The *Drake*'s infrared, local navigation and several other scopes all died.

Flank cursed because his threat analysis program now couldn't tell which ships powered up their weapons. He fired a barrage at the nearest GEC fast attack craft, hitting its slide drive and melting its main heat baffle.

Lemonne fired another volley of monofilament grappling hooks at the *Drake*'s stern. This volley only grabbed vacuum because Tongue spun the ship end over end to stay out of range. Flank targeted the grappling hook turret on the *Charles*' hull and overloaded it with a staccato burst from the port side beam cannon.

Tongue flew the course Flank's tactical analysis program suggested. The program wanted the *Drake* to reverse course towards the *Charles*.

Fly straight into the middle of the squadron's slide-blocking field and into range of every ship's weapons.

"What are we doing?" Barry asked nervously. The tactical board showed they were within range of the *Charles*. Sure enough, the *Charles* poured energy fire into their stern, scorching the hull fungi.

"Tactically, the weakest point on a starslider is the slide drive," Flank explained. "Knock it out and the ship is stuck in local space and without most of its power."

Barry added, "Wouldn't Lemonne have already told that to his new-found friends?"

Flank grinned. "Sure, about us. He's not going to expect us to take advantage of that on him. Unless you want to hold off on this tactic until later, Captain."

The crab ship fired another volley of missiles at them.

"It's later," Barry said with a gulp.

Flank adjusted the threat analysis program, causing the tactical screen to shift its suggestions. "You see that, Tongue?" Flank asked.

Tongue nodded and executed the new course.

The *Drake* was attacking the *Charles*. With the missiles closing on them, Tongue accelerated at and ducked under the *Charles* with barely ten meters clearance.

The missiles were so close they hit both ships. The *Drake* took two shots in the stern, causing a decompression sensor to bleat. A leak in the bathroom behind their personal cabins. The kick's compartment doors slammed shut.

Barry said wryly, "Sorry guys, no showers for a while."

"Bastards," Tongue said.

The dorsal scope showed sections of Lemonne's beautiful porcelain hull shattered and tumbling into the dark.

"Next time use smarter missiles, you shitwits," Flank gloated.

The *Charles* fired another volley of grappling hooks into the *Drake's* hull. These hooks stuck.

Tongue banked to port and sped in the opposite direction from the *Charles*. When they passed by, Flank fired a beam cannon at the *Charles'* black poly-ceramic drive arrays and the monofilament lines stretching taut between them.

Nothing happened. Flank swore under his breath. The cannon was offline. The *Drake* wasn't slicing through any more monofilament line. It couldn't escape.

"What's next?" Barry asked, his face sweaty. The crab ship was maneuvering around the *Charles* to tear them apart with another volley.

"Next," Flank replied with knitted brows, "we fight boarders. Good old hand-to-hand combat."

Tongue gasped in surprise.

"Forget it. It's over, Flank," Barry said. "We're surrendering."

FORTY-THREE

THE COURIER SHUTTLE was towed away by the crab missile ship. One of fast attack craft loaded with human heat signatures docked with the *Drake*.

Flank pitched twenty scenarios for fighting their way past the boarding party, but Barry rejected them all. Barry ordered Flank to open the airlock and they waited in the kick.

Leading the commandos was Jess Forrester, Tongue's girlfriend. Except now she was wearing a GEC commando uniform and stood up straighter, with her hair in a tight military bun. She pulled out a zapper and shot Flank point blank. He collapsed to the deck.

"What the hell!" Tongue demanded.

She pointed the stunner at him. "Step away from the console."

Tongue complied, his mouth hanging open.

Barry's squinted at her. "Who are you? Really?"

"Investigator Jill Stamp."

Tongue let loose an outraged yell and charged towards her. She didn't shoot him. Instead, she pivoted and knocked him into the corridor. The commandos behind her pinned him to the deck with their boots.

"Fox!" Tongue yelled into the deck moss. He struggled against the boots on his back and got more boots for his trouble. "Shit!"

Jill checked on Flank, who was still out. She tapped at the console to wipe out the slide calculations. An alarm trilled; a GEC Monolith slid in three hundred thousand klicks to starboard.

"I'm so glad we could make your day," Barry said as a commando cuffed his hands.

"I am glad no one was hurt," she said.

"I'm hurt," Tongue growled.

Barry asked, "And what wonderful thing will happen to us now?"

"Depends on how cooperative you are. Maybe you get life in prison. Maybe you get sent to Union as refugees."

"You let me believe we had something," Tongue said from behind her. "Fox you."

Stamp said, "We did, baby. I really do care for you. But *this*, this right here, this is my job. This is the best I can do to keep you safe. You don't need to understand," her voice caught. "I hope you realize it at some point. I nearly threw my career away for you."

"I'd like to see that on a greeting card," Barry said.

Commandos advanced into the kick, covered head to toe in combat armor and carrying heavy-duty zappers. They picked up Tongue and shoved him against his own living wall to handcuff him. They trussed up Flank and carried him out.

Finally, it was just Barry left with the GEC troops.

He kept looking at Stamp while the commandos mashed his face down into the console. "You're a massive foxhole," he said.

She smiled evilly.

"I should point out," Barry said to the commando holding him down, "I've seen her bare ass. And it's quite nice."

She opened her mouth to respond, but the kick went dark. She tapped at the consoles, but the screens, dashboards, and telltales were dead. Every console was powered down.

"Unauthorized access to the ship's systems shuts everything down," Barry explained.

"We'll just have to tow it then. Get him out of here," she said to the commandos.

FORTY-FOUR

THE HOLDING cell was like everything else on this damn GEC ship. The walls, ceiling and floor were a dull, gray, steel-based polymer, lifeless and institutional. The first thing Tongue did was to rearrange the furniture, putting his metal chair in the corner, away from the downdraft from the loudly-hissing ceiling vent.

He jogged in place and did abdominal exercises to warm up. The metal chair was a good-enough tool for endurance lifting and yoga. He took the paper gown they gave him to wear and folded it into a makeshift seat cushion to keep the cold metal off his butt and legs. He totally hated cold metal.

He mentally thumbed through the Lucasian relaxation techniques he'd learned. The stillness of self, compartmentalizing toxic emotional states, working through stress and physical pain. Some he could never perform correctly, especially the ones focused on emotional control. It was what kept him from taking the Lucasian rites. His path to serenity meant sneaking around his darker emotions by distracting himself. To prevent himself from going insane in prison, he needed to master self-distraction.

He inventoried the last time he ate, slept, urinated, defecated, laughed, ejaculated, vomited, exercised, and weighed himself. He examined his injured arm and noted the purple-brown bump. He methodically checked his skin for blemishes. He noted the length of his fingernails and toenails. He imbibed the scent of dried sweat on his skin and the familiar tang of body odor.

He considered himself, his physical being, inside and out. Remembering his place in the universe, his location in the galaxy, and how much of the galaxy was completely ignorant of his existence. He dispassionately added layers of perspective. The galaxy teemed with humans. Trillions of humans. And it was one inhabited galaxy among millions of empty ones. His situation did not matter on the level of the sector, galaxy, or universe. Nothing mattered. He stuck his focus on this irrelevance and relaxed.

When the soothing cold emptiness of an uncaring universe thoroughly drained his emotions, he brought his attention back to his situation. He studied the featureless gray wall in front of him. It was a bare single block of gunmetal gray. No markings, indentations, seams, outlets or switches.

Beyond observing it, he contemplated it. Its molecular structure, tensile strength, thickness, weight, and conductivity.

His mind became quieter and more focused. His breathing slowed. Time passed. How much time, he couldn't tell.

The cell's door opened and closed. Tongue kept staring at the wall. He'd been contemplating its intersections and corners for a while. He was quite content.

"Put your clothes on," Jill said.

"I don't want to talk to you. Please leave," he replied.

"There's no choice."

He shrugged, resigned to the hit his emotional state would take. To him, she represented betrayal, his own stupidity, his own gullibility, and a growing set of regrets.

"The gown, Jon."

His nakedness must have made her uncomfortable. It was a metaphor for the pain she caused; stripped his heart bare. If being naked stirred guilt in her, or lust, or any other emotion, he was all for it. Simple. Breathe in, breathe out.

She glanced at his business.

He made his business twitch.

She startled and got huffy. "You need to be serious. We need to talk."

"You talk if you want. *Jess*." Tongue bit down hard on her cover name. His emotions were flaring up and he sought out the careless vacuum sucking at this Monolith's metal hull. If the GEC executed him, the executioners would go home, eat dinner and sleep soundly. Their guilt, joy, sense of justice, none of those feelings would matter in the vast empty universe they existed in. He exhaled through his nose slowly.

He narrowed his focus on the corner until she disappeared in his peripheral vision. He could spend hours contemplating how they manufactured this wall. He assumed it was printed elsewhere and installed here. But what if it was just one part of the rest of this ship section? Was it a separate object at all?

"There are ways we make people talk," she said. "We can make you very uncomfortable without hurting you."

He shrugged. There were a hundred things he could say and do to hurt her, anger her, embarrass her. Especially since the Grids must be recording this.

When he dwelled on how she seduced him, it sparked the cooling embers of his anger. It threatened his inner peace. Better not to engage at all. Let her do what she would. Let her bring in more interrogators. He might talk. Or not. But for now, his mouth stayed shut.

"What about Barry and Flank? Don't you want to help them?"

The Monolith's builders probably manufactured interrogation room walls differently than a typical bulkhead. From the few minutes being escorted through the ship, Tongue saw the GEC ship design was efficient. Standard wall panels were modular, with built-in conduits that could be swapped out easily. But the ships were fragile, more easily damaged. The interrogation room walls, though, must be the thickest, densest, most soundproof walls on the entire ship.

He concentrated on the silence in the room, broken only by two people breathing.

"Jon?" Stamp said.

These very thick, insulated walls allowed him to shut out the entire universe outside.

Eventually, the door opened and closed and the only sound in this room was his own breath.

FORTY-FIVE

FLANK WOKE up face down on a cold metal floor. Maybe that bitch paralyzed him. His vision dimmed and his brain throbbed. He wasn't sure where she hit him. He blinked but saw nothing but grayness around him.

He sat up and found himself inside what could be a walk-in refrigerator unit, a sterile metal box. He was naked under a flimsy paper gown. He had to be onboard the damn Monolith. Shit, this was all absolutely no good.

He collected himself and stood up. He search the room for surveillance equipment. There was nothing obvious, like a camera dome or a hanging comlink. But one non-metallic wall with a hollow sound could be a one way mirror. He didn't believe they were so stupid to leave him in here without surveillance.

The ceiling lights were behind thick glass fixtures that were riveted shut. There was no handle on the door, much less a ringer or control panel. One noisy vent between the ceiling lights, about the diameter of his hand.

He took stock of his raw materials. Furniture included two metal chairs and an end table. The chairs were solid metal, but he pulled off the rubber leg points anyway and hefted them in his hand. The table was bolted together, again with metal, and without some tools there was little he could do to loosen the bolts.

He stacked the chairs on the table to get closer to the lights. The rivets were flush with the ceiling panel and there was no way he could pry them off. Plus, the lights were blazing bright.

He prowled around the room, unable to stay still. The damn gown wouldn't stay velcroed closed and kept exposing his ass. He picked up a chair and tapped it against the wall nearest to him. He held his ear to the wall and tapped again. He tapped the chair down the entire length of the wall. The rear wall was solid metal. He repeated this on the other walls and got similar results. Each wall was thick. So was the door.

His next carefully considered idea was to whip the chair at the wall. It left no mark, dent or scratch. He picked it up and ran it full speed from the door into the wall. Not a scratch.

He swung the chair at the wall, not out of rage, but deliberately. He took practice swings to gauge how much force he was using. The chair bounced off the dull surface and vibrated painfully in his hands. He smashed it against the wall even harder. Nothing to show for it but a small dent. He tried the next wall.

On his third full power smash, the wall gained a dimple. The chair was mangled and bent, too. He smashed the dimple until it was a dent. He couldn't make the dent bigger. He smashed the door, and attacked the other wall. When those attempts weren't more fruitful, he returned to the dented wall. The dent seemed smaller, on its way back to a dimple.

He engaged his biceps and triceps and, for a solid five minutes, smashed the ever-loving shit out of the metal wall. Sweat pasted his gown to his back. But the wall's tiny dent slowly grew into a slightly larger dent.

The cell door opened. Stamp entered, with two guards behind her, ready to put dents in him if needed. The guards were heavily armored and carrying two handed tasers with multiple charges.

Flank planted the chair on the floor. Its bent legs caused it to list to the right.

"No one's ever dented the wall," Stamp said.

Flank cocked his head at a sarcastic angle. "I'm an artist."

"Too bad it won't last," Stamp said with false wistfulness. Sure enough, the dent was disappearing. The wall was made of some pliable substance. He wondered what the hell would damage it.

"Can we talk?" Stamp asked.

Flank grunted dismissively.

"Will you answer some questions about yourself?"

"My time is yours to waste."

"Where are you from? What's your real name?" Stamp asked.

"What do you want my personal history for? I'm not applying for a job, Detective."

"It's Investigator. There are no records on you. We usually work from a psych profile to help you help us." Stamp was earnest about learning about him, acting like he should give a shit about what she wanted.

"Mind foxers? Figures," Flank said. "No shock so many people want to get away from the GEC."

"Tell me about yourself," she insisted.

Flank imagined the recording devices were listening to his respiration, watching his eye movement, and measuring his body temperature, brain activity, and pupil dilation. The only way to mess them up was to tell the entire truth, but in his own way. He spoke quickly.

"I was born and raised on an Exchange planet probably a hundred thousand light klicks away, as the photon flies. Mom and Dad were scientist-engineers killed in a freak accident at a water park. I was raised by a domineering aunt who I could never please and probably warped my personality. I wipe with my left and jerk off with my right. I was best in my school, university, and flight program. I hate seafood, sleeping in, double-speak, and stupid questions. I'm about two meters tall. I believe in the redeeming power of brawling, hard work, brutal honesty, the laws of physics, that Exchange ships will always beat your Grid crates, and rules only keep honest people honest. I'm a guy's guy, and to be honest, of I'm of no use to women unless they're only interested in a bit of plug and play. My biggest fear is becoming incompetent or lowering my standards. I have a deep affinity for vests. I distrust people, contracts, and any social system. I'm happiest around a slide drive or a horny woman. Enough?"

Stamp asked, "Why did you choose to be a pirate?"

"I didn't," Flank sneered. "I was kidnapped by these guys and forced to run their engine. Gambling debts are a horrible thing."

"That is most certainly a lie. Several victims claim you lead the raids and sometimes you assault the crews."

He waved a hand. "Lies to get the insurance adjusters to pay out quicker."

"When exactly did the other two kidnap you and force you into piracy?"

"I was eight. Can you imagine the trauma?"

Stamp crossed her arms. "Why not do legitimate work?"

"We did legitimate work. For decades. And in the end we got stiffed. Epically, galactically, foxing stiffed. With salvage work, there's no outstanding bills."

"Salvage applies only to abandoned vessels. You're depriving people of needed supplies."

"Like the GEC does when it starves the Underseed. We're simply making you Grids atone for your sins."

"Those are not official settlements," Stamp retorted.

"If you don't have the right paperwork, you get to starve? Excuse *me*, you were lecturing me on morality and I rudely interrupted. Please do continue."

Stamp scowled. "You don't know the complete picture of what is going on."

"I'd like to keep it that way, thanks," Flank said.

"It was a fluke we caught you. I never planned to board the *Drake*. You're the best out there. You proved it at Union, you proved it again as pirates. I could pay you a lot to be the best pirate hunters in the GEC."

"Round up fellow Exchangers for you? No."

"Only one. Grand. The rest you can entice into joining you as privateers. What I want is to bring down Eden Overhead and her supporters on the inside of the GEC."

"We work for Grand. Not by choice. We'd have to betray him, which would be a very unwise idea. How about we target someone else?"

Stamp said, "Grand is the way in, because my bosses are after Exchangers."

"Is it because we're running roughshod all over the Mix?"

"Flank, you said you didn't care what the Exchange does."

"True enough. Forget I asked. How much is a lot?"

"Enough for you each to purchase your own starslider and hire a crew," she replied. "If you wanted to. How about twenty-five thousand a month for the three of you?"

"For turning on an Exchange crime lord?" She knew him pretty damn well. He wanted to clutch this opportunity, which she must expect. "The *Drake* could be the flagship of this little fleet you're building," he said.

Her eyes widened with interest, so he continued, "Make Barry do press conferences or something, while Tongue flies the *Drake* and I command the other ships."

She asked, "How much more for that?"

"Fifty thousand signing bonus, thirty thousand a month for the three of us, plus expenses."

"No way."

"Rumor is, Grid prison food is pretty good."

"Tongue won't make it in there. You know that. Come on."

He shrugged. "Thirty-five thousand bonus, twenty-five thousand a month, plus expenses. With monthly payments of five thousand for ten years. We won't need a lot of other ships or crews. You outsource the whole thing to us. We'll take care of it."

"You're trying to pirate me," Stamp said.

Flank shrugged.

"I'll see what I can do," she said. "Let me run this by Captain Spranker."

Flank tried to maintain a good poker face, but Stamp smiled a little. What did he let slip? Shit. Barry would fox this whole thing up.

FORTY-SIX

BARRY WAS IN A VILE MOOD. They gave him a paper gown, drew blood samples, took body temperature readings, scraped cheek cells and made him breathe into a tube. He wasn't contaminated, apparently, so they stuck him in here.

He'd been left to rot for hours inside this gleaming box of a holding cell. He knew there were audio pickups somewhere in here, so he kept his mouth shut. He sat in one chair, put his bare feet on the other, and zoned out.

His mind inevitably tried playing its old favorite, the 'what next' game. Running down the current situation's many angles, figuring out where the smart plays were, positioning and re-positioning himself to take advantage. And making the right move first, before anyone else even realized these angles existed.

But he was in an interrogation room, and his fate was completely in the hands of others. And he was tired of playing what next when the latest game landed him here, naked under a thin paper sheet.

He once believed, fervently, that staying on top of everything could get him to Union first. It did, but in the end, it didn't matter. He thought becoming a pirate in a land of innocent sheep would allow him to get rich and disappear. But he couldn't outrun his past or these

Grids. There was always a hidden angle waiting to rise up and bite him on the ass.

He decided to cease playing the game. Keeping up with ninety-nine percent of the situation was too much effort to still not be good enough. Tongue was right, make your life raft comfortable and ride out whatever waves came at you.

Tongue. He wondered how his friend was holding up. Betrayed by love, probably guilty about what he'd brought down on his crewmates. And Flank was probably trying to bite the guards' necks, if for no other reason than to learn Grid hand-to-hand techniques. Or he was selling out Barry, blaming him for everything.

Investigator Stamp finally came in, dressed in a business suit. Barry stifled the urge to draw his paper gown tighter around himself.

"Captain Spranker, how are you doing?"

He said nothing.

"Can you tell me about yourself?"

"No. You'll have to build your profile the old-fashioned way," he said.

"Sure. You're deeply insecure and narcissistic, willing to hurt others to amuse yourself. The insecurity motivates your charm but your impish nature screws everything up in the end. Plus, you're self-loathing. Does this about cover it?"

Barry grunted, amused. She had misconstrued his joking rebel routine as self-destructive self-loathing. A blind spot in the Grid view of the universe. "I want to be left alone."

"Are you working for the Exchangers?"

"Don't get too clever, Investigator. The Exchange screwed us at Union to screw us, not to give us a plausible reason to harass the GEC on our own."

"And yet, you prey only on GEC shipping, aid the breakaway Underseed settlements. Everything we'd expect an Exchange saboteur to do."

"I'd be happy to knock off an Exchange ship to prove you wrong. Unfortunately, there's not a lot of them out here."

"How interesting. Let's talk about that. Here's my offer: you and your crew work for me as pirate hunters rather than pirates. Against the Exchange. Maybe we'll let you raid Exchange shipping, too."

She had to be toying with him. If not, there were a number of new angles for him to consider. Instead, he said, "No."

"Hear me out, Spranker."

"Don't care."

"Your other option is life in prison."

"Take your offer and shove it right on up your ass. Which I've seen, by the way," he said for any recording devices.

She flushed but said, "Your crew accepted this deal."

Barry snorted. "How much did Flank sell out for?"

"He didn't sell out, he's being smart. You can continue operating under the GEC banner. We need your help. You'd still operate independently. In fact, I may even agree to let you three run the entire anti-pirate operation."

He held up three fingers. "Offer. Ass. Shove." He folded his arms with a papery crinkle. He wondered idly if prisoners were left in paper gowns. Hygienic, but rough on the skin.

Stamp sighed and said, "I'm trying to get you out from under Grand's control. Get you set up with some income, some independence. And then get out of your way as you get revenge on the Exchange."

"I was doing that before you interfered," Barry said. "It's easier to sit in prison. I won't need to dodge Grand's bounty hunters and assassins. Which I would need to do a whole hell of a lot if I turn on him."

"We can protect you. You can be a GEC citizen," Stamp said.

Barry said, "If I have to be in some prison, I'd rather it be an actual one. Leave me alone."

Stamp knocked on the door to be let out.

Barry didn't have to answer to anyone in here. Expectations for the incarcerated were comfortably low. Bonus: Grand would take a financial hit on his pirate rep market when the news broke about the *Drake*.

Barry relaxed and smiled. Ah, freedom.

FORTY-SEVEN

BARRY FIGURED out his new life. If he viewed prison like a vacation from real life, it wasn't really imprisonment, was it? Real life, with its hassles, obligations, rules, conformity, and emotional investments, that was the real prison. And if the GEC correctional facilities were packed with Underseeders who zigged when they were ordered to zag, they might actually be a fun group to hang around.

He needed to trick the legal stiffs into sending him to the right prison. No twitchy, demented killers, but also no cell blocks full of wimps crying every night.

To pull it off, he might need to learn how the Grid criminal justice system worked. No, he was better off not caring. His trial would probably be high profile because the Grids liked celebrity drama no less than Exchange audiences did.

Maybe he could play the part of folk hero, a modern-day Robin Luther Kinghood, who steals from the suits and gives to the disabled. Any Lucasians on the jury, if the GEC had juries, would be sympathetic. On the other hand he must be obnoxious enough to guarantee a jury would return a guilty verdict. It would require a nuanced but obnoxious performance.

Fantasizing about his trial was a great way to pass the time. The outbursts, the mugging for the home audience, demanding the trial be held in the Underseed, insulting the touchy Grids.

What if there was no trial? In the Exchange justice system, only violent crimes went to trial, the rest were dispensed with in day court or contract court. The guilty would pay heavy fines, which typically left them bankrupt and lucky to be scouring garbage cans from food courts frequented by teenage boys.

He feared a plea deal which would preempt his entertaining theatrics. Even worse, what if these corporate goons didn't put him in prison? What if they forced him to be a working stiff? He shuddered.

The cell door opened, and in came a female guard built like a wall. There were two more behind her hefting heavy duty firearms. "Come with me," she ordered, and threw Barry's clothes at him.

"Where are we going?" He dressed quickly and they marched him out of the cell block. The foursome stomped right up to security.

"The admiral wants to see him," the female guard said.

"About time," Barry said enthusiastically. At this point, he'd chat up this morose guard, despite her acting eager to murder him.

This Monolith was an endless series of curving hallways. The décor matched his cell: drab, gray, too brightly lit. GEC personnel he passed made curious or disgusted expressions at him. Word was out about the captured pirates.

They took an elevator ride up several decks, exited, crossed the length of the ship and took another elevator down. Barry asked if they were lost, but no one answered.

Finally, they entered an office suite. The admiral was inside — an older guy, his uniform covered with oval insignia, leaning on a chair.

"I'm Admiral Kleble." He dismissed the guards.

Barry opened his mouth, but the Admiral waved him off. "Keep quiet for a minute."

Jill Stamp arrived and stiffened when she saw Barry. The admiral motioned her to another seat. He sighed and said, "There are events occurring that are out of my control, and they are certainly out of the reach of either of you. So, understand that none of us have any choice here. It's the way it is and there's no point arguing it. Mr. Spranker, his crew, and their ship, will be released."

"Excuse me?" Stamp inquired.

Barry pumped his fist.

Kleble held up a hand. "When you reported the *Drake*'s capture, I'm guessing someone very high up didn't like it. They issued orders to my superiors who issued orders to me. We're calling this a regrettable mistake and we apologize for any inconvenience."

Barry smirked cautiously.

"However, you will pay a fine, Mr. Spranker."

Barry dropped the smirk. "We get unlawfully imprisoned and get apologized for this. Why aren't you paying us?"

"Your mysterious guardian angel, who went to a lot of trouble to arrange your release, believes it would be a *grand* gesture of magnanimity on your part to compensate us for the expense of your detainment."

"*Grand* gesture? Why that slick piece of," Barry said. How was Grand in a position to dictate terms to the GEC? He was an Underseed crime boss. Or maybe he was more than that. Or the GEC wasn't so monolithic. Judging from the look of horror on Stamp's face, the GEC definitely had some internal drama going on and weren't on the same page.

Grand pulled strings to spring them, saving his precious pirate exchange, but made Barry part with a healthy chunk of their net worth. Which meant the *Drake* would be in Grand's grip for that much longer. Very nice, all around, for Grand.

Barry closed his eyes. "How much?"

Kleble named an amount. Barry choked. It was half of everything the *Drake* had stolen to date. Well, at least half of everything they reported to Grand. This would be a serious blow to their financials.

Kleble said, "If it makes you feel better, the money goes to the fleet, in a way. Think of it as fines for each act of piracy."

"I get it. It's a bargain. Lucky me."

Kleble smiled. "Do you really believe you pulled one over on us,

Spranker? We could end the Exchange's piracy in a matter of weeks if we wanted to. And shut down the Underseed. Study your history. Piracy flourishes for a short time, between the opportunity appearing and the law shutting it down. When the authorities want to crush it, it gets crushed."

"Our investors apparently aren't very good history students," Barry retorted.

"We let you exist because it suits our purposes. There are bigger games afoot than you or Investigator Stamp are aware of. If I were you, I'd swear off the pirate's life, go slide into a quiet hole in the Underseed. Take up farming because this sector needs food."

"Before he's freed, I need to report this to my supervisor, Admiral," Stamp said tightly.

"He has already been informed, Investigator."

"He? Lieutenant Susan Wheeler is a she," she replied.

The admiral frowned. "I talked to a Lieutenant Leonard Bozell, commanding the Andiron investigations unit. You're stationed out of there, correct? I don't know a Lieutenant Wheeler." He searched on his desktop tablet. "There is a Lieutenant Wheeler in charge of Andiron's evidence storage room."

Stamp paled two shades whiter than Barry believed was possible. He wasn't sorry for her in the least.

Kleble tapped his comlink and the doors opened. The guards came in, expecting trouble.

Barry stood up, eager to leave while he could. "Stamp, Kleble, no one does incarceration quite like you."

"Wait a minute," Kleble said with disgust. "Do you understand what I'm telling you, son? Here's a second chance to do right for yourself. Because things are changing fast."

Jill Stamp was so pale she her lips were white. The open door beckoned Barry to freedom. Freedom he would be responsible for nurturing and maintaining. It weighed on him. What about a life of carefree prison? But he was a fool not to grab this new lease of freedom, even if it felt like a regrettable mistake.

Besides, there was this devastated look on Jill Stamp's face. He couldn't resist twisting the knife. He smirked and said, "See ya around, Inspector."

"Investigator."

"Whatever."

FORTY-EIGHT

GRAND WAVED HIS HANDS. "And the boss runs over and pulls the deaf bastard out of the machinery and says, 'No! I said *stick* it in your ear!'"

The two feral scouts across from him howled. The three of them were crammed into a shack ten meters outside the settlement's cluster of prefab buildings. Reaching this shack from the rest of the settlement took a fifty-meter slog through cold mud. The shack's floor rang hollow, because it was suspended above the muck. The walls were cheap digitally-printed wood paneling and there were no windows.

Grand missed his estate on Royada. But the big money was out here in the Underseed's barely-settled frontier in Sector 181. Grand needed to personally see that his people properly kickstarted exploration and settlement.

Bixby managed a wide smile at Grand's joke, despite this being the twelfth time he heard it in the last month. Kroger stood nearby, doing his usual routine of trying to melt into the background.

These two scouts, Jim and Bill, emanated a greasy aura from their nervous eyes, stubbly chins, down to the holes in their boots. They smelled like they'd been stuck in a metal can together for weeks. No soap, hot food, or running water.

They were the best available scouts he could find. Not only could they find a new planet, they analyzed its soil, studied its weather, and catalogued its flora and fauna. They were several notches below a professional survey team, but good enough for Grand. He wanted to grab the first-mover advantage by the balls and have Underseed settlements running under his control before the GEC or Exchange even knew about these star systems.

"Bix, how long has Spranker been waiting outside?" Grand asked.

The big man shrugged. "Maybe an hour?"

"Forty-eight minutes and thirty-five seconds," Kroger said.

"Shut the hell up," Grand snarled. Kroger had been irritating him ever since they left Royada. Grand wasn't sure why. The droid's facial expression seem to silently accuse him of mistreating Overhead.

He said to Bixby, "The mud on Spranker's shoes is probably dry now. Bring him in." He said to the scouts, "Thank you for your hard work. Go shower and eat something."

Bixby ushered in a shivering Barry Spranker, who had a sweatshirt hood pulled tight around a stabby facial expression. Grand immediately felt better when he saw his nemesis suffering.

"Jim and Bill, this here is the famous pirate Barry Spranker of the *Drake*. I just freed him from prison, like I did for you two," Grand said magnanimously. "Jim and Bill are scouting new systems for me."

"Did you two discover this charming gem of a world?" Barry asked.

Jim nodded. "We did. About what, two years ago, Bill?"

Bill added something sounding like a cross between a sick dog gargling hot sauce.

Barry blinked at Bill twice.

Jim waved his hand. "Don't worry about it, people can't understand Bill's accent. He's from an isolated Underseed system in the Way Back."

"And what attracted you two to this vacation spot?"

Jim rubbed his nose. "It sure wasn't the stink. Lot of bacteria dying in that mud. No, this continent has one hell of a lot of special metals. Mr. Grand here is going to make a lot of money off the mines here."

Grand added, "These two used to be forward scouts for the Grids. But the GEC dismissed a lot of its explorers. Sound familiar?"

"The GEC told us we could retrain to be refugee aid workers," Jim said. He laughed. "Bill and I don't have the interpersonal skills for aid workers, to be honest with you."

Grand said to Jim and Bill, "Boys, you can get Spranker's autograph later. I need to chat with him right now."

Bill muttered something to Barry, smiled and chucked him on the shoulder. It sounded like 'rotting corpse.' Barry pretended to understand. Bixby ushered the two grimy bastards out the door.

"Did you understand anything that guy Bill said?" Barry asked.

"Jim does most of the talking. Well, all of the talking." Grand said. "How do you like my new planet?"

"I like a little more color in my cold, sticky mud. And a few less toxic chemicals in the air."

Grand had better things to do than listen to Spranker's backhanded insults. "That's the refinery. Costs too much to ship the raw material up to orbit so we refine it down here. There's a lot more to the galaxy than stealing space pizza. There's entire worlds for the taking, if I'm fast enough to grab them."

"They never would have settled this dump back home," Barry said. "The Exchange likes warm worlds with plants and good soil."

Grand shot back, "You have to serve the market. The Grids use these heavy metals. They pay a fox lot to ship them out here from Sector 191 or wherever. But they didn't even glance at the worlds in this sector, besides Andiron and Pergamon. And even there, they tossed down some little outpost. The Underseed could take everything from the edge of the Mix back to the Dogleg. If we move fast enough. There are dozens of unexplored worlds out here. The Mix won't expand out here for decades."

"So are you divvying up the Galactic Habitable Ring amongst your cronies?"

"If I can scrounge up the capital, I'll be the owner and proprietor of several settled planets. Bigger than Eden Overhead ever was."

Barry flicked the gray mud off his shoes. "Not enough to be a pain in the ass criminal overlord, you have to collect planets now?"

Grand sneered. Spranker's lower lip stuck out in a pout and it just tickled Grand right down to his toes. "If that's how you say thank you for springing you from the GEC, you're welcome, you son of a bitch."

Barry bit the inside of his lip, reluctant to say the words. "Thank you," he said.

"How the hell did you let the Grids nab you, by the way?"

Barry shrugged. "Romantic mistake. Pirate groupie trapped us. Turned out to be Jill Stamp. It won't happen again."

Grand pointed a finger. "It better not. I invested a lot of money in you guys. Like I did in the pirate exchange. You fox up like this again, and you'll have so much debt that you'd rather be dead."

Barry on the defensive was sullen. "Yeah, yeah, I hear you. Let me ask, how did you get the Grid juice to spring us?"

Grand reclined in the crappy desk chair, which squeaked in protest. "Let's just say I skillfully played off GEC factions against each other. Some have different opinions about you and the Underseed than the Investigators do."

"Huh, I don't care. You could have just let us rot. You wouldn't have to deal with me ever again."

Spranker was trying to provoke him so he could lift his own mood. Which meant Captain Spranker wasn't happy. Which made Grand happy. "Don't think I wasn't tempted. But I need capital which means I need the exchange to function well and somehow you three are at the top."

"And so you get to milk us of a fat percentage of our profits for a lot longer," Barry said. "How nice for you."

"Actually, I called you here to settle your debts."

Barry leaned forward. "Yes, let's do that," he said. "Especially because it is a figment of your imagination."

Grand smiled mischievously. "I need you to make one more run."

Barry said, "There's nothing out there big enough to be worth it. The ID card haul nearly killed us. We'd need to repeat it about twenty more times to pay off what you think we owe you."

"True. But have you ever heard of the Endor system?"

Barry rolled his eyes. "Where the teddy bears frolic in the woods, in tune with nature? We're not running a religious tourist company."

"Don't roll your eyes at me. It's a real planet. This isn't a scam, or a tourist gimmick."

Barry threw his hands up. "Just because someone calls a planet Endor doesn't mean it's the Lucasian or Janna nirvana." He turned to Kroger. "Droid, how many planets are named Endor in the Exchange?"

"One hundred and eighty-five. More than one per sector."

"I'm not talking about the Exchange versions." Grand activated a small display on the beaten desktop. He held up a data card. "This has the coordinates to the GEC version of Endor. There's only one."

"It's real? Fine. And you know Endor's actual coordinates?"

Grand said, "I know Endor's actual coordinates."

"You know Endor's actual coordinates. Okay. Do you want me to act impressed? Okay, you do. Count me impressed. Did your moronic explorer pals Joe and Buddy discover it?"

Grand smiled. "Believe it or not, no. Eden Overhead gave them to me."

"And how is Eden doing these days?" Barry asked sourly.

Grand acted like he couldn't remember. "Oh, that's right, I sent her off to retirement at Union. An idea I got from what you did to my bounty hunters."

"They tried to kidnap Flank on the *Leggett* so they could steal our ship," Barry replied. "People that dumb need to be cared for by the GEC."

The crime boss wagged a finger at Spranker. "Says the foxhole who was outwitted by GEC cops. Can you imagine what would happen to your share price if news broke about you being nabbed by the GEC?"

"It wasn't my first concern," Barry admitted. "I'm not allowed to invest in your stupid pirate exchange. What do you want me to do with these Endor coordinates? Sell them?"

"No. Not lucrative enough." Grand popped the data card in a reader and several thumbnail vids appeared on the reader's screen. He expanded the first vid, which showed a peaceful green and blue planet, with an orbital facility. Close-ups of the facility showed four construction docks working on mid-sized yachts. The planetside settlement wasn't much bigger than the mudcaked outpost they were currently on. But the Endor settlement looked far more appealing, sitting on a green continent.

The vid didn't appear fake or tampered with. Those were real ships and orbital facilities hovering over a real planet. The map appeared legit, too. Barry would verify it all when he returned to the *Drake*. He probably suspected that it was a scan from some other system entirely. Grand assumed as much because he suspected the same thing, until Kroger had verified it.

Grand said, "It's the juiciest low-hanging fruit you'll ever get. No security, but plenty of cargo coming through. Cargo which won't be reported missing because it's *already* stolen. Someone in the GEC has been stockpiling embezzled resources there. Understand? I want you to sack the whole system. Your share price will skyrocket. And I get rich from the transaction fees you'll owe me and again when trading explodes afterward. We'll be done with each other."

Barry leaned closer to the screen. "You're looking for a bigger payday, I think. The pirate exchange is on a tear lately," he said. "Some would say a bubble."

"Some would say, yes. And I collect a fee every time someone buys or sells. Times are good."

"The ID run boosted our share price dramatically, sure," Barry said. "It tempted more crews to jump into the business, thinking they can strike it rich. That's what you want, isn't it?"

"I invest in each pirate crew on the exchange when they join," Grand said. "To keep me honest. And you never know who is going to do better than you three."

"You also dole out leads to pirates on where to strike. But only to select crews, which boosts them further on the exchange. You know the pirate exchange's bubble is not sustainable. You're manipulating it."

"That's the perks of running your own reputation exchange without any Regulators or markitects involved," Grand said with a big smile. "I get rich on the way up, the way down, and in between." He never thought that Barry Spranker could lift his mood this much. Barry was a smart guy, but it was all the rest he didn't know that made Grand even happier.

Barry leaned back in his chair and a touch of his smugness returned. "I wonder how much you'll make by selling our shares. Not enough to pay for a brand new settlement, like this luxury resort. You need to raise a lot of capital to settle multiple planets. You can make it slowly off the exchange, but that will take a long time."

"You think I'm going to pillage my own pirate exchange for a quick cash grab? That's rich, coming from you, Spranker. I've already been on the losing end of such a scam, remember? It's not turned out very well for you, has it?"

Barry held up his hands. "I bow to your superior intellect."

"You should, because you don't think about the long-game. I'm training the Underseed on how to use a reputation exchange. How to thrive in an Exchange-type economy. I don't want to scare them off by having their first experience go sour. What would happen, Kroger?"

Kroger said, "Humans who lose on a new investment instrument tend to shun it and any similar substitutes. Permanently."

"Exactly. I'm building my credibility in the Underseed, not trying to wreck it. This is just the first reputation exchange. There will be so many more. That will grow my revenue exponentially. I didn't bring you here to ruin you, you foxing dolt. I could have left you in prison if I wanted to do that." He pointed at the screen. "I brought you here to succeed. Wildly."

Barry offered up no pithy, self-serving insult. He smelled lies in everything Grand said now and had ever said. Grand could see that. Barry pointed to the revolving Endor image. "Then what's the catch?"

"It's the biggest smuggling depot inside the GEC. These people are very quiet, very savvy, inside operators. They keep the traffic low to minimize the chance that someone notices. You swoop in and jack the untended ships docked at the shipyards. The heist's audacity will make you legends and immensely rich. I take my share of the proceeds, ride a surge of investing in the pirate exchange and launch several more exchanges. Which will capitalize my exploration operations."

Barry chewed on a knuckle while he thought about it. "Three guys and a small ship can't pull this off," he said. "We hit one, maybe two ships at a time, in deep space where the GEC can reach them in time.

We can't clean out multiple ships right under the Grids' noses. You're talking about assaulting a foxing shipyard."

"That's why you'll be legends." Grand swept his arms out dramatically.

Barry said, "No, we'll go to jail. Or die. Did you say really rich? We need more people. Two ships, loaded with people who can fly the other ships. Maybe it'd work. We'd need a lot of help."

"Expand your operation? I see it. Strategic thinking is why you're at the top of the pirate exchange. You have a month," Grand said. He tossed the data card to Barry.

"Why? What happens in a month?" Barry's brow furrowed.

"Very reputable sources say these smugglers at Endor will jack up security soon. They know they can't hide there forever, what with the GEC and Exchange spreading out in every direction. Nothing you *couldn't* overcome, but enough to cut your take."

Barry weighed the small data card in his hand. "We do this thing and we're done with you, right?"

"Absolutely. Retire on top of the pirate exchange and slide into the sunset. Or stay on top. I don't care. You fill my pockets, no hard feelings between us."

Barry wasn't buying it. Grand rolled his eyes. "I'll even gift you a free plot on a nice colony somewhere. I really won't hold a grudge, Captain, if you make me whole."

Barry squinted skeptically, but put the data card in his pocket. "Hey droid, you record all that? Good. Don't want anyone to forget what's in this deal. I'm agreeing to this, Grand, not because I respect or like you at all. This is just business. I'd rather deal with your droid." Barry cinched the sweatshirt tight around his face and left the shack.

Kroger rolled up to the guest chair. "I don't understand," the droid said. "You gave him the Endor coordinates, which are worth more than your entire *Drake* investment. And you didn't tell me to go long on the *Drake*'s stock."

"That's because, Kroger, as usual you're not aware of everything," Grand said. He listed a series of financial moves he wanted Kroger to execute and explained the reasoning behind each. The droid's facial animation became more and more concerned. Grand finally relented and said, "Relax. Spranker isn't the only one I gave the coordinates. What does that make me?"

Kroger looked down and sighed. "One slick, slimy bastard."

"Damn right."

FORTY-NINE

JILL'S DESPAIR at losing the *Drake* lasted only one hour. Thomas Hewell messaged her from Union: he had arrested Eden Overhead. He found the old gangster stuck on a refugee ship.

Jill sent the squadron limping to Andiron for repairs, while she and Lemonne slid to Union at the *Charles'* maximum speed. She didn't check in with the new lieutenant on Andiron. She wouldn't contact him unless she had to. Jill's imagination tortured her with visions of Eden springing herself from jail faster than the *Drake* crew. Or her new supervisor ordering her to let Overhead go.

Jill tapped her foot impatiently the entire trip to Union. Lemonne's medical droid asked her if she had restless foot syndrome. Jill told her to fox off.

Her foot stopped tapping when the *Charles's* airlock opened to admit her onboard the Monolith *Elizabeta*. It was evening, Monolith time, and she desperately hoped Overhead was still in custody.

A security guard escorted her to an interrogation room in the detention block. When she entered, she only had eyes for the prisoner. Finally, finally, finally.

Overhead's white-haired visage had haunted her dreams for years.

This time the crime queen possessed no sophisticated arrangements, security measures, or shady political ties which could free her.

In fact the woman in the interrogation looked every part a tired, hollowed-out refugee. Overhead was slumped sideways in a wheel-chair. Thomas' report said Overhead was fighting two viruses causing her unrelenting joint pain. The mend would take a few weeks with the right medicine.

If Jill should feel guilty about taking advantage of Overhead's illness, she didn't. "Eden Overhead. I'm Investigator Jill Stamp."

Despite her obvious discomfort, Overhead smiled. "Ah, at last. Well, it's reassuring to know that GEC law enforcement can catch a sick old woman stuck on a refugee barge."

"Tough getting tossed aside by your own people?"

Overhead shrugged off the jab. "You would know."

Jill bit down on a retort. Did she know about Sandra getting replaced? Better to keep it neutral until she figured out what this meant. "What do you know about Grand, his pirate exchange, and the *Drake*?"

Overhead shrugged again. "I bought food from the *Drake* at wholesale prices and sold at a loss to keep the Underseed fed. Strictly a business arrangement." Her eyes suddenly sharpened in anger. "As for Grand, he's smart. He can make money. And he doesn't hesitate to poison his benefac-tor. Despite your best efforts, we were doing fine before he came along. But since he came aboard, I must admit business has been *fantastic*."

Jill wasn't buying it. "The charges lined up against you are tremen-dous," she said. "You'll live out the rest of your days in a place where the prisoners *plead* for transfers to a labor camp. You could cooperate, tell us everything in exchange for a lighter sentence. And some better quarters to recover in. What can you give me that would be worth it, though?"

Overhead's smile was chilly. "Jailing me is your revenge fantasy, dear. And a fantasy is all it will ever be. People higher than you will spring me soon enough."

It was unwise to bring up The Name here in the interrogation room with surveillance equipment recording. Jill would wait until they were safely aboard the *Charles* and away from GEC recording devices. So she refused to take Overhead's bait.

Overhead took the silence as an invitation to continue. "You're too narrowly focused, too rigid. You plod along, turning suspects one at a time, but you lose the big picture. When the Exchangers take action, they accomplish three things at once. The GEC needs to be nimble like them. My partners and I try to be."

"Please enlighten me about this big picture I can't see," Jill said.

"The GEC created the Underseed after it fell behind the Exchange. Our beloved civilization has some serious defects and there have been a steady stream of refugees leaving the GEC in every sector. Underseed settlers are in the tails of the conformity distribution; the troublemakers we're better off without. But the GEC needs the Underseed. We need to bring our people back in the fold to compete against the Exchangers."

"And you ran the beneficial crime syndicate secretly helping the GEC by propping up the Underseed?" Jill said sarcastically.

The former crime boss scowled. "It's not a crime syndicate. It's a GEC operation sanctioned at the highest levels. Above your chain of command, sweetie. Why do you think that you could never bring us in? There is an official way to get things done in the GEC, but there's also the effective way."

"You're an undercover GEC spy, is that your story?"

"'Undercover' is too official to explain my status. I'm not on the pension plan."

She expected Jill to dig further. And damn, Jill wanted to. She could have a real lead to finally crack this internal corruption ring. It was a cancer growing in the GEC, embezzling resources, siphoning off needed talent. Of course the thieves needed to believe their crimes served the GEC's greater good.

"The real problem," Overhead lectured, "the *fundamental security threat*, is the piracy. Hindering GEC exploration and settlement efforts when we are competing against the Exchange for systems and routes. There're millions more Exchangers coming to the Mix than there are from the GEC. The pirates are paving the way for a take over of GEC territory."

Her opinion on piracy matched Sector's take. It lent credibility to her story about being one of the good guys. But nowhere near enough. Jill said, "I've investigated these pirates for months and found no link, no orders, no organization working for the Exchange. They're independent operators, in it for their themselves. Just like there is no evidence that you are working for the GEC."

For the first time, Overhead was worried. "It doesn't matter if they're officially supported by the Exchange or not. We need to stop them. Otherwise the GEC will be forced to take more extreme measures. It will be bloody awful. I can help you bring down these pirates."

Jill folded her arms.

"The pirates are planning to hit a secret GEC installation at a system called Endor. My superiors have set up an ambush. They need your squadron to be the hammer."

"What's at this secret facility?"

Overhead shifted in her chair and kneaded her thigh. "I don't know. My contacts didn't tell me."

"Give us the coordinates," Jill said, her hands suddenly sweaty. She feared for Jon, but that fool had made his own stupid decisions, didn't he?

"You can have them, but in return you must let me contact my people."

Namely, The Name.

"The people who will make sure you're released," Jill said flatly. She expected Overhead to find a way out of prison. Coming right after Spranker and the boys escaped, it stung like hell. Jill dreamed for so long of tossing this woman in jail. And now, with that a reality, she found that she didn't care much about keeping Overhead in prison. There was always a bigger catch for Jill than Eden Overhead. The Name posed his own fundamental security threat to the GEC. Worse than pirates.

"Did you give the pirates the coordinates?" Thomas asked.

"I gave them to Grand, right before he did this to me. He probably gave them to every pirate on his exchange. He wants to cash in. Another reason your squadron has to stop this raid."

Thomas looked to Jill for direction. She didn't want to ignore the threat to the GEC posed by The Name. Doing so would feel like the moral equivalent of scrubbing sandpaper against a bloody abrasion. But The Name wasn't her mission today. Maybe The Name made it that way. Maybe, even worse, it was the right call.

"We'll get you a comm line," Jill said to Overhead, "but I'm not even thinking about releasing you until I have those coordinates."

It was an empty threat, really. Jill could do nothing if The Name ordered Overhead's release. But the old woman in front of her was exhausted and in agony. She recited the coordinates from memory.

Thomas entered them into his handheld. "That's in unexplored space. It's not connected to any slide route."

"The route is secret," Overhead said. "You could map your own route there but you'll arrive there about six months too late. I'll give the you route right now if you promise to release me." She groaned. "And get that mend started."

Thomas said to Jill, "It's your call, Investigator."

Jill nodded. Overhead sang a set of coordinates with a lot of decimal places. "There's only one route in and out. Go to those coordinates and the rest of the route will appear."

A guard wheeled Overhead to the med bay.

Within an hour, Jill and the *Charles* slid for Andiron. She needed to prep the squadron for what she hoped was a final, mortal strike against the Exchanger pirates.

FIFTY

"YOU KNOW, it's weird not having him around," Tongue said, looking at Barry's seat in the *Drake*'s kick.

"Don't get all misty on me," Flank retorted. "He's been gone one day. Essentially out running an errand. He's the *Mandrake*'s problem for now. Are we still locked on to the first beacon?"

Tongue looked at his console and checked over the slide path one more time. The Drake hung at a very specific point in interstellar space. The Endor coordinates included incredibly specific locations to receive the tight-beam beacon transmissions for the next stop along the way. The starslider's sensors had to be positioned in a specific six meter by six meter space in the middle of nowhere to receive the signal.

"We're still receiving. We are blue across my board to slide. It's clear and safe on the other end, it's just, you know, weird to trust some secret navigation beacons that we can't even see."

Flank said, "Having to find the sweet spot where three tight beam transmissions converge is a sneaky way to hide the nav beacons. These Grids know how to be sneaky."

Tongue activated the slide path. They arrived at the first beacon in one piece. Flank started the drive capacitors recharging while Tongue maneuvered to the next tiny spot where they would catch the next set of signals. Unlike most navigation beacons, the one they arrived at didn't relay data from the next beacon. Some other trio of beacons lurked nearby, probably each the size of a flip-flop, tight-beaming one data stream each.

"Got it. It's pointing us to another, uh, you know, point. Just outside the gravity well of a gas giant. Clear of debris and other flight obstacles."

They slid again. And again. The Drake followed a zigzag pattern of slide points that took them farther and farther from any settled system or known slide route. Tongue silently kept track of how far they were from anyone who could help them if they ran into trouble. They exceeded the range for a probe to slide and call for help. Then two probe ranges away. Then five, ten, fifty. They could broadcast a call for help on regular lightspeed that would reach the nearest inhabited system in a century.

"A really evil bastard could create a maze of these points and leave a ship stranded," Flank noted. "One way beacons and you need special coordinates to even find the signal from the next one. We could use that."

"Trick someone to slide there, and then we grab them while they're stuck? Like a spider web of routes." Tongue tugged at his beard while he considered it. "And they have to cooperate to get the coordinates for the beacon that takes them out."

"We could even destroy existing beacons on the GEC's main route, replace them with the hidden ones, and bottle up traffic for easy pickings." Flank grinned. "Grabbing one ship at a time isn't going to work forever. We need to think about the next phase of the business. Especially with your old girlfriend out there with her squadron."

Tongue shook his head. He clammed himself up at the mention of her every time. If he stopped talking, the other guys got the hint and dropped the subject.

The Drake slid to the penultimate stop before Endor. A dusty little nebula. Tongue maneuvered the ship to tap the beacons in the Endor system. Prudent navigation, and curiosity, demanded that he have a peek around, gauge the traffic, scout any defenses or law enforcement, and note any navigational obstacles and opportunities.

But the triangulated signal coming from Endor was the most limited beacon information he had ever seen. It only had data for the location of one slide exit point and a safety certification that it was safe to slide in on that exit point. There wasn't any data on in-system ship masses, orbital stations, or a visual feed of Endor. And no way to get a read on the security arrangements.

"What?" Flank asked.

"It's not telling us anything. Other than, you could slide into this point safely."

"Where's the rest of the data?"

Tongue shook his head. "It's not there. It should be. Standard navigational data, you know? How many planets, how many ships near the beacon, a live optical feed."

Flank scrolled over to the beacon data that Tongue was seeing. "They really know how to keep things zipped up."

"I don't like it. We could be sliding into the side of an asteroid or the hangar of a Monolith."

Flank pulled up a star chart. "We can see them from right here. Standard main sequence star, rough estimate of planets. It's astrometrics. We're twenty year outside the system. Look at our optical scopes, the images are just twenty years old."

There scopes showed one planet with a habitable orbit and atmosphere. The ship energy signatures and broadcast signals they picked up in this spot, although twenty years out of date, indicated a human presence there.

"I would feel a lot better if we could send in a probe," Tongue said. Twenty year old data to a navigator was the same as no data.

Flank shook his head. "I don't want to spook their security."

"Yeah, well, I don't want to slide in there blind. I don't trust Grand."

"Neither do I, but if we send in something shitting out all kinds of energy signatures, they'll know we're coming. Unless," Flank curled his lower lip under his teeth, "unless, I could repurpose a probe to not broadcast anything towards the system. Just a tight-beam transmission through the slide back to us. Like these beacons we've been following."

It took Flank four hours of clanks and grunts for him to strip their smallest probe. The probe was the size of a chopstick and came pre-assembled with a number of lifesaving broadcasters and signaling tech. Flank had yanked out or deactivated nearly everything but a small set of sensors that only beamed information back to the *Drake*. He loaded it in the launch tube.

"Make damn sure you slide this into the *outer* system. They'll notice something sliding in close to the planet."

"Right on the edge of the heliosphere, coming right up," Tongue said. He fired the probe and it slid to the Endor system. The probe arrived and beamed a constant stream of ship mass data and power signatures back to the *Drake* through a wormhole too small for mass to travel. The GEC would need to drop a ship within three meters of the probe to pick up the tight-beam before it disappeared into the wormhole.

Tongue whistled. "Look at what we got waiting for us," he said. Flank came back to the kick from where he had been tidying up his workbench.

"That's a hell of a lot more than one dinky shipyard and a few ships," Flank said.

"This far out, it's hard to tell, but it looks like a major facility and lots of unpowered ship masses." Tongue brought up the scans that Grand gave them to compare. The only thing that matched was the green planet in the background.

"What kind of ships are there?" Flank asked.

"This probe can't tell from this distance. Outer system, remember?"

Flank nodded. "Remind me to build an actual spy probe some day."

"The key thing is, either his data was old, wrong, or he's totally playing us."

"Or someone played him," Flank said. "Do you think Grand knows how to set something up like that slide route we came down? We're way too far from the Underseed. What can we tell about security there?"

Tongue shook his head. "There's energy signatures and encrypted comm traffic. That doesn't tell us much."

Flank waved his hand. "I don't think they have much. Their primary defense is being a secret, with all these trick beacons and such. Secondary defense is being out here in the ass-end of the sector. The GEC doesn't have the resources to go to all this trouble to hide this system and then build more defenses in case all those precautions won't work."

"Yeah, I hear you. It just makes me nervous."

"What I'm worried about is escaping. We'll be flying lumbering cargo ships and other craft that probably can barely slide. We have to get them all the way back to the Underseed, which is like halfway across the sector. This will be for nothing if they can just trap us at the next slide point. They know the escape route."

"So," Flank said, "we need to build our own escape route."

Tongue brought up the star chart of the local area. He superimposed a new slide route over it. Parts of the new route blinked intermittently. "On a public route, you at least know where the beacon was. But if you don't know where the beacon is supposed to be, you can't slide. You're stuck. Navigator's biggest nightmare."

"These are the kind of nightmares you have?" Flank asked.

Tongue smiled. "Never thought I would want to make the nightmare come true. And on purpose. But we can totally do this. We have enough probes."

Flank grinned and clapped him on the back.

FIFTY-ONE

BARRY EXPECTED RECRUITING pirates would require him to tour the Underseed aboard the *Mandrake,* making impassioned appeals to cynical, hardboiled pirates. He visited Jasmine and Murray on the *Leggett* to spread the word. And to expose Jess Forrester as the GEC spy, traitor, and cop Jill Stamp.

But when they spread the word that he was recruiting, pirates offered to meet him. The *Drake's* top position on the pirate exchange worked wonders.

He and the *Mandrake* crew decided to stay at the Underseed system Woodshed so he could hold a pirate job fair.

A home goods warehouse in the outskirts of Woodside offered him two aisles in its store. The *Mandrakers* knew the cavernous place because they bought fluffy pink hand towels for the passenger restrooms on the *Aksamma.* The store's inventory consisted of whatever had been recently nicked from the GEC.

When he started doing interviews, he had the good, the clowns, and the ugly queued up down two aisles. While they were waiting, several of them browsed the end cap displays and scored discounted air fresheners and instapizza rations.

The line meant Barry could be picky about selecting pirate accomplices. He asked: what's your experience piloting GEC spacecraft? Knowledge of GEC shipyards? Melee skills? Zapper accuracy? What's your ship's weapons loadout?

After two days of interviewing, he had enough brutes and pilots but not enough ships. But there was a line still two aisles long of disreputables hoping to land a spot in the raid.

He hunted around for the public address phone and found it hidden behind an end cap display of vegetable peelers. He picked it up and his voice came over every speaker across the store.

"Attention, attention. This is Barry Spranker. All guests who are here for the pirate raid interviews, I have an announcement. We only have positions available for those who have a starship. You must have your own starship."

There were groans and grumbles along the line. Half of the big, dumb monsters shook their heads and left. Someone shouted a question.

"Yes," Barry answered over the intercom. "It needs to be a flyable starship. With a slide drive. Thank you. If you don't have an operating ship, it's going to have to be a no from me."

Nearly everyone left in line sighed.

An employee ran up to him and handed him a note. Barry said, "Oh, and the store wants me to remind you that we're having a special on soybean seeds in Aisle Thirty-Six, next to that flashing, headache-inducing display of Life Day decorations. We also have a shipment of steel deck screws in Aisle Twenty-One. Perfect for all of your habitat-construction needs here on beautiful, arboreal Woodshed. Thank you."

The disappointed would-be pirate recruits took a while to exchange contact info with people they met. Some went in search of the steel deck screws. The trip was not a total waste for everyone.

There were only a dozen people left in line. The first bunch was a crew of Exchangers with a heavily armed shuttle craft. The last group was an Underseed crew that owned an old GEC picket ship named *Forced Place*. According to Grand's pirate exchange, the *Forced Place* ranked in the bottom half and was run by a guy named Mellon.

'Captain Mellon' was good old Clasker who grinned when Barry recognized him.

The hair on Barry's neck rose. Overhead's disappearance was probably Grand's doing, but Clasker could have had a hand in it. Barry didn't understand what a clean-cut guy like Clasker was doing in the pirate business.

Clasker said, "Barry, good to see you. It's been a while."

Barry folded his arms. "Since when did you join the property resettlement business, uh, Captain Mellon?"

"There's so many ways to practice piracy. Some victims are more willing victims than others. Especially when they receive an insurance payoff for lost cargo." Ah, the inside job version of stealing GEC goods. A time-honored Underseed practice with a new sugary pirate coating. No fighting, no space chases, but you could list on the pirate exchange.

Clasker's eyes swiveled about. "Let's take a walk, just you and me."

"Right, sure. Step over to the rugs aisle, if you don't mind."

Barry and Clasker found a quiet spot on the far side of the store amongst the throw rugs, carpet samples, and expensive area rugs suspended on rollers.

"We're not signing up for your raid," Clasker said.

Barry didn't feign disappointment. "What's with the name change? Same old weasely face."

"I dropped 'Clasker' when Grand took over, because his goons have been looking for me."

"What happened to Eden?" Barry asked, his voice muffled by the hideous rugs. He wanted to meet here because this aisle didn't draw much foot traffic and it was almost soundproof.

Clasker idly ran his hand along a thick, scratchy brown area rug. "She visited Grand on Royada and disappeared. She knew my plan was to disappear, too, if she ever did. No regrets, no questions."

"So you turned pirate. You really don't want in on this run? You could use the boost on the exchange." Barry said. He didn't trust Clasker, but he also couldn't believe Clasker could pass up a high stakes job like this one.

"No. And I recommend you pass on it, too."

"Do you even know what *it* is?" Barry asked.

Clasker opened his mouth to reply, looked behind Barry, and shut up. A young couple had wandered into the aisle. The woman was intrigued by the carpeting selections while her male companion kept checking the time on his comlink. She mentioned that last month the carpet section had been cleaned out.

"Excuse me, shoppers," Barry said. "This aisle is closed. Someone saw a varmint."

"A what?" asked the young guy.

Barry got down on his knees and pointed at the dark space under a rolled up rug. "Varmint. Rodent, little thing with claws that likes to poop and lay eggs," Barry explained, making a rodent-like face. The woman recoiled. "Someone brought one of these rugs home and found a dead one rolled up inside, so the manager called us in to check. I told him these things probably live over in cookware, but none of them have been found dead in a wok yet, I guess. Give us ten minutes, all-righty-tighty?"

The guy didn't need any more urging. He tugged on the woman's sleeve to leave the aisle.

"Thanks *super much*." Barry crawled out and stood up, wiping his hands. "I lied to them about the woks. There's been a dead rat in one every day this week."

"Endor," Clasker said. "There are things Eden never looped me in on. High level secrets. Like who her contacts are in the GEC upper ranks. How she was capitalized to found Underseed settlements on the frontier. *And the Endor coordinates.* They're a closely-guarded GEC secret. Part of some big operation."

"A GEC operation? What?"

Clasker raised both hands. "Your guess is probably better than mine. Commodities, precious minerals, currency reserves, toxic waste?"

"Toxic waste?" Barry rolled his eyes.

"I don't know. But I wouldn't go near it," Clasker said. "Someone is shorting the pirate exchange. Including you guys and the exchange's other top crews. Someone expects you all to fail. Getting caught at Endor would do it."

"Grand doesn't allow any short sales on the exchange. He made a point to tell me."

"They must be side bets then, off the exchange," Clasker said. "You can bet on anything you want in the Underseed."

"Who is shorting it?"

Clasker shrugged. "I don't know. Whoever it is has been doing this quietly. I thought you were, so you could take a dive and cash out again. I doubted that this raid of yours was legit and wanted to see for myself."

Barry jabbed thumb at his own breastbone. "We have the Endor coordinates. It's legit."

"That makes me twice as nervous for you and the clowns you signed up."

"Those clowns are the scariest fighters in the Underseed," Barry said. "You act like you're not up to speed any more. What's it going to cost me to know what you know?"

"I'm not plugged in like I used to be," Clasker said. "If you guys are pulling another Connexion scam, shorting your own shares, Grand will kill you."

Barry wasn't double-crossing anyone. Flank cared too much about the pirate exchange rankings. Tongue hated subterfuge even more than usual because of the whole Jill betrayal.

"If it's not you, then someone may know more about this raid than you do. If you don't know who the sucker is, then you're the sucker."

Barry shook his head. Grand needed a big payout. He wouldn't let someone tank his exchange, much less do it himself. How much would Grand have to be compensated in return for sacrificing his prototype for future exchanges? It was likely that Grand didn't know if somebody had other plans. There were too many angles, too many unknowns, for Barry to figure out. But if he was a sucker on the Endor raid, Grand must be, too. That was an interesting development. "I'll put you down as a 'maybe' on joining?" he asked.

Clasker finally smiled. "You've had a hell of a run. It'd be stupid to end it by falling for some mythical star system scam. You may want to figure it out before you go charging in there." He wave. "Either way, safe sliding out there, Captain Spranker."

Barry waved back. "Good seeing you, Captain Mellon."

Clasker walked away to collect his crew. Barry stayed in the rug aisle. He pounded his fist on the roll of thick brown carpet.

"Of course someone's planning to screw me," he muttered to himself. "At this point, I should just expect it. There's just so many suspects to choose from." As he left the rug aisle, he put on happy, care-free face for the benefit of the *Mandrake* and other pirate crews. But inside, his guts felt twisted.

FIFTY-TWO

THE *DRAKE'S* kick hosted an odd scene. The entrance was crowded with onlookers in bushy wigs, spiky metal armor, and scary makeup. They were knockoffs of the Exchange's infamous Death Metal Circus Clowns. Instead of carrying musical instruments, these Clowns made music with zappers, trank guns, and flashbang grenades.

Flank's head floated in mid-air without a body attached. He was testing a skin-tight chameleon body suit.

Barry had only added a zapper to his sweatpants ensemble, mostly to look cool.

"We'll see what's going on there when we slide in," Tongue said. "But it doesn't feel right. This slide beacon is locked down. We don't know where we're sliding to in the Endor system. Hopefully it's not inside an asteroid or too close to the star."

"Such a damned worrier," said Flank's disembodied head. He was pumped to crack skulls. "We scouted the system when we were here last time."

"Here we go," Tongue said.

Barry tried to shoo the Clowns out of the kick. Everyone was too riveted to the show happening on the tactical screens to pay attention to him though.

The *Drake* emerged close to Endor's only habitable world. Half a dozen other pirate ships arrived seconds later. The green and blue planet was directly ahead, and the shipyards were a twenty minute flight away.

"What did I say?" Tongue said, indicating the tactical screens with both hands.

The Clowns gasped.

Flank gulped audibly. "We're foxed. Hard."

The tactical screens showed dozens of active ships. Clusters of three and four were parked at beacons in the outer system. A handful of Monoliths were stationed near the shipyards. They seemed harmless compared to knife-shaped vessels patrolling the shipyards themselves. The tactical screens couldn't identify their class but they each bristled with the power signatures of multiple weapons systems.

The pirates had discovered a fleet of GEC warships.

A text message came in. "*Drake*, this is Admiral Kleble. Stand down and prepare to be boarded."

The other pirate ships frantically commed the *Drake* for instructions. Two captains threatened to leave the second their ships recharged.

Tongue maxed the thrusters. The *Drake* surged forward. "Stick to the plan," Barry replied on the comm.

"Where the hell is the *Mandrake*, they were supposed to draw the heat away," Flank said.

One of the would-be boarders pointed at the tactical screen. "There! She's got a dozen ships closing on her. Is this the time when you tell us you've been in scrapes worse than this?"

"We may be a tiny bit foxed," Barry admitted. He should have listened to Clasker. But he never expected anything *this* bad.

"I'd say a lot foxed," Tongue said. "Those are warships. They have, like, a hell of a lot of weapons."

"With weapons, huh?" snarked Flank. "Tell me, can you name a warship class without weapons, Tongue?"

"Damn it, yes, idiot. Tenders, scout craft, I'm not stupid, you ass. My point is the GEC has its own damn war fleet. That's the secret here. Someone should have told us."

Despite Flank's meticulous preparations they were not prepared to invade a military shipyard. Instead of half a dozen shipyards, there were four dozen arranged in six rows of eight. Multiple ships were under construction at each one.

"The Endor system didn't have any security, Tongue," Barry said, slack-jawed with shock. "You said so. I believed you."

"There's a dozen really heavily armed 'non-warships' intercepting this ship we're in right now," Tongue said. He switched the forward monitors to the tactical view. "We have small craft closing on our stern; the big ships are still vectoring toward the *Mandrake*. The big ones are really slow, like *Leggett Rose* kind of slow."

The GEC ships approaching the stern were tiny, wispy things, mostly just engines with weapons. They had six forward-swept flight wings on a small egg-shaped fuselage. Flank said the weapons were capacitor cannons, meant to disable a ship by overloading its electronics.

These things, whatever they were, were faster than the *Drake*. Within a minute, indicators on the tactical screens lit up. Flank's hands flew across his console. "We're being hit by those cap cannons," he said.

Barry tried not to gulp audibly. "Is this a problem?"

Flank said, "No. If they hit the tiny sensor pods on our hull, the pods will absorb the power and use it for active sensing first. If they are overwhelmed, they'll let the charge carry past into the inner hull. Our only vulnerability is the drive, and only if they overwhelm the capacitors or physically damage the drive arrays. Otherwise, the energy they throw at us shortens our recharge time."

"But we're one of the only starsliders. Most of the rest have metallic hulls, including the *Mandrake*."

"Well, they're kind of foxed," Flank said.

"We're eight minutes out," Tongue noted.

The GEC fighters disabled the *Claw*, a Grid yacht. Its overwhelmed power system shut down and the ship went dark. It continued hurtling toward the planet. There was no point trying to comm to them and they were too far away to rescue.

Another ship, the *Rhyming Plague*, sparked violently on the tactical screen, barely able to absorb the hits it was taking. It returned fire with a barrage from its homemade cap cannons. The tiny Grid ship pursuing it exploded.

"First blood," Tongue remarked morosely.

"Cheer up, those little fighters are remotely piloted," Flank replied. "No life signs in them. Is there any other name for them? Little fighters is stupid."

Tongue shrugged. The cartoonish boarding party was fresh out of suggestions, too.

Barry threw his hands in the air. "Come on, people, say something sharp. We haven't got all day."

Tongue replied, "Spiders?"

"Spiders it is. You'll be famous," Barry said, clapping Tongue on the back. "See? This isn't hard, guys. We're making history every minute on this job."

The other pirate ships opened fire, draining capacitors about to overload from absorbing the GEC's blasts. A running pitched battle developed with the pirates closing on the shipyard and the GEC ships pursuing them. The *Drake* hung back to use its non-conducting hull to shield its metal-hulled allies.

"Target on Spider Three," Flank commed to the other pirates. Spider Three became a dead, dark husk. "Good." He highlighted the spider rated the next highest threat.

The shipyard drew closer. The pirate ships methodically took out a dozen more Spiders. But the spiders kept emerging from the bellies of the oncoming capital ships in a long, steady line. Barry counted a dozen continued to circle the *Drake*.

One of the pirate tubs, *The Naughty Baker*, crapped out, overwhelmed by the GEC's cap cannons.

Tongue whooped. "The *Claw* restarted." The pirate borders cheered. This wasn't supposed to be a suicide mission, after all.

Flank said, "Dead time was four minutes. Having an auxiliary power system cut the restart time by 80 percent. I'm alerting the other ships. Most of them should be able to restart before they get boarded."

The *Drake* jerked violently. Like something punched the ship square in the jaw. Everyone was thrown forward. Barry landed in the corridor to engineering. At the back, the boarding party went down like a stack of psychedelic dominoes.

"Ow," Tongue said, rubbing the spot where his head hit the seat.

"What. The. Fox. Was. That?" Barry asked, his lips mashed into bitter-tasting deck moss.

"That was a warhead. Not a cap cannon," Flank declared matter of factly. He bounced to his feet. He was actually enjoying this.

Barry staggered to standing, leaning on the bulkhead for support. Surprisingly, no body parts were severed.

Tongue returned to his console. "That warhead. Shit."

Barry asked, "What?"

"Stamp."

"No."

"Yes."

"Squadron?"

"Yes."

"After us?"

"Who else?"

"Shit."

Stamp's squadron had slid into the middle of the pirate raiders and had fired the missile at the *Drake*.

"The missile detonation was underneath us. If Tongue hadn't accelerated, our slide drive would be shredded right now," Flank said.

A starslider's main weaknesses were the bow-mounted slide drive, the fragile humans inside the unbreakable shell, and delicate sensors hanging off the stern. A missile, detonated near a starslider's bow, could destroy the slide drive and disable the ship.

Lemonne must have figured out how to take down the *Drake*. And Stamp somehow knew the pirate flotilla would be here. Barry was once again confronting the results of his own smug stupidity. This raid was a trap from the beginning. Like Clasker warned him.

They were boxed in and foxed up.

"Brilliant ideas, anyone?" Barry asked. "Or half idiotic ones?"

Tongue said, "Let's bail. What else can we do, Flank? If Lemonne gets a good shot in, we could lose the drive, or worse."

Flank was disgusted. "Can't you duck and weave, piloting genius, and keep them off of us?"

"I could, Flank, I really could," Tongue said. "The problem is Lemonne and Stamp's people will hit our bow, so we need to keep our stern toward them. But if she calls in her GEC warship pals then we're surrounded by assholes."

Flank grinned and pointed at the tactical screen. "Maybe not."

"What?" Tongue twisted around and put his hands on his hips. "Huh, well, that's really something."

The GEC warships, menacing with their spiky-lethality, had turned from the pirates and were firing on Stamp's squadron. One of her squadron's tugs ate a barrage of spider shots and began to tumble out of control.

The GEC fleet had assumed Stamp's motley squadron was more pirate raiders. Maybe the pirates' main force. Kleble must be screaming at people to correct the mistake.

Or, not? Barry tried playing out the angles on this development but got lost. Had Stamp gone rogue? Was the fleet ordered to fire on anyone who entered the system? Five minutes ago, the secret Endor system was bait to trap the Exchange pirates. But, maybe, the pirate raid was bait to trap Stamp. Or was it a simple coincidence that both the pirates and Stamp stumbled into a top-secret GEC military facility? Why build a ragtag pirate hunter squadron when you already had a whole fleet? Barry scanned the tactical screens, hoping for a clue.

The fleet ships that had not reacted to the *Mandrake*, the pirates, or the squadron caught his attention. They were underway but fleeing the battle. None of them emitted any weapon power signatures, either.

"Bare?"

Barry smirked. Close to one hundred ships were under construction, either at the docks, parked in orbit or on shakedown runs. The warships were slow to react to the pirates. The amount of close-in traffic made Andiron look deserted by comparison. "Can we access the shipyard workers' comms? Hear what they're saying?"

Tongue flipped some switches. Text of the comm traffic scrolled on his console. "Yeah, yeah. They're panicking, they're totally confused about what's happening out here."

The GEC fleet broke out of formation to deal with Stamp's squadron. It was so poorly executed that the ships nearly collided with one another. The comm chatter confirmed the frantic confusion. Maybe it was only Stamp coming for the pirates. The shipyard and the fleet weren't ready for any visits.

Barry keyed the comm to the rest of the pirate flotilla. "Let's have fun, people. We stick to the plan. Stamp won't shoot us down if we snuggle up close to the shipyards, so let's make for it, full speed. We grab the transceiver, you grab all the ships, we all go home."

"Using the drive to help the thrusters will *lengthen* our recharge time," Tongue warned.

Barry licked his lips. "There's going to be so many targets pretty soon, you'll have all the time you need to slide."

"That sounds nice, but, you know, that squadron is coming for this ship right here," Tongue said.

Barry slapped him on the back. "Come with the boarding party and leave this crate. Plenty of fine new ships here to choose from."

"You didn't just suggest abandoning this ship. My ship," Flank said, cracking his knuckles.

Barry rolled his eyes. "That knuckles shit worked, once, in freshman year. And I was half drunk at the time."

"My ship—"

"If a missile nails her square, your ship will be a rock pile with frozen moss inside it," Barry snapped.

Tongue waved to get their attention. "Guys, this is touching and all, but let's just slide the fox out of here. Like right now."

"I was talking about saving the ship, not your flaky ass," Flank said.

"Come on, my plan is so stupid it has to work." Barry said. Discouragement looked unsettling on the Clowns' brightly-painted faces. He added, "I meant that in the best possible way. Uh, boarding party, report to the airlock."

Tongue was apprehensive as he pulled the ship alongside the ship-yard's airlock. "Are you sure?"

Barry said, "I'm sure that paper gowns chafe my thighs. We'll nab that traffic control transceiver before you know it. Slide out as soon as you can."

Barry shooed the metal circus freaks off the kick and down the corridor. The airlock was aft, and the boarding party crowded it. He remembered to grab a stun baton and a short-range zapper. Flank come up behind him, lugging a toolkit.

"No weapons?" Barry asked.

Flank wiggled his arms. "These are lethal weapons."

"So, which one do we take?" one of the Clowns asked.

"Huh?" Barry said.

"Warships or troop transports. Which one should we take?"

The plan called for lifting whatever yachts or shuttles were available. This was different.

"Your choice," Barry said. "Whatever you can fly manually."

"Take the warships, they'll sell for more," Flank said.

"Hell with that, I want a decent pirate ship," said a Clown in a ripped fishnet vest.

Flank was hard to take seriously. The rest of his body blinked out of existence as he activated his bodysuit.

"Good luck," Barry said.

"Go have a good chuckle, Captain," Flank replied.

Tongue's voice rumbled over the speakers. "I'm swinging us below the dock here and will fast-latch to the airlock on the far side. This is the closest I can get to the transceiver station. Best wishes, guys. I'll see you later."

"You are sliding as soon as you can, right?" Flank asked.

"The second she's charged, man."

"Good."

Barry smiled.

Flank said "What? I'm concerned about my ship, not the fruitcake driving it."

"You love us. Admit it."

"Fox you, Barry. Fox you. Let's go."

Barry turned to the airlock. "Come on. What's it take to pop the lock?"

The airlock pressure gauge finally showed a healthy blue and opened with a hiss. They charged inside.

FIFTY-THREE

HALF OF JILL'S squadron was out of action. The Endor fleet, which wasn't supposed to exist, had activated a remote kill switch for one cargo shuttle. Another shuttle was disabled by five shots from these weird little fighters.

"I am a GEC Investigator carrying out legitimate orders from Sector law enforcement," she said into the comm. "It is illegal to fire on any of my vessels." She sent her credentials and the documents permitting her to operate anywhere in GEC space. For the third time.

The comm crackled with a response seconds later. "Investigator Stamp, we acknowledge that you are bona fide GEC law enforcement operating under legal authorization. However, our security protocols supersede your orders and authorization. You have violated those protocols. Stand by to be boarded and taken into custody. Or be destroyed. You have thirty seconds for your ships to comply."

"What are these security protocols?" she asked. "Tell Admiral Kleble that he knows my authority comes from Title 7, Section 460.c of the GEC Criminal Statute."

The response was a terse, "We acknowledge Title 7, but our authority supersedes it. You are not cleared for information on our legal authority. You must comply."

Jill couldn't comply; she refused to comply. This was her best chance to cripple a fundamental security threat in one stroke. It looked like half of Grand's pirate exchange was right here, in range of her weapons. She wouldn't mind if the scary warships wiped out the pirates for her, but she didn't know what this secret GEC fleet would actually do.

Lemonne stood behind her in the *Charles'* kick, on the verge of vomiting. She promised him citizenship in exchange for swiping at his enemies. They never discussed the risk of dying in the process. Especially not due to her own people killing them. There were a lot of lives in her squadron at risk if she decided to fight this.

She toggled the comm. "We're on *the same side*. You and I could trap these pirates. But while you're boarding my vessels, they'll escape. Or you kill us and then you'll be in real trouble. I need them alive and trust me, you need my squadron alive. Let's work together, not against each other."

The fleet ceased firing on her squadron. A small relief. The warships and small mosquito-like fighters were still closing on her ships though, weapons hot.

She continued, "I propose that we dock and send officers to arrest the pirates who just stormed the shipyard. You can arrest us afterwards, if you think you have to, and sort out the legalities then."

Precious seconds ticked by. More pirate ships were docking at shipyards and disgorging invaders.

"Proceed," came the fleet's reply.

Lemonne sighed. GEC security types waving orders and badge numbers at one another didn't seem to faze him, but getting vaporized by a giant warship did.

Lieutenant Fancher shook his head in disbelief and went aft to update his team. He had been sour since the Royada raid failed.

The *Charles'* sensors located the *Drake* when it undocked from the nearest shipyard. Lemonne brought his starslider around to dock at the same airlock.

Jill said, "They've gone inside. They're after something." Because there was little chance Spranker would make this effort to simply trash the place. Well, she couldn't discount the possibility entirely. He may just spray paint his name on the walls.

"Who's flying the *Drake*?" Lemonne asked.

Tongue? Probably not Flank. He wouldn't taxi other pirates to a fight but not join in. No, storming the shipyard wasn't a feint. They must want something here. "Let the *Drake* go." *Maybe Tongue will escape after all*, she thought. It was surprisingly okay with her. She believed he was the least guilty of the three. He was a go-along get-along type. Spranker and Flank were the real problems.

Jill's intuition was confirmed when the *Drake* flew full throttle straight out of the battle area. Maybe the pirates planned to steal spare parts. She rejected the idea that they would take the docked ships. A GEC starship at a high security shipyard had to be well-secured and probably needed several layers of approvals before anyone could fly it.

Lemonne's worried expression was a sour contrast. "We have not gotten a scratch on your ship yet," Jill said.

"No scratches but also no kills," Lemonne responded tartly.

"You can have at the pirates after we disembark. Lieutenant Fancher," she said to the squat man at the kick's entrance, "we go in two minutes."

Lieutenant Fancher barked an order to the twelve hulks in black puffy armor crammed in the aft corridor. They activated their weapons. She followed them to the airlock. With a clank and a hiss, the airlock connected. She followed Fancher and the commandos inside.

The airlock closed behind her. The *Charles* detached immediately. It dropped under the shipyard superstructure and fired its weapons in several directions simultaneously at the nearest pirate ships.

Outside the airlock window were explosions, tracer fire, pirate ships, mosquito fighters, warships, and her own squadron. Her ships were twisting, banking, and firing at the pirates, trying to avoid hitting the fleet. A completely chaotic mess she could do nothing about right now. She ran to catch up with Fancher's team. At least Spranker and Flank were now trapped inside the station.

FIFTY-FOUR

"I'M SO FOXING sorry I didn't steal the wiring diagram of the secret military base which I wasn't aware of until twenty minutes ago," Flank barked. He, Barry, and a dozen Metal Circus Clowns were crouched behind a console. Electrified zapper rounds sizzled against the console's plastic. The wheezing high-pitched retorts of two dozen zappers firing made it difficult to talk. "Who puts a goddamn first aid station under the damn transceiver dish but places the control station somewhere else?"

The shipyard they were inside was a long metallic box with spindly arms branching off. The central corridor was over two stories tall; large enough to run ship components up and down. The transceiver dish slaving the docked ships to shipyard control was seated on the outer hull. The transceiver unit itself was located somewhere else, apparently.

The few shipyard personnel they saw ran away when they saw the Clowns. Flank disabled half a dozen security guards who couldn't draw their zappers fast enough. He, Barry, and the Clowns reached what he expected was the transceiver unit. Three Clowns hit with zapper rounds were napping on the deck's industrial carpet squares.

Barry waited for the fire to die down. "Would you really want me to undermine your quest for excellence by lowering my expectations?"

Flank replied with a gesture indicating what he wanted Barry to do with his mouth instead of talking. "Maybe I can follow the cables from the dish assembly to the control room," he said.

"Did you guys check the station map?" one of the Clowns asked, lip quivering under his greasepaint. He jabbed a finger at the console they were hiding behind.

"Good idea," Barry said. He fired his zapper blindly to cover Flank so he could peep up at the console.

A starslider flashed by the viewports. It was not the *Drake*. Shiny white hull with black decorative stenciling: the *Charles*. Barry said calmly, "Stamp probably has a boarding party coming this way. We need to go."

"Query!" Flank yelled.

"Query," replied the station interface they were crouched behind.

Flank lowered his voice. "Audio directions to the primary local traffic control system."

"Proceed fifty meters towards the bow."

Flank said, "That's behind us. We made a wrong turn when we came in."

Barry shrugged helplessly. They retreated from the guards and took off down the central corridor. The guards' zapper rounds pinged off the metal walls and scorched the carpet squares.

One of the Clowns fell to the deck with a surprised yelp. Barry got a hand under his arm and lifted him up so he could limp on a sleeping leg.

As they passed the docking corridor they entered at, Stamp and her assassin squad came charging towards them. Unlike the first time Barry met her, Stamp was wearing gray body armor and was heavily armed.

"Stamp!" He snarled.

Everyone whirled around. One dumbstruck Clown took a trank dart to the shoulder and slid to the deck. Everyone else scattered.

"Surrender, before anyone else gets hurt," Stamp yelled. The Clowns expected a cue from Barry. He smirked and reloaded. He would never allow her to interrogate him again. It amused him that she thought she had cut off their escape. On the other hand, they couldn't afford to get pinned down in a firefight. The station guards were pursuing them from the other side of the shipyard.

"Get the transceiver unit," Barry said to Flank's floating head. "We're fine. Go." He fired around the corner and shooed the Clowns behind a storage container for better cover. Flank's bald head bobbed down the corridor towards the bow.

He and the Metal Circus Clowns were no match for Stamp's commandos. But the security guards came upon the fight and fired at the commandos and the pirates. Things became awkward and interesting.

The guards ordered Stamp's commandos to drop their weapons and Stamp's people yelled the same thing back. Stamp and a security officer began flashing badges at each other. Eventually they stopped firing.

"Cease fire," Barry said to the Clowns. "Save your ammo. We have to give Flank enough time."

Stamp, the security officer, and the lead commando huddled together for some hushed, angry negotiations. The guards continued pointing their weapons at the commandos. The commandos pointed their weapons at the guards.

Barry was afraid this tiny GEC civil war wouldn't last. He motioned to the Clowns and they quietly withdrew in Flank's direction.

A hundred meters down the hall were two giant engine assemblies on wheeled carts. Each assembly was two stories tall, a clustered mass of metal, diamondwork, and wiring. Good cover — the other side would be loath to shoot up this pricey tech. Barry and the clowns ran for the assemblies.

Behind them, Stamp's lead commando barked new orders. The commandos pivoted and fired their zappers in the pirates' direction.

Two Clowns crumpled. A trank round skipped and bounced across the floor, narrowly missing Barry's calf. But it wasn't a trank round. There was a handgrip on one side. A flashbang grenade. Barry grabbed an unconscious Clown and threw him on top of it.

"Everyone take cover—!" he yelled.

A boom made his ears explode. His hearing went offline. He opened his eyes and only saw billowing purple.

Barry staggered to his feet, groping for the edge of the purple smoke cloud. Two Clowns nearby were clutching their ears.

He reached the edge of the smoke cloud and saw commandos advancing. They weren't taking him prisoner though, dammit. He fired on them, yelling about how lame they were or something. He couldn't hear his own voice. A few functional Clowns joined in and half the commandos went down, zapped and tranked.

His hearing returned like it was riding a distant train barreling into a tunnel. The purple smoke parted momentarily and he saw Stamp running past their position.

"Flank, Stamp got by us. She's coming your way."

Flank's response was garbled and slurred.

"What?!"

"I said," Flank repeated. "I have the transceiver. Let's get out of here. Wait, did you say Stamp?"

Then the commlink went dead.

FIFTY-FIVE

THE TRANSCEIVER UNIT that controlled every unpiloted ship in the shipyard was a hermetically-sealed cube, ten centimeters on each side, with air vents and one data port. The GEC loved to label things and so finding it was easy, once Flank started digging around behind an access panel.

He connected his comlink to it and sent commands to the ships through the transceiver's simple menu system. Dozens of starships obeyed. He disconnected from the unit and tossed it in his knapsack. He lowered the faceshield and powered up his invisibility armor. Flank, the knapsack, and the transceiver unit, effectively disappeared.

The faceshield displayed the armor's power ticking down. Invisibility was a very short-term thing. But he just needed to slip by the hapless shipyard security.

He was chagrined to see Jill Stamp advancing towards him down the corridor, zapper in both hands. The flashes and strobe effects of the battle raging outside lit her up with changing colors. She hadn't seen him. Yet.

He slipped into a dark utility alcove and stayed very still. His armor messed with light but not sound. Luckily the large corridor made it hard to hear breathing or fabric rustling.

She passed the alcove. Her footsteps slowed and then stopped. Shit. If she turned around and took a hard look inside the alcove, he was screwed.

He slipped behind her and jabbed his zapper into her spine. "Hiya, Jill. I never punished you for hurting my friend's feelings."

Her shoulders relaxed. She tossed her weapon to the deck, where it clattered like a plastic toy.

He pushed her up against the nearest bulkhead, keeping the zapper firmly pressed between her shoulder blades.

"How about point blank to the spinal cord? Small chance of permanent nerve damage?"

She didn't say anything. Barry was in his ear, telling him to hurry. He took his hand off of her and began to step back.

She sidestepped to the right and kicked straight back, knocking the zapper out of his hand. Fine.

He dropped into an evasive Lucasian Aikido stance reflexively. He blocked her next kick and sidestepped a hand strike. Tongue would be tickled if he knew Flank had learned techniques of his former order. The only thing he could stomach about that fruity space wizard cult was it had spawned the martial art Lukaido. And Flank was an equal opportunity student of violent and nonviolent combat schema.

An invisible hand grabbed Stamp's wrist and twisted her arm around behind her back. She doubled over and grunted at the discomfort.

"You're wasting your talents on the GEC," he said. "They'll just toss you aside again."

"And what do you want?" She asked, angry. "Best pirate award?"

"For starters."

Barry appeared and smiled when he saw Stamp doubled over and in pain. "Are we taking hostages Flank? For Tongue?"

"Nah, this one's sporting a tracing beacon, I'm sure. I say we knock her out, hide her somewhere."

"She'll miss our big finale."

She sneered. "Where you all die trying to escape from a high security GEC facility?"

Barry fired a trank dart into her thigh. She fumbled at the dart but passed out.

"What are you doing down here? We need to move," Barry yelled at Flank.

Flank ran for the main corridor. Zapper fire was popping off in rapid succession ahead of them. He said, "I started preflight on four dozen ships. We need to hold off Stamp's people long enough." He flashed a grin at Barry, pulled his hood down, and disappeared.

In the main corridor, the remaining Clowns were getting their asses kicked in the zapper firefight. But then one commando fell flat on his face and didn't get up. Another one suddenly toppled over and stayed down. Flank was passing through and around them, leaving each unconscious. Their leader pulled his body heat goggles over his eyes but Flank's invisible hand slammed his head against the wall before he could react.

Amidst the security guards waving zappers in every direction and still falling to Flank, the Clowns gave ground. Something, invisible Flank, grabbed Barry and shoved him into a run down a side corridor. They and most of the remaining Clowns hurried through a door. Flank's hand became visible and hit the door controls. The hatch slammed shut, cutting them off from the rest of the station. Flank pulled his hood down.

"It's time," Flank said. "We have to hurry."

Barry brought the comlink to his mouth and sent a message to everyone. "Go grab a ship."

FIFTY-SIX

"SHUTTLES, pickets, cruisers, transports. This place has everything," Barry panted, running down the corridor with the pack of raiders. "And they're not done building some of them yet."

Flank replied, "We grab these shiny new deathboats. Fast engine, no cargo room, and weapons, weapons, weapons. Would you check out all the tubes on that missile boat."

"I always wanted a foxing cargo ship. Maximum tonnage," said a Clown.

"Can we make some choices here, people?" Barry said. "There's a lot of well-trained people coming to kill us."

"Can we fly them out of here?"

"No," said Flank, skimming their specs. "The cruisers require a crew of fifty, the pickets about ten. Remotely, we can only do in-system navigation and propulsion. We could all pilot one warship."

"They'll destroy it before they let us take it," a Clown said.

Barry waved his hands. "You're right. How about we launch all of the warships remotely. They're bigger prizes. The Grids need to capture them. Meanwhile, we slip out on every transport and shuttle we can grab."

Flank grinned from ear to ear. "Sometimes you can be useful, Bare."

"Won't let it happen again." Barry entered commands to undock. "Here we go."

Flank said, "I'm activating all the ships with an automated departure in five minutes. Everyone grab one before it leaves."

Barry and Flank chose a long-range cargo ship with the designation U-1779-15.

Barry opened the hatch. "I christen thee... pause for dramatic effect... the *Demotion*."

Flank shoved him inside the ship.

They hurried to the bridge. Barry sat at the pilot's station, unsure of the controls. On the *Drake*, any part of the kick's central console could pilot the ship. The notion of needing to position himself in a particular location to use a specific set of physical controls seemed archaic.

Flank sat at the comm console and established a private comm net with the other stolen ships. "I'm relaying the transceiver's signal to the rest of the shipyard so we can launch everything. They shut down comm access to the slide beacons in-system. It limits our range. Name these ships something."

Barry opened up the transponder properties for each ship powering up to leave dock. "*Inkus, Dingus, Porkus, Rinkpus*, the *Feckless*, the *Tangent*..."

Flank plugged the transceiver into the ship. "These other ships are still under construction. Some don't have slide drives, just maneuvering thrusters. I'm warning the Clowns away from them."

Barry focused on the ships unable to slide out, "...the *Yeast*, the *Flourish*, the *Complaint*, the *Interruption*, the *Itch*, the *Appeal*, the *Pretrial Motion*..."

Flank said, "Rotate the transponder information randomly, so the GEC warships can't identify which ship is which. The transceiver will only work while it's in the local grav well; we'll be limited to controlling navigation and propulsion only."

Barry set the transponders to change every two minutes. "So, what? Launch them all. Some can be decoys. When they figure out what's what, we'll be long gone."

"It means we have to be the last to slide," Flank noted, patting the transceiver unit.

"Oh."

Most of the Clowns opted for cargo haulers. Some were former GEC pilots who knew what they were doing in a pilot's seat. Unlike Barry.

"Tongue, are you still here?" Flank commed.

"Above the ecliptic, nearly charged. Still have a squadron of spiders on me. You guys need to get out of there."

"We're sending out all ships out to confuse the Grids. How are things going out there?"

"Man, this navy is, you know, freaking out. Trying not to run into Jill's ships. They're starting to chase the warships."

Flank slapped Barry on the back. He took over at the flight controls and accelerated the *Demotion* away from the shipyard. Already crowded space had become dangerously overcrowded. Flank steered the *Demotion* around all of the small gravitational eddies created by the drives of nearby ships.

Flank pointed at the tactical scope where a quartet of GEC picket ships wer chasing The *Charles* on the far side of the shipyard. The zombie warships were well away from the shipyard, accelerating in all directions. The spider fighters and the warships were moving to intercept them.

Except for a light cruiser and a squadron of spider drones that banked towards the *Demotion*. Like it had caught their scent.

The *Demotion* was a slow, thin-hulled GEC freighter. No weapons, no defensive systems. But it had two life signs in it, which was a dead give away that someone was stealing it. Possibly very dead.

The light cruiser broadcast a demand that the ship halt.

"How much longer until we slide?" Barry asked. The *Demotion* didn't have a screen that showed everyone on the bridge the key stats and diagnostics, like the slide drive countdown.

"Never mind that," Flank said. He pulled Barry over to the pilot's console. "Watch the ship fly its pre-programmed route. And don't touch anything."

"Wait, where are you going?" Barry yelled after Flank. But the bald pirate had already left the bridge.

"If he launches an escape pod, I'm going to ram him," Barry muttered.

FIFTY-SEVEN

FLANK YELLED BACK, but all Barry understood was something about rewiring the drive capacitors.

Barry put the comlink on speaker and called Flank. "What should I do?" he asked, squeezing the flight stick until his knuckles whitened. The slide countdown clock on the pilot's display showed that it was north of fifty minutes.

"Fly the pre-programmed course so they assume we're on autopilot. Don't touch the controls."

Barry pulled his hands off the flight stick like it was infected with flesh-eating plague germs. The *Demotion*'s autopilot was still engaged.

The sleek light cruiser and the spider fighters were closing insanely fast. They'd be within weapons range a whole hell of a lot sooner than fifty minutes.

"They're gonna disable us," he yelled down the corridor in Flank's direction. "Or maybe destroy us."

Barry imagined getting blown into the cold vacuum outside. The shock wave would probably kill him instead of the cold, he figured. What a fun thing to look forward to.

He thought furiously of some shortcut, some opportunity or advantage that he could use to avoid becoming freeze dried. He rubbernecked at the battle, looking for an angle. With a sizable force still pursuing her, the *Drake* slid out of the Endor system. At least Tongue escaped.

Stamp's anti-piracy squadron had returned to fighting the GEC fleet. They were in a running battle with two battleships and swarms of spider fighters. Whatever truce they had was over.

"Okay," Flank said, running back onto the bridge. "We can redirect some incoming weapons energy to the drive and spin up faster."

"And if it doesn't work, we blow up, right?"

Flank grinned. "Makes life interesting, huh?"

"Trying to get dried sand off your feet makes life interesting."

The first blasts of spider weapons fire hit the hull, making a crackling zap noise that echoed through the metal structure. The countdown clock dropped to just over forty minutes.

"Why don't we slide the hell out of here?"

Flank scowled. "We have the transceiver. If we leave, the other ships don't have the slide coordinates and we lose control of the unmanned ones."

It pissed Barry off. For one, he should have realized that. Fear was making him stupider and he hated that. For two, being the last ones out was a fine idea if security was as piss poor as they thought. But not when they were in the middle of a fleet battle. "What the hell is the GEC doing with a navy? Who are they planning to fight?"

Flank grimaced. "Isn't it obvious? The Exchange. The Grids are losing the Mix to the them. You ask me, they figured out how to take it back."

Admiral Kleble had hinted that things were about to change in big ways. Maybe he already knew about this secret navy. A functioning GEC navy would change the rules of the piracy game, too. It would disrupt life in the Underseed. Or end it altogether.

"There may be an all-out war with the Exchange," Flank said. He sounded excited about the prospect, the idiot.

Barry scowled. "There hasn't been an interplanetary armed conflict since the race to Union began. What's that? Tens of thousands of years? A hundred thousand?"

Every control light on the bridge flared when the *Demotion* absorbed energy weapons fire from the spiders trailing its stern. The power surge fed the capacitors and the countdown clock fell to under thirty minutes. But a hull breach vacuumed out the contents of a bunk compartment.

Barry sent the ship into a pre-programmed evasive maneuver. No point in looking like they were on autopilot.

"The closest to a war in the Exchange was the Regulators fought on fraud on the exploration exchange in Sector 162," Flank said. "My grandfather said a lot of good crews lost their reputations because the Regulators accused them of faking entire routes and discovering phantom star systems. They tried to fight the Regulators, the fools."

The whole idea of an interstellar war in the Mix made Barry nauseous and dizzy. It was too much to contemplate.

Stamp must not have known Endor's true status either. Her squadron was out here faring worse than the pirates. They didn't expect to find a fleet here, either, much less to fight it. Stamp's ships were stuck between a hostile fleet and organized pirates. They couldn't adapt to the situation. Barry suspected it was Lemonne's fault; he had been pranking that gullible prick for years.

The spiders made another pass at the *Demotion*, firing at the rear-mounted slide drive. The light cruiser chasing them kept beaming slave codes at the *Demotion* to take control. But thanks to Flank the ship only accepted slave codes from the transceiver that was sitting on the deck, jacked into the *Demotion*'s systems.

The electrical pounding on their aft section from the spider fighters increased. A section of the drive went offline.

"Shit," Flank said. "At least what's left of the drive is charging faster."

"These crates don't have a lot of pickup, do they?" Barry asked Flank.

"No, thanks for noticing. It's a freighter, in case you didn't notice, genius."

Barry held up his hands defensively. "Hey, I asked a simple question. I don't read the specs on every ship. I'm a people person."

"A captain should know his tech."

Barry rolled his eyes. "Just, would you please get us out of here."

The spiders gave up on disabling the ship and began firing higher-powered energy blasts to simply vaporize it. It was great: each shot cut the recharge time by another minute. But it also vented another cargo hold or compartment with each shot. The metal bulkheads groaned as the ship's physical integrity weakened.

Half the bridge consoles blinked out. A muffled explosion jolted the hull. Damage reports scrolled across the screen in front of Barry.

Flank ran out of the bridge. He reported in seconds later, "A capacitor feed on the outer hull failed and a blast breached the hull. We blew an air tank. Our midship dorsal hull section can't be hit again. Fly so we get hit somewhere else."

The spiders were circling the ship now, firing as fast as they could. Barry couldn't hide the midship dorsal hull from them. He asked, "And the chances of this working?"

"I'm not answering that," Flank retorted. He sprinted back on the bridge and over to the engineer's station.

Barry said, "We need another thirty minutes to charge or to take a lot more fire. I'd rather not get shot anymore."

Flank perked up. "We can shrink the slide aperture." He obsessed over slide aperture clearances. The energy beam needed to create a pinhole-sized tunnel in the fabric of space was considerable in terms of both power level and particle composition. Shrinking a tunnel aperture by some multiple of the pin hole energy requirement meant longer slide distances and shorter recharge times. Barry knew Flank's work in optimizing slide drive techniques played a large role in the *Drake* reaching Union first.

"You sure we can drag this wreck through a smaller hole?"

Flank said, "Sure, I'm sure."

"How sure is sure?"

"GEC tolerances for slide aperture are several meters out from the hull. Wastes a lot of energy for peace of mind. My clearances are a few centimeters. Of course, the *Drake* has a streamlined hull without jagged wreckage hanging out. Dropping the tolerance cuts the recharge time by about two-thirds. Down to about ten minutes."

"Is that with or without getting shot by high energy weapons?"

The hull rattled from another round of spider fire.

Flank shrugged. "Without. Eight minutes."

"And with?"

Flank chugged calculations in his wrist cuff. "Three minutes. I'm plotting the slide."

"You're the best, Flank."

"I will be if I pull this off and we aren't crushed at the speed of light."

The entire ship rattled and alarms went off. Barry couldn't understand what the problem was, but Flank's bald head was bathed in the engineering console's amber and red lights.

"They hit a dead conduit and fried the next one," Flank announced. "The capacitor collection grid is failing. The damage is cumulative and they'll overload soon. The system isn't designed to absorb this amount of energy. We need to slide real, real soon."

Something like a table with fragile china crashed in the deck above them. Barry was thankful the GEC installed the bridge in the dead center of the ship. He wrenched the flight controls to flip the ship over. The starfield spun on the external cams. The ship's damaged stern rolled away from their pursuers and they continued at maximum velocity but in reverse. With the slide drive on the stern, there was little chance of a direct hit on it.

The pursuing light cruiser and spiders poured fire on the dorsal hull and the bow anyway. The countdown clock dropped by bits and chunks at about the same rate the damage alarms were popping up.

"This could be interesting," Flank said. "I'm sealing the bridge, just in case." A heavy metal door clanked shut.

"Interesting? I don't like interesting anymore," Barry replied. He flipped through a number of communications menus on his control board. A smirk lifted the corner of his mouth. He cut the drive engine, the exterior lights, life support, and the long-range sensors and activated the ship's distress signal. The *Demotion* drifted, a darkened hulk.

"What the hell are you doing?!" Flank yelled.

The spider fighters stopped firing immediately. A second later, they banked away from the *Demotion*. A distress signal from an unpowered ship apparently triggered a pre-programmed stand down.

The *Demotion*'s countdown clock was now under two minutes. The drive wasn't drawing power any more but the capacitors kept charging.

"Playing the situation," Barry said. He scooted over to the communications console and sent commands to the other slaved ships.

Only a few zombie warships were left that were controlled by the transceiver unit, which was warm against Barry's leg. Each of them was being chased by shuttles that had boarding parties that would take manual control.

He sent new flight plans to each warship and added a few other commands.

The warships all banked to new courses and began broadcasting distress signals. One dove for the sun, which was at least one hundred and sixty thousand klicks away. Another accelerated toward the planet's atmosphere.

A third turned to intercept Kleble's warship. The spider fighters turned to chase it.

The light cruiser banked toward the warship trying to immolate itself in the planet's atmosphere.

"What did you do, Barry?"

The *Demotion* continued to drift. Its countdown clock kept dropping.

"I noticed they didn't recover any disabled ships yet. I figured they wouldn't kill us if it meant losing their precious warships. This transceiver you wanted us to die for was the key to saving our sweaty asses."

The countdown clock reached zero and the *Demotion*, the last functioning pirate ship in the Endor system, slid away.

FIFTY-EIGHT

GRAND LEANED on the edge of his new desk, arms crossed, back straight, delivering his business spiel to four men in front of him. His quarters on the *Leggett Rose* were growing on him. They were tucked behind the casinos in the Chateau, deep in the bowels of the ship-turned-station.

Nothing could replace Royada. Soon, though, he could buy three new Royadas. He'd been recruiting pirates, scouts, and new investors for the pirate exchange for the past several weeks and pocketing a heap of entry and transaction fees as a result. A full-on bubble was underway. The cautious investors had finally jumped in, convinced they had waited long enough to buy into a sure thing. These were the real suckers who bought high, sold low, and got burned. They would be so traumatized by the bubble bursting they wouldn't buy in again until the next bubble was in full froth.

Grand couldn't do anything legitimate about the bubble. The smart play was to cash in on these fools while he could. He could smell their money like it was sweet swamp rot. The Endor raid would pop the bubble nicely.

The would-be pirates sitting in front of him right now, for instance, were falling for his tales of the *Drake*'s glory and riches.

He'd put a copy of the pirate exchange's glossy prospectus into each of their hands. The prospectus touted trends in pirate loot, share value, and market capitalization. The numbers reported in it were going up, up, up. Past performance was no indicator of how much better future performance would be.

Kroger wheeled in but stopped at the entrance: his cue to wrap up the meeting. Grand said, "I don't want to hear your answer today. Don't act rash. Go study the financials. The Mix is a volatile place to do business, and conditions can change rapidly. Are there any more questions?"

The pirates were itching to sign on immediately. Hearing "don't be rash" prompted people to act rash. When one of them said she was ready to sign immediately, Grand insisted they take at least a day to think about it. They would come back twice as committed after the bubble popped. Grand would look like a prudent financial advisor gifted with foresight.

Kroger ushered them out and Grand prepped for a conference call with some Exchange investors who were interested in taking positions on the pirate exchange. There was nothing like new success to wipe away an older tarnished image.

Grand skimmed a report on how the exchanges were performing in Exchange space. He had ignored them for so long, it was like reacquainting himself with a friend who had new teeth and a different hairstyle but the same old familiar personality.

Kroger returned. "Reports are coming in from ships that went on the Endor raid. They returned to a number of Underseed worlds. The raid was a success."

"A success?! For who?"

"Well, sir, the pirates."

The room swam and wobbled in Grand's vision. He gasped, "What about the *Drake*?"

Kroger said, "One of our contacts spotted it at Woodshed a few hours ago. Three captured freighters in tow."

Grand closed his eyes and waited for the dizziness to pass. It was replaced with soul-gnawing dread. He accessed the pirate exchange feed. The entire exchange's total capitalization was now much, much higher. The leading advancers were the *Drake* and the pirates Barry had recruited for the Endor raid. Everything Grant just said to the pirate candidates was dead on.

Unfortunately, that meant he was about to go bankrupt. Again.

Before the raid, Grand made book on bets against the pirate stocks. He also made book against the pirate exchange's average share price. This meant that he accepted bets against individual pirate stocks and the whole pirate exchange increasing in value.

After the Endor raid failed miserably, the exchange would take a sizable hit and he would become richer than ever before.

But these side bets he lost required him to pay off at long odds. Much more than anything he would make from the increased share prices on the exchange or the transaction fees from new investors. The side bets would wipe him out.

Even worse, this time Grand couldn't blame anyone other than himself. When the explorer exchange tanked, it was Spranker's fault. The anti-pirate squadron was supposed to scoop up the *Drake* and the other pirates at Endor and pop the bubble on the pirate exchange. No one knew the GEC was hiding a forbidden fleet of high-powered warships that would block Stamp. The Endor intel was outrageously, scandalously faulty. Nothing he could do about it now. It didn't matter if someone set him up or not. He was done.

His anger looked for an outlet and settled on the droid nervously shuffling his right tread. Grand's mouth fell into a grim line. He up and decked Kroger in the head. Kroger wobbled, but recovered and retreated to the door. Grand kicked him hard in the midsection, his foot sinking two inches into the faux flesh.

Kroger doubled over briefly and brought its arms up in self-defense. Grand was yelling incoherently, he realized. He was able to realize that he was in a blinding rage. He unleashed a series of punches into Kroger's sides, head, and chest.

Kroger whimpered. "Ow. Why do you get so angry? Have I ever told you this, oof, this type of abuse does not injure me in the least?"

"What are you talking about?" Roundhouse kick to the head toppled the droid. "You feel pain."

"I do that," Kroger's voice quavered when a blow rocked his vocalizer, "to soothe your ego."

Grand screamed and tried ripping off one of Kroger's arms. But the damn limb was made of some kind of bio-modified substance much stronger than him. He settled for kicking his droid assistant repeatedly.

"Message incoming from Barry Spranker," Kroger croaked from down on the floor.

Grand wound up and kicked him in the gut again for good measure. "Play it."

Barry's voice dripped with honey-sweet condescension. "Junie, can I call you Junie? We just made you a big old pile of money on your pirate exchange. This more than compensates you for what you lost on Connexion Day. If you were one of the fools who bet against us, well, it's the price you paid for mistreating Eden. Clasker told me to say thanks if you took it on the nose. Suckers are at high risk on unregulated reputation exchanges."

Grand sank to the floor, spent. "I hate him. I foxing hate him! But he is not worth the effort. Not worth the damn effort."

Kroger levered himself upright with his treads. "Are we done here?"

Grand rose and snarled, "Not yet." He pulled his arm back and knocked Kroger's head off of its support stalk. A bone in his finger made a sick grinding noise that probably meant it was broken. Grand welcomed the injury. It was a physical manifestation of the shit his world had just become.

FIFTY-NINE

BARRY'S bare feet left the blood-warm deck moss of the *Drake*'s ramp and sank into the beach's burning yellow sand. He shielded his eyes from the bright sun. Flank and Tongue followed behind him.

No one was there to greet them, thankfully. The last two weeks of raucous, celebratory greetings across the Underseed was enough even for Barry.

The *Drake*'s victory lap, under the guise of selling their loot, stopped at every major Underseed system in the Mix. The story about the raid, the GEC fleet, the lost pirates, a booming pirate exchange, and the defeat of Stamp's anti-piracy squadron made them celebrities. Again. GEC, Underseed, Exchange settlements, it didn't matter, everyone knew. *The Alan Glown Show* devoted a special episode to the raid. Everywhere the *Drake* went, people wanted to buy the crew several rounds of drinks. They even snagged a few invites to Exchange settlements on this side of Union.

Flank squinted at Barry in the bright sunlight. "So, we pissed off the whole universe. You sure you want to hole up here and miss the fun?"

Barry said, "Happy to miss the fun and everything else waiting for us out there."

"I can't believe you're quitting on us, Bare," Tongue scolded.

Barry grinned. "I was going to quit after Connexion Day, remember? And then there was the run-in with Stamp, Grand trying to enslave us, and the Endor raid. That, that was enough. I'm done. The universe can leave me be."

"Let the man enjoy some peace," Flank said. He was only too happy about taking command of the *Drake*.

"You both are welcome to stay, too," Barry said. "The council invited the three of us."

Tongue said, "I can only handle vacation in small doses. I need to keep busy to stay sane, understand?"

Flank affectionately patted the underside of the *Drake*. "Me? I've got a reputation to protect. Investments too. I'll prove I'm a better captain than you could ever be."

An empty hammock in a shady spot right off the beach was calling Barry. He started trudging through the sand. "I'm not competing with you Flank. Go top everything I ever did. I'm *rooting* for you. But I won't be paying attention." He laid down in the hammock and put his arms behind his head. The guys loomed over him.

Flank folded his arms. "Bullshit, Barry. You're not really walking away. Not when we're on top. Who says quit while they're ahead? Quitters. Losers who are afraid to run up the score. You suck, but you're not that bad."

Barry said, "The game's changing out there. It's the right time for me to exit the ride."

Tongue waved his arms around. "What are you going to do here? Swim all day? Run the council? Build a village?"

Barry laughed. "Maybe? Nah. Nothing. I'll only do what I absolutely must to buy triskey and fruit."

Tongue made a disapproving noise. "That's not healthy."

"Says the interstellar pirate about to get chased by an entire warfleet? Come on."

Flank pointed at the *Drake*. "We walk back to the ship and you'll be running after us. We've seen this before. Infidel Valley Bar and Grill."

Barry put his hands behind his head. "Tell you what, you make it to orbit without me calling after you, you'll know you're the captain and I'm staying here. Permanently. Okay?"

Tongue sighed and said, "Each man must set out on his own path and be man enough to do it, I guess."

"A-vo-cado," Barry mumbled in agreement.

The two other men headed up the beach towards the *Drake*, bickering with each other about whether Barry would stay or not.

Barry closed his eyes and swayed in the hammock. His best friends' voices dwindled in the distance. Those two could bicker up the gravity well. He wouldn't miss it.

He sat up to take a last look at the *Drake* parked on the beach. To check if there was any last little tug on the old heartstrings. The ship looked completely out of place, like someone pasted a polished black cylinder on a picture-perfect beach vista. He wouldn't miss the ship or the life it represented.

Tongue looked back at him, hopeful he had changed his mind. Barry waved him off. Tongue shook his head and boarded the ship.

The *Drake*'s main drive activated with an almost silent, ground-shaking woof. The dull red drive arrays on the bow brightened until they glowed.

Barry closed his eyes and listened. The *Drake*'s drive noise crested to a high-pitched keening as it took off. The keening rose and then receded. The sound of breaking waves and squawking birds returned. Barry drifted off to sleep.

BEFORE YOU GO...

Mark says, *"Please help me out. Rate this book. Or even better, review it! An honest rating or review will help other readers decide if this book is toxic trash or something they will love. I would greatly appreciate it."*

IF YOU LIKED THIS BOOK...

You may also like Mark's Kagent trilogy. A cyberpunk thriller about a man who can predict the future, if he can escape his past. 24th century bounty hunters with personal drone swarms. Economic refugees. Lifespeed activists committed to destroying modern society through peaceful terrorism. Offworld utopias. And a band of offworlders who predict and protect the future.

The first book is *Crashpoint.*

WOULD **you like the *Crashpoint* e-book free, along with Mark's newsletter?**

We will only use your information to send you the book and his monthly newsletter. We will never sell it or share it. We will shower you with discounts and early releases. Promise.

CLICK HERE **to grab the newsletter and the *Crashpoint* e-book**

Or   do   it   the   hard   way   and   type   in https://dl.bookfunnel.com/hzy4syu61k

The End

ABOUT THE AUTHOR

Mark Sarney has been writing science fiction since he was a geeky, contrarian kid in Rochester, NY. He once converted his garage into an actual forest for Halloween, has stuck his head inside the Oval Office, and converts sencha tea and long commutes into fiction.

You can follow him at: marksarney.com or twitter.com/marksarney.

Starslider Rejects: Let's be Pirates (#001)

The Obesity Conspiracy Trilogy
The Obesity Conspiracy
The Obesity Pandemic
The Obesity Apocalypse

The Kagent Trilogy
Crashpoint (Kagent Series: #1)
Twistpoint (Kagent Series: #2)
Chokepoint (Kagent Series: #3)

www.ingramcontent.com/pod-product-compliance
Lightning Source LLC
Chambersburg PA
CBHW020934260626
47169CB00006B/1720